HELEN WARNER

The Story of Our Lives

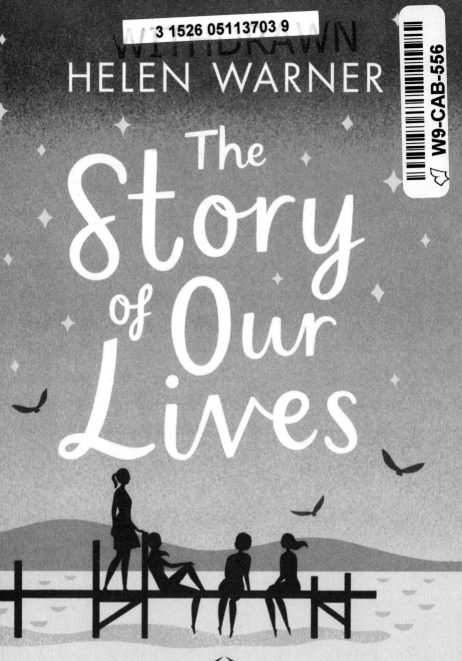

G

GRAYDON
HOUSE

GRAYDON HOUSE

ISBN-13: 978-1-525-82083-0

The Story of Our Lives

BookClubbish.com
GraydonHouseBooks.com

Printed in U.S.A.

Recycling programs for this product may not exist in your area.

For "The Girls"

The Story of Our Lives

AUGUST 1997

"One story dominates the news tonight—
Diana, Princess of Wales, has died in a car
crash in Paris."

SOUTHWOLD

CHAPTER ONE

SOPHIE COULD FEEL HERSELF STARTING TO SWEAT as she tried to heave the stone pot to one side. Could it really be this one that the key was under? Surely they'd have put it under one that wasn't so bloody heavy. Instead of lifting it, she decided to try rolling it. Sure enough, the pot began to move, but the momentum gathered pace more quickly than she had expected and the pot rolled unstoppably towards her foot and straight over her toe. Breathless with pain and almost not daring to look for fear of the damage she might find, she examined her foot.

The toe of her Converse offered very little protection and sagged ominously where her big toe should have been. Gingerly, she pressed with her thumb and winced in pain. She slumped down onto the path, which was still wet from an earlier rain shower, and groaned as her jeans immediately absorbed the moisture. She knew without looking that the damp patch would have spread in a fascinatingly symmetrical fashion across her rear.

Maybe this weekend away wasn't such a good idea after all. The omens weren't great, with the shock waves over Princess

Diana's sudden death still reverberating throughout the country, and although the others had left it to her to organize everything, she knew they would moan about who was sharing with whom and grumble about the house she had chosen from the listings in the *Evening Standard*.

Sophie looked up at the pretty whitewashed and thatched cottage, feeling a sudden stab of annoyance at its old-fashioned beauty. It was the sort of place retired couples would come for a weekend of birdwatching, rather than a group of twenty-something girls looking for a good time.

"What the hell are you doing down there?" The slightly gravelly Midlands accent reached her before its owner appeared at the gate and began to make her way up the path. Wearing tight bootleg jeans and a skinny white sleeveless top that con-trasted with her smooth, dark brown skin, Melissa appeared not to have aged a day since they had first met. Her afro hair had been woven into cornrows that fell to her shoulders, and apart from a slash of bright red lipstick, her pretty face was make-up free.

Sophie struggled to her feet and embraced her friend.

"Hi, sweetie. Bit of a mishap while hunting for the key." She attempted to discreetly run her hand over her bum. Sure enough, it was soaking.

"Did you find it?"

Typical of Melissa to be more concerned with getting into the house than whether Sophie was OK. "No. My suffering was in vain, sadly." As she spoke, Sophie's eyes scanned the area around the door for other pots.

"It'll be under this one!" Melissa cried, dumping her ruck-sack onto the path and darting towards a pretty Mediterranean-style pot that wasn't much bigger than a mug. Sure enough, as Melissa effortlessly lifted it, the key glistened in the sunlight.

She bent down with a balletic lunge and scooped it up. "See?" she said, holding the key aloft triumphantly.

Sophie nodded. This tiny incident summed up their relationship perfectly. Sophie was the hard worker, the one who put in all the effort, only for Melissa to sail in at the end and collect the trophy. Not that she resented Melissa for it. She loved her like a sister. In fact, she loved her more than her own sister, Georgina, with whom she had very little in common, as there was almost a whole decade between them.

"Come on, what are you waiting for?" Melissa threw the comment over her shoulder as she used the key to open the front door, which needed a good shove to dislodge it, and disappeared into the cool, dark hallway. "Christ, it's a bit drab, isn't it?" she added.

And so it begins, thought Sophie, following her friend into the house, noting that she had to duck slightly as she stepped over the threshold, unlike tiny, perfect Melissa.

★ ★ ★ ★ ★

"So how are things going with Steve, then?" Melissa's huge brown eyes danced mischievously as she spoke. They were lying on separate squashy chintz sofas, facing each other, divided by a pine coffee table in the middle.

"Fine." Sophie lifted up her foot and pretended to examine her sore toe. She didn't want to have this conversation. She knew Melissa thought she and Steve were too young to have been in a "boring" relationship for so long.

Melissa rolled onto her side and Sophie could feel herself starting to redden under Melissa's suspicious gaze. "Fine? Talk about damning with faint praise…"

Sophie sighed and turned to face Melissa. "Well, I'm not

sure what else to say. It's fine. No, it's more than fine... It's good. End of story."

"Bollocks!"

Sophie smiled, despite herself, at Melissa's directness. "OK. Well, it's just... Oh, I don't know." She tailed off and sat up, lifting her mug of tea from the coffee table and taking a long, soothing sip.

Melissa mirrored her actions and looked over at her in concern. "Soph? This isn't like you. What's the matter? I thought you and Steve were love's young dream."

Sophie shrugged. "We were. We are," she corrected herself quickly.

"There's a 'but' coming..."

Sophie gazed at Melissa appraisingly. How to explain what she was feeling when she couldn't really explain it to herself? "But I'm wondering if this is it," she said eventually. Hearing the words aloud caused her stomach to lurch. It scared her.

Melissa's dark eyes narrowed slightly. "How's work going?"

God, she was infuriating! How did Melissa know so much about what she was thinking and feeling? "It's great," she replied, her tone of voice at odds with her words.

"And therein lies the problem!" Melissa finished her tea with a satisfied slurp and put the mug back on the table, before crossing her legs underneath her and steepling her fingers in the manner of a miniature tribal chief. "I'm right, aren't I?"

Sophie started to nod miserably, then stopped herself. *Was* she right? Had Sophie really become so shallow that her exciting new job as a TV news producer was causing her to look at Steve in a different light? Did the other guys she worked with at the TV company make Steve's role in HR management look a little, well, *dull* by comparison? As the thoughts skittered through her head, she almost cringed with shame.

She thought back to when she and Steve had met, during their first week at university. They were in the same small tutor group and would often study together in the university library or in Sophie's room whenever Melissa, who was her room-mate, was out. He was funny and clever and, out of all of them, seemed the most likely to succeed. Although Steve was tall, blond and good-looking, it never really occurred to Sophie that he could be anything other than a friend.

But gradually they also started socializing together and before long they were seeing each other most days. It was during a drunken end-of-term house party, when she saw him kissing Natalie Evans—the most beautiful girl in their year, who funded her way through university by modelling for John Galliano and often wore a T-shirt emblazoned with "Galliano's Girls" just in case anyone needed reminding of just how beautiful she was—that Sophie realized with a start that her feelings for him had deepened.

That summer, she invited him to come and stay at her parents' house on the north coast of Northern Ireland. They spent their days going for long walks along the wide white sandy beaches at Portrush and Portstewart, surfing the huge Atlantic waves at White Rocks, then going out drinking and dancing in the evenings. By the time Steve returned home, they were smitten with each other. They had moved in together the following term, despite everyone's dire warnings that it was too soon. They had been together ever since.

"There's someone else, isn't there?" Melissa frowned as she spoke, her expression suddenly serious.

Sophie shook her head but couldn't actually bring herself to deny the accusation aloud. She never lied to Melissa, partly because she didn't want to and partly because she knew Melissa would be able to tell if she did.

Melissa pursed her lips, as if weighing up whether to believe her or not. "It's probably just the seven-year itch. It'll pass." Melissa half nodded as she spoke, as if trying to convince herself of the truth of what she was saying.

"You're probably right." Sophie stood up and walked over to the window, pretending to look out. But all she could see was someone else's face reflected back at her in the glass. And it wasn't Steve's. Her head swirled uncomfortably as guilt mingled with excitement. She didn't get that same frisson when she looked at Steve these days.

"If things ever get a bit difficult, you can always come and stay with me, Soph. Give yourself a break, you know?"

Sophie looked towards Melissa but couldn't quite meet her eye.

"Thanks, but things aren't that bad. In fact, they're great."

"Are you trying to convince me or you?"

A prickle of irritation quivered in Sophie's chest.

"Thing is," Melissa continued, standing up and stretching, showing off her toned stomach as her top rode up, "you can leave Steve any time you want. But what then? Think about it, Soph."

"I'm not thinking of leaving him!" Sophie protested, Melissa's words reverberating around her brain, making it feel crowded with noise. "I love him. Anyway, I know you think he's boring."

Melissa hesitated. "No, that's not true. Maybe I think it's a bit boring to have been with one person all this time, but I don't think *he's* boring. I love him." Melissa gave Sophie a hug. "And I love you," she added, turning abruptly away as if suddenly embarrassed. "Which is why I don't want you to do something you'll regret."

Sophie bit her lip and followed Melissa out into the hallway towards the kitchen. She opened her mouth to protest. To tell her she was wrong. But again, the lie dried in her throat. She tried to think what else to say, but before she could get the words out, the doorbell rang.

"That'll be the others!" Relief flooded through Sophie as she ran towards the front door. Through the stained glass in the front door, she could see two shadows and felt a sudden shiver of excitement. Emily and Amy had caught the train together and shared a taxi from the nearest station. It had been a while since they had last seen each other and she couldn't wait for them to be together again as a group.

There was a shriek of delight as she unlatched the heavy door and swung it open, before both girls enveloped her. As she disentangled herself, Sophie stood back to look at them. "Oh, isn't this just so brilliant!" She could feel tears pricking her eyes as she took in the two beaming faces in front of her.

"Don't you start blubbing or you'll set me off!" Amy reached down to grab her bag, her glossy mane of auburn hair tumbling over her shoulders as she did so. "Right, who's sleeping where?"

"I'm having the biggest room!" Melissa poked her head around the door of the kitchen. "Hey, you guys!"

"Liss!" they squealed, tottering towards Melissa and smothering her in hugs, causing her tiny frame to disappear altogether for a few moments.

Sophie looked at each of her friends with a feeling of deep contentment. They might not have spent much time together as a group for years, but already she could feel the special bond between them reconnecting. This was going to be the best weekend ever.

CHAPTER TWO

~~~~~~~~~~~~~~~~~~~

"I CAN'T BELIEVE YOU WERE ORGANIZED ENOUGH
to bring all the food and booze!" Amy lifted her champagne
flute for Sophie to refill and smiled. "You put the rest of us
to shame. If you opened my fridge, you'd be lucky to find a
pint of milk at the moment." It wasn't true. Her fridge would
never be empty, but she wanted to show Sophie how grateful she was.

Sophie smiled back at her. "Well, you know me and my
stomach. I couldn't risk having nothing to eat. Or worse, nothing to drink." She made a joke of it, but actually Sophie *was*
very organized, and unless she'd brought the food and drink
this weekend, they would have been left with tap water and
cornflakes.

"You'll have to let us know how much we owe you. It's not
fair for you to pay for it all."

Sophie threw Amy a grateful look. "Thanks, Amy, I will."

Amy had lived in the single room the other side of Sophie
and Melissa's double room in their first year at university and
the others had quickly cottoned on to the fact that she was
the only one with any cooking ability and had exploited it

fully. When they all went their separate ways after the first year, Sophie used to say that it was Amy and her prowess in the kitchen that she missed the most.

"Have a look at what I've brought and let me know if there's anything you need that I've forgotten," Sophie said. "I think there's a small shop in the village."

Amy nodded. It was automatically assumed that she would do the cooking. She didn't mind. She loved cooking. It was her passion.

Amy could feel Sophie's eyes on her, scrutinizing her face with a faint scowl of suspicion. "What?" She tried to laugh, but it came out as more of a snort.

"You're looking particularly...well," Sophie began, taking a sip of her cava and narrowing her eyes meaningfully.

Amy raised her eyebrows. Sophie was a TV news producer and a nosy one at that. There was no hiding anything from her.

"There's a reason for that, isn't there, Amy?" Emily blurted, nudging Amy hard, causing her cava to swirl dangerously close to the rim of her flute.

"Hey, careful!" Amy tried to look annoyed, but she couldn't extinguish the smile that had spread across her face or dampen the sudden heat in her cheeks.

"Oooh, I like the sound of this!" Melissa said as they all leaned slightly towards Amy, waiting to hear what she had to say.

Amy knew that resistance was futile with her oldest friends. They could read her so well. And she didn't want to keep it a secret anyway—she was much too excited. "Well..." she began, picturing the pinkness that she knew would be spreading from her neck to her cheekbones. "I've met someone."

"I knew it! Tell us everything!" Sophie demanded.

Amy beamed, before crossing her long legs underneath her

and taking a leisurely sip of her drink, teasing out the moment, as the others held their breath in front of her, their eyes wide.

"His name is Nick—"

"Good name," Melissa cut in, before being silenced by glares of frustration from the others. "Sorry. Go on."

"His name is Nick and I met him through work."

"Colleague or client?"

Amy raised her eyebrows. "Good to see your journalistic training wasn't wasted…"

Sophie shrugged. "It's the obvious question."

Amy smiled. She worked as an events organizer, organizing events for wealthy international clients.

"To be fair, that's what I was going to ask!" Melissa grabbed a handful of crisps and began shovelling them into her mouth one after the other.

Amy paused, looking at each of them in turn, enjoying being the centre of attention for once. "Client!"

Another chorus of squeals followed.

"Is he *very* rich?" All eyes turned towards Melissa in mock disgust but quickly flicked back to Amy expectantly.

"Well, it depends what you mean by *very* rich…" Amy wondered how honest she should be, before deciding that they would only find out anyway. "Yes! He's loaded!"

"But is he a good person?"

"Oh, Emily! Who cares if he's a good person?" Melissa shot Emily an incredulous look.

"No, Emily's right." Amy raised her hands, as if she was refereeing a boxing match. "It *is* important that he's a nice guy…" She paused for a second, enjoying the moment. "But that's the best thing of all—he's awesome!"

An indecipherable sigh swept through the room as each of them digested her news. Amy's eyes were drawn to Emily, wondering what she might be feeling. Even though she was just twenty-five, she was already a single mum to four-year-old Jack. She had fallen pregnant with him in their last term at university, and as far as any of them knew, she had never had anything further to do with Jack's father.

She couldn't be sure of this because none of them actually knew for certain the identity of Jack's father. Emily had always refused to say who it was, and despite years of prodding and cajoling from each of them, either collectively or individually, it had become clear that she was never going to reveal the truth. They all strongly suspected that the father was one of their lecturers, but Emily wasn't confirming or denying anything. She just flatly refused to discuss it.

Emily noticed Amy watching her and smiled, her eyebrows raised questioningly. "Why are you looking at me like that?"

Amy shrugged. "I was just wondering if you'd met anyone new. It seems such a waste someone as gorgeous as you being single." They had all thought it over the years but rarely voiced it, as Emily could be prickly. But it was true. She was a beautiful girl and must have had dozens of offers.

Emily shook her head quickly, her dark eyes clouding as her shoulder-length, raven-coloured hair swished from side to side and she lowered her gaze. "No. I don't have time. There's only one man in my life and that's Jack."

"Aw, how is the little love? Have you got any recent pictures?" Amy was happy to change the subject.

Immediately, Emily's face transformed. She grabbed her large bag from the hall and rummaged in it for a minute, before pulling out a creased photo. They all cooed as they handed it around. Amy's heart jolted as she looked at it. Jack was absolutely gorgeous. His hair was almost white blond and long enough to look cool but short enough to stop it looking ridiculous. His full mouth, which could have given him a sulky appearance, was counteracted by the wideness of his smile, revealing perfectly white milk teeth. His eyes were a bright, piercing blue, and even at four years old, it was already clear he was going to be tall.

"Oh, Em, he's really beautiful." Unlike the others, Amy had always yearned for children of her own, something she had told Nick on their second date, and when he hadn't run a mile, that was when she had decided he could be the one for her.

Emily flushed with pride and reached out to take the photo from Amy's grasp, but she hung on to it. "He doesn't look like you at all..."

"Well, I'm definitely his mother, if that's what you're suggesting—I've got the stretch marks to prove it!" Emily tried to grab the photo, but Amy swiped it out of her reach.

"I'm just trying to think who he reminds me of..." Amy stared hard at the photo. It was one of their old lecturers, she was sure of it. A vague memory of Emily becoming fixated on one of them—Anton, she thought it was—bubbled to the surface, but although she ran through a mental Rolodex of their faces, after four years the images were already too blurred and hazy.

Reluctantly, she handed the photo back to Emily, who looked slightly panicked. For the millionth time, Amy wondered why she didn't trust anyone enough to tell them the truth. Even Emily's parents didn't know the identity of Jack's father and Emily had actually lived with them for the first couple of years after she left university. She had finally moved into a flat of her own, but it was still close to her parents' home in south-east London and her mum looked after Jack all the time when Emily was at work.

"Anyway, Sophie," she said, turning her attention away from Emily, "isn't it about time you and Steve had a baby?"

Sophie's eyes bulged in Amy's direction. "What? Where the hell did that come from? I'm only twenty-five!"

Amy shrugged. "So am I, but if I was in a settled relationship like you, I'd do it while I was still young. Get it out of the way like Emily did."

Emily spluttered on her cava. "Christ! I don't think anyone should follow my example… I love Jack to distraction, but it's been bloody hard from day one. Given the choice, I would've definitely waited until I had established my career and was a lot more secure financially."

"But you haven't got a partner like Sophie ha—" Amy tailed off in embarrassment as she realized too late how tactless her words sounded.

"No. I don't have a partner. Thank you for pointing that out, Amy." Emily looked suddenly furious.

"I'm sure Amy didn't mean it like that." Sophie shot Amy a warning look as she spoke. "No, I'm not planning babies any time soon, thanks, Amy. Anyway, we're not even married," she added.

"What's your name? Jane Austen?" Amy teased, and a low snigger of amusement emitted from Melissa.

"No, it's just…" Sophie stood up and scrunched her long chestnut hair distractedly into a ponytail. She looked flustered. "Well, I can't imagine what it must be like to throw away the condoms and actually plan to make a baby. We've all spent so many years trying desperately *not* to get pregnant after what happened to Em… Sorry, Em, but you know what I mean, don't you?"

Emily nodded, slightly wearily.

Amy's head whirled with thoughts of Nick. She tried not

to get too carried away—after all, they had been dating for only four months. But already she could picture them as parents. Nick was so protective of her and caring. He made her feel special in a way that no one ever had before. She knew she didn't have the wit or the brains or the personality that the others had. She was the quiet one who hated any kind of confrontation and would go along with what everyone else wanted to do in order to keep the peace. But Nick seemed to find her captivating and hung on her every word. He wanted to spend every waking minute with her and told her he couldn't get enough of her. She loved it.

She wondered idly whether their children would inherit her auburn hair and green eyes or Nick's swarthy dark good looks, hoping it would be the latter. He was such a beautiful man—even thinking about him now made her feel weak with longing. She had had many boyfriends in the past, but Nick was different. Special. She already felt that he was "the one."

"Do you think you and Steve will get married, then?" Emily interrupted the silence, cutting through Amy's daydream.

All eyes locked on to Sophie, who seemed to quail slightly as she spoke. "Uh…maybe. I've never really thought about it."

"Oh, you should!" Amy clapped her hands together several times, excitement bubbling up inside her. "It would be so fantastic to have a wedding to go to. I could bring Nick…" She left the thought hanging tantalizingly in the air, imagining already what she might wear, how perfect Nick would look in a morning suit.

"Well, I'm not planning to get married just so that you lot can have a day out." Sophie frowned at Amy. "And you need to stop daydreaming, Amy. You'll frighten him off if you're too keen."

Amy grinned. "I can't help it. You know what I'm like. And it hasn't frightened him off so far."

"True. But then, he hasn't met me yet!" Melissa stood up and stretched languorously, showing off her toned, brown-skinned belly as she did so. Amy laughed, though a tiny prickle of nervousness passed through her. Melissa was a legendary flirt. But despite her sexiness and beauty, she had never enjoyed anything more than flings and one-night stands. Men never seemed to stick around. And she didn't think Melissa was Nick's type anyway. He was always telling Amy how much he loved her because she was so unusual, with her long, slim legs, mane of red hair and dazzling green eyes. She could easily have been a successful model, but standing and posing in front of a lens had never interested her. She was too dreamy. Too creative. If anything, she wanted to be the one holding the camera.

"Anyway, girls, enough of this nonsense. I'm starving." Melissa threw Amy a pleading look. "Amy, get a move on and cook our dinner."

CHAPTER THREE

~~~~~~~~~~~

THE NEXT MORNING, AN EARLY HAZE BURNED quickly away to reveal a cloudless blue sky. Emily's leg muscles throbbed as she pounded along the beach. Running on sand was so much harder than jogging through the park near her London flat. But the salty sea air, the warmth of the sun on her skin and the gentle lapping of the waves on the shoreline were like a balm to her soul and spurred her on to keep running. Every step helped to clear her head a little more after drinking far too much last night. She hadn't drunk that much in years. Since before Jack was born.

Seeing the others was always a bittersweet experience—it churned up so many mixed feelings. Most of all, it made her long to turn back time to their first year of university, when they were all living together in the same halls of residence, young and clueless before life got in the way.

Sophie and Melissa had shared a room, while Emily and Amy had occupied the single rooms either side of them. Naturally, Melissa and Sophie were particularly close, meaning Amy and Emily also paired off. But from the start, the four of them were a tight unit. Emily had loved those days. Looking back through the prism of time, they seemed so carefree and untroubled—when problems weren't really problems at all. They were just excuses for tearful dramas, followed by whole nights sitting up drinking and talking until dawn, dissecting and condemning whoever might have slighted one of them.

Those were Emily's last memories of being truly happy. After that first year, when they all went their separate ways, everything changed. Sophie moved in with Steve, while Amy and Melissa shared a flat. They asked Emily to move in with them, but she chose to stay in halls.

She never told the others the real reason she wanted to be close to the university, but she sometimes wondered if they guessed. Anton was her tutor, and over the course of her first year, Emily had grown increasingly attracted to him. In his late thirties, he was tall, tanned, blond and devastatingly charming. He was also devastatingly married with two young children.

Emily told herself that it was just a crush and that nothing could ever happen between them, but however hard she tried, she couldn't seem to contain her feelings for him. In fact, with each passing month, they grew stronger until he had become something of an obsession. She would find excuses to spend extra time with him, citing the need to go over her last essay in greater detail or to discuss a new theory she had about a particular author. Just being alone with him was enough.

Anton seemed impressed by her dedication to her studies and certainly didn't discourage her from asking for more help. Over time she convinced herself that the attraction was mutual.

The others would sometimes tease her and call her a swot or a teacher's pet, but they never actually asked if there was anything going on between them. The closest they came was when Melissa had wondered aloud whether it was Anton that was the attraction, rather than the Breton Lays in Middle English. Emily had laughed it off, pointing out that even if she did think Anton was very attractive, she would never make a move on a) a married man or b) her tutor. "I would get the blame and I'd be thrown off the course."

Melissa had pondered this for a moment. "He'd be blamed too. He could lose his post."

"Well, it's a good job there's nothing going on, then, isn't it?" Emily had countered, relieved to have been able to deny it so categorically.

After that, it was never mentioned again, and Emily was able to indulge her obsession without being questioned. Her results improved and she was seen as the top student in her year, destined for a first-class degree followed by a big career.

"It's down to you," she had told Anton when she gained the highest marks in her exams at the end of the second year.

Anton had smiled the slightly crooked smile that she had spent so many nights dreaming about and reached out to take her hand. Emily's heart had banged in her chest, wondering if this was the moment he would finally admit his feelings for her.

"There's something I need to tell you."

She nodded, her mouth too dry to speak.

"I'm leaving."

Emily blinked. She must have misheard. It wasn't possible. "Leaving?"

Anton nodded. "I've got a new job. In Durham. I won't be back next term." He was looking at her earnestly. Apologetically.

Emily's thoughts lurched ahead to her third year, stretching out before her like a barren wasteland. He had to reconsider.

"What about me?" she said, realizing as the words left her lips how childish they sounded.

"You'll be fine!" He squeezed her hand, his eyes holding hers. "You're doing so well. Just keep it up and you'll get the first you deserve."

"I don't care about a bloody first!" Emily spat, her thoughts tumbling furiously over one another.

Anton dropped her hand and cleared his throat. "Look, Emily, you've worked so hard. Don't blow it now."

Emily gazed at him in disbelief. As she did so, it dawned on her that this was a common scenario for Anton. Students fell for him all the time. Of course they did. He was gorgeous. She wasn't the first and she wouldn't be the last. The realization hit her like a sledgehammer blow.

"All this time, you must have been laughing at me—"

"No!" The vehemence of Anton's denial made her catch her breath. "No," he repeated. "I have never laughed at you. I... Well, if things had been different..." He left the words hanging in the air between them.

"Don't." Emily stood up and smoothed down her jeans, swallowing back the tears that were thick in her throat. "Just... don't."

Anton watched her as she gathered her bags together. His pale blue eyes glittered slightly, but he didn't speak.

"Well. Thank you. Good luck in your new job." Her words sounded forced. Which was what they were.

"Thank you, Emily. Good luck with the rest of your course. I look forward to reading your first novel one day."

"Yeah. Right." Emily threw him a final glance over her shoulder before closing the door behind her.

It would be almost a year before she saw him again.

AUGUST 1998

"President Bill Clinton has given a nationally televised statement in which he admits that he had an 'improper physical relationship' with White House intern Monica Lewinsky and that it was 'not appropriate.'"

WHITSTABLE

CHAPTER FOUR

~~~~~~~~

MELISSA OPENED THE BOTTLE OF CHAMPAGNE
with a practised pop and expertly poured some into each of
the four glasses she had lined up on the granite worktop.

"Not for me, thanks." Sophie wouldn't look at Melissa as
she spoke, turning away from her and perching on one of the
stools lined up against the breakfast bar.

"What? You're joking, aren't you? I've known you for eight
years now and you've never once turned down champagne."

"I'm not feeling great, to be honest."

Melissa's antennae prickled. Sometimes she thought she
knew Sophie better than she knew herself. Something was
very wrong and she did indeed look like death.

After a moment spent staring at Sophie's back, Melissa
quickly drained Sophie's glass and put it in the sink. Then
she picked up two glasses and handed them out to Amy and
Emily, who were sitting at the pretty cloth-covered wooden
table by the window. They were chatting animatedly and
hadn't noticed the exchange between Sophie and Melissa.

"Here's to Amy and Nick!" Melissa interrupted, striding

into the middle of the room with her own full champagne flute aloft.

Sophie scuttled to the cupboard and retrieved a wine glass, which she quickly filled with tap water. Melissa pretended not to see.

Amy, wearing a short, floaty green dress that showed off her long, toned legs and matched her vivid eyes perfectly, stood up and twirled in delight, sending her long auburn hair swinging behind her.

Melissa watched her, envy scorching through her like heartburn as she raised her glass to toast Amy's engagement. Nick had proposed to her during a romantic weekend in Capri. According to Amy, he had waited until they had arrived by chairlift at the top of a mountain before bending down on one knee and producing a stunning antique diamond ring. He was rich, he was so handsome that it was almost comical and he was madly in love with Amy.

Melissa couldn't understand why she felt so envious. She had no desire to settle down, and anyway, she hadn't met anyone she would want to settle down with. Yet Amy's happiness and radiance made her feel as though she had somehow failed.

How different Amy's life suddenly seemed to the others', having all travelled down such wildly contrasting paths since their weekend away last year. Emily was still scrimping and struggling to support herself and Jack alone, Sophie seemed to have lost her natural sparkle and disappeared into her own melancholy world, and Melissa's love life was non-existent. Well, that wasn't strictly true. Melissa's sex life was excellent. It was just that there wasn't much love involved in any of her liaisons, mainly because the men she slept with were usually married or in long-term relationships. She told herself that she didn't care. She was young and she was having fun. She dismissed the niggling voice whispering in her ear in the middle of the night that sex, however good, was no replacement for love. Nor was it actually very much fun.

"So when's the big day, then?" Emily's voice cut through Melissa's maudlin thoughts as they all pulled a chair around the table and sat down. Distractedly, Melissa picked up a corner of the blue-and-white-checked tablecloth and began to twist it around her thumb, remembering as she did so how, as a child, she used to twist her special blanket in the same way, before sucking her thumb. She had a sudden flashback to her four-year-old self, sitting on the stairs watching her mum and dad scream at each other with pure hatred in their eyes. That must have been the last row before they split up for good. She couldn't remember being in that house after that night.

Amy took a sip of her champagne, the bubbles dancing in the liquid like a perfect reflection of the glints of light in her green eyes. Happiness, Melissa decided, unable to pull her own eyes away from Amy's, was the best beauty product there was. She had never seen anyone look more beautiful.

"I'm not entirely sure, but I think it'll be about this time next year. Nick's in charge—he has very firm ideas about what he wants. I'll just do what I'm told."

"We could make our weekend away next year your hen weekend!" Melissa's thoughts snapped back to the present and she glugged her glass of champagne greedily, eager to shut out the flashbacks to the past. She placed it carefully on the table, before lifting the bottle and refilling, noticing that Sophie made to cover hers with her hand just in case Melissa tried to refill it. But as no one else had drained their glass the way Melissa had, she just returned the half-empty bottle to the table.

"That's a great idea!" Amy paused and looked at each of them in turn, as if she was contemplating whether to say something. "Actually," she began, clearly having decided to say whatever it was, "there's something I'd like to ask you all..."

A whisper of anticipation swept around the table. Melissa's eyes instinctively turned towards Sophie, who raised her eyebrows.

"I wondered if you might consider being my bridesmaids." Amy suddenly looked shy.

"What? *All* of us?" Sophie had a slight look of panic on her face.

"Yes! All of you!" A tiny furrow appeared in the skin between Amy's eyebrows, as if she was suddenly unsure whether she had said the right thing. "Although...only if you want to."

"Of course we all want to!" Melissa threw Sophie a *what the hell?* look. What was going on with her?

"Y-yes!" Sophie stuttered out the words. "We'd l-love to!"

Amy's face relaxed into a wide smile. "Oh, that's amazing! Thank you." She clapped her hands with glee. "And, Em, I was thinking that maybe Jack could be my pageboy."

Emily nodded immediately. "He'd love to! As long as you don't dress him up in velvet pantaloons."

"No pantaloons, I promise." Amy sighed happily and took a sip of her champagne, oblivious to the tumultuous emotions swirling around the heads of all three of her friends.

CHAPTER FIVE

EMILY EMPTIED HER SMALL SUITCASE ONTO THE pretty quilted throw on the bed and looked out of the latticed window towards the beach. The sun was beginning to lose some of its heat and turn from yellow to peach, though it hadn't yet dipped in the sky. She watched two figures making their way out along the strip of shingle that had risen up from beneath the waves as the tide slowly retreated.

Watching them now, it was almost comical. Sophie, so tall with her long, thick chestnut hair, and Melissa, so tiny with her shoulder-length braids, both of them with their heads bowed against the strong breeze, their hair whipping around their faces.

It wasn't hard to guess what they were talking about with such intensity. She had immediately clocked Sophie not drinking and she looked terrible, with her skin almost grey under the harsh rays of the afternoon sun. Emily recognized the symptoms, though she wished she didn't. She loved her Jack so very much. So much that sometimes it physically hurt. But she wished... No, she couldn't even allow herself to think it. Her life had taken a turn that fateful night and she couldn't turn it back.

★ ★ ★ ★ ★

"You're drunk!" She laughed, staggering as he boomeranged between her and the brick wall they were passing.

He ran his hand through his blond hair as he stumbled on. "So are you."

She couldn't deny it. It was rare for her to let herself go, but it had been such a fun night. And such a lovely surprise to see him. They had run into each other by chance at a gig being held at the university. The members of the band had all left at the end of their first year to pursue a music career. Their contemporaries and their lecturers had shaken their heads and mumbled darkly about the "biggest mistake of their lives." But to everyone's surprise, including the band themselves, they had gone on to be very successful and were already selling out huge venues around the world. This gig was a thank-you to their old uni mates and favourite tutors for their early support, so it was a very small and intimate affair.

Emily had gone alone because none of the other girls in her halls of residence were third years and therefore weren't invited. Melissa had been at the gig too, but Emily had lost sight of her early on and assumed she had left.

He seemed as delighted and surprised to see her as she was to see him. They spent the evening getting more and more drunk and sweaty as they thrashed amid the adoring crowd. By the end, they were barely able to stand up, although he was worse than her.

"Can I crash on your floor?" His voice was staccato as he tried in vain to sound sober by concentrating on each word. "I'm not sure I'll make it back in one piece."

Despite her drunken state, she hesitated. "Better not," she slurred.

"No one will know."

That was true. If he left first thing in the morning, it was unlikely anyone would see him. "OK. But you're sleeping on the floor."

"'S'all I need."

★ ★ ★ ★ ★

She was woken by the sound of him stumbling around, crashing first into her desk, then her bed. Still in an alcohol haze, she momentarily forgot why he was there. "What the hell are you doing?"

"Sorry," he mumbled, before lifting the duvet and sliding in beside her.

"What the...?" she started to say, but he silenced her with a kiss and all argument was lost as she melted into him, her body unable to resist as his hands and mouth moved lower.

Afterwards, he fell asleep straight away, with her awkwardly entangled in his arms. She lay there staring up at the ceiling in shock at what had just happened.

As the smudgy light of dawn began to seep over the top of the curtains, she nudged him gently awake and moved as far away from him as she could. His eyes flickered open and she watched as he tried to compute where he was. Slowly, he turned his head towards her, a look of horror in his eyes. "Shit," he whispered.

"It's OK." She sounded more in control than she felt. "Get dressed. Leave. Go home. We can forget this ever happened. Don't worry, I'm not going to stalk you..."

Relief made his features relax and he nodded. He lifted the duvet, then hesitated, as if only just becoming aware of his nakedness.

Emily closed her eyes and turned her head to the wall. "I won't look."

After another second's hesitation, he climbed out of bed and Emily listened as he gathered up his clothes from the floor, then dressed quickly. She turned her head towards him and opened her eyes. He looked far more handsome than he had any right to.

He put his hands in the back pockets of his jeans and bit his lip, awkwardness and embarrassment enveloping him like a blanket. "Sorry," he murmured, glancing longingly towards the door, desperate for escape.

"Go," she said again.

After he'd gone, she tried to get back to sleep but couldn't. The smell of him lingered on her sheets and on her body, bringing with it flashbacks of him thrusting into her, setting her alight in a way that she'd never known before. With an almighty effort, she pushed the thoughts away, got out of bed and began to strip the duvet cover and pillowcases. She threw them into a pile in the middle of the floor and stared at the bare mattress, trying to make sense of what had happened. Already she somehow knew that this night would affect the rest of her life.

★ ★ ★ ★ ★

Watching Sophie and Melissa out on the beach in the evening sunlight, Emily felt a violent stab of jealousy. Sophie's situation was so different from the one she had found herself in. Sophie was in a happy, settled relationship with the love of her life, while Emily had been lost, scared and alone, sworn to secrecy and not even able to share the excitement and happiness of all the milestones along the way—the scans, the birth, the first tooth, the first step. Sophie would be able to share all of that with her Steve, and although she knew it was irrational, Emily hated her for it.

CHAPTER SIX

~~~~~~~~~~~~~~~~

"SO ARE YOU GOING TO TELL ME OR DO I HAVE to guess?" Melissa had borrowed a pair of too-big wellies and an oversized Barbour coat from the house, giving her the comical appearance of a child wearing her parents' clothes as she and Sophie crunched together over the shingle.

Sophie pulled her own leather jacket around her. Although it was August, the temperature still dropped sharply in the evenings, producing a strong breeze that carried with it more than a hint of ice. She looked ahead at the rapidly setting sun, a fierce ball of orange melting into a slate-grey sea. Walking along this narrow strip of shingle, which rose mystically from the water with each low tide, Sophie had a sudden feeling that she was walking on water. That she was invincible. "I'm pregnant."

She couldn't be sure if it was the sound of the wind or a sharp intake of breath from Melissa that whipped past her ears. They crunched along without speaking until they reached the end and couldn't walk any further without wading into the murky depths—the prospect of which Sophie found momentarily, desperately appealing. She hesitated, waiting for the temptation to pass, before turning. Ahead of them, the clapperboard house rose up in its pale blue painted splendour. The last of the sun's tired rays glinted lazily off the latticed windows, giving the impression that the house was slowly but surely dropping off to sleep.

Melissa reached out and took Sophie's hand in hers as they stood, still as statues while the wind continued to buffet them, causing their hair to blow around their faces. Her tiny hand felt strong and safe. "It'll be OK, you know."

Finally, Sophie turned to meet Melissa's eye and wondered if the gleam of tears she saw there was a reflection of her own. "I don't know what to do."

"Why don't you tell me what happened?"

★ ★ ★ ★ ★

Sophie looked up at the clock on the newsroom wall. It was 11:15 p.m. Her eyes felt gritty and sore through lack of sleep, but her heart was still hammering with adrenaline. She had just produced her first ever news bulletin and the buzz it had given her was indescribable. She had felt as if she was literally flying as she heard her words being read out to the nation by one of the most familiar newscasters in Britain.

Gradually, the newsroom had thinned out as everyone else drifted home, but Sophie didn't want to go home just yet. To Steve. Who would probably be fast asleep and snoring by now. She wanted to celebrate.

"So how was that for you, Sophie?" It wasn't just the face that was familiar. The voice was unmistakable too.

"Oh, it was amazing! Thank you. I mean, I know you do this every night, but my God, what a buzz!"

Matt Whitelaw laughed, revealing straight white teeth that

looked even whiter next to his tanned skin. "Yeah, I do it every night, but you know what? Every time is different and I never, ever take it for granted. It's great to see someone so fired up, though. Some of the producers have been around for so long that it seems as if they're just going through the motions."

Sophie nodded, knowing that he was talking about the two senior producers, Simon Tebbutt and Neil Marsh. Between them they had about thirty years under their belts at this company, and while their experience was undoubtedly valuable, they were both a bit too comfortable in their roles and had been secretly described by some of the other producers as "bed-blockers."

"Still, I guess as long as we stay at the top, they won't be going anywhere…" Matt shrugged on his black leather biker jacket and picked up his crash helmet. "Listen, I don't suppose you fancy a swift vino, do you?"

Sophie could feel herself reddening. She glanced around the newsroom to see if anyone had heard, but by now it was deserted. "Won't everywhere be closed?"

Matt tapped his nose. "I know a place… Come on, I've got a spare helmet on the bike." He strode confidently towards the door of the newsroom, clearly expecting no objection from her.

Sophie hesitated, looking down at her Lycra miniskirt and knee-length boots. *Oh, what the hell?* she thought, scooping up her bag and jacket and following him out of the door.

★ ★ ★ ★ ★

"You looked great on the bike in that skirt and those boots." Matt eyed her legs appreciatively as they sat opposite each other on soft red velvet chairs in the private members' lounge he had taken her to. "Did you see that cab driver's face when he pulled up alongside us? I thought his eyes were going to pop out of his head." Matt took a long, slow drag on his cigarette and exhaled, his eyes narrowing behind the tiny wall of smoke, giving him the aura of a fifties matinee idol.

Sophie laughed a little nervously. The evening had taken on a surreal quality. It was gone midnight and she knew that she shouldn't be here, alone with another man. A man she had fantasized about ever since she'd started working for this company just over a year ago.

Matt Whitelaw was the main anchor of the late news show. He was arrogant and vain and had been known to have more than the odd petulant outburst behind the scenes, but he was also undeniably sexy. His pale blue shirt strained against the honey-coloured skin on his taut, flat stomach. His blue-grey eyes were framed by long, dark lashes that gave him a look of innocence, even when he was saying the most outrageous things, which meant that he could get away with just about anything. He had that rare quality that drew both men and women to him in droves and probably stemmed from his sharp intellect and fierce wit. They had been discussing the story about Bill Clinton and the White House intern that was just beginning to surface and Sophie was in thrall as he assessed the mounting evidence. "Watch this space. It's going to cause him trouble, this one…" he finished with a knowing smile.

Sophie smiled back, alcohol dulling her ability to give a meaningful response. Matt then moved on to talking about the team at work, taking apart each character like a surgeon with a scalpel. "I dread to think what you say about me behind my back." Sophie's comment was meant to be light-hearted, but as she finished speaking, their eyes connected and Matt's face took on an intense expression.

"Oh, I do definitely talk about you behind your back." He spoke slowly and deliberately, rolling his words with his tongue. "But nothing for you to dread, I assure you."

Sophie wished he would be the one to look away first, but he had dropped his head slightly and was looking up at her through those lashes in a way that told her he was going nowhere. With an effort, she pulled her gaze away from his and took a sip of her champagne. She felt woozy and slightly sick. She was out of her depth and they both knew it. "I think I'd better go home."

Matt blinked sleepily, not betraying the faintest hint of disquiet. Still he watched her. "No, you don't. The night's only just begun..."

Suddenly, Sophie's senses, which seemed to have been floating in the ether above her all evening, snapped sharply back into focus. "Yes. I really do." She grabbed her bag and jacket and stood up. "You stay. I'll get a cab. Thanks for the drink. I'll see you tomorrow." Her words came out like the rattle of a machine gun, nerves making her gabble. She glanced back over her shoulder as she headed for the door. Matt was watching her with a tiny smirk of surprise. And was it her imagination or did he look ever so slightly impressed?

★ ★ ★ ★ ★

"So how come you were so late last night, gorgeous?" Steve rolled over in bed and wrapped his arms around Sophie, who tensed instinctively, guilt swirling in her stomach. She had arrived back at the flat to find a card from Steve on the kitchen table saying "Congratulations on a brilliant first show."

"I, er, went for a drink with some of the others after the programme."

Steve planted a kiss on her bare shoulder, his bristles scratching her skin in a way that wasn't unpleasant. "That's nice. So how did the programme go?"

Sophie turned over to face him. She loved Steve's "morning face," before he'd had a shave, with his dark blue eyes still crinkly with sleep and his silky blond hair mussed up so that it flopped messily around his high cheekbones. "It went really well. Did you like it?"

"I did." Steve kissed her gently on the mouth. "It looked great, but I meant how did it go behind the scenes? Was Mr Handsome a pain in the arse?"

Sophie smiled at Steve's description of Matt. They had often watched him deliver the news while commenting that he looked incredibly full of himself. "Nah, he was fine. Nice, actually. He came for a drink too." As soon as she said the words, Sophie could feel herself beginning to relax. She might not have told the whole truth, but she hadn't lied to Steve either. Already she was beginning to wonder if she had imagined the sexual tension she had felt last night. Matt had probably just wanted to unwind after the show and she was the only one available to go for a drink with him. It didn't mean he had singled her out at all.

She lifted her hand and stroked Steve's hair away from his face, enjoying the prickly sensation from his stubble on her palm. He took his cue and rolled on top of her, his mouth finding hers so effortlessly, his tongue exploring hers as if it was the first time they had ever kissed. Every nerve ending began to sing as Sophie guided him inside her, the feel of him so familiar yet each sensation so new. She threw her head back and groaned as he began to thrust faster, his mouth on her breasts, her neck, her stomach. Sophie could feel herself teetering on the edge of an orgasm, when Matt's face flashed in front of her closed lids. Suddenly, it was Matt's body above her, thrusting himself into her, pushing her closer and closer to the edge, and she came with an almighty shudder.

"Wow." Steve rolled off her and lay back on the bed, breathing heavily. "That was great."

"It was." Sophie was glad he wasn't looking at her face, because she felt sure he would know what she had been thinking in those final, climactic moments. A feeling of guilt began to gnaw at her. Already she had deceived Steve, and worse, she had fantasized about someone else while he was making love to her.

"I'd better get ready for work." She slipped her legs over the side of the bed and sat up.

"Yeah, me too. Wish I didn't have to, though. Wish I could stay in bed with you all day."

Sophie looked at him over her shoulder and smiled. "Me too." She felt obliged to say it, even though she didn't really mean it. She loved her work with a passion and couldn't wait to get there most days. She had thought it was just because she had fulfilled a long-held ambition when she became a TV producer, but it was more than that. She loved the buzz, the excitement. The people. One person in particular.

Steve quite enjoyed his job as an HR officer for a City bank, but it was a million miles from where his ambitions lay. He was a comedy writer and he dreamed of making it a career one day. For now, though, they had a mortgage to pay on their two-bedroom flat in Balham in south London and they couldn't afford for one of them to give up work just yet. Sophie sometimes felt guilty about it, but more and more recently she had begun to question why he had settled for such a dull career when he could have gone for something more exciting. Like she had.

She still loved him so deeply and couldn't imagine her life without him in it. It was as if her adulthood had only really begun once she met him. But in the newsroom each day, she was surrounded by ambitious, thrusting, handsome, funny men who sometimes made Steve seem a little, well, boring. Every time the insistent little thought niggled at a corner of her brain, she would try to push it away, but it always returned.

Walking into the newsroom later that morning, she was lost in thought and mulling over what news stories might feature in her bulletin, when Keira, another of the junior producers she worked with, sidled up and fell into step beside her. "So, it looks like someone's got an admirer."

Sophie frowned. "Sorry?"

Keira nudged her. "You. And Matt. Jez saw you leaving the newsroom together last night."

Sophie's insides dropped instantly with fear. "What? No. I mean, there was nothing in it. We just went for a drink." She started to stutter and could feel her cheeks burning, making her look guilty as hell.

"Hey, you don't need to defend yourself to me." Keira nudged her gently. "Who wouldn't, given half a chance?"

"No! You don't understand. *I* wouldn't. I have a boyfriend I'm very happy with. Matt's a player. He could have anyone. He doesn't want or need to bother with me."

Keira looked at her closely, as if weighing up whether to believe her. "Seriously? You turned down Matt Whitelaw?"

"No!" Sophie could feel the frustration bubbling up inside her as she reached her desk and dumped her bag on the floor, before slumping into her chair. "I didn't turn him down, because he didn't try anything! We had a drink and I got a cab home. End of story. I don't remotely fancy him and I doubt very much whether he remotely fancies me." Her voice rose as she spoke, and by the time she had finished, she was aware that she had an audience. She looked around to see that Matt had arrived in the newsroom just in time to hear the last sentence.

He smiled at her easily and headed for his own desk, where he sat down and began typing at his keyboard. Keira mouthed the word "Oops" and edged away towards her own seat.

Sophie took a second to compose herself before she turned to her computer and logged in. They had just had new computers installed with an operating system called Outlook Express, which meant they could send emails to one another. Immediately, an email flashed up.

MATT WHITELAW: ACTUALLY I DO REMOTELY FANCY YOU.

CHAPTER SEVEN

~~~~~~~~

"SO WHAT? YOU DIDN'T DO ANYTHING WRONG."
Melissa tucked her hands deep into the pockets of her over-sized Barbour as she and Sophie sat together on the sea wall, looking out over the choppy water while a flock of seagulls squealed through the deepening sky.

"I wouldn't have done anything wrong if I'd left it there." *If only. If only I had left things there.*

★ ★ ★ ★ ★

Sophie let herself into the flat and crept towards the bed-room door, which was ajar. She peeped her head around it and strained her eyes to see if she could make out the figure of Steve asleep in the darkness.

"If you're looking for me, I'm in here."

Sophie jumped. Her heart beginning to pound, she walked to the living room, where she found Steve sitting on the sofa in the dark, his back ramrod straight, staring at the wall.

"What are you doing in here?" She tried to keep her voice

light-hearted, but she had a sudden feeling of foreboding. "Has something happened?"

Steve didn't answer. Finally, he leaned over and clicked on the lamp beside him, bathing the small room in a golden glow. "Come and sit down, Sophie. I think we need to talk."

The bile rose in Sophie's throat. She had never seen Steve look so serious, his lovely dancing eyes now clouded with… something. She couldn't work out if it was sadness, anger, jealousy or disgust. She sat down beside him yet as far from him as possible, as if she was lowering herself onto a cushion of broken glass. How could she possibly be so nervous in the company of the man she had loved for the past eight years? "Steve? You're scaring me. What's the matter?"

Steve's face softened as he gazed at her, and she knew that whatever he was about to say, he still loved her. She could see it, sense it, smell it. He reached out and took her hand, stroking it gently. "I think we should split up."

"No! Oh my God, no!" Her cheeks began to blaze with fear. "But…why?"

Steve reached out and stroked her face, catching her tears in his hand, his expression a mixture of sorrow and love. "I think we both know why."

"I don't!"

"But you do, sweetheart. We've started leading separate lives. Ever since you joined that programme, you've been drifting away from me. I know you so well, Sophie. I can tell. I know that you think I'm boring compared to all those testosterone-fuelled blokes you work with."

"No! You've got it all wrong. I don't think you're boring. I love you!" It occurred to Sophie that it was only now, as she spoke the words, that she realized how true they were.

Steve shook his head sadly and cupped her face in his hand.

His strong, smooth, beautiful hand. "You've had no idea where I've been every evening and I've had no idea where you've been. Why you're always so late home these days when the programme finishes at ten thirty..." He let the words hang in the air for a second and Sophie realized what he was telling her. He knew.

"I..." she began, but she couldn't continue. He was right. She had been so busy covering her tracks that she hadn't ever stopped to find out what he'd been up to all these evenings when she was working. Now she knew. He'd been following her. He would have seen her leaving the building each night with Matt, getting on his motorbike and heading back to his flat near Tower Bridge. Was he sitting outside when she left again an hour or so later and climbed into a cab, wondering if she smelt of him? Hoping that Steve would be asleep so that he wouldn't want to make love?

"But I love you." The words sounded so empty coming from her mouth now. So deceitful. Yet they were true.

"I know. I love you too. But we're done, babe." Steve got up and looked down at her. "I've packed a bag and I'll take it tonight. I'll come back for my other stuff later."

"How can you be so calm about this?" Sophie felt an inexplicable surge of anger.

Steve sighed deeply and shook his head. "Because I've had time to get used to it. When I first realized...I was the complete opposite of calm, I can assure you. I was a mess. But you obviously didn't notice."

Shame and guilt settled around Sophie like a blanket. No, she hadn't noticed. She had stopped taking any notice of her beautiful, loyal, decent partner because she was too busy playing around with her shallow, selfish, arrogant lover.

★ ★ ★ ★ ★

Sophie stumbled through the next few days like a drunk oblivious to everything else except getting the next drink. The only thought in her head was Steve. After he'd gone, she lay in bed listening to the clank and rattle of the pipes that sounded as if they were groaning in protest at the loss of their owner.

She pulled his pillow to her face and let it absorb the tears, which wouldn't stop flowing. The scent of him clung to the bedsheets, causing her insides to cramp with pain and fear. Only now did she really understand how much she loved him. How much she needed him. And that she just couldn't function without him. Without him, it felt as if her life was over.

She rang his mobile over and over again. Each time it would click through to his voicemail and she would leave long, rambling messages, begging his forgiveness, telling him how much she loved him and pleading with him to come home. She didn't know if he listened to them, but she had to try. She had to do everything she could to convince him to give her another chance. Panic engulfed her every time she hung up, wondering how the hell she would ever cope if he didn't.

She called in sick at work, and when Matt texted her, she deleted the texts and deleted his number. Anything she felt for him had evaporated in an instant. She spent the whole time clutching her phone in the desperate hope that Steve would call her back. She wondered where he'd gone and realized with a pang of shame that she had stopped taking any interest in his life around the same time that she had started her job at the TV station. She didn't actually know who his good friends were any more or who he might have gone to in his hour of need.

She lost count of the days, but sometime during the following week, the door opened and he walked in. Sophie leapt off the bed and ran into the hallway, staring at him with her mouth open, hanging on to his gaze, terrified that she might be seeing things and he might disappear again just as quickly as he had appeared. He looked tired and dishevelled but so, so beautiful. His eyes glittered with tears and his mouth moved towards a smile, which quickly became a sob. She crossed the distance between them and threw herself onto him, kissing his face, his mouth, his body. "I'm so sorry, I'm so sorry. I love you so much."

He gripped her just as tightly, responding hungrily to her kisses, and then somehow they were in the bedroom, tearing at each other's clothes, exploring each other's bodies. Later, they lay naked and entwined, Sophie too afraid to move away from him in case he left again. "I love you." She looked into his eyes to try to convey how much she meant it. "I love you so much."

He looked down at her, his expression gentle, the hurt already leaving his features. "I love you too."

"I'm sorry, Steve. I am so, so sorry. I will do anything... anything, to prove to you that I will never, ever hurt you again."

"I'm sorry too."

"Don't. You have *nothing* to be sorry for." Sophie sat up and looked at him fiercely.

Much later, as they drank wine, sitting side by side, still in bed, something occurred to her. "Where did you go? Where have you been?"

Steve blinked slowly and shook his head slightly. "I don't want to talk about it."

"OK." It was understandable. It had been such a painful

time for both of them. "But I want you to know that I am there for you, Steve. I am going to put you first from now on. No more leading separate lives."

Steve smiled slightly and leaned forward to kiss her. "And no more looking back either. I just want to forget the past and move on."

Sophie's eyes filled. She felt like the luckiest woman alive. He was going to give her another chance. And there was no way she was going to blow it this time.

★ ★ ★ ★ ★

The darkness had begun to encroach and the sky was losing the last pink traces of the day. The waves continued to crash around them and the strip of shingle that had risen out of the sea's murky depths had now submitted to it once more.

Melissa looked at Sophie, frowning in confusion. "But that's all good, isn't it? I know you might not necessarily have planned to get pregnant just yet, but you're back with Steve, you're madly in love again... What's the problem?"

Sophie wrapped her arms around herself. She didn't know if she could voice what the problem was, or admit it, even to herself. In the end, she didn't need to.

"Oh." Melissa didn't have to say any more. She understood.

"So, as I said, I don't know what to do."

Melissa nodded and Sophie could see the fear in her eyes on her behalf. Her stomach churned like the sea stretching far out in front of them.

"Well," Melissa began, hesitant at first, then more confident, "it's almost certainly Steve's, isn't it?"

"Yes. Almost." God, how she hated that word right now.

"But…surely you used something with…the other one." Melissa stuttered over the words.

Sophie nodded. No need to tell Melissa about that last time when the condom came off. She hadn't thought anything of it at the time. Why didn't she think anything of it? How could she have been so stupid?

"And with Steve?"

"Not that first day, when he came home."

"So Steve will definitely think it's his?"

Sophie nodded again, still hugging herself, not so much for warmth but for some kind of comfort. Yes, Steve would believe that the baby was his. But what if it wasn't? Could she live with such a lie for her whole life?

"Have you told Steve?" Melissa stood up from where they were sitting on the sea wall and faced Sophie.

"No. Not yet. I'm still trying to deal with it myself."

"Well, if you want my advice…"

"I do."

Melissa's face softened and she reached out to hug Sophie. "Tell him. And tell yourself the same thing. And live your life looking forward, not back."

CHAPTER EIGHT

~~~~~~~~~~~~~~~~

AMY THREW ANOTHER SLICE OF BACON INTO THE scorching frying pan and watched with satisfaction as it immediately started to sizzle and crisp. There was no sign of any of the others yet, meaning she had the kitchen to herself, which was how she liked it. She wasn't alone very often these days, ever since she moved in with Nick, so it was a rare treat.

It was lovely to see the girls, but there was a strange atmosphere this year. Something that Amy couldn't put her finger on. Sophie in particular seemed out of sorts and down. She didn't look great either. And Melissa was drinking them all under the table, more so than usual. Even Emily seemed a bit low.

Amy sighed. She was so very happy right now and she felt bad that she couldn't share some of it with her closest friends. It seemed inappropriate to gush about how well things were going for her when clearly the others were having issues of their own that meant they were slightly distant and distracted.

She thought about Nick and what he'd be doing this Sunday morning while she was away. He had opined that he wouldn't know what to do without her and would spend every moment she was away waiting for her to return. Amy grinned to herself. She could never in her wildest dreams have imagined finding a man like Nick, who was so unashamedly obsessed with her and was happy to tell everyone how much he loved and adored her.

He had wanted to get married quickly, suggesting they jet off to a paradise island and do it as soon as possible. But Amy had gently resisted. She was an only child and she knew how much it would hurt her parents not to see her married. She wasn't good at standing her ground. Usually, she would go along with things to keep everyone happy, even if it meant that she sometimes went against her own instinct. But on this she was absolutely adamant. "I want my parents there and I want the girls there. They're like the sisters I never had and I have to have them at my wedding."

A flash of irritation had crossed Nick's face. This was probably the first and only time she had insisted on anything. But after a moment's thought, he had nodded and smiled. "Fine. I just love you so much, Amy, I want you to be mine as soon as possible."

Amy had beamed back at him, buoyed by her tiny victory, and wrapped her arms around him. "I am yours, darling. I have been since that day we first met. I always will be. Being married will be wonderful, but it won't change anything."

Nick had kissed the top of her head. "But that's where you're wrong. Being married will change everything because we will both know that we are together for ever and nothing will ever come between us."

Remembering his words now made Amy feel as though she was glowing from the inside out. She was so certain of his love and devotion that she had never experienced even the slightest scintilla of doubt about their relationship. He wanted her to give up work after the wedding so that they could try for a baby and Amy couldn't wait. She loved her job, but Nick was her priority now. Nick and the family she knew they would have together. She couldn't wait.

As she placed the crispy bacon slices on a warmed plate and began to whisk eggs together, Emily wandered into the kitchen and sat at the island in the middle of the room. "Well, aren't you a sight for sore eyes… That looks and smells like heaven, Amy."

Amy grinned. "That's what Nick says to me every morning when I cook his breakfast."

"I bet he does." Emily reached over to sneak a piece of bacon, but Amy slapped her hand away, causing Emily to giggle. "He's a very lucky man, Amy. I wish I had you to cook my breakfast every day."

Amy smiled and poured the eggs into the sizzling pan, deftly flipping them around the pan as they began to bubble and solidify into an omelette. "I would happily cook you breakfast every morning, Em. Just get yourself over to my place by seven thirty and it'll be waiting for you."

Emily laughed. "Don't tempt me!"

Amy crumbled the crisped bacon into the omelette and folded it over, before cutting it in half and serving it onto the two plates she had warmed. She took them to the table, where she had prepared a jug of freshly squeezed orange juice and a plate of thick-cut toast. Emily groaned, before launching herself towards the table and beginning to devour her food. "Will you rethink marrying Nick?" she managed between mouthfuls. "And marry me instead?"

Amy watched her with satisfaction. She felt a deep swell of love and admiration for Emily, who had had such a tough time bringing up Jack on her own yet never whined or moaned about being tired or broke, both of which she most definitely was. "So how are you, Em? And how's my darling Jack?"

Emily nodded slowly as she poured herself some orange juice. "We're both well. Jack's a dream. Life is good."

Amy raised her eyebrows. "I just thought you seemed a bit, I don't know, distracted or something last night. Are you sure everything is OK?"

Emily smiled fondly. "You're always worrying about other people, aren't you? There's no need on my behalf, honestly. I'm fine."

Amy shrugged. Emily was always such a closed book, she knew there was no point in digging any further. "OK. And what about Sophie? She doesn't seem herself at all."

Emily opened her mouth to answer, but before she could speak, Sophie herself arrived in the kitchen, looking pale and tired. "What about me?" There was a weary defensiveness to her voice.

Amy could feel herself reddening instantly. She jumped up and ushered Sophie into her seat. "Nothing. I was just making breakfast," she gabbled. "What can I get you?"

Sophie shook her head. "I'm not feeling great, Amy, thanks all the same. I'll just have some dry toast."

"What's wrong, do you think?" Emily fixed Sophie with an incisive gaze as Amy watched nervously. There was a sudden tension in the air that she didn't quite understand.

Sophie sighed. "Well, I might as well tell you both. You'll find out anyway—"

"You're pregnant," Emily cut in, her voice flat and toneless.

Sophie swallowed and nodded. "I'm pregnant."

"Oh my God!" Amy threw herself towards Sophie and wrapped her arms around her. "That is fantastic news! Congratulations!" Sophie's body felt stiff and unyielding, so Amy stood back and waited for a response.

Eventually, she replied, "Thanks. Although I'm still trying to come to terms with it myself."

"What did Steve say?" Again, Emily's tone was flat.

Sophie took a deep breath. "I haven't told him yet."

Amy gasped. The idea of telling her friends something so huge before telling Nick was unthinkable. "Why not?"

Sophie shrugged wearily. "Because I've only just found out. Because I haven't come to terms with it myself yet. Because, as per usual, Melissa knew before I did."

Amy pulled up a chair and sat down beside her. "But you're happy about it, aren't you?"

Sophie bit her lip. "Of course. Just…adjusting. It's a shock, that's all." She looked at Emily. "You must have felt the same, Em."

Emily's face, which had been set hard, softened slightly. "You can say that again. But once you're over the shock, it's the best thing you'll ever do. And at least you've got Steve…" Her words hung in the air for a few seconds, the admonishment unspoken.

Sophie nodded. "Yes. I know. I'm very lucky." Her words sounded robotic and forced.

Amy watched the exchange. It was as if there was a whole other scene being played out that she wasn't part of. There was a definite undercurrent and she couldn't for the life of her work out why.

"Where's my breakfast?" Melissa staggered into the kitchen, wearing a tiny pair of denim shorts and a white sleeveless top, the faint sheen of sweat on her forehead the only sign that she was hungover. She pulled up a chair and slumped down, before looking up at the others curiously. "Oh. I take it you've told them, then?"

Sophie nodded.

"Isn't it the most fantastic news?" Amy couldn't understand why no one else seemed to be pleased or excited. If it was her, she would be jumping up and down with glee.

Sophie and Melissa exchanged a glance. "Yes, of course it is," Melissa said. "It's brilliant news and you're thrilled, aren't you, Sophie?"

Sophie gave a small, tired smile. "Yes," she said. "I'm thrilled."

JULY 1999

"American cyclist Lance Armstrong has won his first Tour de France title."

BRIGHTON

CHAPTER NINE

~~~~~~~~~~~

"RIGHT, MADAM, YOU HAVE SOME CATCHING UP to do after all those months not drinking. Cheers!" Melissa clinked her glass against Sophie's and they both drank greedily. The effect was almost instant, as Sophie's spirits soared with each sip and her head began to swim in a pleasurable way. They sank down into the two armchairs and beamed at each other.

"That's more like it!" Melissa sighed. "Wonder where the others are."

As if on cue, there was a knock at the door. Sophie made to get up but found that her legs were surprisingly wobbly. "Jesus, I'm such a lightweight… I feel pissed already!"

"Good!" Melissa leapt out of her chair and ran towards the door, which she swung open with a flourish.

"Helloooo!" came a cry as Amy and Emily tumbled into the room, both of them looking distinctly dishevelled.

"I see you've located the champagne Nick sent and demolished it already."

Melissa put her hands on her tiny hips as if in a gesture of disapproval, but she couldn't hide her delight. "Oh, it's so great to see you—come on, group hug!"

With an almighty effort, Sophie hauled herself out of her chair and joined the others in a mini rugby scrum of a hug. Four different scents combined with the alcohol fumes to make her senses swim. She had felt so dislocated and strange for so long now that it was overwhelming to be surrounded by so much love and such a feeling of belonging.

"Sophie! Are you OK? What's wrong?" Amy pulled back as she spoke and broke the circle. All eyes turned towards Sophie with expressions of concern and bafflement.

Sophie shook her head roughly, trying to shake out the wooziness, embarrassed. "Sorry, I'm fine. I'm just…happy to see you."

"You're such an old softie!" Melissa reached up and put her arm around Sophie's back, giving her a squeeze. "I think it's more likely that it's the first alcohol you've had in ages and it's gone straight to your head."

"You're probably right." The tension began to seep out of Sophie's body. She knew that it was more than just the effect of the alcohol, but she didn't care. She desperately needed to let out some of the emotion she had been bottling up for so long.

★ ★ ★ ★ ★

The look of joy on Steve's face was like a dagger to her heart. "Oh, wow, that's amazing. Really, really amazing." He gazed at her in wonder, as if he was seeing her for the first time. "Are you sure?"

Sophie tried to smile, her lip wobbling. "I'm sure. I've done four tests so far. All of them with the same result."

A sudden shadow flickered across Steve's face. She knew what he was thinking.

"It's definitely yours, Steve."

He nodded and looked down. "But presumably you can't know that for certain."

Sophie swallowed hard and took a deep breath. She had to make this convincing. "I can and I do. We always used something. Whereas when you first came home…"

"We didn't," he finished for her. Still he was looking down, unable to meet her eye.

"When the baby's born, if you want, I'll have a DNA test done…" Part of her hoped he'd agree. It would give her the answer she needed. Even if it wasn't the answer she wanted.

"No." Steve's voice was firm and he looked up at her, as if decided. "No. No need."

Sophie could feel her face beginning to burn, but this was how it had to be. Even if she wasn't certain, she had to make them both believe it.

"Wow," Steve said, his face softening again. They were in a pizza restaurant, a large, noisy one where the clatter of plates fought with the hubbub of chatter and laughter. She had chosen it deliberately, unsure if she could cope with the well of emotion swirling around inside her if they were alone. She was scared that tears and words would come tumbling out in a waterfall of confession and regret.

Steve reached across the small marble-topped table and took her hand. "I am so, so pleased. How are you feeling?"

Sophie bit her lip. "Scared."

A flicker of confusion passed over his face, his bright blue eyes clouding momentarily. "Just scared? Nothing else?"

Sophie smiled. "I'm excited too. Just…can't imagine it, you know?"

Steve nodded. "I know."

But of course, he didn't.

She asked for a transfer at work so that she wasn't producing the late news, claiming that the hours were too difficult for her to cope with while pregnant. Matt had texted her a few times, so eventually she invited him to go for a coffee and told him that she was pregnant.

The look of horror and fear in his eyes was in such stark contrast to Steve's delighted reaction that she wondered for the millionth time why she had ever been stupid enough to get involved with him. "It's not yours," she had told him bluntly, almost wanting to laugh as his face relaxed with relief. They had finished their coffees and parted company for what she knew would be the last time. Matt had only ever been interested in her for sex, so there was absolutely no point in continuing to see each other if that wasn't on offer.

She and Steve sold their flat and moved into a small house not far from where Steve's parents lived in Richmond in time for the baby's arrival. On the surface, everything seemed perfect. Steve's mum was going to act as the childminder once they both went back to work and Steve had had a promotion at work, which meant that they weren't even going to be worse off financially.

But she couldn't help feeling like a fraud. And worse, much worse, she was starting to resent the baby. Things got slightly better after the twenty-week scan, when the sonographer revealed that she was expecting a girl. At least it wouldn't look like him. She found herself clinging on to the hope that as soon as the baby was born, she would hold her in her arms and fall in love with her, all doubts forgotten.

The pregnancy was difficult. Not physically but emotionally. She couldn't shake the feeling that she was cheating Steve by pretending that she was certain about the baby's paternity, and without intending to, she started to mentally distance herself from him. He was so thrilled and excited about the baby that she wasn't sure if he had even noticed, but she could feel an invisible wall building up between them.

After a long and painful labour, when the midwife placed the slippery, snuffling little bundle into her arms, she felt nothing. She cooed over her, as she knew everyone would expect her to do, but in stark contrast with Steve's tearful, heartfelt welcome for his firstborn, all she felt was a cold detachment.

During the days and weeks that followed, she went through the motions of motherhood, all the while wondering when the surge of love she knew she was supposed to feel for her beautiful baby would kick in. But it didn't. She watched Steve's face melt every time he looked at Emma and felt a little spike of something that felt uncomfortably like jealousy shoot through her.

Emma was an easy baby. She smiled a lot and slept well, but Sophie still found her exhausting, and although she would never admit it to anyone, even herself, she found motherhood a drudge. Whole days went by in a mundane blur of washing, ironing, changing nappies and feeding. When Steve went back to work after taking two weeks off, Sophie felt as if she had slumped into a pit of loneliness and despair that even the sweetest baby in the world couldn't pull her out of.

All the girls came to visit. Melissa surprised her by scooping Emma up and cuddling her as if she had done it a million times before. She didn't even seem to mind when Emma spewed up over her pale blue cashmere jumper. Amy and Emily came together, and once they had done the obligatory oohing and aahing, they both seemed keen to get away. She understood why. The house felt claustrophobic and stuffy, as if her mood had settled like a blanket of dust over everything in it.

Lots of other friends and family came to visit in the early days too, but they had their own busy lives to lead and gradually the visits dwindled away to nothing, leaving her to find ways to fill the achingly long days. The first six weeks of Emma's life were the longest of Sophie's. The minutes, hours and days stretched out before her like a marathon course she felt she had no hope of ever completing.

When Steve came home from work, he was so thrilled to see Emma, he seemed not to notice that Sophie was gradually retreating into herself. He was as affectionate and loving towards her as ever, but she could tell that his main focus had moved away from her and she didn't like it one bit.

Amy's hen weekend had been in the diary since before Emma was born, and from the moment of her birth, it had taken on a huge significance. Every day she looked at it on the calendar like an oasis in the desert of her life and lurched towards it, willing it to come quicker. It was her escape. Her salvation. She imagined that just a couple of days away would turn her into the mother she knew she ought to be.

And now that day was here and she still didn't feel the all-consuming love that she had heard other mothers talking about. Instead, she was already dreading the weekend being over and having to return to the drudgery of her everyday life.

"So, Soph, how are you finding motherhood?"

Sophie spun around to find Emily looking up at her with an expression that she couldn't quite read. "Um, good. Really good." It was the same answer she always gave. It had become a habit.

"Is she a good baby?"

Sophie smiled. "She is. She sleeps really well and she's turning into quite a porker!"

"Have you got any new photos? I'd love to see them."

Sophie hesitated. *Had* she brought any photos with her? It hadn't occurred to her. She had been so excited about packing her own things. "I'm not sure where they are…" She reached for her bag and rummaged through it, feeling as she did so her cheeks starting to flame. "Oh no!" she said, feigning regret. "I must have left them on my bed at home."

Just then, Amy came to her rescue. "Hey, you two!" she beamed, wrapping her arms around both their shoulders and pulling them into her embrace. "I hope you're both ready to paaaarrrtaaay!"

"She looks so happy, doesn't she?" Emily motioned towards Amy as she danced off to refill her glass.

"She does." Sophie looked enviously at Amy, her long auburn hair shining, her porcelain skin glowing and her beautiful face set in a permanent smile of even white teeth. She had so much to look forward to. It seemed unlikely that she would ever find herself struggling with life the way Sophie was right now.

"So...bit of a shock to the system, isn't it?" Emily's dark eyes were boring into her, as if she could read Sophie's thoughts.

"Well, in a word, yes. But you'd know all about that. Honestly, Em, I can't imagine how you did it on your own. It's so..."

"Relentless?" Emily found the word for her. "I know, but I wasn't on my own. Not really. I had more help than you'd think."

Sophie felt a swell of admiration that Emily could play down what must have been such a difficult time for her. "I know your mum and dad were great, but not having a partner must have been really tough. I don't know what I'd have done without Steve these past few months." She paused before continuing. "He's really taken to fatherhood. He's better at it than me, if I'm honest. It seems to come more naturally to him."

"I'm sure that's not true." Emily reached out and touched Sophie's arm. "It's just that you're having to deal with all those hormones as well as the day-to-day drudge. It's hard. Nothing can really prepare you for it."

Sophie smiled her gratitude, unable to speak for a few seconds. The relief of hearing someone else voice what she was feeling was immense. Maybe she wasn't so hopeless after all.

"It's not unusual to find it a struggle, Sophie. I think it would be weird if you sailed through it with no problems or feelings of doubt. God, the number of times I cried because I was such a useless mother!"

"You?" Sophie was dumbfounded. Emily had always seemed so strong. So sure. So capable.

"Yes, me! And every other new mother too. The only words of comfort I can give you are that this feeling will pass. It's a bit like the birth itself. You forget very quickly how painful it was."

"I feel…" Sophie paused, trying to formulate her words. "I feel guilty. There are so many other people who are desperate for a baby. And then there's me, who wishes…" She couldn't finish the sentence. Couldn't say out loud what she really felt.

Emily blinked and nodded slowly. "You can't worry about other people, Soph. You have to concentrate on yourself. Don't you think I've often thought how much easier my life would be if I'd met some rich, handsome man like Amy has? But that's not her problem. It's mine."

Sophie nodded gratefully. Emily was always so wise. So calm. "And I'm sure you'll meet your Mr Right one day, Ems."

Emily's dark eyes clouded momentarily. "Maybe. Then again, maybe I already did."

CHAPTER TEN

~~~~~~~~~~

"COME BACK TO OUR ROOM AND LET'S CARRY on the party there!" Melissa tripped drunkenly up the steps of the hotel and reached out to stop herself falling, forgetting that she was clutching an almost empty bottle of champagne. The bottle smashed and Melissa screamed in surprise as her hand landed heavily on one of the exposed shards of glass.

There was a communal gasp of horror from the others as the palm of Melissa's hand began to bleed. "It's nothing…" Melissa lifted up her hand and looked at it dispassionately, seemingly not noticing the blood dripping onto her white jeans in artistic splatters and apparently feeling no pain.

"Liss! It's not nothing…" Sophie's head, which had been swimming just moments earlier, cleared instantly. She fished in her bag for some tissues and found a travel pack of baby wipes. "Right…let's wrap your hand in this." She removed a baby wipe from the packet and, after checking that there was no glass left in the wound, tied it around the cut.

Melissa snatched her hand away impatiently. "It's fine! Stop fussing. Come on, everyone, let's keep this party going!" She stood and staggered drunkenly up the remaining few steps, before turning around and looking down at them expectantly.

Sophie and the others stood for a moment in shocked silence. Finally, Amy spoke. "Well, I don't know about you guys, but I'm actually really tired. It's been such a brilliant night—maybe we should quit while we're ahead?"

A murmur of agreement rumbled through the trio as they began to climb the steps. "I think we're all too tired to carry on, Liss," Sophie told her as they reached the top.

Melissa sneered in disbelief. "Jesus, tell me you're joking! We're not a bunch of pensioners on a coach trip. We're here to party. To celebrate Amy's hen weekend…" She paused momentarily and frowned to herself, as if she had lost her train of thought. "Come on! Let's get another drink!" She hooked her arm through Sophie's and tried to pull her towards the hotel bar, which was still open, although there were just a couple of men propping it up.

"No, Melissa!" Sophie snapped as a worrying thought occurred to her. "I'm tired. And I need my bed."

"Well, I'm not!" Melissa retorted, her eyes glinting, and Sophie noticed for the first time how dilated her pupils were. It wasn't just alcohol that Melissa had been partaking of that night. "You lot go to bed. I'm carrying on." She strutted towards the men at the bar, wiggling her tiny hips suggestively. "Right, which one of you lucky boys is going to buy me a drink?"

Sophie watched her helplessly, unsure what to do. She didn't feel that she could leave her alone, but she was utterly exhausted. She glanced at the other two, who were yawning and looking at their watches.

"She'll be fine." Amy shrugged. "You know what Melissa's like—she can look after herself. Go to bed, Soph."

Sophie glanced back at Melissa, who by now was perched on a bar stool between two men, laughing loudly and demanding champagne "for medicinal purposes" as she held up her roughly bandaged hand.

"She'll be fine," came Emily's voice with more than a hint of irritation. "I'm certainly not going to sit up all night drinking with a couple of sad, middle-aged businessmen."

Sophie hesitated, before slowly turning to follow the others towards the lifts, trying to ignore the niggling feeling of doubt in her mind. Amy was right. Melissa was a big girl now and she could take care of herself. Sophie made her way back to her room, suddenly feeling old again after the most fun night out she'd had in years. They had eaten at a small seafront restaurant, before heading out clubbing, something Sophie hadn't done for years. She had felt young and vibrant for a short while. Now she felt even more tired and old than before.

She let herself into the hotel room. The debris of their earlier partying was everywhere to be seen: empty champagne flutes and several empty bottles littered the coffee table and bedside tables. Wearily, Sophie gathered them all up and put them on a silver tray that she placed outside the door. Then she brushed her teeth, climbed into bed and fell into a deep, fitful sleep.

★ ★ ★ ★ ★

"So what do you do, exactly, working for a record company?"

Melissa frowned as she tried to focus on what he was saying. Her head felt thick and her senses were starting to blur. She had drunk far, far too much champagne. And she had managed to do a couple of lines of coke when the others were preoccupied earlier. She wondered vaguely if she should maybe do another one now to help clear her head a bit. The bottle they had ordered when she first joined the men at the bar was now empty and they had moved on to whisky. "Very glamorous. Very, very glamorous," she managed.

"A bit like you," the one called John—or was it Joe?—replied.

Melissa smiled prettily. He wasn't bad-looking. Mid-forties, with icy blue eyes and a strong jawline. He was wearing a wedding ring, but if it didn't bother him, Melissa certainly wasn't going to let it bother her. He looked like he had a good body under his suit. He wasn't paunchy like his friend Mark, who seemed to have realized when he was beaten and was now yawning into his whisky.

"I think I'll call it a night," he said, draining his glass and getting to his feet a little unsteadily. "Have fun," he added, giving a lascivious wink, as he staggered out of the bar.

"So…" Joe—or was it John?—raised one eyebrow at her meaningfully.

"So…" Melissa had been here before. Men picked her up all the time. She sometimes wondered if she should play harder to get, but she simply didn't know how. Occasionally, she would stop to think about why she was the way she was and she knew that it wouldn't take a genius to work out that she was desperate for approval. And love. In the absence of any decent men asking her out, meaningless sex with married strangers gave her a tiny, fleeting taste of both.

"My room or yours?" He grinned. He had a nice smile. He also had no hint of doubt that she would sleep with him.

"Have to be yours. My room-mate won't appreciate us barging into mine…"

He smiled again. She wished she could remember his name. "Mine it is, then. Shall we?" He slid off his stool and crooked his arm for her to take. She slipped her arm through his, taking care not to hurt her roughly bandaged hand, and together they made their way out of the bar.

"Goodnight!" the barman called after them.

Melissa turned to wave and recoiled slightly at the look he gave her. Did he think she was a *hooker*?

"Ignore him, he's just jealous," Joe or John said, guiding her towards the lifts with a sudden urgency.

"Worried you'll be spotted by a friend of your wife's?" Melissa said as the lift doors closed behind them.

Immediately after the doors closed, he pushed her up against the mirrored lift wall and kissed her hard, his tongue finding hers and his hands moving under her top to find her breasts, which he squeezed roughly. "My wife doesn't understand me," he murmured, unzipping her white jeans and sliding his hands down to cup her buttocks. He lifted her up as if she was weightless and Melissa wrapped her legs around his waist, fumbling for the zip of his trousers. They dropped to the floor and she caught sight of his bare behind in the mirror as he slid inside her.

"No!" she gasped as he began to thrust.

He stopped abruptly and looked at her in shock. "No? Bit late for that, isn't it?"

"I meant, we need to use something."

His face softened and he pulled out of her, letting her drop gently to her feet. "Shit. Of course. Sorry. Couldn't help myself."

A loud ping made them both jump and simultaneously they pulled up and zipped their trousers just in time for the lift doors to open. He grabbed her hand and led her out of the lift, Melissa scurrying to keep up with his long strides. Within seconds he had opened the door to his room and pulled her in. He raced to the bedside table, where he retrieved a condom and held it up triumphantly. "There!" he said, his eyes narrowing with undisguised lust. "Now, where were we?"

★ ★ ★ ★ ★

The next morning, Sophie awoke with a start. She immediately glanced over to Melissa's bed. It was empty. The niggle of discomfort she had felt last night instantly became a huge, pressing weight as her stomach dropped with fear. She should never have left her. What sort of friend was she to have abandoned her, knowing she was drunk and high on coke? She picked up her mobile phone and looked at it, praying for a message. There was none. She found Melissa's number and dialled, tensing as she did so. It rang out, before clicking through to an answering service. Sophie hung up without leaving a message.

She climbed out of bed and walked to the window, aware that a cold sweat of panic had broken out on her forehead. Where the hell was Melissa? Just as she was wondering whether she should call the police, there was a familiar click and whir as the door opened and Melissa crept in, looking almost comical as she tried to tiptoe across the carpet, seemingly not noticing Sophie standing by the window.

"Where the bloody hell have you been?" Sophie yelled, fear and panic and relief coursing through her veins all at once. She knew she sounded like a mother scolding her naughty child, but she didn't care. She was suddenly filled with a simmering rage.

Melissa's already huge eyes widened as she looked at Sophie in surprise. "Oh, hey, Soph. I was trying not to wake you." She swallowed a giggle as she spoke, infuriating Sophie even more.

"Well, as you can see, I'm already awake. Mainly because I was bloody well worrying about where you were!"

Melissa sighed deeply. "I'm fine! You didn't need to worry about me. I can look after myself." She pulled off her blood-spattered white jeans to reveal a tiny black thong that showed off her perfectly formed bottom. She then took off her top and slid into bed. "God, I'm seriously knackered, though." She snuggled down and closed her eyes.

Before she knew what she was doing, Sophie had crossed the room and pulled back the duvet, causing Melissa to yelp in shock as she tried in vain to grab it back.

"Where have you been?" Sophie demanded, clutching the duvet to her chest.

Melissa rolled her eyes. "I spent the night with that guy..."

"What guy?"

Melissa frowned and sat up, pulling her knees to her chest to protect her modesty. "The one in the bar. Jesus, Soph, I don't know what the big deal is."

Sophie sat down on her own bed. She didn't really know what the big deal was either, but she was so angry. Was she jealous? "But you don't know anything about him. He could be an axe murderer. He could be married..."

"He is," Melissa said in a matter-of-fact tone. "Well, he's not an axe murderer, obviously. But he is married."

"And doesn't that bother you at all? Sleeping with some-one else's husband?"

Melissa raised her eyes for a second, as if pondering the question. "Nope."

"Well, maybe it should," Sophie said, feeling about a hun-dred years old.

"I don't think you're in any position to preach to me about

morality, Sophie." Melissa's voice was gentle, but her face had hardened slightly.

Sophie quailed. Melissa was right. She was in no position to lecture anyone. She stood up and threw the duvet at Melissa, before turning and heading for the bathroom.

"Soph!" Melissa called after her. "I'm sorry. I didn't mean—"

The rest of her words were lost as Sophie switched on the bath taps and ran herself a deep, hot bath. She wanted to cry, but, like yesterday, she couldn't. She hadn't cried for a very long time and it was only now that she realized just how odd that was. She turned off the taps and walked back out into the bedroom.

Melissa looked up at her with wide, wet eyes. "Are you OK, Soph? I'm really worried about you."

Sophie frowned. "No, I don't think I am. I think I might need help."

JULY 2000

"In entertainment news, a new reality game show, *Big Brother*, airs for the first time in Britain tonight. The show sees twelve contestants kept in a custom-built house, with their every move monitored on camera. Each week one housemate will be evicted by public vote."

BATH

CHAPTER ELEVEN

~~~~~~~~

SOPHIE PRESSED HARD ON THE BRAKES AS SHE drove down the steep, winding road towards the centre of Bath. To her right she could see the city laid out beneath her, rows and rows of honeycomb-coloured houses in their Regency splendour. It was a damp, misty day, when the sun hadn't quite been able to burn through, but nothing could dampen Sophie's excitement at seeing everyone again. It had been a year since their last get-together at Amy's wedding and she wished now that she had been in a better frame of mind to enjoy what was probably the most glamorous wedding she had ever been to.

★ ★ ★ ★ ★

"Well, this looks pretty special." Steve got out of the car in the shingle-covered car park in front of the ancient greystone church. It stood in the middle of the Wiltshire countryside, secluded from the rest of the world by woods and fields that had remained unchanged for centuries. He looked around him in wonder for a few seconds, before his eyes alighted on Sophie. "And so do you, sweetheart. You look absolutely stunning."

Sophie flushed under his gaze and self-consciously smoothed down her strapless cappuccino dress. "Thanks, but I feel like a fairy elephant beside the others. You look great, though."

It was true. Steve looked almost film-star handsome in his dark, slim-cut suit, which contrasted with his blond hair and sparkling blue eyes. His face was tanned and Sophie felt a sudden swell of pride that he was with her. She took his hand and led him towards the church, where the others were waiting. They had all stayed overnight together with Amy at the luxurious hotel just a hundred metres away where the reception was going to be held and Sophie had found the whole night a struggle.

She had started taking antidepressants straight after the hen weekend in Brighton and she was still suffering with some of the side effects. Her head felt as though it was permanently stuffed with cotton wool, which perfectly matched her horribly dry mouth. She couldn't have any of the free-flowing champagne that the others had vigorously enjoyed last night, especially Melissa, and she felt generally leaden and out of sorts. Her feelings of worthlessness were only exacerbated by the breathtaking beauty of everyone else around her. She felt embarrassed for Amy that she would be spoiling her otherwise perfect wedding photos.

As they reached the church, Melissa bounded over to them. "Hey, gorgeous!" She reached up to wrap her arms around Steve's neck and pulled him towards her in a warm embrace. Steve glanced nervously at Sophie as Melissa finally let him go, but she couldn't give him the reassuring smile she knew he wanted. She wouldn't blame him for fancying Melissa when he was stuck with someone as fat and unattractive as her. Melissa's strapless dress clung to her perfect curves as if she had been poured into a liquid milk chocolate mould, and her black afro hair had been swept up into a chignon that showed off her toned brown shoulders and elegant neck.

Emily and her six-year-old son, Jack, who was the pageboy, stood off to one side and Sophie steered Steve over towards them, safely away from Melissa. "Hi, Em. Hi, Jack." Steve crouched down so that his face was at the same level as Jack's. "Love the suit, buddy!" He tugged at Jack's miniature dark grey suit. Amy had delivered on her promise not to put him in pantaloons, much to everyone's relief.

Jack gave Steve a wonky, gap-toothed grin. "Mum said I only have to wear it for an hour and then I can get changed into my comfy clothes."

Steve shook his head vehemently. "Oh, no, no, no, that won't do! You need to wear it all day so that everyone thinks you're the same age as the rest of us."

Jack's eyes widened. "Do you think they will?"

"'Course they will. But only if you wear your suit. In your comfy clothes they might mistake you for a six-year-old or something."

Over the top of their heads, Sophie caught Emily's eye and smiled. Steve stood up. "Thank you," Emily mouthed to him silently.

"That was a sweet thing to do," Sophie murmured, giving Steve's hand a squeeze as they walked off. "She's such a great mum, isn't she?"

Steve glanced back at Emily and shrugged. "Who knows? I mean, I don't know her like you do, but she's always seemed a bit cold to me. I bet she's not as good a mum as you are."

Sophie smiled, despite herself. It wasn't true, but she loved Steve for saying it.

Steve reached for Sophie's hand again. "Listen, I'd better get inside and leave you to do your duties." He kissed her on the lips, then whispered in her ear, "You look beautiful. Don't forget that."

Sophie watched him stride into the church with a mixture of feelings. She wanted to believe that she was enough for him. But she couldn't allow herself. How could she? Beside the others, she felt dull, lumpy and colourless. Amy, standing ahead of her, preparing to walk down the aisle, looked like she had stepped straight out of a Pre-Raphaelite painting. Her smooth, creamy skin was perfectly offset by her flowing, diaphanous ivory gown and tumbling mane of gleaming auburn curls.

"Steve looks gorgeous in his suit."

Sophie looked down at Melissa, who had come to stand beside her and linked her arm through hers.

"He does."

"And you look gorgeous in that dress. You make the perfect, gorgeous couple." Sophie knew that Melissa was just trying to make her feel better, but even so, she was grateful. That was what Melissa always did. She would say or do something spectacularly annoying or upsetting one minute and the next she would give the most insightful, wise advice and show incredible kindness.

Sophie watched Emily as she smoothed Jack's hair and dabbed at an imaginary smudge on his cheek, making her think about Emma. They had decided not to bring her to the wedding, even though Amy had made it clear that she was welcome. They had left her at home with Steve's mum, who was all too delighted to have her. But watching Emily and Jack now, Sophie felt a small ache of yearning. It was an unfamiliar sensation, but it was unmistakable. She liked it.

From inside the church, the sound of a string quartet playing drifted out over the still, summer afternoon and Amy turned to look back at them. Her eyes shone with happiness and excitement. Sophie wondered if Amy had ever suffered a crisis of confidence. She doubted it. "No turning back now." Amy grinned. "Let's go."

★ ★ ★ ★ ★

"Let's go."

Sophie looked up at Steve in surprise.

"Really?" She couldn't hide her relief. It was almost ten o'clock and the evening was in full swing, but she was desperate for it to be over. "Won't it look bad if we leave now?"

"I'm not sure anyone will notice if we just slip away."

They stood for a moment longer, watching the shenanigans on the dance floor, which mainly centred around Melissa. She had been like an Exocet missile for available men all day, and now that they had run out, she was busy infuriating numerous wives by making a play for their husbands. Sophie watched her with a combination of envy and unease. Envy because Melissa seemed to find it so easy to let herself go and have fun. Unease because, just like in Brighton, she seemed out of control.

Sophie strongly suspected that it wasn't just the effects of alcohol she was witnessing and that Melissa was also getting an extra kick from somewhere. Working for a record company, Melissa had often talked about how many people used cocaine. Sophie didn't particularly disapprove—there were plenty of people in TV who used it too—but she worried about the situations Melissa was getting herself into, especially when it came to men.

As for Amy, she had glided through her big day as if she was walking on air and she was still positively glowing as she danced with Nick now. It was as though they were caught in their own private, beautiful bubble. She and Nick both looked as though they had stepped straight out of the pages of *Vogue* and they seemed so happy together. Sophie hadn't always been sure about Nick. He was almost too good to be true. And it worried her that he had persuaded Amy to give up her job. But then again, she reasoned, Amy had never made any secret of the fact that she was desperate to start a family and she had never been particularly passionate about her career either.

Watching them today, there was no doubting the love they felt for each other, so Sophie had buried any misgivings.

She had done her bridesmaid's duties and smiled obligingly throughout the day, all the while feeling as if she was standing apart, watching someone else. The strain was huge and she wasn't sure how much longer she could stand it.

"Come on—I can see how hard this is for you."

Sophie's stomach dropped. "Is it that obvious? I thought I was doing a really good job of pretending."

Steve put his arm around her tense shoulders and pulled her to him, kissing the top of her head as he did so. "You are. I'm really proud of you. But I can tell that you've had enough. If we go now, we can be home by midnight."

Sophie wrapped her arms around him, breathing in his smell and enjoying the warmth from his body. "I love you." It was the first time she had said it for months. Probably because it was the first time she had felt it for months.

"I love you too," Steve murmured with a slight crack in his voice.

★ ★ ★ ★ ★

From the distance of a year, it was hard to remember how bad she had felt back then. Sophie's insides curdled with shame if she thought about it for too long, especially how she had felt about her darling Emma, now eighteen months old and only just starting to toddle. Sophie smiled as she pictured her little girl, with her cloud of silky blond hair and her huge navy-blue eyes that always made Sophie melt. It had taken so long to bond with her, but when she finally did, it was like a dam bursting and now she couldn't get enough of her. She'd made sure she'd packed plenty of photos to show the others this time.

It seemed like a lot longer than a year since they had all been together. A new millennium had dawned and Sophie certainly felt as though she had lived a whole life in between. Becoming a mother had changed her. It had shaken her to her core, but she had survived and emerged stronger than before.

The fact that Amy—or rather Nick—had organized the Brighton weekend instead of her had added to her general feeling of being out of kilter. But now, having returned to work as a producer on a big new reality show called *Big Brother*, and literally being back in the driving seat, she could feel herself regaining some of the vitality she had lost.

She pulled into a side road that took her to the parking spaces behind the tall Regency town house she had rented. It was so much easier now that she could go onto the Internet and book online, seeing the house properly before actually booking it. She climbed out and stretched, looking up at the gleaming sash windows with the sun glinting against the inky blackness, and smiled to herself. It was exactly as it had looked online. She took her bag out of the boot and made her way to the back door.

She was casting around for the pot under which the owner had hidden the key when the door flew open. "Sophie!" yelled Amy, tumbling over the step in her hurry to embrace her.

Sophie hugged her tightly, burying her face in Amy's silky

auburn hair, which smelt of summer and combined with her Hermès scent to make Sophie feel light-headed with happiness. They broke apart and held each other at arm's length. "You look incredible." Sophie shook her head slightly as she spoke, unable to believe that Amy could look any more beautiful. But she did. There was something new. Something unmistakable. "You're not pregnant, by any chance?"

Amy gave a tiny squeal and clamped her hand over her mouth quickly. "Don't say anything to the others yet. I'm only eight weeks. I don't want to jinx it."

Sophie grinned. "I'm not sure you'll be able to keep it a secret. They'll know the second they clap eyes on you."

"Is it really that obvious?" Amy's green eyes danced as she spoke, radiating happiness.

Sophie's gaze moved down to Amy's belly that, typically, was still as flat as ever. "Maybe it's only obvious to me because I recognize the signs. Emily will probably clock it too."

"That's why I got here early, so that I could see you alone. I've been so desperate to speak to someone who'd understand how it feels."

Sophie nodded, remembering with a sudden, horrible clarity the terror she'd felt at this point in her own pregnancy. She couldn't possibly identify with Amy's emotions because she had no experience of the joy that anyone actually intending to become pregnant might feel. "Well, let's go inside and crack open the water to celebrate! To be honest, Amy, they'll all know the second you refuse a glass of champagne anyway."

They made their way through the flagstoned lobby into a vast kitchen equipped with all the latest mod cons. Sophie ran her hand longingly over the granite worktop, thinking of her own tiny Ikea galley kitchen back at home.

"Amazing, isn't it?" Amy filled the kettle and put it on to

boil while Sophie pulled out a wooden chair and sat down at the huge, stripped oak table.

"I'm sure it's not that dissimilar to yours." Sophie looked around her in awe as she spoke. She hadn't been to Amy and Nick's house in Notting Hill yet, but she knew it was spectacular from Melissa, who had crashed there many times after a boozy night out. Apparently, there was a separate flat in the basement that she could use whenever she liked. Melissa had tactlessly told Sophie that the flat alone was bigger than Sophie and Steve's whole house.

Amy made a cup of tea for Sophie and a cup of hot water for herself. "I've gone right off tea," she mused as she placed the steaming mug in front of Sophie.

"I did too, but it'll come back, don't you worry. So, how's Nick taken the news?"

Amy sat down opposite Sophie and sighed prettily. "He's thrilled. We'd been trying for a while and we were both starting to get a bit worried. It's weird, though—I just *knew* when I was pregnant."

Sophie nodded, enjoying Amy's delight but envying her too. Her own emotions had been such a mess when she discovered she was pregnant. She couldn't say she had felt happy at any point in her pregnancy. There was just a cloud of guilt and doubt hovering over her all the way through that tarnished it. Made it less special.

"Were you the same?" Amy prompted.

Sophie's attention snapped back to the present. She had to let all the negativity go. She couldn't change what had happened, so she had to accept it and move on. "Um, not really. Emma was a surprise in every way. A happy accident."

Amy beamed, clearly not guessing for one second that Sophie had been anything other than delighted by her pregnancy.

At least she could comfort herself that she had managed to put on a convincing act. Only Melissa knew the truth, which was that at one particularly low point, she had rung a helpline to investigate a termination. But by then it was too late. The thought made her skin prickle with horror now. The idea that her little darling might not have existed was one that she couldn't contemplate.

"Have you got any photos? I'm dying to see what she looks like now."

Sophie reached for her bag and pulled out the envelope she had stuffed with pictures of Emma.

Amy took them and began to leaf through them. "Oh, Soph, she's perfect!"

Sophie could feel the tears burning at the backs of her eyes. "Yes. She is."

"God, she looks so much like Steve!"

People said that all the time. But Sophie couldn't allow herself to hope. To believe it.

She stood up and walked to Amy's chair, looking over her shoulder at the photo she had in her hand. In it, Steve was sitting with Emma on his lap on the sofa in their tiny sitting room. He was tickling her and she was arching her little body away from him, but her face was split with a wide, milky smile that perfectly matched Steve's. She *did* look like him. But then, Sophie sometimes thought that at certain angles she also looked a bit like Matt. The mind played tricks like that all the time.

She would have liked to forget what Matt looked like and could easily have blotted his face from her mind if it wasn't for the fact that his star had continued to rise and he was now presenting several of the major news bulletins. She always switched channels, but it was impossible to avoid him altogether. He always seemed to be on somewhere, reading the news. She and Steve had never discussed Matt after they were reconciled. It was as if they had an unspoken rule that he should never be mentioned. Maybe it was the only way both of them could cope with it and it certainly suited Sophie. She just wanted to forget.

At that moment, the doorbell rang. "I'll get it," she offered eagerly. The ground floor was up a flight of stairs that led to a grand, tiled hallway and Sophie gazed around her as she made her way to the door. The house was vast and stunning. It made her tiny terrace look like a shoebox. The seeds of dissatisfaction with her own humble surroundings that were beginning to take root were quickly forgotten as she threw open the wide, heavy door to reveal Melissa and Emily, who had travelled down together by train.

They gave a united squeal of delight before enveloping Sophie in a barrage of hugs, amid cries that she had "lost so much weight!" and her hair looked "fantastic." Sophie returned the hugs, smiling ruefully to herself at the unspoken suggestion of how truly awful she must have looked the last time they saw her.

Clattering down to the kitchen, dropping bags and jackets as they went, they gabbled various compliments about the house and moans about the train journey before they swamped Amy with yet another blanket of squeals and cries of delight.

Sophie put the kettle on and sighed happily. Things were definitely looking up for them all.

CHAPTER TWELVE

~~~~~~~~~~~~~~

MELISSA LINKED HER ARM THROUGH SOPHIE'S AS they strolled beside the river on their way into the centre of Bath. It was a warm day without being stifling and already the streets were packed with tourists and shoppers making the most of the summer weekend. "You seem really good, Soph. And you're doing so well at work! *Big Brother*'s a huge hit. You must be pleased."

Sophie looked down at Melissa and smiled. "I am. I'm much more suited to producing this type of show than news. I wish I'd switched years ago…" She left the words hanging in the air for a second, imagining how different things would be if she had. "I'm really sorry about…well, how I was last year. It all got a bit too much, you know?"

Melissa nodded and bit her lip. "I'm sorry too. I was a bit of a mess myself, with nothing like your excuse."

Sophie didn't reply, unsure what to say. Melissa seemed together enough, but she didn't look great. Her black hair was dull and lank and her skin, which normally glowed with good health, now looked spotty and blotchy. "I know, I know. I look like shit." As always, Melissa voiced what Sophie was thinking.

"You don't look like shit. But you don't look yourself either. What's going on? Is everything OK?"

Melissa unlinked her arm from Sophie's and thrust her hands into the pockets of her jeans. It was a defensive gesture and made her look both young and vulnerable.

"You don't have to tell me. But you've always been there for me when I really needed you and I'd like to do the same for you, Liss. I want to help."

Melissa gazed up, her large brown eyes swimming suddenly. "I'm fine."

Sophie reached out and put an arm around Melissa's tiny shoulders. Instinctively, Sophie recoiled, shocked by how thin Melissa felt to touch, the bones jutting out to fill the palm of her hand. "You're not fine. But you don't have to talk about it if you don't want to. I just wanted you to know that I'm here."

"Thanks." Melissa gave a wan smile and sniffed hard. She did a lot of sniffing, Sophie noticed.

"Look, it's probably none of my business, but it might help if you didn't do coke any more."

Melissa shook Sophie's hand from her shoulder roughly. "You're right." She marched quickly ahead of Sophie with a purposeful stride, before turning her head and locking eyes with Sophie, her chin tilting upwards defiantly. "It's none of your business."

★ ★ ★ ★ ★

After the Brighton weekend, Melissa had gone back to work on Monday morning, wondering why she couldn't shake off the sense of unease that had been bugging her ever since her row with Sophie. She had made Sophie promise to see her doctor, as it seemed obvious that she was suffering from postnatal depression. In return, Sophie had asked her to promise that she would stop doing coke.

Melissa had rolled her eyes indignantly. "I hardly ever use it! Just when I'm on a big night out. Loads of people do it. It just gives me a bit of an extra kick."

Sophie had narrowed her eyes slightly, as if trying to make up her mind whether or not to believe her. "You honestly only do it occasionally? It's not a regular thing?"

Melissa had tutted. "No, of course it's not! I'm not stupid."

"I know you're not stupid," Sophie had countered quickly. "I just worry about you, that's all. I don't want you getting yourself into situations you can't handle."

Melissa had grinned knowingly. "You don't need to worry about me, Soph. I'm a big girl now and there are no situations I can't handle."

But as she snorted a quick line off the toilet cistern at work that Monday lunchtime, she was reminded of Sophie's words and a little niggling voice inside her head whispered that maybe she was getting a bit out of control. That the sordid night she had spent with a married man whose name she couldn't remember and whom, in the cold light of day, she didn't remotely fancy was exactly the sort of situation Sophie was referring to.

As the cocaine hit her bloodstream, she could feel the uneasiness seeping away, to be replaced with confidence. Sophie was wrong. She didn't *need* coke. She just liked it. And where was the harm if she wanted a little pick-me-up from time to time? Everyone in the music industry did it.

The aftermath of Amy's wedding was even worse. This time she couldn't even remember why she might have upset some people—she just knew from the churning feeling in her stomach that she had. Over the weeks that followed, she had several sharp flashbacks to angry faces turned in her direction, with one particularly awful memory of a woman slapping her face in the toilet. She had convinced herself it couldn't be real. Surely things hadn't got that out of hand.

The thing that no one seemed to understand was that she could stop at any time. She just chose not to.

★ ★ ★ ★ ★

They had arranged to meet for lunch at 2 p.m. at a small restaurant up near the Royal Crescent. They were shown to a table for four in the pretty courtyard garden. By the time Melissa and Sophie arrived, Amy and Emily were already waiting for them, their numerous shopping bags laid out around their feet.

"Someone's been busy!" Sophie climbed onto the bench beside Amy, who appeared to have the most bags.

"Well, you can't come to Bath and not spend money," Amy protested, giggling as she sipped on a glass of sparkling water.

"Hear bloody hear!" Melissa slid in beside Emily and immediately waved to the waiter. "Bottle of champagne, please!"

Emily shot Melissa an irritated glare. "It's all right for those who've got the money!"

Melissa tutted. "Look, you chose to be a single parent. Doesn't mean the rest of us have to be penny-pinchers too."

A sudden anxious silence descended around the table. "I'm sure Melissa didn't mean—" Amy began, but Emily cut across her.

"And you choose to spend all your money on coke, but that doesn't mean the rest of us have to behave like free prostitutes too."

There was a loud, collective gasp. Melissa sucked in her cheeks and dropped her eyes to the table.

"Em, I think that's out of order." Sophie broke the silence. She gave Emily a *what the hell?* look.

Emily blinked twice before her face softened. "I'm sorry, Melissa. Just...a bit under pressure right now." At that moment, the waiter appeared. He took one look at the scene and put the bottle and four champagne flutes on the table. "I'll leave you ladies to pour, shall I?" He didn't wait for an answer before scuttling away.

Amy, who was sitting closest to where the waiter had left the champagne, picked up the bottle. "Come on, let's have a glass of bubbly and enjoy ourselves. These weekends together are so precious. Let's not spoil them by arguing."

There was a murmur of agreement as each of them reached out to pick up a champagne flute. Amy poured out three glasses, then put the bottle down.

"I'm not feeling great, to be honest," she said in answer to the questioning looks. "I think I'll stick with water for now." Amy looked away as she took a sip of her water and two strawberry-sized patches appeared on her faintly freckled cheeks.

As they slowly began to chat amongst themselves again, Amy looked up and caught Sophie's eye, with an almost imperceptible shake of her head. Sophie returned the gesture as she took a long sip of her own champagne.

CHAPTER THIRTEEN

SOPHIE WAS THE FIRST ONE TO WAKE UP ON
Sunday morning. She padded downstairs into the wide, airy
kitchen, enjoying the coolness of the flagstoned floor beneath
her feet, and automatically reached for the kettle. It wasn't
surprising that she was the first one up. None of the others
had a toddler at home who thought 7 a.m. was a lie-in.

She walked to the French doors and looked out over the
small, pretty back garden. She could already feel the warmth
from the sun and smiled to herself. She loved the summer, with
all the happiness it seemed to bring. She pictured the scene at
home, as Steve fed Emma her breakfast, before taking her into
their postage-stamp-sized garden to feed the birds. As she did
so, she could feel an unmistakable ache inside to hold her baby
girl and bury her face in her cloud of silky, messy golden hair,
inhaling the scent of soap and sleep from her warm head. It
was a newish sensation and one that she welcomed.

"Typical that it's the mums who are up first!" Emily came
into the kitchen and joined Sophie at the French doors.

Sophie smiled. "I know! Who's got Jack this weekend?"

"Mum and Dad. He loves going there."

Sophie nodded, suddenly feeling immensely grateful that she had Steve and thinking for the millionth time how hard it must be for Emily to be a single mum.

"So Amy's pregnant, then?"

Sophie started in surprise. "Oh! You clocked it, then? I wasn't sure if you had."

"Impossible not to."

The kettle flicked off. Sophie walked over to it and threw teabags into two mugs. "Are you OK, Em? It's just…well, yesterday, it got a bit heated there with Melissa for a minute. You were pretty tough on her."

Emily shrugged. "I know, but she makes me so cross. There I am, struggling to bring up Jack on my own with hardly any money, and she's just so…irresponsible. It pisses me off. And she *is* using way too much coke—maybe you should speak to her, Soph? She listens to you."

Sophie bristled, her instinctive protectiveness towards Melissa rearing up. "I have. She insists she only does it occasionally. She works in the record industry, Em. They all do it."

Emily shrugged irritably. "Supposedly, everyone in TV does it too, Soph, but I don't see you nipping off to the loo during lunch to do a line."

Sophie bit her lip. She had wondered if anyone else noticed Melissa excusing herself yesterday and returning to the table with a telltale persistent sniff.

"She might be able to kid herself that she hasn't got a problem, but she can't kid me," Emily muttered, almost to herself.

Sophie couldn't think how to reply, so she said nothing. She finished making the tea and rejoined Emily at the French doors. As always, she felt huge and ungainly beside her. Even without a scrap of make-up and wearing her pyjamas, Emily still managed to look effortlessly beautiful. Her huge dark eyes

were framed with even darker lashes and combined with her
olive skin and high cheekbones to give her an exotic, other-
worldly appearance. Her bare arms were smooth and toned in
a way that Sophie knew no amount of press-ups on her part
would ever achieve for herself.

Yet again she wondered why Emily had remained single.
Yes, she had a child, which might put off some men, but with
her beauty, there was bound to be a queue of others who
didn't mind.

Maybe she gave off the wrong signals, Sophie mused as they
sipped their tea in a companionable silence. Steve had often
commented that he thought she was a bit stand-offish and
cold and it was true that there was always a sense with Emily
that she was holding back. She had known her for over ten
years now and yet she had never seen her really let herself go.
When the others got blind drunk, Emily always knew when
to stop drinking and switch to water. She never blabbed anything in a moment of indiscretion or got involved in bitch-
ing sessions. There was an apartness about her, which meant
that, although Sophie loved her dearly, she had never felt as
though she actually really knew her.

"Only we know what Amy's got ahead of her…" Sophie
looked at Emily and grinned conspiratorially.

"Hmm. Except that I imagine Amy will have an easier time
than both of us did. You know what she's like—she glides
through life without a hitch. Her pregnancy will probably be
much the same and no doubt her baby will sleep all night,
every night from the start. And even if it doesn't, she won't
have to worry—I'm sure they'll have maternity nurses to do
those horrendous night feeds!"

Sophie nodded. "Would you change it, though, Em? I

mean, if you could go back and do it all again? Would you do it differently?"

"I wouldn't change having Jack, obviously." As ever, Emily's words were chosen carefully. "But would I change the circumstances of his birth? Yes."

It was the most blunt Sophie had ever heard Emily be and she raised an eyebrow in surprise.

"How about you?" Emily prompted, deftly turning the conversation away from herself.

"Yes, same." Sophie almost wanted to laugh at how much neither of them was saying.

"But why? Weren't you both over the moon when you found out you were pregnant?" Emily looked steadfastly ahead as she spoke. Sophie wasn't sure, but she wondered if she could detect a note of bitterness in her voice.

"Steve was thrilled. I...well, I guess I was in shock. And then after Emma was born, I found it really hard to bond with her. Were you like that with Jack?"

Emily considered for a minute before speaking. "No. I wasn't. But I can see how it can happen."

The corrosive swirl of guilt that had slowly but surely been eating away at Sophie since she'd first realized she was pregnant intensified and took another bite at her insides. Even Emily, who had no partner on the scene to help her out, no one to share all those incredible "firsts" with, hadn't struggled to bond with her baby. Just Sophie, who had only herself to blame for what had happened. She felt like the worst mother in the world.

They lapsed into another silence and sipped their tea, both deep in thought.

Finally, Emily cleared her throat. "So...what shall we do today, then?"

Before Sophie could answer, Melissa appeared in the kitchen doorway. "I need coffee!" she intoned as she slumped dramatically into a chair. They had eaten at home last night, with Amy doing the cooking as usual. She had thrown together a chicken-and-chorizo dish followed by home-made tarte au citron without breaking a sweat. Sophie had watched in quiet admiration as she deftly kept everyone's glasses topped up, while drinking only water herself.

Melissa had polished off two bottles of Prosecco single-handedly and was very drunk by the time she staggered off to bed. "God, I feel like death," she wailed now. She did indeed look grey and sickly.

"I'm not surprised, the amount of booze you put away last night!" Emily drawled, without turning away from the French doors.

"I didn't realize you were counting..." Melissa shot back. Then, a little more gently, "Make me a coffee, will you, Em? Pretty please?"

Emily's face softened. Such was the effect Melissa had on people. She could be exasperating one minute and utterly irresistible the next. It was impossible to stay angry with her. As Emily filled the kettle, the unmistakable sound of retching came floating down from above.

They all instinctively looked up, as if they would be able to see the source of the noise through the ceiling. Sophie caught Emily's eye and held it for a split second.

"It sounds like Amy caught my hangover from hell." Melissa leaned her elbows on the table and put her head in her trembling hands, her dark braids falling forward and masking her face completely. "Ugh, I think I might be following her into that bathroom."

"I don't think she's got a hangover." Emily's voice definitely contained more than a hint of bitterness.

"What? What's wrong with her, then?" Melissa looked up quizzically.

"She's pregnant," Emily said, her voice flat.

"Oh God, not another one!"

"Melissa!" Sophie spun towards her, ready with an admonishment, but Melissa continued unawares.

"Well, you're all at it. It's so boring!"

"What's boring?" Amy breezed into the kitchen. Her face had a slight sheen, but other than that, there was no hint that she had just been violently ill.

There was an awkward beat of silence before Melissa spoke, still from underneath her curtain of braids. "Everyone getting pregnant."

"She's joking, of course. Aren't you, Liss?" Sophie glared in Melissa's direction, and even though she wasn't looking at her, Melissa must have sensed it.

"Hmm. 'Course I am."

Amy nodded uncertainly and joined the others at the table. Sophie looked from face to face, wondering how they had all become so dislocated as a group. Each of them had a secret, internal life that none of the others knew about. She wondered distractedly if they would ever recover that special bond they had once had. "Right," she said, determined to salvage what was left of their weekend together. "Who wants bacon and eggs? I'll give Amy the morning off and take over as chef."

There was a collective groan, coupled with a burst of laughter, and the bubble of tension burst. For the time being.

SEPTEMBER 2001

"Almost three thousand people have been killed and another six thousand have been injured in a series of coordinated attacks by Al-Qaeda in the United States."

CAMBER SANDS

CHAPTER FOURTEEN

THEY WERE HAVING AN INDIAN SUMMER THIS year, and although it was September, the temperature was nudging 80 degrees. Melissa turned up the air conditioning, but still she could feel the beads of sweat trickling down her forehead. Her hands shook, even though she was gripping the steering wheel. She wondered if there might be anywhere to stop for a "pick-me-up," but there was no sign of a service station—just the endless motorway stretching ahead of her in the shimmering heat.

She was dreading this weekend. No, that wasn't quite right. She loved seeing the others. They were the closest thing she had to a family. Especially Sophie. But the past couple of times they had been together, she could just sense a wave of disapproval coming from them. She didn't really know why. So she did the odd line of coke now and then. So what? A lot of people in the music industry did it. And the TV industry for that matter. She was almost certain Sophie must have done it. And Amy probably had too—well, her husband, Nick, anyway. She knew for a fact that he did it, because she'd done it with him... Although thinking about it now, she decided that perhaps it might be best not to mention that to anyone. They would probably get the hump, which was ridiculous. It wasn't as if she'd forced him.

Her hands were sliding on the steering wheel now. She wiped them on her jeans, but they refused to dry. Why wasn't her air conditioning working? She wrenched at it furiously, and as she did so, the car swerved across two lanes into the fast lane, narrowly avoiding the crash barrier. The radio still carried wall-to-wall coverage of the terrorist atrocities in America. Melissa tried to retune to a music station—it was all too depressing and she didn't like to think how close she had come to being caught up in it, having left New York only the day before the planes flew into the World Trade Center. Again, the car swerved as her attention wandered. Behind her, a horn blasted angrily and Melissa instinctively flicked a middle finger up in the rear-view mirror.

She manoeuvred the car back into the slow lane, her whole body now shaking as well as sweating. She needed a coffee and a cigarette. She rummaged in her bag, which was open on the passenger seat, and retrieved her packet of cigarettes but couldn't locate her lighter. She shook the pack, so that all the cigarettes tipped out onto the seat, and grabbed one. She pressed the cigarette lighter and drummed her fingers impatiently on the wheel as she waited for it to heat.

She had a vague, uneasy sense that Amy might be a bit pissed off with her, but she couldn't quite remember why. She often crashed at Amy and Nick's if she was in west London. They had a self-contained flat in the basement of their lovely house in Notting Hill, which Amy had generously said she could stay in for a while when she was flat-hunting. She hadn't seen that much of Amy, probably because she was so busy with her new baby, but she seemed to see quite a lot of Nick. He would pop down for a sneaky fag or "to get away from the chaos" upstairs but usually stayed for only half an hour or so.

Melissa liked Nick's company. He was good fun, and although he was rich and successful, he was still down to earth and liked a laugh. He was also as big a flirt as she was, which she enjoyed. Amy seemed very wrapped up in the baby, so he probably just wanted a bit of attention.

Nick moaned that Amy had changed since having the baby and Melissa could see his point. She was always so sunny and ditsy before, but now she just seemed worn down, as if she had the weight of the world on her shoulders. Sophie had been the same. It almost put Melissa off having kids. Almost. She would never admit it, even to herself, but every time one of the others got pregnant, she felt a stab of jealousy so powerful that it physically hurt.

It wasn't that she desperately wanted a baby. She didn't. Especially not now, when she was doing so well at work and having so much fun. But the thought of having someone to whom you were the whole world… Well, there was no doubt it was a powerful tug.

She thought about her own mother. After her parents split up, it was just the two of them for three blissful years. Until her mum met Graham. Graham was fat, funny and successful. Her mum was captivated by him and so was Melissa. He seemed to idolize them both and spoilt Melissa rotten, much to the annoyance of her own dad, who had also moved on to a new relationship with Sara.

Then, almost overnight, everything changed. Her mum had two girls in quick succession, Molly and Ruby, just fifteen months apart, and Sara had a boy, Sam. Having been the centre of the world for all these adults, suddenly Melissa felt invisible and forgotten. She loved all of her half-siblings, but they were a lot younger than her and no one seemed very interested in what she thought or felt. Things didn't improve as they got older either. Molly and Ruby were so close that there was no room in their relationship for their older half-sister and she rarely saw her dad, Sara or Sam.

By the time she left for university, Melissa could sense the relief on her mum's part at finally getting her off her hands. She hadn't been an easy adolescent and she knew there would be no chance of her boomeranging back home afterwards. She was on her own. Meeting Sophie and sharing a room with her had been like finding her family for the first time since she was seven.

Melissa lit her cigarette and took a long, hard drag, the nicotine hit instantly soothing her rattled nerves. Sophie also seemed a bit pissed off with her lately, which hurt more than she liked to admit. Sophie was her rock. More of a sister than her own sisters had ever been. She decided that she would use this weekend to build a few bridges and get back to the easy, happy relationship they had had before. Right now, though, she really needed to find somewhere to stop and give herself a little boost.

★ ★ ★ ★ ★

The temperature was nudging an unseasonal 80 degrees as Sophie headed down the A21, watching the tail lights of the cars that snaked out in front of her, stubbornly refusing to move on the steaming asphalt. She mentally said a prayer of thanks for the invention of air conditioning.

Emma had been poorly with a raging temperature the previous month and the doctor had told Sophie and Steve to keep her cool, which proved to be impossible. In the end,

Sophie had resorted to driving her around in the car all day with the air conditioning on full blast. It probably wasn't good for Emma's breathing, but it certainly succeeded in keeping her cool.

It must have worked, because Emma recovered remarkably quickly and was back to her beautiful, bouncy self within days, much to Sophie's huge relief: She had missed Emma's non-stop chatter in her strangely gravelly voice and the way she would convulse with laughter, throwing her head back with the complete abandon that only small children can enjoy. Instead, she had just wanted to curl up on Sophie's lap, her tiny thumb in her mouth and all her energy and curiosity seemingly gone. The only good thing to come out of it was that it helped to further strengthen her bond with Emma, after their difficult first year.

Sophie couldn't wait to see Amy, who had given birth to a little girl, Megan, almost six months previously. She had been to visit her in the very exclusive Portland Hospital and had been unsurprised to see her propped up on her snow-white pillows, looking like a beautiful Pre-Raphaelite painting, nursing a perfect little bundle in a white blanket. Nick had hovered beside her proudly, almost unable to tear his eyes away from his wife and new daughter.

All Sophie's early reservations about Nick had long gone. He really did seem to be the perfect husband and now father. It wasn't his fault that he was impossibly good-looking, rich and charming with it. She sometimes felt a cramping ache of jealousy whenever she compared Amy's situation to her own, but surely that was natural, wasn't it? There wasn't a person alive who wouldn't envy Amy's lifestyle, her beauty and the way everything always worked out perfectly for her.

"I don't envy her," Melissa replied when Sophie mentioned

it the last time they spoke. Melissa had called her from New York, where she was accompanying a band on the US leg of their world tour.

"What, not even a tiny bit?"

There was a pause, during which Sophie could hear Melissa taking a long drag on her cigarette and exhaling. She pictured her sitting in her hotel room, surrounded by God knows what kind of detritus. Strangely, the motherly instinct that had taken so long to kick in with Emma was a constant whenever she thought about Melissa. She worried about her far more than she should. "Well, maybe I envy the house and the money. Not the marriage, though."

Sophie had wondered what she meant at the time but couldn't bring herself to ask. She had enough to think about without getting into discussions about the state of other people's relationships. She and Steve were gradually getting back on an even keel and she needed to focus on him. She owed him that. He had been so patient. So giving. Now it was her turn to give back. He had come to hate his job in HR at a bank in the City and her plan was to make enough money for him to be able to give it all up and make a go of his writing.

After *Big Brother*, Sophie had moved into the development department of the TV company, where she discovered that she had a talent for coming up with new ideas and formats. One day, she took a phone call from a man named Mark Bailey, who had just started to come to prominence as a judge on a new wave of reality shows, some of which Sophie had developed. He was setting up his own production company and wanted Sophie to help him run it.

Despite his reputation for being demanding and expecting those who worked with him to forget any kind of a personal life, Sophie didn't hesitate. She could sense that Mark Bailey was going places. She wanted to be riding whatever tidal wave she suspected he might create in the years to come, and if things went well, it would set her and her little family up for ever. She definitely wanted a better life. Preferably one like Amy and Nick's.

Finally, after what seemed like hours, the cars in front of her began to move and in the distance Sophie could see the blue flashing lights that signified the cause of the hold-up. As she snaked past the scene of the accident, she tried to re-sist the urge to look, but it was impossible. A black Mini had crashed into the central reservation and its driver was stand-ing beside it, talking to a police officer. Sophie frowned as a thought occurred to her and instinctively she braked, trying to get a glimpse of the driver. Behind her, a car horn sounded, its driver incensed at the prospect of any further delay to their journey, and Sophie accelerated past.

An hour later, she drove down a sandy track leading to the house, her breath catching in her chest as the sea came into view, spread out like a carpet of glinting aquamarine jew-els in front of her. Having grown up living beside the sea in Northern Ireland, the sight of it always had a profound effect on her, making her think of freedom. Of escape.

She parked the car and switched off the engine, still unable to tear her eyes away from the breathtaking scene in front of her. She climbed out and stretched, inhaling the salty tang as deeply as possible before striding across the pale powdery sand towards the shore. The beach was deserted, apart from some-one sitting at the water's edge, their back to Sophie.

As she drew closer, she could make out the dark hair bil-lowing in the breeze and recognized the narrow shoulders. "Hey, Emily!" she called gently, not wanting to alarm her.

There was a slight pause before Emily turned and waved.

Sophie could sense that Emily had quickly rearranged her features and she slowed her pace to give her time to recover from whatever mood she had been in.

She leaned down to kiss the top of Emily's head, before sitting next to her, mirroring her position of hugging her knees to her chest.

"Amazing house, Sophie. You've surpassed yourself this time!" There was a dampness around Emily's eyes, but she was smiling as she spoke.

Sophie turned to look back at it. She had been so busy admiring the sea that she hadn't even noticed the house itself. It was truly stunning, built of glass and steel, taking full advantage of its spectacular setting right on the shore front with huge plate-glass windows covering almost every wall. "Wow. It's even better than I expected. Shall we go and explore?"

"Sure." Emily elegantly stood up, showing off her toned physique, while Sophie scrambled clumsily to her feet. She always felt so big around the other girls. Ungainly. Why couldn't at least one of them be as large as her? As they reached the house, Sophie rummaged in her bag for the keys and opened the enormous front door. Inside, the house was dazzlingly light and airy, with simple white walls and spectacular views from every window, all of which seemed to have been cleverly designed to capture the sea view.

"This is fabulous!" Emily's voice echoed in the huge space and ricocheted off the walls, making them both laugh and triggering more echoes.

"How are the others getting here?" Emily opened the giant American-style fridge and picked out the complimentary bottle of Prosecco that had been left inside.

"Both driving, I think." An image of a smashed-up black

Mini flashed into Sophie's mind. "By the way, did you come down the A21?"

"Hmm? I did, yes." Emily poured two glasses and gave one to Sophie. She chinked her glass against Sophie's and took a long sip. "Why?"

Sophie shook her head. "Nothing. I hope."

★ ★ ★ ★ ★

"Well, I guess I'll be off, then." Amy watched Nick's stiff, broad back as he stared out of the window.

There was a long pause. "Yup."

"It's only for two nights, Nick."

Another pause. "So you keep saying."

Amy frowned. Nick went away on business all the time. She couldn't understand why he was being so offhand about her having a weekend with the girls. She'd always done it and she needed it more than ever this year. She was desperate to get some time to herself and it was the first time she had left Megan overnight in the six months since she had been born. It wasn't even as if Nick had to look after her. Amy had arranged for their nanny, Suki, to move in for the weekend and he wouldn't have to do a thing if he didn't want to.

She picked up her bag. If she wavered any longer, she would end up cancelling and she needed to see her friends. Well, she needed to see Sophie and Emily, anyway. She already saw plenty of Melissa, as she was always crashing in their basement flat.

She walked over to Nick and put her hand on his arm. "I love you," she said, looking up at him hopefully.

But Nick's face was set like stone and he refused to look back at her. "Just go, Amy."

Amy swallowed hard. He was being so cold. He was acting as if she was leaving for good, instead of a quick weekend catching up with her friends. For a second, she considered not going, before a little spark of long-forgotten defiance sprang up inside her. She wasn't doing anything wrong.

She turned slowly away and began to walk towards the front door, her legs seemingly moving on autopilot.

"Have a nice time without us!" he shouted suddenly, and she turned to see him glaring at her with a look of white-hot anger in his dark eyes.

Amy hesitated again. She hated it when he got like this and she already knew that he would sulk for days after she got back. Was it really worth the grief? For a moment, she wasn't sure. But again, that spark of defiance flared within her and she opened the front door. "I will," she said, before stepping out into the sunshine.

★ ★ ★ ★ ★

It was getting late and they were all hungry. "Where the hell is she?" said Emily, staring out at the sea from the huge plate-glass window in the sitting room. The sky had taken on a pink hue, signalling that the sun was beginning to set.

Amy looked at her watch and tutted. "If we don't eat soon, the salmon will be ruined."

Sophie looked again at her phone, willing it to burst into life with a call from Melissa. A strange sense of uneasiness had settled around her, as the image of a smashed-up black Mini refused to budge from her brain. Was it Melissa? She wasn't sure what car she owned at the moment. The last few times she had seen her, she had travelled by train. "Let's give it another ten minutes, and if she's still not here, we'll eat."

She had called Melissa's number repeatedly over the past couple of hours, but each time it went straight to voicemail. Sophie's messages, at first irritated and frustrated by her lateness, had switched to pleading for her to get in touch. But still she heard nothing.

Suddenly, her phone burst into life, causing all of them to start as the loud, jangling sound reverberated off the double-height walls.

Sophie didn't recognize the number but snatched it up regardless. "Hello?"

There was a muffled sound, like someone blowing their nose. "Soph? It's me."

"Melissa!" Relief made Sophie's insides swim. Amy and Emily turned as one. To an onlooker, it would have seemed as though they were playing a game of musical statues, as they all froze simultaneously. "Where the hell are you?"

"At the police station." She blew her nose again.

Shock rendered Sophie speechless for several seconds as her brain tried to compute the information. "Police station?" Two sets of eyes widened in front of her as she spoke.

"Can you come and pick me up, Soph? I need to get out of here…" Her voice was swallowed up by a sob.

"Oh no! I can't… I've had too much to drink…" Sophie's eyes scanned the faces of the other two as she tried to think what to do. She hadn't been keeping count, but surely everyone had had too much to drive?

"I'll go." Emily was already shrugging on her denim jacket and scooping up her car keys from the stainless-steel table where she had dropped them earlier. "Tell me where she is."

"Oh! Em's coming to get you." Of course, Emily hardly ever drank too much. She had had a couple of sips of her Prosecco before switching to water.

"Can you come with her?" There was a pleading tone to Melissa's voice.

Sophie hesitated. She knew exactly why Melissa didn't want to be alone with Emily. She was terrified of her disapproval. At least with Sophie, she could feel that they were on even terms. Whatever Melissa did, however bad, she knew Sophie's guilty little secrets too, which made Sophie less likely to judge her as harshly as Emily. "OK, give me the details and we'll be there as soon as we can."

CHAPTER FIFTEEN

"WELL, AT LEAST YOU WEREN'T HURT. OR WORSE, you didn't hurt anyone else."

Melissa took a long swig of her Prosecco and nodded mutely. The dark circles around her brown eyes had deepened and her skin was blotchy and spotty. Her signature braided hair was lank and dishevelled. On the CD player, a U2 album played gently in the background, reverberating softly off the walls.

"Are you sure you don't want any food?" Amy came in from the kitchen and put her hands on her hips while giving Melissa a look that Sophie couldn't read.

"No. Thank you." Melissa drained her glass and picked up the bottle from the small occasional table beside her to refill it. A couple of foamy drips oozed out and Melissa frowned in confusion, as if she was puzzled that it was empty.

"There's none left, Liss. You finished it off!" Emily tried to laugh, but it stuck in her throat and became an embarrassed cough.

Around the room, they all exchanged glances. Sophie and Emily had collected Melissa from the police station in Rye, where she had been cautioned for driving without due care and attention. Sophie was hugely relieved to hear that she hadn't been charged with anything worse, such as drug possession. Melissa, on the other hand, seemed irritated and unconcerned.

As Melissa had rightly predicted, Emily gave her a stern talking-to in the car back to the house. "What if you'd killed someone?" She looked in the rear-view mirror at Melissa, who was draped casually over the back seat of Emily's Renault.

"I didn't, though, did I?" Melissa shot back. "Anyway, I hadn't taken any drugs, so that wasn't why I crashed the car. I just got distracted for a minute."

Emily pursed her lips. "Yeah, yeah, yeah. Tell it to the judge. Listen, you might have got away with it this time, but you won't be so lucky next time. And someone might get hurt. You need to grow up and take some responsibility for yourself, Melissa!"

A thick, sulky silence was the response from Melissa for the next few minutes, until she seemed to forget the conversation entirely and began to chatter inanely about the brilliant new album by Jay-Z that had just been released.

Emily had tutted in disgust, while Sophie desperately tried to calm her own urge to throw Melissa out of the car. She seemed so unaware of how irresponsible and dangerous her behaviour was. Sophie had always made excuses for her, citing her age, her single status, her lack of family support, but actually, now that they were all nudging thirty, the excuses were becoming thinner and thinner, much like Melissa herself.

As they arrived back at the house, Amy greeted her nervously, as if she didn't know what to say or how many questions to ask. But Melissa seemed not to notice and immediately threw herself onto one of the sofas, declaring that she was "desperate for a drink."

Having drained a bottle of Prosecco single-handedly, Melissa now looked as though she was ready to drop off to sleep.

"Why don't you go to bed, Liss? You must be shattered after such a stressful day." Emily's voice was measured and patient.

"Yes, Melissa, that's a good idea. Let's just forget today ever happened and start afresh in the morning." Sophie tried to emulate Emily's patient tone, but it was so at odds with how she felt that she failed. She suspected that even Melissa would detect the annoyance behind her words.

She needn't have worried. Melissa gazed at Emily, as if she was trying to focus, or possibly even remember who she was. Then she frowned slightly, her smooth forehead crumpling momentarily, before nodding.

Emily crossed to the sofa and helped Melissa to her feet, as if she was assisting an elderly patient. Then the two of them shuffled out of the room together, looking like participants in the world's slowest ever three-legged race.

The moment they'd gone, Amy emerged from the kitchen and brought her mug of camomile tea to the large table in the middle of the room. "Thank God for that!" Sophie followed suit and pulled up a chair.

"Emily's being so patient with her!" Amy took a sip of her tea and shook her head incredulously. "I don't know why— she doesn't deserve it."

Sophie looked at Amy in surprise. Amy had never expressed irritation with Melissa before. It just wasn't her style to bitch. Melissa often used Amy and Nick's basement as a crash pad and she suddenly wondered if Amy was getting fed up with her unwanted guest.

"If it was just the drinking and the drugs, that would be bad enough. But it's the…other stuff," Amy continued.

Sophie frowned. "Other stuff?"

Amy's pale skin flushed slightly. "Yes. Like the penchant for married men and the sleeping around. I think she needs a bit of tough love. We've tried being understanding and helping her out of the sticky situations she seems to keep finding herself in. Maybe now's the time to tell her that until she gets a grip and takes responsibility for her actions, we don't want to see her."

Sophie inhaled sharply. "I'm not sure I could bring myself to do that…"

"I could." There was a new steeliness to Amy's voice that alarmed Sophie. Had Melissa made a move on Nick? Surely even she would draw the line at seducing a friend's husband, especially so soon after the birth of their first child. But even as she told herself that no one could be that callous, she somehow knew that was what had happened. *Was* she too soft on Melissa? Was tough love the answer? She just didn't know.

★ ★ ★ ★ ★

The next morning dawned clear and bright, the sun already comfortably warm by 8 a.m. Sophie quietly opened the French doors and walked out onto the balcony of the bedroom she was sharing with Melissa, who slept on, oblivious to the ructions she had caused.

The wide white sandy beach stretched out in front of her, the sea twinkling azure under a matching sky, and her breath caught momentarily. She loved the sea so much. Whenever she stood in front of an ocean, she would fantasize about taking a boat, sailing into the horizon and disappearing.

They had stayed up late last night, talking over what to do about Melissa. Sophie was worried about the idea of telling Melissa that she wasn't welcome until she pulled herself together. "But don't you think she needs our help?" She had looked from one to the other, trying to find some agreement, but Sophie could see that Amy and Emily had made up their minds and she too had eventually come to the conclusion that there was no alternative.

She loved Melissa. She just didn't love what she was doing with her life at the moment. And even though Amy hadn't confirmed anything, Sophie felt sure that something dubious had gone on with Nick. That was a line too far for Sophie. The only way to give Melissa the shake-up she needed was for them all to distance themselves from her. They had always been there for her and it would shock her to her core if they suddenly weren't.

Her family background meant that, despite appearances, Melissa was vulnerable and needy. There was a horrible possibility that losing her friends would tip her over the edge into something even worse. But to carry on supporting her while she behaved so badly was unthinkable. Sophie took a deep breath and prepared herself, before letting herself back into the bedroom.

Melissa slept soundly, looking peaceful and more beautiful than she had any right to do. Her braids fell around her smooth brown shoulders, giving the rather fitting impression of a black halo around her. The irony wasn't lost on Sophie as she slipped out of the room and down the sweeping steel staircase.

She found Amy in the kitchen, emptying the dishwasher. Her long auburn mane of hair was scrunched into a messy bun on top of her head. She wore a matching pale blue silk camisole and shorts, showing off her long, long legs and toned arms. Her pale skin was flawless, except for a smattering of freckles across her pert little nose. She didn't look like a woman who had recently had a baby. She looked up as Sophie came into the room and smiled. "Morning! Mums up first."

Sophie grinned back. "Yup. Emily will be down next, I guarantee it. It's ironic, really, as we're the ones who need a lie-in most, but your body clock just goes haywire, doesn't it?"

Amy nodded and poured Sophie some coffee. "Here. Shall we take it out onto the beach?"

"Sure." Sophie took the mug gratefully and headed outside onto the wide strip of sand in front of the house. Amy followed and they walked towards the water's edge, Sophie savouring the feeling of the warm sand between her toes. She sat down, taking care not to spill her coffee. "God, this is heaven, isn't it?"

"It is." Amy dropped down beside her, gracefully crossing her legs beneath her. "I'm so glad I came. I nearly didn't."

"Why not?"

Amy shrugged. "Nick wasn't too happy and it's hard leaving Megan."

Sophie nodded. "I know. But you need a break, Amy. And even though it's hard to leave them, it's amazing how quickly you get over it—usually after the first glass of Prosecco!"

Amy laughed. "That's true."

"So…" Sophie scooped up some sand with her spare hand and let it fall through her fingers, a peculiarly satisfying sensation. "How are you finding motherhood?"

Amy reached up and untied her hair, which tumbled down her back in copper-coloured ripples. "It's hard." She tilted her chin up towards the sun and closed her eyes. "I don't know how you coped, Soph, and I *definitely* don't know how Emily coped. Jesus, imagine having to do it by yourself…"

"I know. She's pretty amazing." Sophie gazed out to sea for a minute, thinking. Amy had an army of people to help her. She had probably never had a sleepless night, thanks to the maternity nurse she and Nick had hired. Yet even she had found it tough going. It made Sophie feel better somehow. She and Steve had managed it all between themselves with very little help. Maybe she wasn't such a hopeless mother after all.

"And what about Nick? How's he taken to being a dad?"

There was a beat too long before Amy replied. "Great. He's been great...but he works a lot. You know how it is."

Sophie didn't know. Steve had never prioritized work over Emma. He had doted on her from the second she was born and couldn't get home quickly enough to see her. But then again, maybe Nick enjoyed his work more than Steve did. She wasn't quite sure what Nick did, but it seemed to involve property and travel. Whatever it was, it made him a lot of money.

"What's she like? Megan, I mean."

Amy's face melted into a wide smile. "Oh, Soph, she's perfect. Just so sweet and so good! We got her into a routine from the start and she never seems to stop smiling. I just didn't expect to feel the way I do about her. It's like falling in love for the first time."

That old familiar prickle of guilt caused Sophie's stomach to clench. She should have felt like that about her little Emma from the start. Emma, who had also smiled her way into the world, who had always fed and slept well and whose huge blue eyes twinkled with the sense of humour she was already starting to display. She wondered if she would ever forgive herself for the indifference she had felt towards her cherished little girl in those early days. "I know exactly what you mean." The well-worn lie tripped off her tongue all too easily. It was what people expected and it was less complicated than having to explain how you really felt.

They sat in silence for a while, each of them breathing in

the sharp, salty tang of the sea and enjoying the moment. Eventually, Sophie spoke. "Amy, last night, when we were talking about Melissa…"

Amy's expression hardened instantly. "Hmm?"

Sophie hesitated, unsure whether to continue. "Well, I got the feeling that maybe something had happened between you and her. Something bad."

Amy didn't reply, but she pursed her lips slightly.

"It's fine if you don't want to talk about it…" Sophie swallowed, regretting bringing it up.

"No, it's OK," Amy said eventually. "Nothing happened between me and her."

"Oh. OK." Sophie frowned to herself, nonplussed.

"But unfortunately I'm not sure the same could be said for her and Nick."

"Oh…" Sophie said again. "I did wonder—"

"I saw them, late one night," Amy cut in, her eyes drifting, as if they were running from the tears that were chasing them. "Megan was six weeks old."

A sudden burst of boiling rage shot through Sophie. Whatever issues Melissa had, this was unforgivable. She had crossed a line that no woman should ever cross and she was glad that Melissa wasn't within physical reach.

"She doesn't know I saw them." Amy's voice jolted Sophie out of her fury. "Neither of them do."

"Oh God, Amy. I'm so sorry. I honestly don't know what to say."

"It's fine. And it could have been worse. It was just a drunken kiss… I don't think it went any further than that. Trouble is, it was obvious they both wanted it to, even if they didn't actually have sex."

Sophie shook her head, trying to find an upside to what

Amy was saying, but there wasn't one. Knowing that your husband *wanted* to sleep with one of your best friends was almost worse than discovering that he had. Any hesitation she might have felt about cutting Melissa out of the group for a while dissipated in an instant. There was no other option. She finished her coffee and stood up purposefully. "Right, I'm going to tell her to leave. I don't want her spoiling what's left of this weekend."

"No." Amy stood up and faced Sophie, her eyes narrowing and her lips set in a straight line. "I'll do it. With pleasure."

★ ★ ★ ★ ★

Melissa was still asleep when Amy barged into the room. She could feel her rage boiling to the surface when Melissa didn't even stir, despite the disturbance. Amy grabbed the duvet and hauled it off her, revealing Melissa's perfect, petite frame, wearing just a sleeveless top and a thong. For some reason, the sight of her looking so perfect enraged Amy even more. "Melissa! Get up. Now!"

Melissa's eyes shot open in alarm and she sat bolt upright, looking around her in confusion and shock. "What? What's going on?"

Amy clenched her fists, aware that if she didn't leave the room now, she might very well punch Melissa. "Get some clothes on and come downstairs. I want to talk to you."

As she stalked out of the room and headed for the stairs, she could hear Melissa muttering to herself. "Can't you just bloody talk to me here? Fuck's sake!"

Emily emerged from her bedroom, frowning as she pulled her robe around her. "What's going on?" She followed Amy down the stairs.

Amy swept into the huge living room, where Sophie was waiting, chewing her lip nervously.

"Amy, what the hell's going on?" Emily asked again.

"Yes, what's going on?" Melissa appeared, having thrown on a pair of cut-off denim shorts and a T-shirt.

Amy leaned against the glass table for support—she was shaking all over. "We'd like you to leave. Now."

Melissa immediately looked at Sophie, who shook her head and dropped her eyes. "What? Why?"

"Because I saw you and Nick. Together. Kissing. I know what's been going on, Melissa, and I'm not going to take it any more. I've discussed it with Sophie and Emily and we'd like you to leave."

Melissa's cheeks flamed instantly. "Nothing's going on, Amy! I don't know what you think you saw, but it was nothing." She wrung her hands together, looking at Amy with a pleading expression.

"I know what I saw and it wasn't nothing!" Amy's voice quavered and she swallowed hard. "Megan was six weeks old, Melissa!"

"Jesus," Emily muttered, before coming to stand beside Amy in a gesture of support.

"So," Amy continued, drawing herself to her full height and tilting her chin up, "we'd like you to leave. And you are not welcome at my house again."

Melissa slumped into a chair and put her face in her hands. "I'm sorry," she whimpered. "It meant nothing. It was just a drunken kiss. I'm really sorry."

"Get up!" Amy was shocked at the vehemence of her own words, but all the hurt and anger she had been bottling up for so long was now erupting in a torrent and she couldn't stop herself. "Get up, go upstairs and pack your things and get out. There'll be a taxi waiting by the time you come back down."

Melissa looked up slowly, her thin face wet with tears. "Please, Amy. I'm so sorry. I'll make it up to you. Please don't—"

"I said, get out!" Amy yelled, making all of them jump.

Melissa stood up shakily and threw Sophie a pleading look. "Soph?"

Amy looked at Sophie and could see she was wavering. Finally, she shook her head. "No, Melissa. You've crossed a line here. You need to leave."

"Is this…for ever?" Melissa sounded like a frightened child, her eyes huge in her tiny face.

Sophie glanced at Amy before speaking. "You need to sort yourself out, Melissa. Don't contact us again until you have."

Melissa burst into noisy tears and rushed out of the room, leaving a stunned silence behind her.

Amy sank down into a chair, all the rage leaving her body instantly. She felt weak and wrung out. Sophie knelt down beside her and put an arm around her shoulders. "It's OK, Amy. It's hard, but she needs a bit of tough love. Otherwise, she'll never sort herself out."

Amy nodded. Already she felt guilty, but Sophie was right. This was the only way to make Melissa take responsibility for her behaviour. She just hoped it didn't push her over the edge.

JUNE 2002

"The Queen's Golden Jubilee celebrations continue tonight, with a party in the palace taking place to celebrate the monarch's fifty years on the throne. Queen guitarist Brian May kicked off the event by performing a solo on the roof of Buckingham Palace."

PORTRUSH, NORTHERN IRELAND

CHAPTER SIXTEEN

~~~~~~~~~~~~~~~~~~~~~

SOPHIE STOOD IN THE ARRIVALS HALL AT BELFAST International Airport, watching the arrivals board. Flying to Belfast used to be such a tense affair, but these days, Belfast was a vibrant, bustling place. Since 9/11, Irish terrorism had been succeeded by a new, more sinister threat. Their flight landed twenty minutes ago, so they should be through soon. The butterflies in her stomach danced a little harder with every passing minute. She wasn't entirely sure why.

Steve and Emma had flown home that morning. Sophie was staying on for a couple of extra days and had invited the girls to come for the weekend, the final part of her thirtieth birthday celebrations.

It had been such a lovely week so far. Amazingly, for almost the first time she could remember, the sun had shone every single day and they had spent their time eating, drinking and watching Steve surf the huge waves at White Rocks beach, reminding Sophie of that first magical summer when she had got together with him. The big difference this time was that they had their little Emma with them. At three years old, she was like a tiny cloud of golden energy, always laughing, always talking and, it seemed, always on the move. She never sat still for a minute and grabbed every second of every day as if it was her last. Sophie was besotted with her.

Over dinner on her birthday, she told Steve the news she had been keeping to herself until she was sure. It was so different in every way from her pregnancy with Emma. This time she felt almost ecstatic. Seeing the blue line so clear, so bold and so positive was like a sign that she could finally put her mistakes behind her.

Steve's lovely face crumpled with emotion as she told him. "What's wrong?" she said, a sharp cramp of fear clutching her insides, in case he wasn't happy.

"It's you." He shook his head and drew a hand across his face. "The difference in you from before, with Emma…"

"I'm sorry. I was just scared."

"I know. You have nothing to apologize for…"

Sophie dropped her gaze. She had so much to apologize for that if she started now, until the end of her life it wouldn't be enough.

"You have nothing to apologize for," Steve repeated. "I'm just *relieved* to see you so happy this time."

Sophie lifted her eyes to his. "I am happy, Steve. And I'm relieved too. I really want this pregnancy to be different. To make it up to—"

"—yourself," Steve interrupted. "You need to make it up to yourself. No one else."

"God, I love you so much." The tears Sophie had been holding back began to stream down her cheeks. "And I love Emma…"

Steve reached out and took her hand. "We know you do. And we love you too. Everything is going to be OK."

★ ★ ★ ★ ★

Sophie sniffed and blinked quickly as two familiar faces came into view in the arrivals area. Emily's shiny black bob had grown out to just below her shoulders and hung in a sleek, dark sheet, in sharp contrast to Amy's auburn mane, which was piled up on top of her head. No Melissa. Sophie's heart dropped slightly, even though she had known she wouldn't be here, because she hadn't invited her. She had spoken to her a couple of times and she seemed to be getting herself back together, but Sophie wanted to make sure Amy was completely comfortable before bringing her back into the fold.

Emily and Amy were deep in conversation, hauling their weekend cases behind them, and Sophie felt a sudden, deep surge of affection for them both. They had never been to Ireland to visit her before and she was touched that they had made the effort. As she watched them, they looked up and smiled in unison.

"Welcome to the Emerald Isle," she said, adopting her best tourist-guide smile and giving a brief curtsy as she swept her arm expansively around the arrivals hall.

"It looks…breathtaking!" Emily laughed, hugging her with her free arm. "Oh, it's good to see you, Soph. I can't believe it's been so long."

"I know. It's absurd. Still, you're here now." Sophie reached out to hug Amy. "And you have no right to look as good as you do, young lady! Where did your baby weight go?"

Amy shrugged and grinned, but Sophie noticed that the laughter didn't reach her eyes. "It'll be back soon enough…"

"Seriously?" Sophie's mouth dropped open in surprise. "You're pregnant again? Wow! Congratulations."

Amy sighed. "I'm really sorry, Soph. I don't want to be a killjoy on your birthday weekend."

"I wouldn't worry—that makes two of us who'll be drinking water, then..." Sophie waited for the penny to drop.

"Oh, great!" Emily cried in mock frustration. "So I'll be the only one enjoying the Guinness, then, I take it?"

Sophie nodded. "Yup. I'm pregnant too."

"Oh, Sophie, I'm so happy for you!" Amy's eyes, which had looked so lifeless a few moments ago, now lit up with genuine delight. Sophie tried not to let her confusion show. Maybe Amy was still in shock at being pregnant again so soon after Megan was born.

"So how did Nick take the news?" Sophie asked as she led them out towards the car park.

"He's delighted. It was him who was so desperate for another one." Amy sounded exhausted at the mere thought of it.

"But you're happy too?"

Amy hesitated. "Actually, I would rather have waited another year, but he wouldn't let it drop."

Emily looked up and caught Sophie's eye. Sophie decided to change the subject.

~~~~~~~~~~~~~~~~~~~~~~~~~~

CHAPTER SEVENTEEN

AMY SIPPED HER SPARKLING MINERAL WATER AND
tried to ignore her phone, which she could feel vibrating in-
cessantly in her bag on the floor. The other two were chatting away, oblivious. She didn't need to answer it to know it
would be Nick, checking up on her. There had been the most
almighty row about her coming this weekend, but she had
put her foot down. She wasn't going to miss Sophie's thirtieth birthday weekend, whatever he said.

★ ★ ★ ★ ★

"Amy!" Nick bellowed from downstairs. Upstairs in their
bedroom, Amy tensed. Megan was asleep and his shouting
reverberated all over the house. She quickly finished applying
her lipstick and scampered out of the bedroom and towards the
stairs. Nick was standing in the wide hallway, a heavy scowl
crumpling his smooth, chiselled, handsome face.

As she appeared at the top of the stairs, he looked up. "There
you are!" The scowl deepened as she reached him. He looked
her up and down with narrowed eyes.

"What?" She tried to laugh, but it died in her throat. When had she become so tense around him? It was ridiculous.

"Is that a new lipstick?"

"Yes." She touched her lips in an involuntary movement.

"When did you get it?" His mouth had set in a hard line.

Amy frowned, wondering why he had become so critical. There was a time, not so long ago, when he used to smother her with compliments, telling her endlessly how beautiful she was. The compliments were becoming rarer and rarer. "This morning, when I took Megan for a walk."

Nick nodded curtly. "I don't like it. It doesn't suit you."

Amy's stomach dropped. "Right. I guess I won't be wearing it again, then." She sighed heavily and shook her head, before walking past him into the kitchen. She hated any kind of confrontation and lately Nick seemed determined to start a row about absolutely anything.

"Amy! Don't be so sulky." Nick followed her into the kitchen and grabbed her arm roughly, spinning her around to face him.

"I'm not sulking." Amy rubbed her arm surreptitiously and rearranged her features into a smile. "Anyway, dinner's nearly ready. Why don't you go and freshen up and I'll pour you a drink?"

Nick pursed his lips, as if deciding whether to pursue an argument or to let it go. Eventually, he seemed to make a decision. "OK. I'll be back in five minutes. Maybe you could wash off that horrible lipstick in the meantime?"

★ ★ ★ ★ ★

Amy looked at Sophie across the table, envying her the glow of happiness that seemed to envelop her. Her large blue eyes shone and her skin was clear and dewy. Despite what she said,

Sophie had lost the extra weight she had put on during her first pregnancy and her face had taken on a new definition, with high cheekbones and a toned jawline. Her long chestnut hair was thick and glossy and she was holding her head high again, embracing her height instead of trying to hide it.

Amy had had that glow too, with Megan. But not this time. This time the glow had been replaced by a knot of dread in her stomach. When had everything changed so drastically? She tried to pinpoint a moment, a day even, but it was so gradual, so seeping, that by the time it had happened, it was too late to reverse it. She didn't recognize herself any more. Back then, at the beginning, she had been so full of—she grappled for the right word—joy. Yes, she had been joyful.

A tiny scintilla of light made her smile fleetingly at the memory of what she had been like, before the walls of her brain closed in, smothering it. "Smug," he had told her. "You were unbearably smug."

And he was right. That was the worst part. Who did she think she was, being so full of herself? Being so infuriatingly *happy* all the time? She actually made herself sick, let alone anyone else.

But Nick loved her, despite all her faults. She swallowed hard, trying not to think of what would be waiting for her when she got home. He was so angry that she was leaving him and Megan for the weekend. He couldn't understand how she could do it. How she could care so little about their child that she would prefer to go off gallivanting with her friends, no doubt trying to pick up men along the way.

The mere thought of Amy trying to pick up men was laughable. She couldn't remember the last time she had even smiled at another man. Actually, that wasn't true. She used to smile at the postman and enjoyed a chat with him most mornings. Until

Nick told her that she was embarrassing herself by flirting. After that, she had taken in her parcels with nothing more than a cursory "Thank you," prompting an initial small, puzzled frown from the middle-aged, round-faced, eternally jolly postman.

She *did* feel guilty leaving Megan to come away this weekend, but she really needed some space. The pregnancy had only added to her increasing sense of being trapped. She sometimes felt as though she was holding her breath for days on end, waiting for Nick's next outburst. It wasn't as if he had ever physically hurt her—except for a couple of times when he had shoved her a bit roughly—but he could be vicious with his words.

And yet he was incredibly generous too. He was always buying her clothes, shoes, bags, jewellery and just about anything she could possibly want. In fact, now that she thought about it, he had bought everything she owned. He decided what she should wear and had very clear ideas about how she should look. There was no point in her buying anything for herself, as he'd make her take it back, telling her it made her look fat and frumpy. Whenever he was home, she could feel him watching her, assessing her faults. It was exhausting.

Watching Sophie and Emily now, as they discussed the struggle to pay the mortgage, she felt a sharp stab of guilt. She was so lucky. She lived in a beautiful house and had more money than she could ever spend. She had plenty of help around the house and a nanny on tap for Megan, while both Sophie and Emily were constantly juggling the demands of being working mothers. She had absolutely nothing to complain about. And yet...

For a moment, she thought about telling them what she was feeling. She could almost taste the relief at finally unburdening herself to someone. But she already knew that the words wouldn't make sense. She would be accusing him of loving her *too much*. It would sound ungrateful and insane. Which was what she was, as Nick told her regularly. This was what she had wanted. She had wanted Nick to love her and look after her. Why couldn't she just enjoy it?

"Have you heard from her?" Sophie looked expectantly across the table at Amy.

Amy frowned, trying to catch up with the conversation. "Who?"

"Melissa. I wondered if you had heard from her after…" Sophie's words dropped into thin air as she tailed off, looking uncomfortable.

"I did, yes. She called to apologize."

Sophie tilted her head slightly. "That's good, isn't it? It means she realizes what she did was wrong. What did you say?"

"I thanked her for the call and hung up."

Amy felt Sophie flinch. "Oh. Right." There was a pause. "Did you tell Nick she'd called?"

Amy shrugged, a gesture completely at odds with how she felt. She'd told Nick about Melissa's call that night and it had resulted in the biggest fight they'd ever had.

"What are you suggesting?" he had snarled, his handsome good looks temporarily rendered ugly with temper. "I hope you're not insinuating that I've done anything wrong." The cadence of his voice dropped and became menacingly quiet. "Don't ever question me, Amy, OK?"

Amy had swallowed hard as a punch of fear hit her in the stomach. "I wasn't."

"Good. Because you need to start appreciating what you've got, Amy. Don't you think I could have had my pick of women? But I chose you. And what do I get in return? Non-stop fucking nagging!"

Amy had mustered her courage. "I know. I'm sorry. But you do know that I saw you that night…kissing Melissa?"

"I said, don't fucking question me!" Nick had yelled, a sudden blush spreading from his neck to his face. He looked guilty as hell. Maybe it wasn't just a kiss after all.

"Nick, don't be like this," Amy had pleaded, searching his face for signs of the loving charmer who had wooed and beguiled her not so very long ago. But there was a coldness in his eyes that seemed set like concrete. "I'm sorry," she had said again.

Nick had shaken his head and pursed his lips with disappointment, but at the same time he reached out and encircled her with his arms. "Look, whatever you saw, it was nothing. Melissa did throw herself at me, but that's what she's like, isn't she? She's just a slag. Probably best you don't see her again anyway."

"I hope she's OK," said Sophie, breaking into Amy's thoughts. She looked away for a second. "And I know you won't want to hear this, Amy, but I miss her."

Amy glanced at Emily and gave a small nod.

Emily took a long sip of her wine. "Well, the truth is, we both miss her too."

Sophie looked from Emily to Amy, a little spark of hope igniting in her eyes.

Emily smiled slightly before continuing. "So that's why we've invited her this weekend. It's your thirtieth birthday weekend, Soph. It doesn't feel right to celebrate it without Melissa."

Sophie's eyes filled with tears and her face broke into a wide, incredulous smile as she looked at Amy, shaking her head. "I can't believe you did that for me, especially you, Amy. How do you feel about it?"

Amy took a deep, shuddery breath, unsure how she was supposed to feel. On the one hand, she still felt betrayed by

Melissa. But on the other, she knew what had happened really did mean nothing. It was just a drunken—and perhaps something else—kiss. In truth, she didn't really care that much. She had been too exhausted and preoccupied at the time with the baby. "I'm fine about it, Soph. Really."

"When is she coming?" Sophie couldn't hide the excitement in her eyes.

"Tonight. She's picking up a hire car at the airport."

"Are you sure that's a good idea? Look what happened last time she was driving—she smashed up her Mini and ended up being arrested." Sophie chewed her lip nervously.

Emily shrugged. "Honestly? I don't know for sure, but I think she's really trying to sort herself out. Last year in Camber Sands gave her a real shock. We're like a family to her—closer than her own family for sure—so throwing her out was the wake-up call she needed. I think it might be time to give her another chance."

"Thank you." Sophie reached out and took Amy's hand. "Thank you so much. I know how hard that must have been for you."

Before she could stop herself, Amy had burst into tears. "Sorry," she said, wiping her eyes and blowing her nose on a napkin. "It must be the hormones."

Sophie picked up her hand again. "Are you OK, Amy? You don't seem yourself at the moment."

"I don't know what 'myself' means any more," Amy muttered, before giving Sophie's hand a reassuring squeeze. "I'm fine. Really!" she added, seeing the sceptical frown on Sophie's face. "I'm glad Melissa's coming. I've missed her too."

Across the table, Emily and Sophie exchanged a glance and Amy retracted her hand. "I'm just nipping to the loo—back in a minute."

CHAPTER EIGHTEEN

～～～～～

"SOMETHING'S VERY WRONG, ISN'T IT?" SOPHIE
watched Amy as she walked towards the toilets. Even her posture was different. Before, she had walked like a ballerina,
with her head held high and her beautiful, long neck poised
and elegant. Now her head was stooped and her shoulders
rounded, as if she was trying to fold herself away. Trying not
to be noticed.

"It's him," Emily replied, her dark eyes narrowing. "I knew
he seemed too good to be true. Have you seen that he doesn't
stop ringing and texting her? He's constantly checking up on
her. And yet he's the kind of man who tries to have sex with
his wife's friend just weeks after she's had a baby. I know Melissa was in the wrong too, but at least she's got the excuse
that she was probably off her face. I bet he's at it all the time."

Sophie nodded, wanting to scoop Amy into her arms and
tell her it was all going to be OK. But that would be a lie.
Things were clearly far from OK.

"I think she should stand up to him more—tell him to piss
off and stop checking up on her."

"Hmm." Sophie gave Emily a rueful look. "That's just not

her, though, is it? She's not like you and me—she'll do anything to avoid a row."

Emily shrugged. "I suppose you're right. But the irony is that if she was to stand up to him, he'd probably have more respect for her and treat her a bit better."

"Yes, but that's why he went for her and not either of us." Sophie shook her head sadly. "All that money...that lovely house. But even though it's a struggle sometimes, I wouldn't swap my life for hers. Would you?"

Emily shook her head vehemently. "No way."

"You know, Melissa always said that too."

"Did she? When?"

"Probably after he'd tried it on with her a few times. She used to say she wouldn't mind the money, but she definitely wouldn't want the marriage."

"She's surprisingly insightful sometimes."

Sophie smiled. "She is. Thanks so much for inviting her this weekend, Em. It's really made my birthday celebrations complete. Do you honestly think Amy will be OK with her?"

"I'm sure she'll be fine." As Emily spoke, Amy came back into view. She was pushing her phone into her handbag and her eyes looked damp. "Well, she'll be fine about Melissa," Emily added under her breath. "Whether she's fine about being married to an arsehole is another matter."

"Shall we go back to the hotel?" Amy said as she reached the table, her upbeat tone at odds with her miserable appearance. "We told Melissa to meet us there."

The hotel they were staying at stood on a white cliff above a wide sandy beach. The views were spectacular—on a clear day like today they could even see the Scottish coast—and the suite Sophie had booked so that they could all share was vast and luxurious. Sophie opened the door to the balcony and stepped out into the late-afternoon sun. It never got really hot here—there was too much of a breeze blowing off the Atlantic Ocean stretched out before her—but it was certainly warmer than she had ever known it. What a perfect week it had been and Melissa coming would be the icing on the cake. She was aching to see her.

As she looked out over the sea, she was reminded of their weekend in Whitstable, when she had confided in Melissa that she was pregnant with Emma. She had felt so scared, so confused, and her emotions were in turmoil. This time there was no turmoil—only delight. She ran her hand over her stomach and smiled to herself. The bump was rounding nicely. She didn't even care that she would be losing her hard-fought flat stomach. She could get it back again afterwards. It would be worth every extra ounce of weight she put on to have the chance to get it right this time. To enjoy the new baby, instead of feeling nothing but abject terror and loneliness.

Just then, a small red VW pulled into the car park below her. Even before the car door opened, Sophie knew it was Melissa.

As she stepped out, Melissa looked up and caught Sophie's eye. For a fleeting second, a shadow of worry passed across her face and she bit her lip nervously, her eyes sliding away from Sophie's.

"Melissa!" Sophie yelled, waving frantically. "You're here!"

Melissa's face melted into a wide smile. "It was supposed to be a surprise!" she shouted back.

"It is! It's the best surprise I could have had—get yourself up here right now!"

Within what seemed like less than a minute, Melissa was hammering on the door. As Sophie swung it open, Melissa flung herself into Sophie's arms and burst into noisy sobs.

Sophie hugged her tiny frame. "No, Melissa! No tears allowed on my birthday weekend!" Although in truth she was fighting them back herself.

"Sorry." Melissa hiccoughed, wiping her hand across her eyes. Sophie took the opportunity to examine Melissa's face. Even allowing for the tears, she looked a lot better than the last time they had seen her. Her skin was clear and her eyes were less bloodshot.

"Hello, you," said Emily, coming forward to give Melissa a hug. "It's lovely to see you."

"You too, Em." Melissa disengaged herself from Emily's embrace and looked anxiously around the room. "Where's Amy?"

"I'm here." Amy emerged from the far corner of the room, where she had been sitting furiously texting ever since they arrived. She looked at Melissa evenly. "I'm glad you're here. We all are."

Relief flooded Melissa's features. "Amy...I just want to say—"

"It's fine," Amy interrupted in a tone of voice she rarely used but which brooked no argument. "Really."

Melissa hesitated and made as if to reach out her arms towards Amy, before seemingly changing her mind and just nodding instead. "OK."

There was an awkward pause, before Sophie clapped her hands. "Right! Let's get this party started!"

"Don't get your hopes up too much, Liss," said Emily. "It's only you and me drinking."

Melissa frowned and looked from Sophie to Amy, before realization dawned. "Oh my God! You're both pregnant? That's amazing news—congratulations! And, Emily, I hate to rain on your parade, but I'm afraid I'm not drinking at the moment either. I'm… Well, let's just say I'm trying to 'work through my issues.'" She made quotation marks with her fingers as she spoke.

Emily put her hands on her hips and sighed. "Well, that's just great, isn't it? Oh, sod it! There's no point in drinking on my own. Looks like it's a teetotal weekend for all of us, then."

CHAPTER NINETEEN

~~~~~~~~

"I'M SO PLEASED FOR YOU—ABOUT THE BABY."
Melissa linked her arm through Sophie's as they walked barefoot along the beach in the early-morning sun, the sky a vivid
watercolour of orange and blue and the sea a vivid indigo,
topped off with fluffy white swirls of surf.

Sophie smiled. "Thank you. It's a bit different to the last
time…"

"I know. You weren't in a great place. We lost you for a
while there."

"You can talk!" Sophie smiled ruefully down at Melissa,
who looked fresh and pretty, with no make-up and her braids
pulled back into a jaunty ponytail.

"I'm sorry. I was a mess and it was inexcusable."

Sophie shrugged, walking closer to the sea so that the
water splashed over her feet. It was freezing, despite the warm
weather. "Everyone has a reason why they behave like they do,
Melissa, and you're no different. I'm sorry for cutting you off
like that. I just didn't know how else to get through to you."

"I'm glad you did." Melissa pulled Sophie to a halt and they
stood side by side, paddling in the shallows and gazing out

over the waves. "It was what I needed. And I'm trying really hard. I'm not there yet, but I am definitely better than I was."

Sophie put her arm around Melissa's tiny shoulders and gave her a quick hug. "That's fantastic. I'm so proud of you."

Melissa nodded. "I'm quite proud of myself, if I'm honest. I know I have a problem. I just couldn't see it. Didn't want to see it."

"No. Well, in that respect you're no different from the rest of us. We all have things we don't want to admit."

"But you're OK now? You're happy with things at home?"

Sophie nodded emphatically. "I am. Steve and Emma are just amazing and this pregnancy feels like the final piece of the jigsaw. It feels like a second chance to get things right."

Melissa's brown eyes clouded. "You're so lucky, Soph. I'd give anything to have what you and Steve have."

"You've changed your tune—I thought you thought we were Mr and Mrs Boring."

Melissa smiled ruefully and shook her head. "Not any more... Now I'm the boring one, being permanently single."

"Is there nobody on the scene?"

"No. The truth is, I've spent so long hopping from one unsuitable man to another that I've got no idea how to have a normal, healthy relationship."

"I'm not sure anyone really knows that. There's someone out there, Melissa. You just haven't met him yet."

Melissa laughed, showing her even white teeth. She really was a natural beauty and it seemed inconceivable to Sophie that she couldn't get a boyfriend. But then again, until now, she had been a bit of a handful.

"Amy doesn't seem quite as happy as you to be pregnant..." Melissa began as they moved off along the beach again, arms linked companionably.

"No. Em and I are a bit worried about her, actually. She's not herself at all."

"In what way?"

"It's as if she's lost her..." Sophie paused as she grappled for the word. "As if she's lost her mojo."

Melissa nodded.

"And...I'm not sure things are great between her and Nick."

"Really?" Melissa shot Sophie a worried look. "Oh God, it's not because of me, is it?"

"No!" Sophie shook her head. "No, not at all. It's just that he seems to be chipping away at her confidence. I mean, you remember how she was before? She was so carefree and always happy. I don't ever remember seeing Amy in a bad mood. Now she's so...wary. It's as if she's having to think about her every move. You used to say that you wouldn't mind the money and the house, but you wouldn't want the marriage, and I never really understood. But I think I can see what you meant now."

"He's a bastard." Melissa's words were carried away on the breeze, but they were unmistakable. "I know I was wrong to hang out with him and kiss him when Amy had just had the baby. But if it had been up to him, it would have gone a lot further..."

Sophie nodded, not really wanting to hear any more. She had envied Amy so much, but now she only pitied her. No amount of money would make up for being trapped in a gilded cage the way Amy was. Sophie thought about Steve and how lucky she was to have him. He wasn't possessive at all, yet he more than anyone had a right to be. She had cheated on him and maybe even fallen pregnant by someone else... But still he trusted her.

And he was right to trust her. The only consolation of all that had happened was that Sophie would never, ever make the same mistake again. She had come so close to losing him that she had learnt the hard way how precious he was to her. She knew without a shadow of doubt that he was the only one for her and that no one would ever tempt her to stray again. She wanted to grow old with him and bring up their children and grandchildren together.

As they wandered further on down the beach, Sophie considered what Melissa had said about how lucky she was, and just how good her life was right now. For the first time, Sophie realized that she was right. Not only was her relationship the best it had ever been, but work was also going amazingly well. Her decision to join forces with Mark Bailey had turned out to be an inspired one and she could feel already that she was going to make a lot of money out of their association.

Knowing very little about TV, Mark had relied on Sophie for everything when setting up his own production company, and in return for her sharing her knowledge, he was extremely generous. She owned a large number of shares in the company, and although it was still very early days, business was booming.

She hadn't told him yet that she was pregnant, because she knew he wouldn't understand and suspected he might even be a bit disappointed in her. He had a regular stream of girlfriends but seemed to have no intention of ever settling down and having children, despite the fact that he was over forty. But she couldn't allow herself to worry about what Mark thought. This baby came first.

She put her hand instinctively to her stomach. Protecting him—and somehow she knew it was a boy—was her priority now. It was still such a new sensation to feel this way. Instead of being full of dread about what lay ahead, she felt only hope and excitement.

"You've gone very quiet." Melissa nudged Sophie gently. "Are you OK?"

Sophie shook her head, enjoying the salty tang of the sea and the warmth of the sun on her face. "No, not OK," she said, grinning. "I'm great."

JULY 2003

"Britain is sweltering in the grip of a heatwave that has seen temperatures soar to a record-breaking 101.3 degrees Fahrenheit. Today was the hottest day since records began, bringing misery to commuters, who have had to endure train delays and speed restrictions to prevent buckled rails."

NOTTING HILL, LONDON

CHAPTER TWENTY

AMY TOOK ONE LAST LOOK AROUND THE SUMP-
tuously furnished sitting room, her well-trained eye searching for any signs of dust or clutter. She straightened a cushion
and swept her hand over the plush sofa for the second time in
five minutes. As she bent over to pick up a stray white thread
from the charcoal upholstery, she caught sight of herself in the
huge, gilt mirror hanging above the marble fireplace.

Who was that woman staring back at her? She was thirty-
one years old but looked and felt at least forty-five. She was
just so very tired. Tired of being continually examined and
cross-examined by Nick. Tired of being a corporate wife and
tired of being a mother. Most of all, she realized as she stared
at her reflection, she was tired of being lonely, even though
she was very rarely actually alone in the house. Yes, there were
the nannies, a housekeeper and a gardener, but she imagined
that they probably despised her. A spoilt little rich girl with
everything she could possibly want, yet who was still as miserable as sin.

There was no girls' weekend away this year. None of them
could muster up the enthusiasm after what had happened. Amy

had more than a sneaking suspicion that Nick wouldn't have let her go anyway, even if they had wanted to. So they were meeting for dinner at Amy's house instead. It had been a battle, but Nick had finally, grudgingly agreed to it. He hadn't specifically asked if Melissa was coming, but she knew he assumed they still didn't speak.

Amy used to so love cooking and entertaining. It was her passion. But even that no longer excited her. Nick said she used too much salt, too much sugar, too many spices. Until finally she lost all confidence in her abilities and he hired a cook—a beautiful, vibrant, sexy Latina girl named Benedetta, who seemed to delight him with her culinary prowess just as Amy once had. He was probably screwing her. She couldn't even summon up the energy to be upset about it. She honestly didn't care.

Thinking about Nick having sex with someone else caused an ache between her legs, but it wasn't an ache of longing. It was a physical ache, as her body remembered his rough hands forcing her legs apart and slamming into her last night after he arrived home late from a dinner with God knows whom. He was drunk and high on coke and Amy had learnt long ago that resistance was futile when he was in that state. He was stronger than her and trying to fight him off only resulted in more bruises. It was easier to acquiesce and hope it didn't last too long.

As always, the morning after almost made it worthwhile. Almost. He was tender, loving and attentive, just as he had been in the beginning. Every time, Amy found herself believing that this was the real Nick. This was the man she had fallen in love with. He never apologized—that would involve talking about it and they never, ever discussed what was happening. But he would bring her coffee in bed and kiss her slightly swollen lips with what she knew was genuine love. On these mornings, she really did think she was happy again. For a while. Until the next time.

In a way it was lucky that it had happened last night, so that he was in a good mood today. Otherwise, she knew she was in danger of him deciding not to let her host the girls after all. He hated her seeing them, claiming they were a bad influence on her. She could see why he might think that, after what happened when she returned from Northern Ireland last year...

★ ★ ★ ★ ★

Amy walked through the arrivals hall, pulling her little case behind her and carrying the weight of dread on her shoulders. She had persuaded the others to wait at the baggage carousel with Sophie, while she hurried ahead. Nick had insisted on meeting her at Heathrow, despite her protestations that she was happy to get the train, and she was nervous that he would make a scene in front of them.

As she spotted him, she allowed herself to relax a little. He was smiling and handsome, clutching a bouquet of white roses. Maybe it would be OK after all. Maybe she had imagined it. As she reached him, his eyes flickered over her shoulder. "On your own? Where are the others?" His smile remained fixed in place.

"They're still waiting at the baggage carousel. I thought I'd come on ahead."

"Wanted to avoid me meeting them, eh?" Nick's dark brown eyes glinted slightly as he spoke.

Amy tried to laugh. "Of course not! Shall we go?"

Nick glanced once more over her shoulder. "Yes, OK. I got these for you, by the way." He thrust the roses towards her, just slightly too hard, so that they crushed into her chest and the head of one of them dropped off. They both watched it fall to the floor and roll towards Amy's foot. She looked up and caught his expression as he took her arm forcefully and pulled her along with him. She knew then that she hadn't imagined it. This was going to be bad.

"So, I bet you spent the entire weekend slagging me off and whining about how badly I treat you…" Nick began, once they were in the car.

Amy watched him nervously out of the corner of her eye, her heart hammering. His jaw was set and his face wore a mask of anger. She could feel the boiling hot fury coming off him in waves, and for the first time, she was scared.

"Nick, don't be ridiculous. We didn't even discuss you."

It wasn't true, of course. Only that morning, Sophie, Emily and Melissa had sat Amy down and told her outright that they were worried about her. "Is everything OK at home?" Sophie had prodded. "Is Nick treating you well?"

When Amy didn't reply, Emily had jumped in. "You can tell us, Amy. We're here for you and you know you can trust us."

Automatically, Amy's eyes flickered towards Melissa, who reddened but held her gaze. "Amy, I am deeply ashamed that I flirted with Nick and kissed him, but I swear that's all it was and I would never, ever do anything to hurt you again. Emily's right, you can trust us. All of us."

Amy imagined for a fleeting minute how wonderful it would feel to talk about it. To unburden herself about what she was going through. But trying to put it into words was like trying to catch smoke in a bucket. It was too indefinable and kept drifting away. What would she say? That she felt trapped because he loved her too much? That she wished he'd let her choose her own clothes, jewellery and shoes because otherwise she felt like she was losing her identity? How spoilt and ungrateful that would make her sound. So, in reply to the three concerned faces around her, she said simply, "I'm fine. Honestly."

There was a short, awkward pause before Sophie tried again. "What about your mum, Amy? Could you talk to her? If we're worried, I'm pretty sure she's worried too."

"Talk to her about what?" Amy tried to laugh it off, but even as she spoke, it occurred to her how distanced from her mum she had become over the past year. Nick had made it clear that she wasn't welcome at the house, ever since Amy's mum had taken her shopping after Megan was born and bought her some new clothes and make-up that he didn't like. "You look like a cheap whore," he said when she showed off the leather skirt, top and boots they had bought from Zara. Amy had almost jumped in shock, having expected him instead to compliment her on getting her slim figure back so quickly after the baby. Although the clothes weren't designer, she knew she didn't look cheap or tarty either. But she never wore them. And because she didn't want her mum to know, she stopped inviting her over.

She still met with her mum, although much less frequently, when she would take Megan over to her parents' house in Surrey. But for reasons she didn't quite understand herself, she never mentioned the visits to Nick.

"I don't believe that for a second," Nick said, jolting Amy back to the present. "I bet you had a great time going through all my faults. Moaning about me. Bit rich, considering Melissa was the one doing all the chasing, by the way. At least she wasn't there. I'm glad you all finally saw her for what she was."

Amy swallowed but didn't say anything.

"Though, actually, I don't think it's good for you to see any of those girls," Nick continued. "Every time you come back, you're different. It's about time you called an end to these weekends altogether."

Amy's heart dropped. Her weekends with the girls kept her sane. She couldn't imagine what she would do if they suddenly stopped. They were the only real friends she had. Everyone else was a work associate or old school friend of Nick's. No one else really knew her or even liked her for that matter. She couldn't allow him to take that away from her. She clenched her fists and mustered her courage. "I like seeing them, Nick. They're my friends." Her voice wobbled as she spoke and she wondered if she might cry.

"I like seeing them, Nick. They're my friends!" Nick mimicked. "Jesus, Amy, how old are you? You're pathetic, you know that, don't you?"

Amy blinked hard and looked straight ahead, willing the tears that were burning the backs of her eyes not to fall. At every set of traffic lights, she thought about opening the car door and jumping out. But she couldn't bring herself to do it. Megan was at home waiting for her and she needed to see her little girl. To hold her and kiss her. She couldn't just run away. And anyway, she tried to tell herself, maybe it would be OK. Maybe it was just an almighty sulk that would pass after a night's sleep. Nick would never hurt her. She was almost sure of it.

As they pulled up in the drive, Nick switched off the engine and sighed heavily. Then, without looking at her, he got out of the car and lifted her case and the flowers from the boot. Amy hovered, unsure whether he wanted her to go into the house before him or after. "Well, what are you waiting for?" he snapped, answering her question.

As she made her way up the steps, it occurred to her that this must be how it felt to climb a gallows, knowing what was waiting for you at the top. With a shaking hand and a dry mouth, she put her key in the lock and opened the front door. Ahead of her, beyond the hall, the kitchen light was on and she could see the shadow of a figure moving about. Of course, Megan's nanny, Suki, was here. Relief flooded through her, making her feel weak-kneed. As if on autopilot, she headed for the kitchen, aware that Nick was close enough behind her to almost feel his breath on her neck.

"Hi, Suki," she managed in a strangled voice as she rounded the corner.

Suki was busy unloading the dishwasher and looked up at her with a smile that didn't reach her pale blue eyes. "Oh, hi, Amy. How was Ireland?"

"Good." Amy put her keys on the table and took off her jacket, watching Suki with a feeling of unease. Somehow she knew that Suki had spent the whole weekend with Nick. That she had probably slept in her bed, playing happy families while Amy was out of the picture. Yet there wasn't a trace of guilt about her. A part of her almost admired her brazenness. "How's Megan been?"

"She's been just fine, hasn't she, Suki?" Nick's voice came from behind her, startling her, even though she knew he was there.

"She certainly has." A tiny smile flickered across Suki's face as she spoke. "She's slept like a log." She closed the dishwasher and stood up to face Amy. "Anyway, I'll be off, now you're home. You'll want some time alone together." Amy didn't like the way she said the word *together*, as if she was mocking her. Which of course she was.

"No, don't rush off!" Despite her misgivings, Amy was

suddenly desperate for Suki to stay. Anything to put off being alone again with Nick.

"Anyone would think you weren't pleased to be home, Amy." Nick wrapped his arm around Amy's shoulders and gave her a squeeze. Amy swallowed, knowing they were playing a game at her expense, yet she had no idea of the rules.

Suki smiled. "I'll see you guys tomorrow, OK?" She directed her words only to Nick. Amy stood helplessly as Suki picked up her bag and let herself out of the front door, closing it with what sounded to Amy like a sickening thud.

The silence that followed was thick and heavy with tension. Amy's heart began to pound. Nick's arm around her shoulders tightened and seemed to increase in weight. "So," he said, his lightness of tone at odds with the atmosphere and all the more sinister for it.

"Nick, I—" she began, but he was too quick for her. In one movement his hand was on her throat and he slammed her head against the wall. Amy's eyes watered instantaneously and her legs buckled, which only served to tighten Nick's grip on her throat as he held her upright. Amy began to panic as her airway closed. She could feel her eyes bulging and then, as suddenly as it started, he released her, watching contemptuously as she slid to the floor.

For a second, there was a shocked silence, before Amy began to cough and sob simultaneously. He could have killed her. He really could have actually ended her life there and then. He had chosen not to but had proved beyond doubt that he was easily capable of it.

Gulping for air, suddenly aware how precious breathing was, Amy put one hand to her throat and the other instinctively to her belly. Nick's contemptuous expression instantly melted into one of anguish and he slumped down beside her. "Oh God, I'm sorry, baby."

Amy looked at him nervously. He had never apologized to her before. That must mean it was really bad. But he wasn't looking at her face. He was looking at her stomach. He was talking to the baby. "I'm sorry," he repeated, scrambling to his feet and putting his hand out briskly to Amy. She considered refusing to take it, thinking it might give her back a tiny bit of control. But she couldn't. She was too scared. So instead, she allowed him to pull her to her feet, her legs shaking and unsteady beneath her. Her neck hurt and it was as if there was a giant, jagged lump in her throat when she tried to swallow. Her eyes met his for a second before she dropped them again. He looked confused and disappointed, as if somehow she had failed him.

With a shuffling walk, she headed out of the kitchen and into the hall. Nick didn't move at first, but when she reached the bottom of the stairs, he dashed over to her. "Here, let me help you," he said, taking her arm and gently guiding her up the stairs. Several times he kissed the top of her head. In their bedroom, he sat her on the edge of the bed and took off her boots. "Lie down, sweetheart," he said. She watched him warily, noticing that he kept glancing towards her throat. She wondered with a slightly morbid fascination what she would see when she finally looked in the mirror. "Megan..." she tried to say, but her voice was too croaky to get any words out.

"Shh..." He put a finger gently to her lips. "She's fine. She's asleep. You'll see her in the morning."

Amy nodded obediently, too tired and too sore to argue. Nick pulled the duvet over her and tucked her in. "Just try to get some sleep. You'll feel fine by the morning." He stood up and ran a hand through his hair, biting his lip nervously, as if he didn't know what to do next. She liked this side of Nick: the caring, solicitous, loving husband, taking care of his pregnant wife. It was almost worth what had preceded it. And maybe it was a one-off. He was obviously under a lot of stress and had just let it get the better of him. He clearly regretted it already.

He bent down to kiss her tenderly on the lips. "I love you," he said, a small sob escaping as he spoke. "I love you so very much."

"I love you too," Amy said, attempting a smile, as her eyelids drooped. And at that moment, she really meant it.

The next morning, she woke with a start. Although it was light, she could tell it was still early by the dullness of the daylight seeping over the top of the curtains. Gingerly, she sat up, grimacing at the pain and stiffness in her neck. She looked towards Nick's side of the bed in the dim light. It was empty. She wondered distractedly where he had slept.

Padding to the bathroom, still dressed from the night before, she felt old beyond her years. In the en-suite, she switched on the light, illuminating the bulbs around the large mirror above the sink. The reflection that stared back at her caused her to gasp in shock. The pale skin on her neck was slashed with an angry red weal, and under her chin, the bruising was already turning blue. Around her eyes, her make-up had smudged, giving her the haunted look of someone dressed up as a Halloween ghoul.

Robotically, she reached for a make-up wipe and began to remove the dark streaks from beneath her eyes. When all traces of mascara and eyeliner had gone, she rubbed moisturizer over her face and tentatively tried to dab some onto her neck, but the skin was too raw and she winced in pain. She would be wearing scarves for several days to come. As the tears began to trickle in a steady flow down her cheeks, she slumped onto the toilet seat and put her head in her hands. Looking down, something caught her eye and she became aware that a dark red patch was rapidly spreading down her legs.

★ ★ ★ ★ ★

A year later, there had been more "incidents"—more than she wanted to remember. But there were also periods of genuine happiness in between. She still loved him, despite what he did, and it almost seemed like a small price to pay for the happy times. It was after one of these incidents when he was in a solicitous, loving mood that she had persuaded him to let her have the girls over for dinner. "I won't go away for the weekend again," she said, hopeful that this would feel like a concession to him. She didn't need to tell him that none of the others wanted to go away either.

"Sure." Nick had smiled, stroking her face and kissing her forehead. "But can I ask one thing? Don't talk about me. It does my head in to think about you picking over my faults and slagging me off…"

"I won't!" she assured him, desperate to secure this tiny victory. "I'll change the subject as soon as they mention you."

"Oh, so they *do* talk about me, then?" Nick's mouth wore a wryly amused smile, but there was a hard glint in his eye.

"No…not really," she stammered, the lie tripping up her words. "Just general stuff, like how you're enjoying fatherhood. Nothing deep."

Nick held her eye for a few seconds. "Well, make sure you keep it that way and don't be concocting any of your fantasy stories about what an ogre I am. Do you understand?"

Amy nodded rapidly, not caring what he was insinuating.

She had absolutely no desire to talk about what was happening between her and Nick. She just desperately needed to see her friends. To feel reassured that she hadn't lost herself completely. That there was still some of the old Amy left inside her.

CHAPTER TWENTY-ONE

~~~~~~~~~~

"ARE YOU DRIVING TONIGHT?" STEVE WAS SITTING on the bed watching Sophie getting changed.

"Yes." Sophie slipped a black silk top over her head and peered at her reflection.

"You look gorgeous." She met Steve's eyes in the mirror and smiled. He was always complimenting her, even when she knew herself that she didn't look great. The pregnancy had left her with a belly that would never be flat again, even though she was slim enough everywhere else.

"You know, you *could* drink, Soph. I'm sure it wouldn't do any harm."

Sophie shook her head.

Steve got off the bed and enveloped her in a hug. "It wasn't your fault," he said into her hair.

"I know." It was such a well-trodden conversation between them. He had said it so many times. One of these days she'd believe him.

"Anyway…" She pulled away from him, suddenly claustrophobic in his embrace. "I'd better go."

Steve nodded and looked at her in that way he had, as if he

could see right into her deepest core. "It'll be good for you to see the girls again…" His words were measured and he spoke carefully. "Even if it's only for dinner."

Sophie smiled. "It will." But although she was looking forward to seeing them, she was apprehensive too. Especially about seeing Amy. None of them had wanted to go away for a whole weekend after what happened last year, but even if they had, Sophie certainly didn't have the stomach to organize it. And left to the others, nothing would get done.

"I just hope Nick's not there…" Sophie mused as she applied her lipstick.

"Keep an open mind. You don't know anything for sure."

Sophie turned to look at Steve. "We do, though. You can just sense it. I've done enough stories about it in the past to spot the signs."

"Well, be careful, then. I don't want him turning on you." Steve's lovely blue eyes narrowed.

Sophie reached up and wrapped her arms around his neck. "I love that you're so defensive of me…"

Steve kissed the top of her head. "Pah! As if you need anyone to defend you! I certainly wouldn't want to get on the wrong side of you, that's for sure."

Sophie laughed. Steve was only half right. For the most part, she could be ballsy and feisty, but only he knew how vulnerable she really was. The past year had been so successful professionally and so hard personally. There had been many times when all she wanted to do was curl up and hide from the rest of the world and Steve was the only one who could coax her out of it when she felt particularly low.

She took one last look at herself in the mirror. Long black silk top to hide the lumpy tummy, expensive bootleg jeans and high-heeled silver designer wedges. Her previously thick mane of hair had thinned, but not catastrophically, and it now shone to her shoulders. Even to her own hypercritical eye, she thought she didn't look too bad. "Right, I'll be off, then."

"Try to have fun, sweetheart." A small shadow passed over Steve's face as he spoke, and for the millionth time, Sophie felt as if she'd somehow failed him. He'd been so patient and kind, supportive and encouraging. There must have been times when he was in agony emotionally, but he held it all in to focus on her.

As she walked out to the street, she turned to look back at the small terraced house that had been their home for the past four years. Just inside the miniature front wall, there was a *SOLD!* sign that the estate agent had put up with unseemly haste just one hour after they accepted the offer. The house was small. It was ever so slightly tatty. But looking at it now, Sophie felt a pang of affection for it. It had been a place of safety and security. Yes, there had been turmoil and grief, but on the whole it was a happy house. She would miss it.

Melissa was waiting outside Notting Hill tube station as Sophie pulled up. "Hey!" she beamed, clambering into the passenger seat and leaning across to kiss Sophie. "Crikey, it's hot, isn't it? Oh, Soph, you look great. Really great."

"Well, I couldn't look worse than the last time you saw me, could I?" Sophie immediately regretted the remark. "Sorry," she added, before she put the car into gear and pulled away.

There was a beat before they both said in unison, "I hope Nick's not there tonight…" and burst out laughing, immediately breaking the tension.

"I'm amazed he agreed to us coming over. I bet he's given her a hard time about it." Sophie glanced at Melissa, who was applying her lipstick in the mirror.

"Probably preferable to letting her go away for the weekend, where he can't keep an eye on her every move. I bet he never lets her go away again."

"I hope you're wrong about that. But I have a horrible feeling you might be right."

Sophie pulled to a halt at a red light and turned to look at Melissa. "So how are you, Liss? You look good. Are you still behaving yourself?"

Melissa looked down into her lap. She didn't reply for a moment and Sophie's heart sank.

"Mostly," she replied eventually. "But it's hard. Especially when everyone around me is getting off their faces all the time. I've fallen off the wagon a few times." She gave Sophie a sheepish look.

"Well, as long as you get back on again, that's all that matters."

"It's so boring, though, Soph. You have no idea."

"Actually, I do." In front of her the light turned green and she pulled away again.

"Are you still not drinking?" Melissa sounded aghast.

"Nope." Sophie smiled. The reaction was always the same. People didn't seem to be able to conceive of a life without alcohol.

"You know it wasn't your fault, don't you?" Melissa began.

Sophie put a hand up to stop her. "Don't," she cut in. "I can't go there. Not yet."

Melissa nodded. "So, work seems to be going well!" Her voice rose a couple of octaves, as if to emphasize that she knew she was changing the subject.

Sophie relaxed. "It is. Actually, it's been my saviour over the past year. I love it."

"I'm not surprised. You certainly picked the right man

to hitch your wagon to. I wish I'd got in there now. I knew Mark Bailey when he was a nobody in the music industry."

Sophie laughed. The idea of Mark Bailey being a nobody was hard to imagine. His star had risen sharply over the two years since they'd set up their company and he was starting to attract a lot of attention in the US. The company was making a fortune, thanks to a huge commission from the network, and the format had already been sold to several other countries around the world. Sophie had always felt that Mark was going places—she just had no idea that it would all happen so quickly.

"He's really quite attractive, I think," Melissa said.

"I wonder if you thought that before he made his first million," Sophie countered, grinning at her.

"Well, of course I did!" Melissa looked mock indignant, then burst out laughing. "Although now you mention it, maybe a bit of fame and fortune has added a certain *je ne sais quoi* to his charms."

"I think we all know what it's added!" Sophie said drily.

"Seriously, though, Soph, has there never been any kind of frisson of attraction? You're working together *very* closely..."

"Stop it. I really love working with Mark, but I would never fancy him in a million years. And he'd never fancy me. I'm definitely not his type."

"Well, that's probably a good thing..."

"Yup." Sophie pulled into the driveway in front of Amy's huge white stucco house. It was in a quiet, leafy square and boasted some of the most expensive properties in London. She looked up at the facade before her and exhaled. "Different world, isn't it?"

"It won't be long before you're living in something like this, Soph, the way you're going."

"Hardly!" Sophie scoffed. Their new house wasn't anything like Amy's and it certainly didn't have such an exclusive postcode. But it was a huge step up for them, with five bedrooms, so that the children could have their own rooms as they got older. Assuming they had more children. And she did assume it. In fact, she yearned for it. Had become obsessed by it.

Amy opened the door with a flourish and for a moment it seemed as if she was back to her old self. "Helloooo!" she squealed, grabbing Sophie and Melissa into an embrace with both arms, squashing the bottle of champagne and bouquet of flowers they were clutching. "I am *so* happy to see you! Come in, come in!" She stood aside to allow them to step into the wide, oak-floored hallway. Outside, the temperature was sweltering, but inside, it was noticeably cooler.

Sophie gazed around her as she followed Amy through to the large, airy kitchen. Every inch of the house was perfect. There wasn't a single speck of dust or a piece of chipped paint anywhere. "My God, Amy. Your house is so pristine. How the hell do you manage to keep it like that? Especially as you were always so messy!"

Amy's face clouded as she followed Sophie's gaze. "I don't," she said, almost contemptuously. "I have a housekeeper every day."

"You lucky cow!" Sophie pulled out a stool and perched at the huge marble island in the centre of the room, where Amy had lined up four champagne flutes and a bottle of champagne. "My house is like a rubbish tip. We're both as bad as each other, so our poor cleaner really doesn't make much of a dent in it for her fifty quid a week."

Amy looked at her longingly. "I'd love a bit of mess. But Nick's unbelievably fussy. I think he might have OCD. He goes mad if anything is out of place."

Melissa and Sophie exchanged glances as they took a seat.

"So," Melissa said, cutting through the awkward pause, "when's Em getting here?"

"She should be here any moment." Amy picked up the champagne bottle and began to pour.

"Not for me," said Sophie, unable to meet Amy's eye. "I'm not drinking."

Amy nodded but didn't say anything. She finished pouring the champagne into two glasses and put the bottle down on the worktop. Then she opened the huge American-style fridge and retrieved a carton of cranberry juice. "How about this?" she said, smiling.

Sophie smiled back. "Perfect."

At that moment, the doorbell rang. Amy ran to answer it.

"Thank God he's not here," Melissa whispered as soon as she was out of earshot.

Sophie nodded. "I know. And however hard she tries, you can see it in her eyes. She's not happy, is she?"

Melissa shook her head just as Amy returned, ushering Emily into the kitchen.

As they hugged their hellos, Sophie wondered if she was imagining that Emily seemed more awkward around her than usual. To be fair, lots of people did. She wished they didn't.

Once all their glasses were filled, Amy lifted hers. "I'd like to make a toast," she began, before stopping. She bit her lip nervously and took a deep breath. "Here's to you, Sophie. I can't imagine how you've got through the past year. But you have. And we all love you."

Sophie's eyes filled. She could barely see to lift her own glass, which she clinked against the other three. "Thank you," she whispered.

★ ★ ★ ★ ★

"Bloody hell, the flight's only from Belfast," Melissa moaned. "Why are the bags taking so long to come through?"

Just then, the alarm sounded and the carousel began to move. "At last!" Emily sighed. "My feet are going numb. Sophie, you look a bit peaky. Why don't you go and sit down? We can get your bag."

Sophie began to object but thought better of it. As she stumbled towards the seats, she realized that the nagging pain that had started in her back was now in her stomach too and it was getting worse. It felt as if something was gnawing at her insides. As she slumped down onto one of the chairs, she felt a rushing sensation and yelped in agony.

Everyone waiting at the carousel turned to look at her in shock. "Help," she managed to whisper as a pool of red formed around her and feet came running from all directions.

★ ★ ★ ★ ★

"It's not your fault." It was the first of many, many times she would hear those words. Steve held her hand and looked at her with bright blue eyes that were dimmed with tiredness and grief. But it didn't matter how many times she heard it. She would never believe it. It was her fault. Before she knew she was pregnant, she had been more than a little bit merry on several occasions. Once, at an awards ceremony with Mark and the team at work, she had been properly drunk. It was payback for what she'd done in the past. She knew it.

"It was a boy, Steve."

Steve's eyes filled and he nodded.

Don't say it, she willed him. *Please don't say it.* Other people would say it, but she didn't want him to.

Steve made as if to speak, then seemed to think better of it. He nodded again and squeezed her hand instead.

Yes, *they could try again.* Yes, *she was still young enough.* Yes, *at least she knew she could get pregnant.* All the platitudes that other people trotted out, wanting to help. Not realizing how utterly futile they sounded. As if they were talking about a pair of shoes that didn't fit. She didn't want to try again. She wanted *this* baby. Only Steve really understood and she loved him so much for it.

Going back to work was easier than she had expected because she hadn't told anyone about the pregnancy in the first place, something she was eternally grateful for now. She had just worn baggier tops and looser trousers, safe in the knowledge that no one would notice.

Mark might have thought that she was putting on weight, but it would never have occurred to him that she might be pregnant. It wasn't that he was unkind or selfish. He was just a very rich, single man without children, who would have been baffled by the idea of anyone actively wanting to have a baby.

Their relationship was very close, but it was purely professional. Mark never asked about her home life and she never volunteered any information. Likewise, although her natural journalistic nosiness meant she was quite interested in his love life, she had sensed right from the start of their partnership that it was best not to pry. Anyway, she could read about his high-profile liaisons in the papers whenever she wanted to.

Melissa and Emily had both been fantastic. They had gone with her to the hospital that first, awful night and then called or texted her regularly for weeks. They managed to keep their distance at the same time as letting her know they were there for her if she needed them.

Amy was a different matter. Emily had told her what had happened and she had called Sophie in floods of tears. "It should have been me...not you!" she wailed.

Sophie had reeled in shock. "What? God, no, Amy, don't say that."

But Amy's words were unstoppable. "I don't even want this bloody baby, Sophie," she continued. "I thought I was losing my baby too...the day after you. And I was glad! I *wanted* to lose it."

Sophie stared at the phone in horror, completely at a loss for what to say. "No..." she stuttered eventually. "You don't mean that."

"I do mean it! If I could swap places with you, I would. This is all so wrong."

Sophie's legs felt wobbly and she had to sit down. "If you're trying to make me feel better, Amy, it's not working."

Amy continued to sob on the other end of the line while Sophie listened. "Amy?" she said when the crying eventually subsided to a hiccough. "What's going on? What's made you feel like this? If it's guilt on my behalf, then please don't. There's no need."

"It's not guilt. Well, yes, it is guilt, I suppose. It just all feels so wrong, Sophie. You really, really wanted your baby. And I really, really don't."

Sophie gasped.

"I know!" Amy continued. "I know it's an evil thing to say. But it's how I feel. Oh God, I don't know what to do..." She descended into another bout of sobbing so violent that Sophie began to feel seriously alarmed.

"Right," she said, trying to sound controlled and firm. "You need to calm down. Do you want me to come over?"

"No! No…" There was genuine panic in Amy's voice. "You mustn't come over. Promise me you won't come over."

Sophie frowned. "OK, OK! I won't come over. But you're worrying me, Amy. You need to talk to someone."

Amy blew her nose on the other end of the phone. "I'm talking to you, aren't I?"

Sophie shook her head. She was worried about Amy, but she couldn't deal with this right now. She had enough worries of her own. "Look, Amy…I'm going to get Emily to call you, OK? I'm in no state to offer advice and I just can't…" She tailed off as the tears began to overflow. Amy was right. It was so unfair. She had wanted her baby so much. But now he was gone. Yet Amy's was still there—growing, kicking, alive. Unwanted. How could that be right?

"I'm so sorry, Soph," Amy started to say. But Sophie had rung off.

She locked herself in the bathroom and allowed herself to cry for five minutes. Then she wiped her face, blew her nose and stood up straight. She couldn't afford to crumple. She owed it to Emma and Steve to get through this and stay strong.

Emily answered immediately, "Soph? Are you OK?"

Sophie took a deep, shuddery breath. "Yes, I'm fine. But Amy's not. Can you call her, Em? I just don't have the strength to deal with it right now…"

"Of course." Emily's tone was brisk and businesslike.

"I'm worried about her. She's in a bad way."

"Worse than in Ireland?"

"Yes. Definitely worse. But I offered to go over and she panicked. It's him…"

Emily sighed. "I know. God, what a mess. Listen, Soph,

you shouldn't be worrying about this now. Leave it to me. I'll call her."

"Thanks, Em. Will you let me know how you get on?"

Emily hesitated. "I'll only tell you what I need to. You've got enough on your plate."

"OK. Thank you."

It would be another month before Sophie spoke to Amy again, by which time she sounded much calmer and seemed to have got her head together. They didn't discuss her earlier outburst, and when Sophie asked how the pregnancy was progressing, Amy had breezily assured her it was fine.

CHAPTER TWENTY-TWO

AMY OPENED THE DOOR NERVOUSLY, LIKE SOME-
one who was terrified of being attacked on her own doorstep.
As her eyes alighted on Emily, they widened in horror. "Em!
What are you doing here?"

"I've come to see you." Emily tried to keep her face pas-
sive, but she was so shocked by Amy's appearance that it was
a huge effort. It was only a week or so since she had last seen
her, but she seemed to have aged years in that time. "Aren't
you going to invite me in?"

Amy hesitated and for a moment Emily thought she might
refuse, but eventually, reluctantly, she opened the door a bit
wider and moved to one side. Emily stepped into the hallway
and immediately shivered. It was a beautiful house. Perfect,
in fact. But there was something cold and forbidding about it.
The air seemed to hang thick with tension. They faced each
other awkwardly. "I was worried about you. Sophie told me
about your phone call. I thought it best I come round."

Amy reddened. "I'm fine. I just had a bad moment. I felt
terrible for Sophie. About what happened."

Emily nodded. "Why are you wearing a scarf? It's boiling hot."

Amy's eyes slid away. "Sore throat," she muttered. "I thought it might help. Anyway, do you want a coffee?"

Emily nodded. "Yes, please. Where's Megan?"

Amy busied herself making coffee while Emily pulled up a chair at the kitchen table. "She's out with her nanny."

Emily watched Amy as she moved around the kitchen. She was hunched over and her hand kept moving to her neck to adjust the pale blue cashmere scarf she had wrapped around it. It was obviously irritating her. "Why don't you take that scarf off, Amy? It looks really uncomfortable."

Amy stopped spooning coffee into the cafetière and turned to look at Emily. Without her saying a word, Emily knew.

"Look, Amy, you don't have to stay. You have options."

"No. Actually, I don't."

There was such a defeatist tone to her voice that it made Emily prickle with annoyance. "There are always options, Amy. You could come and stay with me for a while."

"In your little flat?" Amy put the coffee down in front of Emily and shook her head. "There wouldn't be enough room for us all."

Emily sighed with frustration. "We'd manage. For goodness' sake, Amy, the most important thing is your happiness… And your safety," she added, aware that she was overstepping a boundary.

Amy picked up her cup and took a sip of her coffee, deep in thought. "But Megan… He'd make sure…"

"Bring her with you, of course," Emily urged, trying to keep the impatience out of her voice. "Pack a few things and come with me now. Before he gets home."

Amy's hands started to shake. "I don't know…" she said, her breath catching. She looked like an animal caught in a trap.

"You *do* know. Come on, Amy, you need to leave. You can't carry on like this."

Amy's face hardened, as if she was steeling herself for battle, and she stood up shakily. "Oh God," she whispered to herself. "What am I doing? OK," she said, giving Emily a pleading look. "OK. Wait here."

Emily waited, her heart pounding. It was ten past four. As the hands of the clock creaked through the minutes, she inwardly prayed that Nick wouldn't come home early for some reason. She hated to admit it, but she was scared of him. It seemed impossible and ridiculous to be scared of that handsome, charming, thoughtful man, who had so beguiled them all at the beginning. She imagined how it must be for Amy, living with that fear day after day.

By the time Amy reappeared, clutching a large overnight bag, it was almost four thirty. Emily stood up and swallowed, meeting Amy's terrified eyes with what she hoped was an encouraging expression. "OK. Let's go."

Amy's eyes widened. "I can't go without Megan! We have to wait for her to come home."

Emily's heart sank. "Of course." She sat back down. "When will she be back?"

Amy looked at her watch. "Soon. They've been gone an hour."

Emily nodded. "OK. Well, just make sure you've got everything you need so that we can leave straight away."

"I have." Amy sat down opposite Emily and stared at the clock, as if willing it to stay put. After what seemed like an hour but was only five minutes, the front door opened. "That's them!" Amy jumped up and ran to greet the young nanny, who was pushing Megan in an expensive, upmarket buggy.

She wheeled her into the kitchen and gestured towards Emily with a quizzical expression. "Oh...Suki, this is my good friend Emily." Amy gabbled the introduction.

"Hi," Suki said, without looking at Emily.

Emily took an instant dislike to her. "Hi," she replied, her chilly tone matching Suki's.

Suki bent down and began to undo Megan's straps.

"Oh, no! It's OK, leave her. We're going out." Amy picked up her bag.

"Really? It's nearly time for Megan's tea." Suki tilted her head so that her mane of golden hair fell in perfect ripples over her right shoulder. She was undeniably beautiful, but Emily could tell from the malicious glint in her cold blue eyes that she was as hard as nails. She was no friend of Amy's, that was for sure.

"Yes, Amy's coming shopping with me," Emily said, standing up. Without realizing it, she had automatically squared up to Suki.

"Oh. OK." With a last suspicious scowl at Emily, Suki shrugged and unhooked her handbag from the buggy. "Well, I guess I'll just go and watch TV for a while..." As she walked out of the kitchen, she was already texting on her mobile phone.

Emily looked at Amy, who she could see was quivering with fear. How the hell had Nick had this effect on her? And how could she stand sharing her child with someone as vile as Suki? "Ready?"

Amy hesitated. "Yes. No."

Emily tried not to let the prickles of irritation she was feeling show. Amy bent down and stroked Megan's face.

The little girl tilted her dark head towards Amy's hand and smiled a gummy smile, instantly reminding Emily of Jack at the same age. It was such a magical time, when they were just beginning to talk and walk. "Drink?" Megan said with another imploring smile. She was adorable.

"You want a drink, darling?" Amy kissed Megan's forehead. "OK, Mummy's going to get you a drink and then we're going out."

"Get out?" Megan replied, tugging impatiently at the straps holding her into her buggy.

"No, sweetheart, just stay there for a minute while I get you a drink." Amy was already filling a baby cup with water.

"Want to get out!" wailed Megan, her bottom lip protruding. Emily knew there was an almighty tantrum brewing. She recognized the signs. "Why don't I take her out of her buggy and carry her?"

Amy nodded, flustered. "Sure. Oh, damn!" The cup she was trying to put a lid on tipped over and the water pooled onto the floor. While Emily undid Megan's straps and lifted her out of her buggy, Amy was mopping up the spill with kitchen paper.

Emily looked at the clock nervously. "Come on, Amy. We really need to go."

"I know!" Amy finished mopping the floor and refilled the cup.

"Right, put your bag in the pram and I'll carry Megan. Oh no…" She tailed off as a familiar smell reached her nostrils.

"What?" Amy looked up at her in alarm.

"I think someone's nappy needs changing. But, look, let's just leave and we can find a loo somewhere along the way." As if on cue, Megan burst into noisy tears, her little fat cheeks flaming red.

Amy instinctively reached out for Megan and cuddled her to her chest, stroking her hair. "No, I'll change her. It'll only take a couple of minutes." She whisked her out of the room before Emily could object.

The sense of foreboding that Emily had started to feel began to grow. She somehow knew what was going to happen next before it happened. Sure enough, the front door opened and Nick walked in. "Hi, Emily," he said with a wide, even smile. He kissed her on both cheeks and threw his arms out. "This is a lovely surprise."

Emily narrowed her eyes at him. He was convincing, she'd give him that. No one would ever guess what a nasty piece of work he was. "Hi, Nick."

"Where's Amy?" He gazed around the kitchen, as if expecting her to materialize from one of the cupboards. As he did so, his eyes alighted on something. Emily watched in fascination as he walked over to the large sideboard behind the table and moved a candle just a couple of centimetres to the right. Then he swung around and smiled again at Emily, sending a chill down her spine.

"She's just upstairs changing Megan."

"Ah…" There was an awkward pause. Then Nick spotted Amy's overnight bag. "Going somewhere, were you?"

Emily hesitated, aware that this was potentially a dangerous situation. "Shopping," she said, her tone as light as she could make it.

Nick's smile slipped a fraction and he looked at his watch theatrically. "Odd time to go shopping. Ah, and here she comes," he added as Amy's footsteps could be heard on the stairs.

Amy rushed into the kitchen carrying Megan and sat her in her pushchair, seemingly not having noticed Nick leaning against the sideboard. "Sorry, that took longer than I thought." She did up Megan's straps and stood. "Right, let's go quickly before I change my mind."

"Why don't you leave Megan here, darling? You don't want to be bogged down with a pram on your shopping trip."

Amy jumped as if she'd been shot. "Nick! What are you doing home so early?" she stammered, her pale cheeks flaming instantly.

"Oh, I got a text from Suki. She wanted me to help her with something. Anyway, sweetheart," he continued, unstrapping Megan and lifting her out of her buggy, while Amy watched open-mouthed, "at least you can go shopping unencumbered, eh?" He cuddled Megan and began to bounce up and down on the balls of his feet, making her giggle with delight.

Amy looked helplessly at Emily. Emily felt a sudden, desperate urge to punch Nick hard in his smug, handsome face. Only the fact that he was holding Megan prevented her. "Nick's right," she said, knowing that her voice was quavering with anger. "We can shop unencumbered, Amy. Come on, let's go." But she already knew that Amy wouldn't be coming with her. She couldn't. If she left without Megan, he would see to it that she never got her back.

Amy shook her head, almost imperceptibly. "Maybe another day?" Her voice was barely louder than a whisper.

For a moment, Emily considered snatching Megan out of Nick's arms and telling Amy to run, but there were too many risks, and besides, he was so much stronger than her. Instead, she nodded, holding Amy's desperately sad eyes with her own, trying to convey to her that everything would be OK. But she felt defeated. As she made her way towards the door, she turned to look back at Nick. "I like Amy's scarf," she said, fixing him with a cold stare. "A nice present from you, I take it?"

Nick's dark eyes clouded and he pointedly turned his back to her. "Goodbye, Emily. Lovely to see you, as always."

As Amy opened the front door to show her out, Emily hugged her, whispering in her ear, "Call me as soon as you can. It doesn't matter what time of day or night it is. I will come and get you. You can't stay here."

Amy let out a low, guttural sob. "I can't leave either," she whispered back, her voice hoarse.

As the door closed behind her and Emily trudged down the beautiful stone steps, she felt as if she had just abandoned a puppy in the middle of a motorway.

CHAPTER TWENTY-THREE

"CAN I SEE HIM?" SOPHIE HAD FOLLOWED AMY out to the kitchen after the main course.

Amy put down the plates she was holding and looked up at Sophie with a slight frown. "Are you sure that's a good idea?"

Sophie nodded. "As long as you're OK with it."

Amy ran a hand over her forehead. "Yes, of course. Follow me."

They climbed the stairs to the first floor. Amy tiptoed into a darkened room, where a little bundle was sleeping soundly in his cot. She switched on the moon-shaped lamp on the chest of drawers and Sophie gazed down at him in the soft light it threw out. He was lying on his back with his arms stretched out either side of him, his palms clenched into tiny fists. His mouth was slightly open and his breathing was snuffly as his chest rose and fell inside his snow-white Babygro. Beside him lay a small, white, fluffy dog.

Sophie reached out to touch his soft, downy head. "He's perfect, Amy."

Amy put her arm around Sophie and leaned her head on

her shoulder. "He's why I couldn't leave, Sophie. Him and Megan."

"I know. We all know." Sophie continued to stare at the sleeping child. George, they had named him. Sophie had never told anyone, but that was the name she had chosen for her baby boy. In a strange way that she couldn't really understand herself, she took some comfort that Amy had used the same name.

And she felt comforted in finally seeing him too. She hadn't been ready before. It was too raw. So she had lovingly chosen a present and sent it by post instead. It was the fluffy dog that was lying beside him now.

"I'm so sorry you lost your baby, Sophie… And I'm sorry for what I said when I called you. I didn't mean it."

Sophie pulled her eyes away from the baby and turned towards Amy. "Thank you. I'm sorry I haven't been able to see him before now. But I'm so glad I have. It helps, in a weird sort of way."

Amy nodded and gave Sophie a quick, slightly embarrassed hug. "Shall we go back and join the others?"

As they walked down the stairs, Sophie put her hand on Amy's arm. "How are things now? Between you and Nick?"

Amy didn't look up. "Good. Fine. Everything's fine." The words rattled off her tongue unconvincingly. Sophie decided to let it drop. Maybe having another baby had helped. Amy certainly seemed calmer and less stressed.

★ ★ ★ ★ ★

"Resigned," Melissa corrected her as they drove away from Amy's later that evening. "She's not calm. She's resigned to her fate."

"Oh God, don't say that." Sophie glanced at Melissa as she drove towards the tube station.

"Melissa's right, I'm afraid," said Emily from the back seat. She sounded frustrated and annoyed. "She's completely trapped. If she was to leave him, he'd come after her. I can't believe she's still got that same bloody nanny, too. She's seriously bad news and I guarantee she's sleeping with Nick."

"There must be something we can do." Sophie wasn't used to being helpless. To not being able to solve a problem.

"Well, I've told her that she can come to me any time of the day or night. I'm not sure what else we can do but make it clear we're there for her." Emily sighed. "I'm actually more worried about her now than I was before. This resignation and acceptance are more terrifying than if she was hysterical and screaming blue murder.

"He's so bloody clever, that's the problem," she continued. "He'd make out she was a mentally unstable danger to the kids. And that bitch of a nanny would back him up."

They lapsed into silence for a few moments while they each contemplated Amy's situation.

Suddenly, Emily sat up and leaned forward. "We could stage an intervention!"

"What? *Kidnap* her?" Sophie looked at Emily in the rear-view mirror in disbelief.

"We wouldn't be kidnapping her," Emily said, a slight note of irritation detectable in her voice. "We'd be rescuing her. It's very different."

"Jesus," Melissa muttered under her breath. "I can't believe this is happening."

"I don't know, Em…" Sophie said. "I was talking to Steve about it earlier. He said we don't know for sure that he's violent towards her—"

"We do," Emily cut in firmly. "We might not have actually witnessed it, but we've seen the results with our own eyes. And when I confronted him last year, he didn't even try to deny it. He just smirked in that creepy way he has."

"Yes, but whatever we think of him, he's still the father of those kids. He will always have to be a part of her life." Melissa's words fell into a vacuum of silence.

At last Sophie spoke. "I've got room in the new house for all of them."

Emily sat up straighter and leaned forward. "And he doesn't know where the new house is, so there'd be no chance of him tracking her down, at least to begin with. Let's think how we could do it."

"I'm not sure…" Melissa cut in. "It could go horribly wrong. We might make things worse."

"Nothing could be worse than him killing her, Melissa," Emily snapped. "And if we don't do something, I'm seriously scared that's what might happen."

SEPTEMBER 2004

"In entertainment news, a brand-new talent show, *The X Factor*, is launching tonight. It is the brainchild of *Pop Idol* star Simon Cowell, who will sit on the judging panel, along with Louis Walsh and Sharon Osbourne."

WELLS-NEXT-THE-SEA, NORFOLK

CHAPTER TWENTY-FOUR

THEY CLIMBED OUT OF THEIR FORD FIESTA AND
Emily lifted their bags out of the boot. Jack hovered uncertainly, his hands shoved deep into the pockets of his jeans. "What's wrong?" she said, motioning to him to follow her up the path.

Jack shrugged. "Nothing…"

"Just feeling a bit shy?" Emily finished the sentence for him.

Jack nodded. "A bit."

At that moment, the door flew open and Emma came flying down the path. "Jack!" she squealed in delight, throwing herself at him so that he had to take a few steps to stop himself from toppling over.

"Hello, Emma." He grinned, glancing up at Emily.

"Will you come to the beach with me?" she implored, her big blue eyes widening as she grasped his hand and tried to pull him towards the seafront across the road.

"In a little while, sweetheart," said Sophie, coming down the path and giving Emily a huge hug. She looked stunning, in a pale pink loose waterfall cotton cardigan over a matching tunic dress. Her eyes seemed to be shining and her skin glowed under her tan, making Emily feel plain and tired-looking beside her. "Let Jack and Emily put their things away and let's get them a drink first, shall we?" Sophie said.

"OK," Emma agreed cheerfully, pulling Jack towards the house instead. "Come on, Jack, I'll show you where you're sleeping."

Emily and Sophie watched them go. "Oh, Sophie, she's such a little cutie." Emily linked her arm through Sophie's and they walked up the path towards the door together.

"She's exhausting!" Sophie said with a laugh. "But yes, she's gorgeous. And Jack is getting so tall and handsome. You've done such a great job with him, Em."

Emily smiled proudly. "Thank you. He's a good boy. Are the others here?"

"Yup. All inside."

"How are things?" Emily stopped before she reached the front door and turned to face Sophie. She really was looking fantastic—Emily wondered if maybe she was pregnant and the thought made her prickle slightly with envy.

Sophie glanced towards the house. "I'd say she's good, considering. But she's also... Fragile is probably the best way of putting it."

Emily nodded. "Not surprising really."

"No," Sophie agreed.

"What about the kids?"

"Hopefully too young to understand, although Megan's very, very shy, especially compared to Emma. Makes you wonder how much she's taken in."

Emily nodded, suddenly nervous about seeing Amy. "She doesn't blame us, does she?"

Sophie bit the inside of her cheek as she thought about it. "You know, I'm not sure. Maybe a bit."

Emily's heart sank. "We did the right thing, though, didn't we?" She desperately wanted Sophie to agree with her.

"Yes, we did. Of course we did. Sometimes it takes people a while to accept what the right thing is, though, doesn't it? Especially when you have as little confidence as Amy."

Emily nodded, although there was a horrible nagging doubt at the back of her mind. It had all been her idea and she had been so forceful in persuading the others. If it turned out to have been the wrong thing to do, she knew in her heart that she was the one who was most to blame...

★ ★ ★ ★ ★

It was lunchtime, two months after the meal at Amy's house. Sophie was driving her SUV. Emily was in the passenger seat. They had told Melissa she didn't need to come as there wouldn't be room for Amy and the two kids if she did and she had agreed with what seemed to Emily like undue haste. Sophie parked on Amy's drive and they looked at each other nervously. "Ready?"

Emily gazed back at her with wide eyes. "Not really. I'm terrified. What if that bloody nanny's there?"

"You distract her. Tell her you're looking for someone to look after your son and you want to ask her advice and to see if she can recommend anyone. I'll get Amy and the kids out as quickly as possible."

"OK." Emily looked slightly calmer. "Let's go, then. No point in waiting any longer..."

They climbed out of the car and walked up the steps together. Emily rang the bell and they waited in silence. After a few minutes, the sound of heels on a wooden floor could be heard. Amy opened the door a few inches, just enough to allow her to peer out nervously.

She visibly jumped in shock as she registered Sophie and Emily. "No!" she hissed. "You can't be here."

She made as if to close the door, but Emily was too quick for her and put her foot on the step. "Amy, can't you see how ridiculous this is? This is *your* house! We're *your* friends. Why on earth shouldn't we be here?"

Amy's pale, frightened face crumpled instantly. "Because he doesn't want you here!" She dissolved into tears and put her hands up to cover her face, allowing Emily and Sophie to step into the hallway.

Emily closed the huge front door carefully and scanned the hall for clues as to who else was in the house, but as usual, everything was so pristine that there was nothing.

Sophie put her arms around Amy and hugged her. "Amy, we've come to get you. You can't stay here."

Amy's wet eyes widened in terror. "No!" she growled. "We tried that once before—Emily, tell her—and it didn't work. He'll make sure I don't see the children."

"We're taking the children with us," Emily said in what she hoped was a calm, reassuring voice. "He won't know where you are."

Amy put her hands over her face again and leaned against the wall for support. "He'll find me. You don't know what he's like."

"We need to report this to the police—" Sophie started to say, but she was silenced by a yelp from Amy.

"No! No! You mustn't involve the police. I just couldn't bear the shame. What if my mum and dad find out? And he's a good father... He really is... He loves the children so much.

And he loves me! He just…" She stopped speaking suddenly, as if her words had run out.

Sophie ushered Amy towards the kitchen, where they sat shakily either side of her at the table. "Look, Amy," she began, taking Amy's hand in hers. It was freezing cold. "Do you love your children?"

Amy frowned. "Of course I do. You know I do. Why would you ask that?" She looked in confusion from Sophie to Emily.

"She's asking because it's the reason that you are going to go upstairs and pack a bag. You are going to get the children up from their nap and you are going to put them in Sophie's car…"

Amy was shaking her head furiously all the time that Emily was speaking. Emily ignored her and continued calmly. "You are going to leave this house and you are going to leave Nick because it's not safe for you to stay. If you love your children, as we both know you do, you won't put them in harm's way."

"He'd never hurt the children!" Amy looked at Emily in disbelief.

"He's already hurt them," Sophie said gently. "Do you honestly think that by beating up their mother, he's not hurting the children?"

"But he doesn't beat me up…" Amy looked confused.

"He might not punch you or kick you," Sophie said, tilting her head so that she could make eye contact with Amy. "But he's violent towards you, isn't he?"

Amy blinked several times in quick succession. Emily held her breath. Amy had never admitted it before, maybe not even to herself. But Emily could understand why not. There was something terrifying about hearing the words spoken out loud. It somehow made it seem more real. "I…I'm not sure," she mumbled.

"You're scared of him, Amy," Sophie continued. "And there's a reason why you're scared of him. It's not your fault. I'm scared of him too, and so is Emily…"

Emily nodded ruefully. "It's true. And we have nothing like your reason."

Amy's head dropped. "I just haven't got the guts to leave. I'm not like you two. I can't stand on my own two feet. I'm useless."

Sophie reached out and lifted Amy's chin. "You are not useless, Amy. He's made you believe that you are, but you're not. You are a fantastic cook, a loving mother. You're beautiful, clever, a great photographer, and you are a very, very special friend to us. We love you and we're worried about you. If you stay, you aren't just condemning yourself to a life of violence and fear, but you're condemning your children too. We know that's not what you want. What damage do you think it must do to Megan to see her mum in such a state?"

A large fat tear ran down Amy's porcelain cheek. "I don't want that."

"We know you don't, sweetie." Emily put her arm around Amy and rubbed her narrow back. "Do the right thing. Come with us now. It's the best chance you'll have."

"Where would we live? What would we live on?" Amy shook her head as she spoke. "It's impossible."

"You can live with me and I'll support you until you get yourself together."

Emily looked at Sophie in admiration. It was a huge commitment she was taking on and yet she had absolutely no qualms.

"No." Amy shrugged wearily. "I couldn't do that, Sophie. You've got your own family…"

"Yes, and I've spoken to Steve and he's completely happy.

Amy, I couldn't have offered it a year ago, but now that we've moved into this new house, we have enough room for you. And…well, Nick hasn't got a clue where it is, so he won't be able to find you."

"Oh, he'll find me." Amy grimaced. "He'll always find me."

Emily caught Sophie's eye and gestured to her watch. She didn't want a repeat of what happened last time. At least that bitch Suki wasn't here this time.

Sophie nodded. "Amy, you need to come with me now. I'm not leaving here without you and the children. It's not safe for you to stay."

"Come on, Amy," Emily added. "This is the best chance you'll get. Take it while you still can."

Amy looked from one to the other helplessly. "You're not giving me a choice, are you?"

Sophie shook her head. "No, we're not. But you have to trust us. We are doing this for your own good—and for the good of Megan and George. Those children need their mum back. *We* need you back. Let's go and get your things together." She stood up and looked down at Amy expectantly.

Something in Amy's face changed and set hard. She stood up and faced Sophie. "Do you promise me it will be OK?"

Sophie blinked before replying. "Yes," she said clearly and firmly. "I promise."

Amy nodded, holding Sophie's gaze. "Then let's go. But we'll need to be quick. Suki's due here at two."

Emily looked at the clock. It was just gone one. "We can pack and get out before then," she said, already heading for the stairs. "And that's another reason why you need to leave, Amy. You can't have that vile bitch anywhere near you or your children."

"You're right," Amy said, suddenly energized as she climbed the stairs two at a time. "I hate her."

Emily and Sophie both laughed.

The journey to Sophie's house took over an hour. George slept in his car seat, while Megan curled up in Amy's lap and sucked her thumb. Emily watched her, noticing that even at the tender age of two and a half she looked troubled.

Amy had quickly returned to being a quivering wreck, after almost an hour of seemingly superhuman energy, in which she packed up all her own things, as well as the cornucopia of baggage that accompanied each of the children. Once it was loaded into Sophie's SUV and they had pulled out of the drive, she seemed to deflate like a popped balloon. Silent tears began to pour down her cheeks and dissolve into Megan's dark hair.

Steve came out of the front door as they arrived. He peered into the back seat at Amy and the children. "You made it, then."

"Yes." Sophie got out of the car and gestured towards them. "No hiccoughs, thank God."

"Are you sure this is OK, Steve?" Amy's voice was small and croaky as she leaned forward.

"I'm absolutely certain," Steve said, throwing Amy an encouraging smile as he began to quietly unload the car. Emily watched him, envy scorching through her body. Sophie was so lucky to have him. She couldn't imagine what it would be like to have that sort of support. Yes, she had her mum and dad, but it just wasn't the same as having a partner to help with everything. Sighing to herself, she unstrapped George's car seat and carried the still-sleeping baby into the house.

Inside, it was big, light and airy. It had all the same luxury of Amy's house without the added tension. And it looked lived-in, unlike Amy's, which had always seemed like a show home, rather than a family home. Emily looked up at the vaulted glass ceiling at the back of the kitchen, thinking how different it was to her boring little B&Q kitchen in her boring little flat. It made her sad to think that Jack would probably never live somewhere like this, with a pretty garden that stretched into the distance, and a trampoline and swings for the children to play on. Now that she thought about it, she didn't ever remember seeing any toys in Amy's garden. Nick probably thought they were too messy.

"Are you OK, Em?" Sophie was behind her.

Emily turned and nodded. "I am. I'm relieved it's over."

Sophie glanced at Amy, who was sitting at the kitchen table with Megan, feeding her a biscuit. "I'm not sure it's over. In fact, I've got a feeling this might just be the beginning."

"I think what you're doing for her is incredible, Soph." Emily reached out and hugged her. "You're a good friend."

"So are you. We're lucky to have each other."

Emily smiled. "Anyway, I'd better be off. They're going to be OK, aren't they?"

"They'll be fine."

Emily walked over to where Amy was sitting. Megan had climbed onto her lap again and the two of them made a pitiful sight. Amy looked dazed, her eyes not quite focusing, and Megan was sucking her thumb again. Beside them on the floor, in his car seat, George slept on, oblivious. "Look, Amy, I've got to go, but I'll come back at the weekend, OK?"

Amy nodded mutely.

Emily crouched down so that she was at eye level with her. "This is the right thing for you, Amy. For all three of you. Sophie and Steve will look after you and you don't have to be scared any more, OK?"

Amy nodded again, but her gaze was vacant and unseeing.

Emily reached up and ruffled Megan's hair. "I'll see you very soon, sweetie, OK? And I'll bring you something nice when I come back."

Megan shrank even further into Amy's stomach, but she managed a wary smile.

Emily stood up again. "So, bye for now. Bye, Steve," she called.

Steve broke off from where he was making tea and came over to Emily. "Bye, Em," he said, giving her a hug. "Well done."

Sophie motioned to him to follow her and Emily out into the hall. "Let's keep in touch. If we hear anything from Nick, we'll let you know…"

"And I'll do the same," Emily said, shivering slightly at the prospect. "Might be a good idea to take her phone too?"

"Done it already. I'm hoping she won't notice until the worst is over."

The first text came from Sophie a few hours later.

He's ringing her constantly. I only listened to the first voice-mail… Steve said not to listen to any more. He'll be on to you next…

As if on cue, Emily's phone buzzed in her hand, making her jump. The number was withheld, but she knew it was him. For a moment, she considered answering it. But something stopped her and she let it click through to voicemail.

Once the message alert sounded, she pressed her voice-mail with shaking hands. His voice was clear, confident and charming. *"Hi, Emily,"* he said, before pausing. *"Look, this probably sounds a bit ridiculous, but I've just got home and Amy and the kids aren't here."*

There was another long pause, as if he was collecting himself. *"I'm just a bit worried. If you get this message and you know where they are, could you give me a call? Thanks, Emily."*

Emily stared at the phone. He was so plausible. So charming. It was hard to imagine him being the monster she knew he was. She deleted the message and decided to switch off her phone for a few hours so that there was no possibility of her taking any more of his calls.

When she switched it back on just before going to bed, it buzzed into life angrily and she could see that there were six new missed calls. All from him and all with accompanying voicemail. She wondered if she should take Steve's advice, but something compelled her to listen to them.

In the first message, he managed to maintain his worried yet charming tone, but by the sixth, he had given up all pretence:

"Listen, you fucking conniving bitch, I know you know where they are and I know you're to blame for them leaving. Call me back and tell me where they are or I will track you down, and I promise you, you don't want that to happen…"

Emily's heart began to pound with a mixture of outrage and fear. This was what poor Amy had been living with all this time. She couldn't help wondering, what if he did track her down? He was so menacing and she knew what he was capable of.

But, she rationalized, he had never been to her flat and wouldn't have a clue where she lived—would he? Amy had taken her phone with her and she was fairly sure her contact details wouldn't be written down anywhere else. With a trembling hand, she deleted the voicemails and texted Sophie:

He's threatening to track me down… I'm a bit scared. How is Amy? X

Sophie replied almost instantly.

Do you want to come here? We could squeeze you and Jack in too. Amy's gone to bed. She's like a zombie but at least she's safe.

Emily thought for a moment how wonderful it would be to be looked after by Sophie and Steve. But even though it was tempting, she didn't want to involve Jack in this mess, and if she was honest, she didn't want to put either of them in harm's way any more than they already were.

No thanks but I'll call tomorrow xx

Over the next week, the volume of Nick's calls increased. Emily stopped listening to them and would delete them in bulk at the end of the day. Then, just as suddenly as they had started, they stopped.

She rang Sophie. "He's stopped calling."

"Hmm. He's stopped calling her and us too."

"It worries me more than the abusive voicemails. He must be up to something."

Sophie was silent for a few minutes. "I know what you mean."

"How's Amy?"

"Good, actually. It's as if she's waking up from a coma. She seems angry, which I think is a good thing."

"Me too," Emily agreed. "I'll come over tonight if that's OK? Jack's at my mum and dad's house."

"Sure. Amy would like that. Stay for dinner."

Emily arrived at around seven in the evening. The house was a scene of happy chaos, with Steve cooking while Amy watched the kids playing. "Where's Sophie?" Emily hung up her jacket and took a seat beside Amy at the huge kitchen table.

"Still at work," chorused Steve and Amy together, before laughing.

"Well, you certainly seem a lot happier than when I last saw you." Emily reached out and took Amy's thin hand in hers.

Amy glanced nervously towards Megan, who was playing dolls with Emma in a corner of the room and seemed oblivious. "I'm not sure 'happy' is the right word," she began. "But I definitely feel better. I'm just terrified Nick's going to turn up here. Poor Steve—I won't let him out of my sight in case he does."

Emily looked up at Steve, who was cooking at the island in the middle of the room. He caught her watching him and smiled. "It's nice to be so in demand. I'm not used to women wanting my attention all the time."

Emily laughed.

"Joking aside," Amy continued, glancing at Steve, "I can't stay here indefinitely…"

"Yes, actually, you can." Steve's voice was firm. "You can stay as long as you need to." He finished the stir-fry he was making and deftly scooped it into three dishes, which he placed on the table, before taking off his makeshift tea-towel apron and sitting down opposite them. "Dig in," he said, pouring a glass of red wine for each of them.

"Thanks so much, Steve." Amy picked up her fork. "I don't know how I'd have coped without you and Sophie."

"Shh! None of that talk," Steve said, already wolfing his food down. Emily thought it was a peculiarly satisfying sight to see someone enjoying eating so much, especially with Amy picking at hers like a tiny bird. It was no wonder she was so thin.

The doorbell rang, causing them all to start. Steve jumped

up and headed for the front door, wiping his mouth with a napkin. "Sophie's forgotten her keys again," he said, before disappearing.

Emily and Amy continued to eat in silence while they waited for Steve to return. Minutes passed. Finally, Emily frowned and stood up. "Where's Steve got to?"

Amy's eyes widened in fear and instantly she shrank back into herself. "Oh God," she whispered. "What if it's Nick?"

Emily noticed Megan turn towards them curiously. "It won't be him," she said, trying to keep her voice steady as she headed out into the hallway. Even before she reached the wide-open front door, she knew something bad had happened. "Steve?" she called tentatively, before going out onto the front step.

In the neatly paved driveway, Nick's Range Rover was parked erratically, and beside the open driver's door, Steve had pinned Nick up against the car.

"You can't fucking stop me seeing my kids!" Nick snarled as a thin trail of blood snaked from one nostril, pooling onto his top lip.

"You don't deserve to see them!" Steve snarled back, pushing his fist further into Nick's chest, causing him to yelp in pain. "Funny how you're not quite such a big hard man when you're faced with someone your own size, isn't it?"

Nick tried to shake himself free from Steve's grip, but he was no match for Steve's greater height and strength.

"No, you prefer beating up women who are half the size of you, don't you? You're pathetic." Steve loosened his hold for a second, and in a flash, Nick's fist came up and connected with his chin, sending him spinning off balance. As Steve hit the ground, Nick kicked hard at his ribs and he howled in pain.

"Steve!" Emily cried, running towards Nick, who was

about to land another kick in Steve's stomach. Without pausing
to think, she threw herself at him and began to rain blows at
his head. The anger she had felt against him for so long over-
flowed in a steaming torrent of rage as she pummelled him
with a strength she had never known she had.

The next thing she knew, she was lying on the ground,
waking up to find Steve crouching over her, his face creased
with concern. "Em? Em, are you OK?"

Emily frowned and rubbed her eyes. "What happened?"

Steve reached under her back and helped her to sit up. "Nick
caught you with a right-hander. Nothing compared to what
you did to him, though." He smiled ruefully.

"Where is he?" Emily tried to turn her head to look for
him but immediately felt dizzy.

"He's gone. Jumped in his car and took off. He'll be lick-
ing his wounds for a while, I think."

"Are you OK? He gave you a bit of a kicking there."

Steve winced. "Think he may have cracked a rib. Hope-
fully, he came off worse, though. Come on, let's get inside."
He reached out to take her hand and pulled her to her feet.
Emily's legs wobbled under her and she lurched against him.
"Whoa! Steady on there. Take it slowly."

As they shuffled back into the kitchen, they found Amy
cowering in a corner of the room, covering her eyes with her
hands and sobbing violently. Emma and Megan were staring
at her with a mixture of horror and curiosity.

"Hey," Emily said, crouching down beside her. She tried
to take her hand, but Amy had folded herself into a ball and
it was impossible. "It's OK. He's gone."

"But he'll be back." Her voice was little more than a whimper.

"And if he does come back, we'll be ready for him," Steve
said. He tried to crouch but winced in pain and decided to

stay standing. "It's OK, Amy. He's a typical bully. Knowing he'd have to get past us will put him off, I promise you." He gave a dry chuckle. "You should have seen Emily go for him. Remind me never to upset you, Em."

Emily laughed. "Well, the same goes for you."

Slowly, Amy unfolded herself until she was sitting with her back against the wall. She wiped her eyes with her hand. "Thank you," she whispered, giving Emily a watery smile.

There was a bang as the front door slammed, making them all jump. "Jesus, what the hell's been going on in here?" said Sophie, taking in the scene as she walked into the kitchen, bringing the last remnants of the late summer evening with her. She scooped Emma and Megan up in either arm and planted a kiss on each of their heads. "I take it a certain someone's been here?"

Steve, Amy and Emily all nodded. "It got a little...messy," Steve said, instinctively putting his hand to his stomach.

Sophie's mouth dropped open. "Oh my God! Are you all OK?" She put Megan and Emma down on the floor and reached out to take Steve's hand. "Did he...attack you?"

"Well, yes. But we attacked him more." Steve gave a rueful smile. "Especially Emily. I definitely know not to get on the wrong side of her in future."

"Oh God, how awful. Well, at least he's gone."

Steve nodded. "Yup. I think we can safely say we've seen him off."

"Until the next time," Amy muttered.

CHAPTER TWENTY-FIVE

"SO, I HAVE SOME NEWS..." SOPHIE HAD WAITED
until the children were in bed and it was just the four of them
curled up in the cosy sitting room of their rented holiday cottage. They had lit the real fire in the inglenook fireplace—
even though it was the middle of summer, there was a distinct
chill in the breeze that blew off the sea—and drawn the heavy
drapes across the pretty latticed windows.

Melissa, Emily and Amy all sat up and looked at Sophie
expectantly.

"I'm pregnant. Again."

"Oh, Soph, that's fantastic news!" Melissa threw herself at
Sophie and hugged her tightly.

Amy beamed as she tucked her legs underneath her. "I'm
pleased that having us three there hasn't stopped you...well,
you know." She tailed off as a flush spread up her pale cheeks.

Sophie laughed uproariously. "No, of course it hasn't. Quite
the opposite, actually. Gorgeous baby George would make
anyone broody."

There was a murmur of agreement. "Congratulations,

Sophie," Emily said, raising her glass of red wine. "How pregnant are you?"

Sophie ran her hand protectively over the nicely rounded bump she had carefully kept covered with an oversized sweater. "Five months. Almost twenty weeks."

"Well out of the danger zone," Emily said. "I'm pleased for you, Sophie."

Sophie couldn't stop smiling. She really felt as though everything was going to be OK this time. She was convinced that having Amy and the children living with them was the key that had unlocked whatever was causing their problems. She was so distracted by the children in particular, who were both adorable, that she sometimes even forgot to obsess over getting pregnant again.

It was Steve who had suggested she do a pregnancy test as they lay in bed one night. "Oh! Do you think so?" she had replied, startled, her brain immediately whirring back through dates.

"I do." Steve had propped himself up on one elbow in bed beside her. "Call it intuition or call it the fact that your boobs are noticeably bigger..."

Sophie had laughed, wishing she could leap out of bed and run to the chemist right at that moment.

The next morning, she bought a test on the way to work and did it as soon as she arrived. Sure enough, the blue line was clear and bold. It felt like a new beginning. A second chance.

"So how's Mark Bailey taken the news?" Melissa said, bringing Sophie back to the present.

"I still haven't told him."

"And it's not like he'd notice with everything that's going on at the moment..."

"No," Sophie agreed. Mark was starting to make waves in

America and had sold a huge format to the networks there. It meant he was spending less and less time in the UK, leaving the day-to-day running of it all to Sophie.

"What will he do without you?" Melissa sat up and leaned forward.

Sophie considered for a moment. "He'll have to either find someone to take over while I'm on maternity leave or come back and do it himself."

"I could do it," Melissa said with a slightly embarrassed laugh, but Sophie could see that she wasn't joking.

She looked at her curiously. "Would you want to work in TV? You've never shown any great interest in it before."

Melissa shrugged. "I'm a bit old for the music industry and a bit bored of it. I fancy a change, and of course, I know Mark of old…"

The other three all turned towards her simultaneously, their radars suddenly alert. "When you say 'know him,'" Sophie began, "are we talking in biblical terms?"

Melissa shrugged again. "It's the music industry, Soph. Everyone dates everyone else."

Sophie's mouth dropped open. "I can't believe you've never mentioned this before!"

"Well, it didn't seem important. It was just a one-night stand…or a one- or two- or three- or four-night stand, to be more precise."

Sophie felt a brief prickle of something approaching jealousy and mentally swatted it away. She genuinely didn't fancy Mark in the slightest, but she did feel a bit possessive over him. It threw her off balance to discover that Melissa had known him intimately before she had even met him. "Would you have liked it to carry on?"

Melissa sighed. "Maybe, but you know what Mark's like.

He doesn't understand the concept of monogamy. I knew I'd end up getting hurt, so I put a stop to it."

Sophie gave Melissa an admiring look. "Wow, that's a very mature thing to have done, especially if you were keen on him."

Melissa smiled. "I suppose it was really, considering I was probably off my face at the time!"

★ ★ ★ ★ ★

The next morning, all four of them, plus the four children, headed over to the beach for breakfast. Amy had prepared a feast of smoked salmon and cream cheese bagels, beautiful exotic fruit salads, plus bread and croissants she had freshly baked herself. Over the months she had spent living with Sophie and Steve, she had begun to cook again, much to all their delight. Once she got back into her stride, it was obvious she hadn't lost any of her talent. They had never eaten so well.

They spread a huge blanket on the pebbles and unloaded all the goodies from the picnic hamper they had found in the cottage.

"Amy, this food is incredible," Melissa groaned, tucking into her third croissant. "We're all going to be enormous by the time this weekend's over."

Amy smiled shyly as she broke a roll in half and gave it to George, who was sitting between her legs, beaming contentedly as he stuffed the bread into his mouth and chewed it with great concentration. Sophie watched him, entranced. Having him in the house had helped heal her heart, which used to break every time she looked at him. Now she could just delight in him without feeling that ache of longing for her own little boy.

She ran her hand over her rounded stomach and smiled to herself, imagining the little life that was busy growing inside her. A brother or sister for Emma. She didn't really care what sex it was, as long as it was healthy. She'd heard others say it in the past and never really believed them, but she really meant it.

It had been good for Emma having the younger children living with them. She was a good-natured, generous little girl and had taken on the big-sister role with great enthusiasm. Sophie watched her now, walking hand in hand with Megan across the pebbles, stopping now and again to pick up any that caught her eye and showing them to an ever-obedient Megan.

Sophie worried a little about Megan. At three years old, she still carried a prematurely careworn expression and seemed anxious and jumpy. It wasn't surprising, given what she'd been through in her short life, but Sophie wondered when, or if, she would ever grow out of it.

"Fancy a little stroll, Soph?" Melissa said, jolting Sophie out of her reverie. Melissa stood up and held out her hand expectantly.

"Sure." Sophie took Melissa's hand and clambered to her feet, not caring for once that she felt huge and ungainly beside her. She had the best excuse possible.

"So, how's it been, really? Having them all living with you?" Melissa's braids blew across her face and she pushed them back impatiently.

"Surprisingly good. I know it sounds weird, but I feel like they've brought me back to life after...well, you know."

Melissa nodded. "Amy's still very fragile, though, isn't she?"

"He did such a good job of taking her apart, bit by bit, that it's going to take a very long time to get her back. I'm not sure if we ever will."

"Any more unwanted visits?"

"Yes, unfortunately. And he's demanding access to the children, which is difficult as she can't really stop him seeing them."

"Of course she can! He was violent towards her!" Melissa interjected furiously.

"I know. But she doesn't want that becoming public knowledge. And if he takes her to court, it would have to. Steve and I are helping her as much as we can, but I sometimes worry that..." She stopped as she tried to find the words. She hadn't been able to voice it to anyone before.

"What?" Melissa turned towards Sophie so that the sun framed her face, giving her an ethereal glow.

"Well, he's changed his tack and is on a charm offensive. I worry that she's falling for it. And worse, I worry that she blames us for breaking them up."

"But that's ridiculous. He was violent. If we hadn't done something, he might have killed her."

"I know that and you know that. But Amy is so down on herself. She has so little confidence that she can't see it. And boy, is he charming when he turns it on."

"Yes, well, I certainly found that out..." Melissa gave Sophie a rueful shrug. "You don't think..."

"I don't know. I wish I could say for sure that she'd never go back to him, but I really don't know."

"What does Steve think?"

Sophie grimaced. "He doesn't know her the way I do, so I don't think it would occur to him that she might consider going back after what Nick's done. Steve doesn't see Nick's charm. Especially after he cracked one of his ribs."

"No," Melissa said, giving a half laugh. "Well, that's understandable. Is there anything we can do?"

Sophie thought for a minute. "I'm not sure. I think we've

just got to keep supporting her and build up her confidence
so that she has the courage to divorce him and put some clear
water between them. I do know one thing for sure, though.
If she does summon up the courage to file for divorce, there
will be fireworks. He doesn't like losing. Or not being in control." She turned to look at Amy sitting on the blanket with
George, while Megan and Emma skipped happily around
them. They suddenly looked so very vulnerable.

"God, that's a frightening thought. Aren't you scared?"

"A bit. But we've got Steve on our side and Nick's probably
more scared of him. Anyway, every time I get a bit panicky,
I imagine how it must have been for Amy, living under that
kind of threat day in, day out. She's never really told me the
whole story—and I'm not sure I want to hear it either—but
it must have been a living hell."

Melissa nodded and followed Sophie's gaze towards Amy
and the children. "Then we've got to do everything in our
power to convince her never to go back."

JULY 2005

"The Queen gave a defiant message to the terrorists behind the 7/7 London tube bombings that 'They will not change our way of life.' She was speaking during a visit to meet survivors of the blasts."

VALE DE PARRA, PORTUGAL

CHAPTER TWENTY-SIX

"WELL, THIS IS THE LIFE!" MELISSA SIGHED HAPPILY. "I can't say I'm sorry to be well away from central London at the moment." The others nodded and sipped their champagne. They were sitting around a silver bistro table at a beach bar, with an uninterrupted view of the powdery white sandy beach and deep turquoise Atlantic Ocean beside them. Although the temperature was nudging 80 degrees, the constant breeze blowing off the sea meant it was pleasantly hot, rather than uncomfortably scorching.

Emily turned to Amy, who had been quiet all morning. "You OK, Amy?"

Amy blinked quickly and nodded. "Hmm? Oh, yes, I'm fine. Just thinking about the kids. I can't believe Steve's looking after all of them on his own. I hope he's OK."

"He'll be in his element!" Sophie had almost finished her glass of champagne and was already reaching for the bottle to pour another. Since she had started drinking again, she seemed determined to make up for lost time. "And, actually, Jack's a real help now that he's older. He's another pair of hands, not another liability."

Emily smiled proudly. Sophie was right. Jack was definitely more of a help than a hindrance. He had loved the idea of staying with Steve and the other kids for the weekend while they went away together for a couple of days.

This trip was being paid for by Amy. The others had objected strongly, saying they were happy to pay for themselves, but Amy had insisted. "It's my way of repaying you," she said. "Although it's not really possible to put a value on what you did for me."

Melissa had happily accepted, while the other two had agreed reluctantly. "It'll make her feel better," Melissa had said. "Just go along with it."

And she was right. Emily could see that Amy was already gaining in confidence. Not that she could have had any less confidence after what happened…

★ ★ ★ ★ ★

Amy stared at her phone, her hands shaking slightly and her eyes blurring as she read the text message:

I love you so much. I love the children. I can't live without you. If you don't come home I don't see the point in carrying on.

She looked out into the garden, where the children were playing under Steve's watchful eye. He was pushing George in the baby swing, his little legs kicking in delight, while Megan and Emma tended to their dolls in the playhouse. It looked like such a happy, idyllic scene of a family enjoying their garden in the last days of summer.

But of course it wasn't a happy family scene. Steve wasn't

the children's dad, even though over the past months he had been more of a father to them than Nick ever had...

No, she told herself sternly, that wasn't fair. Nick loved the children, but he had spent so much time working that he couldn't be there for them the way Steve was. And he was in such agony being away from them. Maybe he had changed. He certainly seemed like a different person recently. Now that she had shown him that she was serious, that she wouldn't be used as a punchbag, maybe things would be how they used to be in the early days.

She had loved him so much. Surely that person couldn't have disappeared altogether? Maybe all he'd needed was the shock of almost losing her to make him appreciate what he'd got.

She bit her lip, thinking about the reaction of the others if she was to voice what she was thinking. She already knew what they'd say. *A leopard never changes its spots; don't be fooled by him; be strong.*

But she was different from the others. She wasn't strong compared to them. She needed someone to lean on much more than they did. She couldn't imagine how her life would have been if she had found herself in Emily's situation, having to cope by herself and being the sole carer and breadwinner, bringing up a child on her own.

Even when she had finally left Nick, it wasn't under her own steam. She had been forced into it by Emily and Sophie and had been looked after by Sophie and Steve ever since. She would never have managed without them.

A small voice in her head whispered that if she'd stayed, he would have killed her, but she mentally swatted it away. Over the sea of time that had elapsed since then, she couldn't even remember the violent Nick. All she could remember was the loving husband and father, who had cried at the birth of both of the children. It must have crucified him to have those two adorable little people snatched away from him so cruelly.

Every time she met him so that he could see the children, she could feel herself softening towards him a little more. Could feel herself being drawn back towards him like a magnet. And Sophie could feel it too. Whenever Amy returned from seeing him, she would have to sit through a debrief with Sophie, who seemed determined not to let Nick redeem himself in any way.

Steve was a little more forgiving. This was surprising, considering Nick had cracked one of his ribs, but Steve would argue that it was a terrible punishment for any dad to be separated from his children. Sophie always rounded on him furiously if he defended Nick, but Steve always quietly stood his ground. "What he did was wrong," he would say firmly. "But that doesn't mean he shouldn't see his kids."

"He doesn't deserve to see them after what he did," Sophie would say, scowling angrily.

Amy would sit between them, feeling increasingly uncomfortable. It was as if her opinion counted for nothing.

It had been a year since she left him, and although she would never have dared voice it to anyone, she missed him. She couldn't help it. He was like a drug to her. He was so handsome, so tender and so broken. She knew, in a way that no one else would understand, that he had changed. She wanted to go back to him.

She looked again at her phone. At the words he had written. With another glance into the garden to make sure Steve couldn't see, she typed:

I love you. I never stopped loving you.

Before she could change her mind, she pressed "send."

Almost immediately, the phone beeped with a return message:

Come home. Come tonight. I'm here waiting for you.

A little thrill of excitement shot through her as she remembered his hands on her body, his mouth on hers. The way he could set her alight with one kiss. Then, just as she was tingling with lust at the thought of his touch, other memories began to crash into her head. His rough hand on her neck, squeezing until she almost blacked out. The agony of her hair being pulled out in clumps as he thrust his face into hers, so close that she could feel his breath on her skin, screaming that she was a useless whore.

She swallowed hard and blinked, trying to shut out the images that had filled her nightmares over the past year. He had learnt his lesson. Promised that it would never happen again. Had sworn it over and over, with tears of remorse filling his beautiful dark eyes. She believed him.

Getting up, she walked to the French doors. Steve stopped pushing George's swing and looked over at her curiously. "You OK, Amy?"

Amy nodded and smiled. "Yes, I'm fine. I just…thought I'd nip over to Mum's for a couple of hours. Would you be OK to have the kids?"

A shadow of something Amy couldn't quite read passed over Steve's face. "Uh, sure. Wouldn't your mum want to see the kids too?" He resumed pushing George on the swing.

Amy looked away. She hated lying to Steve at all, but lying to him when he knew she was lying was excruciating. "Yes, but she's not feeling too great, so I don't want to risk them picking up whatever it is she's got."

Steve nodded. "OK. I'll see you later, then?" He gave Amy a look that went through her, before she turned and walked out of the house. He knew where she was going. She just hoped he wouldn't tell Sophie.

When she arrived at the house, she stood at the entrance to the drive for several minutes, her heart racing and her mouth suddenly dry as she looked up at the imposing white stucco building. She hadn't been back here in over a year. Whenever they met, it was in a "neutral" place like a park or a coffee bar. She hadn't wanted to meet at the house, which was a place filled with horrible memories and a deep-rooted feeling of fear. For a moment, she considered turning around and leaving. This was wrong and pointless. She would never forget what had happened within these walls. But she would also never forget how distraught he had been as they said goodbye after their last meeting. The way he looked at her wasn't just an act. He loved her deeply. She knew he did. And she loved him.

With shaking legs, she climbed the white stone steps. She lifted her hand to ring the bell, but before she could press it, the door swung open and Nick was standing there in front of her. He was wearing a pale blue linen shirt, with the sleeves rolled up to reveal his tanned forearms, and he had bare feet, giving him a sexy yet vulnerable appearance. He had obviously just showered as his dark hair was still damp and she could smell the scent of fresh soap on his skin. The prickles of fear immediately melted into a wave of lust as he reached out to her and wrapped her in his arms.

Kicking the door shut behind him, Nick picked her up as if she weighed nothing and carried her up the stairs to their bedroom. She couldn't think about anything except being with him as he laid her on their bed and began to undress her, covering every part of her body with light, feathery kisses.

Amy reached up to undo his shirt and moaned as her fingers connected with his skin. It was like the first time they had ever made love, only a million times more intense.

As she undid his jeans, she pulled him into her, desperate to feel him inside her again. No man had ever been able to make her feel the way Nick did. As he began to move in and out of her, she cried out and he looked at her in concern. "Amy?" he whispered.

"It's OK, don't stop," she groaned, arching her back as she climaxed in an almighty shudder.

"Oh God, I love you so much," he murmured, his mouth devouring hers.

Afterwards, they lay naked and entwined on the bed, Nick stroking her hair and caressing her face. "I have missed you more than you could ever know," he said, kissing her on the lips.

Amy looked up at him, thinking she had never seen such a beautiful face, all the more beautiful now that it was reflected in the faces of their children. All the pain and fear she had felt seemed to have dissipated into the ether. All she could feel was a deep longing to stay like this for ever, lying in each other's arms, in a bubble of happiness and love.

"Come home," Nick whispered. "I need you. I need you all."

Amy wriggled into a sitting position and pulled her knees to her chest. "I want to. I really do. It's just…"

"It'll be different this time, I promise. Everything will be perfect, like it was in the beginning. I've changed, Amy." Nick looked up at her imploringly. "I've learnt my lesson. I will never, ever hurt you again. You know that, don't you?"

Amy nodded. She did know, as surely as she knew her own

name. "But…how will I tell the others? What about Sophie and Steve? They've been so good to me."

A wave of annoyance passed across Nick's face. "It's nothing to do with anyone else, Amy. Them being involved is half the problem. I know they mean well and they've been good to you…but they've also actively encouraged you to walk away from your marriage. Tried to stop the kids seeing their own father—that's not the best thing for them, is it?"

Amy shook her head slowly. He was right. Sophie in particular had taken it upon herself to make sure she divorced Nick. Yes, they'd had their issues, but she could see in his eyes that he was a changed person and that he was serious about wanting to make it work. "I'll think about it."

"I love you. I need you. Come home."

"If I do come home…there are some things that will need to change."

Nick nodded eagerly. "Anything. Anything you want."

"I don't want any more employees. No Suki…" She left the name hanging in the air just long enough to register with Nick that she knew what had gone on between them. His cheeks coloured slightly, but he didn't speak. "No Benedetta…" she continued, thinking about the sexy young Latina Nick had hired after telling Amy that she couldn't cook, something that had been like a dagger through her heart at the time.

Nick nodded. "Anything. I'll do anything. Just come home."

It was as if a river of warm honey was trickling through her body. After all this time, after all this pain, she felt loved. She felt wanted. There was no doubt in her mind—she was going to come home. Now all she needed to do was work out how to tell Sophie.

CHAPTER TWENTY-SEVEN

"SOMETHING'S GOING ON WITH AMY." STEVE rolled over onto his side so that he was facing her.

Sophie thought about rolling over onto her side too, but her bump was too big. "I know. It's him, isn't it?"

"I think she's been seeing him."

Sophie frowned. "We know she's been seeing him. I thought you were the one who said it was important for him to see the kids."

Steve sighed. "I was. I am. But she's been seeing him without the kids."

"What?" Sophie scrambled up into a sitting position, cradling her bump. "When? Why didn't you tell me?"

Steve sat up and leaned against the headboard. "Because I wasn't sure. It was more of a hunch than a certainty."

"How come you're sure now?"

Steve shrugged. "Because she's so sly about it. She always waits till you're not here. Always lies about where she's going. Tonight she told me she was going to see her mum again—she's been saying that a lot."

"Well, maybe she was?" Sophie's mind was whirring, casting

about for a rational explanation that wasn't the one she didn't want to hear.

"Her mum called while she was out."

"Oh." Sophie felt instantly tearful. It somehow felt as if she had discovered that Amy was cheating on her. And it hurt just the same. What the hell was she thinking?

The next morning, Sophie took Amy a cup of coffee before she left for work. Amy was sitting in bed reading to the children, who were snuggled in either side of her. She looked up. "It should be me bringing you coffee—not the other way around."

Sophie laughed. "The exercise will do me good. Hey, guys, Emma's persuaded Steve to make pancakes this morning. Do you fancy them?"

Megan and George both nodded vigorously and clambered out of bed, before toddling off down the stairs. Sophie waited until they'd gone before she sat down on the side of the bed. Amy bit her lip nervously.

"Steve thinks you've been meeting up with Nick. Is that true, Amy?"

Instantly, a flush spread from Amy's chest up to her neck. "Yes. But you knew that." She pulled the duvet around her defensively.

"I knew you were meeting him so that he could see the kids. I didn't know you were meeting him on your own too."

Amy made as if to shake her head with an automatic denial, but something in Sophie's expression must have made her think again. "I... We... We're getting on really well, Soph. I think he's changed."

A combination of irritation and frustration made Sophie want to grab Amy's tiny shoulders and give her a shake, to shake the stupidity out of her. "He hasn't changed," she said as patiently as she could. "No one could go from behaving the way he did to suddenly being Mr Nice Guy. Don't let him fool you, Amy."

Amy bit her lip again but didn't say anything.

"He almost destroyed you. For God's sake, can't you see how dangerous he is? What about the children? Don't you worry about them? You could be putting them in danger if you got back with him."

"No!" Amy protested, her cheeks now flaming. "He would never hurt the kids."

"How do you know?" Sophie thought she might burst with frustration. "How do you know for sure? He was quite happy to hurt their mother!"

"Because he loves them. And he loves me. You don't know him like I do, Sophie. He's learnt his lesson. I'm not stupid, you know."

There was a new spark of defiance to Amy's demeanour, which a part of Sophie was pleased to see. She had been so broken for so long now that it was good to see her getting some of her old self back. Yet it worried her too. She knew how convincing Nick could be. Once he'd got her back, she'd be trapped again, only worse this time because she'd be too embarrassed to ask for help.

"I know you're not stupid, Amy. But I also know what Nick's like. He can be so convincing. I just don't want you making a huge mistake. And it's not like you haven't got any-where to go—you can stay with us for as long as you need to."

Amy nodded. "I know. And I'm really grateful to you and Steve. But you've got your new baby on the way and you won't want us three here, intruding on your family time!"

"We love having you here!" Sophie's response was as instinc-tive as it was heartfelt. They had grown so used to having Amy and the kids around, it was unthinkable that they should leave. She had always known that one day, when Amy was back on her feet, they would get a place of their own, but it seemed a long way off. "Emma would be bereft without Megan and George!"

Amy smiled. "And they without her, but she'll have a new little brother or sister to play with. She'll be fine."

"You sound like you've made up your mind…" Sophie thought for a moment she might cry. She had grown to love those children almost as much as her own and Steve definitely had. He had spent so much time with them. He would be devastated.

Amy took Sophie's hand in hers and squeezed it. "Don't hate me, Sophie. But I do really love Nick and surely it's got to be better for us to be together as a family, making it work?"

Sophie swallowed back the tears that were gathering in her throat. She nodded. "Yes, as long as—"

"I know," Amy interrupted. "I know. And we'll see you all the time."

Sophie hoped, rather than believed, that would be the case. Nick would hate her even more than before and she knew, with a sinking sense of foreboding, that it wouldn't be long before he would persuade Amy that it was best not to see her friends. "When are you going?" she asked, holding her breath for the answer.

"Well, maybe we should go sooner, rather than later? Give you a chance to really prepare for the baby." Amy's tone was conciliatory, cajoling. It was almost as if their roles had reversed in just a few short minutes.

Sophie's shoulders sagged, but she mentally gave herself a shake. It was Amy's life and Sophie couldn't dictate what she did and didn't do. "Well, as long as you know that whatever happens…"

Amy shook her head with a confident smile. "It won't."

"*Whatever* happens," Sophie repeated, "you will always have a home here, with us. You must promise to call me if you're ever in trouble."

"I promise." Amy squeezed Sophie's hand again. "But I know it won't come to that. We're so good together now. He's a changed man and he's so lovely to me."

"OK." Sophie stood up, unable to stomach any more of Amy's praise for a man she knew to be completely undeserving of her. There was no point in telling her what she point-blank refused to hear. But then again, maybe she was wrong. Maybe Nick really had learnt his lesson and they would live happily ever after. But she doubted it.

Although both she and Steve were dreading them going, in the end they didn't have time to miss them too much as Sophie went into labour just a couple of days after they left. Their son, Theo, arrived a few weeks early, but Sophie joked that he was so big, it was a damned good job he was early or she might have been in danger of breaking a world record for the heaviest baby ever.

All she could think was how different it was to when she'd had Emma. This time she thought she might burst with happiness that she finally had a healthy little boy who was already the spitting image of Steve. She just wanted to spend all day, every day, staring at him. Steve and Emma were the same. It was as if none of them could get enough of him.

"He's so beautiful, Sophie," said Melissa, cradling him in her arms. It always took Sophie by surprise just how good Melissa was with babies. Sophie always imagined Melissa wouldn't want to get puke on her designer jeans and would be repelled by the thought of changing nappies, but she was exactly the opposite. She was a real natural, and in return, children seemed to love her too.

"Well, I'm biased, but yes, he is. I feel so different to when I had Emma. God, it makes me feel terrible to look back at what a mess I was."

Melissa put Theo over her shoulder, his mouth dangerously close to her pale green silk top, and rubbed his back tenderly. "Yes, well, you had your reasons. Now you need to put all that behind you and enjoy both of your gorgeous kids. Has Amy been to visit?"

"Yes. She brought Megan and George with her."

"Not him?"

"Nick? No, thank God. I have to admit I was slightly surprised she came. I was convinced he'd have persuaded her to stay away from us."

"Well, they're still in the honeymoon period, I guess." Theo started to cry half-heartedly, so Melissa handed him back to Sophie with a laugh. "Back to Mummy, I think…"

"Maybe he really has changed, Liss. Maybe it'll work out for them."

"I hope so, but I can't believe it, can you? We need to keep a close eye on her."

Sophie nodded. "So, how are you getting on at Merlin?" Melissa had recently started working at Mark Bailey's company, after Sophie persuaded Mark that she would be a real asset with her experience in the record industry. Mark had remembered Melissa with a definite glint in his eye and didn't take much convincing.

Melissa grinned. "A-m-a-zing! Honestly, Soph, I totally love it."

"And how are you and Mark getting on?" Sophie raised a mischievous eyebrow.

Melissa shook her head decisively. "Not gonna happen this time. He's got his pick of glamorous women. Why would he be interested in me?"

"Because you're gorgeous, glamorous and really, really fun?"

"Yeah, well, look where's it's got me. Thirty-three and single." Melissa pulled her beautiful, full mouth into a fake pout.

"Is there no one on the horizon?"

"Not at the moment. But who knows what the future holds? Maybe now that I've stopped looking, that's when I'll find someone."

Sophie certainly hoped so. Melissa had really turned her life around from her wild younger days and she deserved some happiness.

The next couple of months passed by in a blur. Unlike the first eight weeks of Emma's life, Theo's whizzed by. Sophie wanted to grab the hands of the clock and make time stop so that she could hold her life exactly where it was. She and Steve were besotted with the children and each other, all the pain of the past now melted away, hopefully to be forgotten for ever.

All too soon, Sophie was expected back at work. She could have taken a lot longer on maternity leave, but Mark had made it clear that he wanted her back as quickly as she could manage, with the company growing so fast. She loved her job, but it was still a wrench leaving Steve and the kids on her first day back. "They'll be fine," Steve told her, kissing her tenderly over the top of Theo's head as he cradled him in his arms.

And although it was hard work, being back was also great fun, especially now that Melissa was working for the same company. As a result, it was several weeks before Sophie noticed that Amy hadn't been in touch and then it was only because Steve mentioned it.

"Oh!" Sophie said, climbing into bed and snuggling up to him. "I hadn't thought about it, but yes, it's been ages."

Steve kissed the top of her head and pulled her into his arms. "Have any of the others heard from her?"

"I don't think so or I'm sure they'd have mentioned it."

"You should call her, make sure she's OK."

Sophie immediately felt a swirl of guilt. What if Amy was in trouble again? She hadn't even given her a second thought recently. "I will. I'll also call Emily to check if she's been in touch."

The next morning, she called Emily on her way to work. "No," she said. "I assumed she'd have been in touch with you."

Sophie furrowed her brow in concern. "I'll call her."

With shaking hands and a feeling of dread in the pit of her stomach, she dialled Amy's number. Amy answered after three rings. "Hi, Sophie!" she said brightly.

Relief flooded through Sophie. "Hi! I'm just calling up to see how you are. I haven't heard from you in *ages*."

"No, sorry. I haven't called, but I thought you'd be up to your eyes. How are the kids?"

Sophie beamed, even though no one was watching her. It still gave her a thrill whenever anyone asked about "the kids," rather than just Emma. "They're fantastic. We miss you guys, though. How are you all?"

"Good! How's it been going back to work? Was it a wrench?"

"God, yes. But it's getting better. It really helps that Melissa works there now."

"I bet it's a hoot." There was a wistful note to Amy's voice. "How is she?"

"She's great. She's settled in so well at Merlin. I'm slightly worried she'll nick my job next! Why don't you come over one evening and I'll invite her and Emily so that we can all catch up?"

"Um, yes, that would be lovely. How is Steve?"

A prickle of concern began to niggle at Sophie. Amy was deflecting everything away from talking about herself. "He's good. But, more to the point, how are you?"

"I'm well. Really well. How's Emma getting on at school?"

"Yes, she loves it, although she hates leaving Theo…"

"I bet."

There was an awkward pause while Sophie waited to see if Amy would add anything further about herself or the children. When she didn't, Sophie couldn't help herself. "Why don't you tell me how you really are, Amy?"

"I've told you."

Instead of the indignance Sophie would have expected, there was a fearful quaver to Amy's voice, immediately making Sophie feel guilty. "I know, I'm just worried about you. Are you sure everything is OK?"

"Yes, yes! Absolutely. It's all going brilliantly."

"OK, well, that's good to hear." Sophie could tell that Amy was putting on an act for the benefit of someone who was listening. It wasn't difficult to guess who. "So, let's make a date for you guys to come over. When would suit you?"

"Um, I'll check my diary and get back to you if that's OK?"

The sudden brightness in her voice confirmed for Sophie that Nick was not only listening but telling Amy what to say. She could tell that she was desperate to get off the phone and end the conversation.

"Can't you check it now?" Sophie wanted to do anything to keep Amy on the line There was something going on and she didn't like the feel of it.

"No, I have to go now, but I'll call you back."

"Promise?"

There was a moment's hesitation before Amy spoke. "Yes. I promise. Bye now."

The line went dead and Sophie stared at her phone with a mounting sense of unease. Amy wouldn't be calling her back.

CHAPTER TWENTY-EIGHT

"SO WHAT DO YOU SUGGEST WE DO?" MELISSA took a large slug of her wine and looked from Sophie to Emily. "We can't kidnap her again."

"Well...we could, actually." Emily raised her eyebrows. "We did it before."

"I know," Sophie butted in. "But we had more proof then. You had actually seen him in action, Em. This time she insists everything's fine, so it's just a hunch. Maybe she wants to focus on putting her family back together and doesn't want to rock the boat by seeing us."

"But don't you see how screwed up that sounds?" Emily's face darkened. "No normal relationship would suffer just because someone wanted to see their oldest friends. If he's stopping her from seeing us, he's right back to where he was before—controlling her... And God knows what else he's doing."

The three of them lapsed into a gloomy silence. Emily could feel a fountain of frustration bubbling up inside her. She had always felt mainly responsible for their intervention with Amy and even more so when Amy got back together with him. Had she been poking her nose into something that didn't concern her? Had she got it wrong? At the time, she had been entirely convinced, but the months that had elapsed since had made everything blurry. She didn't want to abandon Amy to her fate, yet part of her felt angry with her for putting herself in that situation again. Last time, Emily had been more than ready to take Nick on, but this time she wasn't sure she had the stomach for the fight. "Well," she said, taking a sip of wine and shrugging her shoulders, "I guess we just wait until she contacts us."

"But that might be never!" Melissa looked shocked. "What if she's too embarrassed to admit she's made a mistake and ask for help?"

"You can go round there and check on her if you like." As soon as she said the words, Emily felt mean. Melissa had her own reasons for wanting to keep away from Nick. And the truth was Amy had probably never mentioned to Nick that she was still in contact with Melissa. He would naturally have assumed that they would have fallen out over Melissa's dalliances with him.

"You know I can't do that. But I do think one of you should…"

"Last time I came face-to-face with him, he knocked me out. Funnily enough, I don't fancy a repeat performance." Emily finished her glass of wine and stood up. "It looks like it'll have to be you, Soph. Sorry, guys, I have to go."

"Where?" Sophie looked at her watch, then narrowed her eyes at Emily. "I thought you said Jack was staying with your parents tonight."

Emily grinned. "He is. See you." She walked out of the bar feeling as though she had just scored a tiny victory over

Sophie, who was expert at extracting information. She didn't want to tell anyone yet. It was too soon.

She couldn't believe it when he got in touch through Friends Reunited. The general catching-up questions had quickly moved on to deeper conversations. He was working in London, had split from his wife and had apparently *never stopped thinking about you and that amazing night we spent together*. Well, she could certainly understand that because she had never stopped thinking about him or that night either.

He wanted to meet. Wondered how much she would have changed in the twelve years since they'd last seen each other. In his profile photo, he was side on to the camera, part of his face in shadow, but he still looked every bit as beautiful as she remembered. The thought of him caused her stomach to flip over. Yes, there had been plenty of other men over the years. But none had ever lasted beyond a brief affair and now she understood why. None had ever come close to him.

"Emily?" His voice hadn't changed at all—it was still that mix of gravelly and melodic that she had always loved listening to. She smiled to herself before she looked up at him. He had aged well. Almost fifty, he looked at least a decade younger. His hair was still blond, with tiny flecks of grey starting to show through, and his tanned skin was a little more weathered, but the blue eyes still glittered and the smile was as slow and sexy as ever.

As he leaned down to kiss her, the years rolled away and she was instantly transported back to that bedroom. "Hello, Anton."

He sat down in the chair opposite, his eyes never leaving hers. "My God, I had forgotten how lovely you were."

Emily smiled at the cheesiness of it all. With anyone else she would have laughed in his face and told him to practise his chat-up lines. But out of Anton's mouth, they were the only words she wanted to hear. It was what she had dreamed of for all these years. And now that he was here, she realized she had known all along that he would come back for her. She had expected it and she had been waiting for him.

As they left the bar together, there was no discussion about where they would go. They hailed a cab and held hands chastely as it sped through the streets back to her flat. As soon as the front door closed behind them, he was pulling at her jacket, her dress, his mouth on hers, kissing her whole body as if he wanted to devour every part of her.

Emily steered him towards her bedroom, undressing him as she went, dropping his clothes in a trail behind them. All she could think about was fulfilling the desire that had been pent up inside her for all these years.

They fell onto the bed in a tangle of naked limbs, kissing each other hungrily. Emily lifted herself up and slid him inside her. As she rocked back and forward, he cupped her breasts and held her gaze with his, watching with liquid eyes as she gave a moan of pleasure. "I have waited so long for this," he gasped, rolling her over onto her back and thrusting into her in one fluid movement.

Emily arched her back towards him and her whole body exploded with an orgasm. Anton continued to thrust into her, kissing her neck and setting her alight again until he came with an almighty groan.

Lying down beside her, Anton picked up her hand and placed it flat against his chest. "Can you feel how hard my heart is beating?" He grinned. "That was incredible."

Emily sighed with happiness. This was truly her perfect moment with the man she loved. The man she had always loved. "It was. Just as I knew it would be."

Anton nodded and traced his thumbnail over her flat brown belly. "I can't believe that you were still here. I was so sure you'd have been married with God knows how many kids by now..."

Emily stiffened. He wouldn't know about Jack. She thought about her Friends Reunited profile and whether she had ever mentioned him. She didn't think so. Her heart began to race and she rolled away from him. He looked at her in surprise. "What's wrong?"

"Nothing—just going to get us a drink." She left the bedroom and closed the door, her eyes immediately drawn towards Jack's room. Luckily the door was shut. She headed for the kitchen and glanced around, looking for clues that might give away his existence. She gathered several pictures and clippings held by magnets to the front of the fridge and shoved them into a drawer.

She did the same in the sitting room, guilt causing her stomach to clench as she hurriedly stashed the many photos that depicted his journey from toddler to pre-teen into the chest that served as a coffee table.

Then she grabbed a bottle of wine from the fridge and two glasses, before returning to Anton in the bedroom. "I don't think we've had quite enough yet..." she said with what she hoped was a seductive smile.

Anton, who was sitting up naked, reached for her and pulled her on top of him, putting the bottle and glasses onto the floor with one deft movement. "I agree. And I'm not talking about the wine."

CHAPTER TWENTY-NINE

AMY GLANCED AT THE CLOCK. IT WAS NEARLY SIX
thirty and Nick would be home in half an hour. She scooped
George up out of his high chair, where he was busily demol-
ishing a bread roll and throwing the crumbs onto the floor.
He squirmed in her arms and reached back towards the chair,
wanting to finish his snack. "No, sweetheart," Amy chided,
whisking him out of the kitchen. "You need to get in the bath.
Come on, I'll race you. You too, Meggie."

She raced towards the stairs and made George giggle as she
climbed them on all fours, pretending to be a dog. Megan was
less easily amused, following at a more sedate pace and looking at Amy suspiciously. Amy ran the bath and dunked both
children into it for a perfunctory wash, before chivvying them
into their bedrooms and into their pyjamas.

Back downstairs, she kept looking nervously towards the
clock as she found a dustpan and brush and cleared up the debris from the children's tea, wiped the table and stacked the
dishwasher. She didn't miss Suki one bit, but she certainly
missed what she did around the house. Looking after two
children on your own was hard work.

As the hands of the clock snaked inexorably towards six thirty, she dashed into the downstairs bathroom to run her hands through her hair, slick on some lip gloss and spritz herself with Nick's favourite Hermès perfume. By the time he walked through the door ten minutes later, Amy was posed serenely on the sofa, with a child under each arm, reading *The Gruffalo.*

He put down his briefcase and beamed at them. "Well, isn't that a welcome sight for sore eyes," he said, kissing Amy and the children one by one.

Amy quietly exhaled and allowed her shoulders to relax, only now realizing how tense she'd been for the past few hours. He seemed in a really good mood. She could never be sure until he walked through the door. It varied so much. "Good day?" she asked, getting up and going to fix him a gin and tonic.

Nick loosened his tie and took her place between the children on the sofa. "Good now work's over," he said as George scrambled onto his lap and immediately demanded he play "horsey." Nick happily obliged and within seconds George was screaming with laughter. Amy watched Megan, who had inched very slightly away from Nick. She was a carbon copy of Amy in miniature form and shared her mother's nervousness around him. Nick had never mentioned it, but Amy wondered how much he noticed.

He certainly made no secret of favouring George. His son was too young to remember any of the really bad moments, so he took Nick at face value and idolized him, whereas Megan was serious and tense in his presence. Forgetting what had gone on clearly wasn't an option for her and it made Amy feel physically sick with guilt.

They had been back almost six months now and she had

to remind herself every day that she had done the right thing. Nick had wooed her with a passion that had swept her off her feet when they first came home and she had found herself falling in love with him all over again. It was exciting, magical, thrilling. It was just like it had been in the very beginning.

She had understood when he said he didn't want her seeing "the girls" any more. He said they would poison her against him, just like they did before. Amy acknowledged that this was true. They hated Nick. There was every chance they would use any opportunity to persuade her not to stay with him. So her visit to see Sophie and Steve when baby Theo was born had to be the last. Nick was very firm—they didn't stand a chance if she wouldn't agree to that. So she did.

She missed them, though. All of them. And so did Megan. She often looked up at Amy with her big, imploring eyes and begged to know when she would see Emma again. Amy would smile reassuringly and lie that it would be soon. She hoped that after a while she'd forget. Unfortunately, forgetting wasn't something Megan did.

"I said, what did you do all day?" Nick was suddenly standing behind Amy, catching her unawares. She dropped the crystal glass full of freshly mixed gin and tonic she was holding and it shattered onto the hard tiled floor. The liquid splashed up Amy's legs before settling in a puddle by her feet.

There was a beat of silence before Nick leapt back in shock. "For fuck's sake!" he yelled, mopping himself down, although Amy was pretty sure none of it had reached him. Out of the corner of her eye, she saw Megan's head turn towards them sharply.

"Sorry," she said, trying to muster a reassuring smile. "You go and sit down. I'll clear it up and bring you another one."

Temper blazed in Nick's eyes, but he reluctantly returned

to the sofa, shaking his head and tutting. "Horsey!" George cried, leaping onto Nick's lap the minute he sat down.

Nick shoved him off roughly. "No! For God's sake, all I want after a busy day is a bit of peace and quiet. Instead, I have to come home to a bloody pigsty!" He stood up and stomped out of the room, leaving Amy and the children gaping after him. George started to cry, his face crumpling in confusion. Megan stayed silent and chewed at her thumbnail.

Amy put down the dustpan and brush she was using to clear up the broken glass. She sat on the sofa and pulled George into a cuddle. "Shh, now, darling. Daddy's just very tired. Now, how about we all go up to bed and I can read you the rest of *The Gruffalo?*" George sniffed sulkily but nodded.

"Meggie?" Amy ruffled Megan's hair and looked at her questioningly.

Megan pursed her lips. "Is Daddy getting angry again? I don't like it when he gets angry. It scares me."

Amy's stomach dropped. "No! Don't be daft. He's just very tired because he's so busy at work. He'll be happy again in the morning."

Megan frowned. "I hope so."

Later, when the children were in bed and Amy was cooking dinner—a dinner she had no idea whether Nick would eat—he reappeared in the kitchen. Amy felt his presence before she saw him. It was as if he carried a black storm cloud into the room with him. She glanced at him and recoiled at the look in his eyes. It was a look she'd seen too many times before and she knew exactly what would happen next.

He sat at the table and stared at her through the thick silence. Amy's throat dried as she finished simmering the Thai green curry and served it onto two plates. She placed one of the plates in front of him. He looked at it in disgust. "What the fuck is this?"

Amy shook her head and sighed. "Nick, please... Don't start with this again..."

The movement was so quick that she didn't have time to react and in a split second he had pinned her against the wall, his hand around her neck. His eyes were blazing with a manic rage as he pushed his face forward until it was just millimetres from hers, their noses almost touching. "Don't...WHAT?" he snarled.

All at once, the terror and tension seeped out of Amy's body and she sagged forward so that his hand pressed harder into her windpipe. She didn't care if he killed her. She just wanted it to be over. Nick's eyes flickered with panic and he pulled his hand away as if he'd been electrocuted, causing Amy to crumple into a heap on the floor at his feet.

For a moment, Amy didn't move. She wondered vaguely if she was dead. The thought didn't scare her. She found it strangely soothing. Then Nick's feet shifted and she realized with a slight sense of disappointment that she was still alive. "What did you do that for?" Nick's voice was genuinely perplexed, all his rage now replaced by genuine concern.

Amy swallowed. Her throat felt raw and she knew that the old, familiar bruises would already be reappearing on her neck, as if her skin had a memory. As if they had been lying dormant all this time, just waiting for their moment to reappear. She didn't want to get up. She wanted to carry on lying where she was.

Nick crouched down and stroked her hair tenderly. "Amy? Sweetheart, are you OK?"

Amy smiled to herself. It was almost impressive, the way he was able to detach himself. As if her lying on the floor with strangulation marks across her throat had absolutely nothing to do with him. It was as though he had stumbled in and found her there.

"Amy?" He took her hand in his and pressed it to his lips. "Come on, darling, say something."

But Amy couldn't speak. There were no words. She had put herself in this situation and it was all her fault. She had come back to him, always knowing subconsciously that they would end up here again. And only now it dawned on her that she had wanted it all along. What kind of a woman was she, that she wanted her husband to kill her? That she was disappointed that he had failed? What kind of mother would do this to her children? The very worst kind, which was exactly what she was. She was worthless.

CHAPTER THIRTY

~~~~~~~~~~~~~~~~

"HAVE YOU STILL NOT HEARD FROM HER?" STEVE looked up from the rocking chair, where he was feeding Theo, who was guzzling greedily from his bottle, making a satisfied smacking sound with each mouthful.

Sophie spun around from the wardrobe, where she was putting away a tiny mountain of white Babygros. "Amy? No."

"Aren't you worried?"

Sophie bristled at Steve's tone of voice. "Yes, Steve, of course I'm bloody worried! But what do I do? We effectively kidnapped her once before and look what happened... She's made it really clear she doesn't want to see us."

"I think we should pay them a visit."

Sophie closed the wardrobe door and sighed. "I do too, but I'm scared that we might make things worse. What if they're perfectly happy, but he doesn't want her to see us again because he knows we'll try to turn her against him? Let's face it, he'd be right, wouldn't he?"

Steve tutted. "I suppose so. I just can't believe she'd be happy to cut us off after spending a whole year with us. I mean, how must Megan feel not seeing Emma?"

His face softened as he spoke about Megan and Sophie felt her heart squeeze with love. She knew how much he missed

Megan and George, even though he had his hands full with his own two. "I know. And we all miss *them* so much. They were such a part of the family. It feels like a bereavement. I would love to see Amy again..." She tailed off as she thought about how close she and Amy had become and how painful it felt to have lost her again so abruptly.

"Well, like I said, I think we should just show up there."

Sophie bit her lip nervously. "OK. But I don't think we should take the kids."

Steve nodded his agreement. "What about Emily and Melissa? Should we tell them?"

Sophie considered it for a moment. Emily had got a mysterious new boyfriend and was so loved up that she seemed to be in a world of her own lately, and Melissa was travelling so much to America with work that she wouldn't be able to offer much in the way of assistance. "No, let's just do it ourselves. It'll look a bit more believable if we pay a friendly visit as a couple than if the whole lot of us turn up mob-handed. That way, if there's no problem and they're all perfectly happy, we can just have a coffee and leave."

"I'm not sure I can promise to be civil to him." Steve smiled ruefully. "He did crack my rib the last time I saw him."

Sophie laughed. "Well, I'm not exactly his biggest fan either, but let's give him the benefit of the doubt."

Theo, who was lying over Steve's shoulder, having his back rubbed, let out a gigantic burp. Steve grinned at him proudly. "OK, that nails it. It seems my son shares my opinion of the lovely Nick. Let's go tomorrow, shall we?"

★ ★ ★ ★ ★

The following evening, having asked Steve's mum to baby-sit, they set off for Notting Hill. As they drew up outside the house, Steve whistled through his teeth. "Maybe I'm beginning to understand why Amy didn't want to leave him after all."

Sophie looked up at the beautiful white stucco mansion. "I hate it. It gives me the creeps. But maybe it's because I know what's gone on here."

They parked the car and walked up the front steps. "I'm really nervous."

Steve took her hand and gave it a squeeze. "Me too. It'll be fine. It's the right thing to do. Hopefully, we'll find that all is well and we can go home again feeling reassured."

Sophie rang the bell. After a few moments, they heard footsteps echoing down the hallway. Sophie's heart started to race and she immediately regretted coming. She was just looking back down the steps, wondering if it was too late to make a bolt for it, when the heavy black door swung open.

Nick frowned slightly, as if trying to place who they were, before recognition dawned. "Oh. It's you."

"Hi, Nick!" Sophie's voice sounded much brighter than she felt and it slightly startled her. "We were in the area and we thought we'd pop in for a coffee."

Nick closed the door just a fraction, but enough to make a point. "Right. Only, we're a bit busy at the moment."

"That's OK," Steve said affably, taking a step closer to the door. "We won't keep you long."

Nick shook his head. "Sorry, but it's really not convenient. Maybe another—"

His words were interrupted by a loud squeal from the hallway. "Steve! Sophie! You came!" Megan slipped around Nick's legs and dived into Steve's arms, taking him unawares and almost causing him to lose his balance.

"Hey, Meggie! Wow, you have grown soooo much!" Steve

lifted her up so he could get a better look at her, causing her to giggle in delight.

Sophie watched Nick as his face folded in fury. "Megan!" he snapped. "Get inside. Now!"

Megan's mouth dropped open in shock. "But it's Sophie and Steve. Mummy always said we'd see them soon."

"Well, you've seen them now. Please go back inside."

Sophie's skin prickled at the sinister tone of Nick's voice. Like a gently bubbling volcano about to erupt. "Is Amy in?" she said as loudly as she could, hoping that Amy would hear her and come to the door.

"As I said…" Nick reached out and pulled Megan roughly from Steve's arms. "She's busy. Please leave."

Steve shrugged. "No, I really don't think so, Nick. We've come to have a coffee with Amy and that's what we're going to do."

Nick turned away and attempted to kick the door shut, but Steve put his foot in the gap. "Move your foot now or I'll call the police." Nick fixed Steve with a look of pure hatred.

"Oh, I don't think we want the police involved, do we, Nick? We might mention a few things to them ourselves and you might find yourself being marched off in handcuffs."

Sophie swallowed hard and her eyes kept being drawn to Megan's bewildered little face. Sophie was scared for herself and Steve, but she was more scared for Amy and the kids. Nick would make her pay for this. "Maybe we should go, Steve?"

Steve looked at her in surprise. "What? No, I think we shouldn't go anywhere until we've seen Amy. I want to know that she's OK."

Nick shook his head. "I think you should take Sophie's advice and leave."

"I will." Steve matched Nick's steely tone. "When I've seen Amy."

Nick hesitated for a moment, then tutted loudly. "Oh, for fuck's sake... Amy!" he yelled over his shoulder. Sophie squirmed on Megan's behalf at her dad's bad language, but she was obviously used to it and didn't flinch.

After a few moments, Amy appeared, moving falteringly down the hallway. Sophie's hand flew to her mouth. Amy looked as if she had aged at least ten years since she had last seen her. Her eyes looked haunted and she walked with a stooped, shuffling gait. "Amy..." she began, her voice breaking as the tears gathered. "What's happened to you?"

Amy managed a wan smile. "I've just had the flu and it's taking a long time to shift it."

Sophie so desperately wanted to believe her. She didn't want to think that she had let her friend walk back into a deathtrap and had then been so wrapped up in her own life that she had barely given her a second thought over the months that had passed since. She looked at Steve for some kind of reassurance, but she could see that his face was a mask of confusion.

"Right, you've seen her—now you can leave." Nick used his own foot to kick Steve's out of the way and slammed the door hard in his face.

Sophie gasped. "Shit. What do we do now? Do we leave?"

Steve was biting the inside of his cheek as he stared fiercely at the black-painted door, as if somehow he would be able to see right through it if he stared hard enough. "No," he said at last. "We're not leaving."

Sophie followed as he walked down the steps and looked into the passageway that led to the back garden. There was a tall wooden gate blocking the path. Steve tried the latch and shrugged when it was locked. Taking a few paces back, he ran at it and gripped the top, before propelling himself athletically up and over it. Sophie gasped with a mixture of admiration and fear. "Steve!" she hissed. "Don't do anything stupid!"

She heard the sound of the lock being undone and the gate opened. Steve grinned. "Not bad for an old man, was it?"

Sophie rolled her eyes. "Seriously, Steve. What the hell are we going to do now?"

Steve's grin faded instantly and he became serious. "We're going to make sure she's OK. That's what we're going to do."

Sophie nodded, relief flooding through her as she realized that this was what she had hoped they would do. They couldn't just walk away, knowing they might have put Amy in even more danger.

She followed Steve down the narrow path. Dusk was rapidly encroaching and the garden was bathed in an eerie mist that made Sophie shiver but at least provided a level of camouflage. There were steps up to the French doors at the back of the house, through which they could clearly see the kitchen and day room, illuminated against the darkness outside. Steve lay on his stomach at the top of the steps and motioned to Sophie to do the same. She obeyed, by now shaking at the prospect of what they might see.

George was sitting on the floor near to them, playing with his Lego, apparently oblivious to any commotion, while Megan was standing to one side, looking back into the hallway. "I can't see them," Steve muttered. "Can you?"

Sophie shook her head and squinted to try to get a better look. "No. They're obviously still in the hallway. That must be what Megan's looking at."

They continued to watch for a few more minutes, until suddenly Megan visibly jumped with fright and ran crying into the hallway. After a few seconds, she reappeared with Nick, who chivvied her back into the kitchen, before disappearing again, looking flustered. "Where's Amy?" Sophie looked at Steve. "I don't like the feel of this."

"Neither do I." Steve scrambled to his feet and made his way to the French doors near to where George was sitting. He crouched down and knocked very gently on one of the square panes of glass.

George looked up in surprise and beamed with delight when he saw Steve's face at the window. He stood up and came towards him, pressing the palms of his small hands to the glass. Steve waved. "Hi, Georgie! It's me, Uncle Steve. Can you open the door so I can get in and give you a hug?"

George frowned in confusion, before looking up at the lock that was above his head. "Just turn the key, Georgie!" Steve said, giving him a smile of encouragement.

George pondered for a second longer, then reached up and turned the key, looking enormously pleased with himself as he did so. Clearly, this was a new trick for him. Steve opened the door as gently as he could and crept into the house. He scooped George up and gave him a tight squeeze. "Good boy, George. Well done."

Sophie followed Steve into the house and headed towards the hallway, her heart thumping furiously. She could hear Megan sobbing but couldn't see her. Finally, she realized the noise was coming from under the table. She bent down and looked underneath. Megan was curled into a ball, her thumb in her mouth, crying piteously. "Oh, sweetie." Sophie reached out to touch her, but Megan instinctively recoiled. She was looking past Sophie with a look of abject terror in her eyes.

Sophie turned slowly to follow her gaze. The hallway was in darkness, but she could just about make out the silhouetted shape of someone standing above a mound of some kind. Her mouth dried with fear, but as if on autopilot, she began to walk slowly towards the figure. She reached for the light switch and flicked it, flinching as the hallway flooded with light, blinding her temporarily.

As her vision cleared, she heard a scream, realizing after a second that it had come from her. "Sophie?" Steve came running into the hall from behind her and kept moving until he reached Nick, who was standing over Amy's slumped form. In one fluid movement he twisted Nick's arm up behind his back and slammed him against the wall. "What the hell have you done?" he yelled, his voice querulous with anger. "Sophie, call an ambulance and call the police!"

CHAPTER THIRTY-ONE

THEY WERE SITTING OUT ON THE TERRACE OF their Portuguese villa, around a long wooden table laden with delicious food that Amy had prepared. The villa was up on a hillside, with a breathtaking view down towards the sea and a natural lagoon where a flock of pink flamingos was wading in the burnt orange light of the spectacular Algarve sunset.

"So, Emily, how do Jack and Anton get on?" Sophie asked, taking a huge green olive and popping it into her mouth.

When Emily didn't reply, they all turned to look at her curiously. "Em?" Melissa prompted. "Sophie just asked you how Anton and Jack get on."

"I know." Emily's tone was curt, as if she was drawing a line under the conversation.

Melissa rolled her eyes. "Oh, for God's sake, Emily. Why do you always have to be so secretive? You know every bloody thing about us, but you won't tell us a single thing about you. We know now that Anton's his father, so why the need to be so cloak-and-dagger? It's really not a big deal any more."

Emily's dark eyes narrowed. "Because it's no one else's business, that's why!"

"But, Emily," Sophie cut in, "we're not just anyone else. We're your best friends. Why don't you trust us? You should know that we'd never judge you or blab anything you didn't want us to."

Emily's face softened slightly. "It's not that I don't trust you…"

"Well, you obviously don't, or you wouldn't have kept Anton such a secret all these years." Melissa scowled impatiently as she speared an asparagus tip and bit off the end. "And to be perfectly honest, we knew all along anyway."

"Oh, did you really?" There was a sharp tone to Emily's voice that made Sophie sit up a bit straighter. Like Melissa, she found it frustrating that Emily wouldn't tell the rest of them anything about herself, while knowing every single thing about them, both the good and the bad. She had always put it down to Emily not wanting anyone to know about Anton, because he was married and her lecturer. Now she wondered if there was a bit more to it. "Come on, Em, Melissa's right. And it was a simple enough question. How does Anton get on with Jack?"

A succession of emotions passed over Emily's face. Finally, she exhaled, as if she had come to a decision. "He doesn't know about him."

There was a long silence as each of the others digested what she had just said.

Sophie frowned. "Jack doesn't know about Anton or Anton doesn't know about Jack?"

Emily shook her head slightly. "Both."

★ ★ ★ ★ ★

Emily swung her legs over the side of the bed and sat up. Beside her, Anton groaned and pulled her naked body back towards his, his hands roaming over her skin. "Don't go," he whispered hoarsely. "Stay the night."

"I can't." Emily tried to disentangle herself from his arms, but his touch was like a magnetic force, pulling her further into him every time she tried to move away.

Anton kissed his way down her body. "There's no reason to leave," he whispered, using his tongue to set every nerve ending on fire. "Stay here and let me devour you all night long."

Emily moaned with pleasure. She was helpless to resist him, yet she had to go. "Just...one more time," she gasped as he entered her and began to thrust, sending shudders of ecstasy through her whole body.

"Now I really, really do have to leave," she whispered as they lay entangled in each other's arms, both slick with perspiration. She rolled away from him and stood up.

"God, you're beautiful."

She looked back at Anton, who was grinning up at her with that sexy, lazy, slightly crooked smile of his. Even the sight of him made her tingle. She had never felt this way with anyone else. He was so comfortable in his nakedness, so animal in his obvious lust for her that it made her less self-conscious and more insatiable than she had ever been. He made her feel like a goddess.

"I have to go." She reached for her dress, which was draped over a chair in the bedroom of Anton's flat.

"Let's get married."

Emily pulled the dress over her head and gaped at him. "What did you say?"

"I said, let's get married."

Emily shook her head, as if it would help to make sense of the words. "I don't understand... Why would we get married?"

Anton looked wounded. "Seriously, you have to ask that

question? I love you. You love me. And we have already wasted far too many years. Let's not waste any more time. I want to spend the rest of my life with you, Em. I thought you felt the same way."

Emily sank down onto the side of the bed. "I do... It's just...I need time to think about it."

Anton raised his eyebrows quizzically. "What is there to think about?"

Emily sighed. What was there to think about? Well, for starters there was Jack. It had been just the two of them for so long, without any kind of father figure in the picture. How would he react to Anton's sudden presence in his life? She hadn't told him about Anton. She wasn't sure why. It all felt too complicated and would open her up to questions she wasn't sure she was ready to answer yet.

And, rather crucially, she still hadn't told Anton about Jack. The guilt she felt about this chewed at her insides constantly. But once she had started with the omission, it was impossible to put it right. She couldn't just come out with "Oh, and by the way, I have a twelve-year-old son that I haven't told you about."

"Just...things. Can I have some time to decide?"

Anton shrugged. "Sure. I'm not going anywhere."

★ ★ ★ ★ ★

"Well!" Melissa raised her eyebrows. "That is just weird. How the hell have you managed to keep that a secret?"

"We always meet at Anton's flat, so it's not hard to keep it from him. And Jack's always out these days, so he doesn't seem to be aware that I'm not home either. I'm always there to pick him up from football or band practice or wherever he's been, so he hasn't cottoned on."

"What about the weekends? School holidays?" Sophie couldn't imagine how Emily could pull off such a huge deception.

"Anton goes back to Durham to see his girls every weekend. Same with school holidays. Being a lecturer means he gets the same holidays as them."

"I thought they were older."

"They are. Sixteen and fourteen. Still at school."

There was a long pause.

"But don't you *want* Jack and Anton to know about each other?" This time it was Amy speaking, her green eyes burning with curiosity.

Emily looked suddenly sad. "Of course I do. But the more time that passes when I haven't said anything, the harder it seems to be to tell them."

"That's why you shouldn't be so secretive," Melissa said, earning a silencing scowl from Sophie.

"Well, it's done now, so we just have to help you work out how to broach it." Sophie took a sip of her red wine as she mulled the problem.

"There's more," Emily said, causing them all to gape at her in surprise. After all these years of saying so little, suddenly it was as if a dam had burst and she now wanted to tell them everything. "He's asked me to marry him."

"Oh, Em, that is amazing news!" Amy leapt out of her seat and hugged Emily, who remained strangely still.

"Congratulations," Sophie said, lifting her glass in toast. "It *is* good news, Emily, isn't it?"

Emily's eyes clouded. "Not really. How can I marry him? How do I suddenly announce I have a son that I haven't mentioned before?"

"Hmm." Melissa nodded as she chewed on a piece of bread.

"Especially as it's his kid too. He'll probably be furious that you kept it from him."

"Yes, thanks for that, Melissa!" Sophie cut in. "I'm sure Emily is well aware of that. But on the other hand, Em, he might be absolutely thrilled."

Emily gave Sophie a strange look that she couldn't read. "You see, this is why I always keep everything to myself. No one knows the answer, so it's pointless discussing it."

"No! It really isn't," Sophie reassured her. "We'll figure it out together. The most important question is whether you want to marry him."

Emily smiled. "I do want to marry him. I've always wanted to marry him. He's my Mr Right. He always was. I just wasn't sure if it would ever happen."

"Well, then." Sophie rubbed her hands together. "You are going to marry Anton and we are going to help you work out a way to break it to him about Jack."

"Honesty is the best policy," Melissa declared confidently. "Just say you didn't tell him before because you didn't want to freak him out."

Emily raised her eyebrows. "It's that simple, is it, Melissa?"

Melissa nodded furiously. "It's only as complicated as you want to make it. You've spent too long keeping things bottled up and it only leads to trouble."

Later that night, Emily lay in bed, thinking. Maybe Melissa was right. Maybe she was wrong to always bottle things up. It had certainly felt like a huge relief to talk to the others about Anton. It was the first time she had unburdened herself and it was a new and cathartic experience for her.

Down the hallway, Amy was also lying awake, staring at the ceiling. Coming here to this beautiful place had done her so much good, but the spectre of Nick always loomed large at the back of her mind. She wondered if it always would. He couldn't get to her physically any longer, but the emotional damage was much slower to heal. She would never be able to forgive herself for going back to him. For putting Megan and George in such a vulnerable position.

Her therapist had helped. Had shown her that she was the victim and that she shouldn't blame herself for what happened. But how could she not? Sophie had warned her so many times that he wouldn't have changed, but she hadn't listened. She had let him dupe her because she had wanted to be duped.

Sophie and Steve were her saviours and she would never, ever be able to repay them for saving her life. When she woke up in the ambulance on the way to hospital that awful, fateful evening, Sophie was by her side, holding her hand and telling her everything would be all right.

"It won't be all right," she had whispered, unable to speak aloud because of the excruciating pain.

"Shh." Sophie shook her head. "Don't try to talk, sweetie."

"But you don't understand." Amy had to find a way to voice it. To say the unsayable. "I *wanted* him to kill me. I just wanted it to be over."

Sophie frowned, her blue eyes crinkling in confusion. "No, you didn't, Amy. You wanted the violence to stop. That's not the same as wanting to die."

But Amy knew the difference. She wanted to die because she was worthless. She was a worthless mother, a useless wife, an ungrateful friend and a daughter who had deliberately distanced herself from her own, loving parents. She didn't add anything to the world and she knew that it would be a better place without her in it.

Lying here now, months later, with her physical wounds

gone and the psychological trauma starting to recede, she couldn't imagine ever feeling that way, but at the time it had been so very real. Nick would be going to prison, and while she knew that he deserved his punishment, she couldn't shake the feeling that she deserved to be punished too.

The future stretched out before her and she was scared of what it might hold. Living with Sophie and Steve was wonderful, but they wouldn't be able to stay there for ever. She would have to find a job and get a place of their own, however many times Sophie told her she was welcome to stay for as long as she wanted.

She needed to show Megan and George that she would look after them, after letting them down so badly. And she needed to make it up to her parents too, for shutting them out of her life and keeping their grandchildren away from them. Her mother's face when she came to visit Amy in hospital would stay with her for ever. "Why?" she kept asking through the tears that poured down her cheeks unchecked. "Why didn't you tell us what he was doing to you? We would have helped you."

"I was embarrassed," Amy croaked. She had told her parents that she had left Nick the first time because things weren't working out and had been slightly surprised by their reaction, which seemed to be one of relief. "Well, hopefully, we'll at least get to see a lot more of you," her mother had said, causing Amy to cringe with shame that she had allowed Nick to squeeze them out of her life. But her parents had both stopped short of criticizing Nick, as if they somehow sensed that they might not have seen the last of him. And when they first got back together, Nick was expansive and generous towards them, making them all think that perhaps they had misjudged him. But it didn't last and very soon Nick was suggesting that it was better when it was "just the four of us. We don't need anyone else."

"I never liked him," her father had muttered darkly, shaking his head in disgust as they sat by her hospital bed that awful night. "I'm glad he's been arrested or I don't know what I'd have done…"

"Don't, Richard." Amy's mum put a shaking hand on his arm. "It doesn't help to talk like that. And he's gone now. Hopefully for good."

They had suggested that Amy and the children move in with them, but Amy wanted to return to Sophie and Steve's, where she felt safe and secure. It was also perfect for the children, with Emma acting as the bossy big sister, while baby Theo provided a welcome distraction for them all. She felt useful there too, looking after the children while Steve worked on his scripts. He had been getting more and more work recently and she could see that his career was about to take off the way Sophie's had.

She was luckier than most because money would never be a problem for them. She would never need to work again. But that didn't mean she didn't want to. She needed to do something with her life to prove to herself and everyone else that she wasn't worthless. She just hadn't figured out what it was yet.

MAY 2006

"Sir Paul McCartney and his wife, Heather Mills, have announced they are to separate after four years of marriage. The couple said the split was amicable and they remain friends."

DEDHAM, ESSEX

CHAPTER THIRTY-TWO

"WHERE'S EMILY? SHE SHOULD HAVE BEEN HERE
by now." Sophie paced around the long, low-ceilinged sitting room of the sixteenth-century cottage they had rented.
"I hope she's coming."

"I'm sure she'll be here soon." Amy came through from the
kitchen carrying a tray of home-made canapés. As usual, they
looked mouth-wateringly delicious. "Probably just caught up
in the traffic out of London."

Sophie looked at her watch. "Well, we came out of London
too and we didn't get held up. I can't help feeling that there's
something wrong." She was worried about Emily. Had been
worried about her for a little while now. She had been increasingly difficult to get hold of and seemed remote and slightly
prickly whenever they spoke.

After their wonderful weekend break in Portugal last year,
they had returned home having convinced Emily to come
clean with Anton about Jack. "The sooner you do it, the better," Melissa had said on their last night. "Promise us you
won't prevaricate any longer?"

Emily had nodded firmly, seemingly determined to sort things out once and for all. "I promise."

But in the following weeks, it was clear that she still hadn't told him. "What are you waiting for?" Sophie asked her, perplexed as to why she was even hesitating over something so important. Jack had been to stay with them a few times and it was also obvious that he still knew nothing about Anton, making it difficult to speak openly for fear of blabbing within his earshot.

"Things are just not as straightforward as you make out. God, I wish I'd never told you lot anything—it was so much easier when I kept things to myself," she added, causing Sophie to recoil, feeling hurt.

The next time she saw Emily, she deliberately didn't ask. At first, Emily didn't say anything about Anton either, making Sophie assume that she still hadn't told him. But as they said goodbye at the end of the evening, Emily cleared her throat. "I've told Anton. About Jack," she added needlessly.

Sophie nodded encouragingly. "Oh, that's great. How did it go?"

Emily turned her head away, the light from the street lamp above her catching her hair, making it gleam. "He was upset that I hadn't told him sooner."

Sophie bit her lip. There was something about Emily's tone that made her think she wasn't telling her everything. "Well, that's understandable, isn't it? He's got a child he didn't know about. It's a huge shock. But he'll get over it. He'll be pleased when he sees what a fantastic boy he is." She shivered in the chilly evening air.

Emily looked back and met her eye. For a moment, it seemed as if she was about to say something important, but then she hesitated and instead just exhaled loudly. "I guess."

"What about getting married?"

Emily shrugged. "I don't know. I think he might have got a bit carried away with the romance of it all and just said it in the moment. Or maybe he's changed his mind. Especially now…"

"No, surely not!" Sophie hushed her. "If anything, he would want to get married more than ever, now that he knows you have a son together."

Emily exhaled loudly.

"What?" Sophie frowned and bent her head slightly, trying to read Emily's expression. "What aren't you telling me?"

Emily closed her eyes for a second. "Nothing. It's nothing. Look, I'd better get home. Jack's home alone tonight."

Sophie smiled. "God, I can't wait until mine are old enough to be left alone. It seems a million years off."

"Don't wish it away, Soph." Emily's face took on a wistful expression. "I would happily have kept Jack at six years old for ever. They're so much easier at that age."

"I know, it's a great age." Emma was six now and Sophie had often wished she could hold on to time to stop her getting any older. "I suppose you need to tell Jack now, about Anton?"

"Yes, and I'm not looking forward to it either." Emily gave a little wave as she walked away. "I'll see you soon, Soph."

But she hadn't seen her soon. She hadn't seen her at all. They had exchanged emails and Emily had agreed to come when they booked this weekend back in the winter, but other than that, she had kept herself to herself.

"Emily's always been a bit offish. You know what she's like about her privacy," Melissa said now, wolfing down one of Amy's canapés. "Don't worry about it, Sophie, she'll be here, I'm sure."

Just at that moment, as if on cue, a car pulled up outside.

"What did I tell you?" Melissa said, standing up to peer out of the window. "She's here."

Sophie hurried to the front door and swung it open. "Hello, stranger!" she called as Emily climbed out of the car and smoothed down her T-shirt and capri pants. "Long time no see!"

Emily looked up at Sophie and promptly burst into tears.

"I'm fine!" Emily protested, half laughing as the others ran around, treating her as if she was a sick patient.

"Drink this," Amy ordered, handing her a perfectly mixed gin and tonic. "Best medicine there is."

"Well, if you insist." Emily sipped the drink obligingly. "God, that's good."

Melissa planted a bowl of crisps in the middle of the chunky wooden coffee table and Sophie came and sat beside her on the sofa, tucking her legs underneath her, as if she was settling in for a long session. "Right, why don't you tell us what's wrong?"

Emily sniffed and shook her head wearily. "I honestly don't know where to start."

"Start at the beginning," Melissa ordered. "From when we got home from Portugal."

★ ★ ★ ★ ★

"Thanks so much again, Steve," Emily said for the tenth time.

Steve smiled obligingly. "Honestly, Emily, it was no trouble. I love having him here. He helps me keep my sanity when the little ones get too much, don't you, buddy?" He nudged Jack playfully.

Jack smiled shyly as Emily looked at him proudly. Whenever she was apart from him, she seemed to see him through new eyes on her return. He was getting so tall that he was almost catching Steve up. She knew how much he loved visiting this mad, noisy, fun household, and whatever he might say, she also knew how much he loved being around the younger kids. Growing up as an only child with a single mother had been quite a lonely existence at times, however close he was to her parents. These weekends with the other children had given him the sense of family he seemed to yearn for.

In the car on the way back home, she took a deep breath and prepared to tell him about Anton. Melissa was right. She had prevaricated too long and it was time to be open with him. But just as she was about to speak, Jack looked over at her with a wistful expression. "I wish Steve was my dad," he said.

Emily's heart thumped. "Wow," she replied, wondering how to react. "Where did that come from?"

"And I wish I lived with them in that cool house. It's so much fun."

Emily felt as if she had been punched in the stomach. She opened her mouth to formulate an answer, but all that came out was a strangled sob.

"Mum?" Jack looked at her in concern. "Are you OK? I'm sorry. I didn't mean I don't like living with you. I just meant that I wish we could all live together in that big house."

Emily nodded furiously, tears momentarily blinding her view of the road ahead. "I know, darling," she managed at last. "Sometimes I wish it too." Now, she decided, was definitely not the right moment to tell him about Anton.

And as the weeks passed, there never seemed to be a right moment. Every time she spoke to any of the others, they always asked if she'd told him yet, and because she felt ashamed that she hadn't, she stopped returning their calls.

Telling Anton about Jack should have been easier, but still she hesitated. What if he hated her for keeping it from him? He would certainly not think her much of a mother for keeping her child a secret. He didn't often talk about his ex-wife, but when he did, he always conceded that she had been a brilliant mother to their two daughters.

In the end, it was a simple slip of the tongue rather than a planned-out conversation that revealed the truth. They had been out for dinner at an Italian restaurant and were walking home, hand in hand. Emily had had a couple of glasses of wine and was feeling slightly light-headed and pleasantly woozy.

"You need to stay the night tonight," Anton told her, kissing the top of her head. "I hate waking up with you gone."

"I can't." Emily sighed. "We've got an early start tomorrow."

Anton stopped walking and looked down at her curiously. "We? Who's 'we'? And you said earlier that you'd got tomorrow off."

"Did I?" Emily tried to remember. She couldn't get her thoughts straight. This was why she didn't usually drink. It got her into all sorts of trouble.

"Is there something you're not telling me, Emily?" Anton's face became suddenly serious. "You haven't got another man, have you?" He narrowed his eyes suspiciously.

Emily bit her lip. It was now or never. She could almost hear her own heart beating in her chest. "Um, not exactly."

"What's that supposed to mean?" Anton tried to laugh, but she could see the annoyance and apprehension in his features.

"I've been wanting to tell you for a long time…"

"Tell me what? Seriously, Em, you're worrying me. Have you met someone else? Please tell me you haven't." Anton's face was thrown into darkness under the amber light of the street lamp, but she could still tell that his expression was one of genuine fear.

"No, no, nothing like that." Emily put the palm of her hand flat against his chest, in a gesture of reassurance, but also to support herself as her legs wobbled. "Anton, I had a baby. After I last saw you… A son."

In the silence that followed, Emily felt the ground rushing up on her and wondered if she might faint. Anton stepped back slightly so that she could see his face clearly. "A son?"

Emily took a couple of breaths, desperately trying to steady herself. "Yes. A son. He's thirteen now. He's called Jack."

Anton shook his head in disbelief, his eyes widening in shock. "And you didn't think to mention it?"

"It…it's complicated."

Anton looked away, distractedly running his hand through his wavy fair hair.

"Anton, say something. I'm sorry I didn't tell you. I should have told you, but I was worried it would scare you off. And I'd waited so long for you to come back…" Emily tailed off, suddenly tearful. "I couldn't bear to lose you again."

Anton looked down at her, his expression already beginning to soften. "I know. I get it. Look, we all have skeletons in our closet. Why should you be any different? I just wish you'd trusted me enough to tell me."

Relief flooded through her body and she reached up to cup his face in her hands. "Thank you," she whispered, pulling him down so that she could kiss him.

★ ★ ★ ★ ★

"What did he mean by 'we all have skeletons in our closet'?" Sophie almost didn't want to ask the question, but her antennae had pricked as soon as Emily said it.

Emily looked at Sophie with huge, mournful brown eyes. "I knew you'd pick up on that."

"He probably didn't mean anything by it." Melissa waved

her hand dismissively. "And he's right. We all do." She glanced briefly at Sophie, then looked away quickly.

"No." Emily shook her head and took a long sip of her gin and tonic. "He definitely meant something by it. I just didn't find out what it was until earlier this week."

★ ★ ★ ★ ★

"When are you going to introduce me to Jack, then?" Anton rolled onto his side and propped himself up on his elbow so that he could look at Emily.

Emily mirrored his pose. "There might be a little bit of an issue I need to deal with first."

"What sort of issue?"

"Well…" Emily hesitated. "I haven't actually told him about you yet."

Anton raised his eyebrows and exhaled. "Wow. You really know how to make a man feel good about himself, Em. We've been seeing each other for almost a year now. Are you ashamed of me?"

"No!" Emily protested. "Of course not. It's just, well, it's difficult. Jack and I are very close and it's always been just the two of us. I'm worried about upsetting him with such a huge revelation. He's a sensitive boy."

Anton sat up and leaned back against the headboard, pulling the duvet up to cover his naked body. "He's thirteen, Em. I'm sure he could cope with it."

"But you don't know him like I do." Emily sat up and pulled her knees up to her chest. "And there just never seems to be the right moment. Every time I go to tell him about you, something seems to crop up. It's as if fate keeps intervening. It's made me a bit superstitious that it's a sign."

Anton tutted irritably. "That's ridiculous. I think you're treating him like a baby, rather than a young man."

"Well, while we're on the subject, you haven't introduced me to your daughters, have you?"

Anton shifted uncomfortably. "That's different."

Emily frowned. "No, it's not. How is it different?"

"Because they don't live here. They live in Durham."

"Have you even told them about me?"

Anton didn't reply.

"You haven't, have you? Why not? What happens if we get married?"

A sudden flush spread up Anton's neck. Still he didn't speak.

"You do remember that you asked me to marry you, don't you?"

Anton nodded. "Of course I do." His voice had dropped to almost a whisper.

"But you've changed your mind?"

"No! Yes… Well, it was just me being a romantic fool. I thought it… Oh, what does it matter? You turned me down anyway."

"I didn't turn you down, Anton. I just said I needed time to think about it. It's not the same as turning you down."

"Look, forget I said anything. Let's leave things as they are. You're right. It's probably best I don't meet Jack yet. It's just that I want to spend more time with you." Anton flashed her his most beguiling smile and leaned over to kiss her, his hands moving towards her breasts.

Emily pushed him away gently. She wasn't letting the conversation drop that quickly. "We wouldn't spend that much more time together anyway, even if I told him about you. You always travel back to Durham to see your girls at the weekend, so you're never around."

Anton sighed. "I know. I just want to be able to spend the night at your place for once. The whole night. I hate that you always scuttle off back home after sex. It makes me feel cheap." He grinned at her to show that he was joking, before leaning down and playfully kissing her breast.

Emily tried to stay focused. She somehow knew that this was a significant and important conversation, but she couldn't concentrate as his mouth began to move all over her body, covering her with butterfly kisses. She wanted to resist him, but she was just as helpless with desire now as she had been right back at the beginning. They could talk another time.

★ ★ ★ ★ ★

"So how did you find out, then?" Sophie reached out and took Emily's hand in hers.

"Find out what? OK, so I'm really confused now." Melissa threw her hands up in the air in frustration as she sat cross-legged on the floor beside them.

"That he's still married." Sophie looked at Emily. "I'm right, aren't I?"

Emily nodded as large fat tears began to spill over her dark lashes and roll down her cheeks. For someone who'd had so much trauma in her life, she rarely cried and it was hard to watch.

★ ★ ★ ★ ★

It was Facebook that did it. It was still a fairly new innovation in the UK and Emily didn't go on it very often, or even know how to use it properly. But once Jack turned thirteen and wanted to use it, she thought she should be a responsible parent and keep an eye on what he was up to on there.

One day, she was scrolling through, not taking much notice of the various dreary update posts from her friends, when she had a sudden flashback to Anton's first message to her on Friends Reunited and the feeling she had had when she first read the words that she had dreamed of for all of those years. *I never stopped thinking about you.* She suddenly wondered if he was on Facebook and typed his name into the search box. Immediately, his profile popped up.

The side-on profile picture of him was beautiful. He was on a boat somewhere sunny and looked as blond and tanned as she had always remembered him. She clicked on the photo to look at it more closely and it took her to Anton's profile page.

To her surprise, he had been tagged in quite a few photos, clearly taken by his daughters. She clicked on the profile of Lucy, the elder daughter. Amongst the dozens of pictures she had posted were numerous ones of both her and her sister, Isobel, along with another, very attractive older woman, presumably their mother.

Emily peered at the pictures, fascinated by how good-looking Anton's ex-wife was. From the few things Anton had said, he seemed to suggest she had "let herself go a bit" in recent years. But the woman in the photos had shoulder-length, shiny dark hair, a petite, slim figure and a pretty, unlined face. She looked strikingly similar to Emily, in fact. Her daughters were both miniature versions of her and nothing short of gorgeous.

In a couple of the photos, it was just Anton and the woman, beaming at the camera, their arms wrapped around each other. Above, Lucy had captioned it: *My mum and dad—the lovebirds!* X

Emily felt a pang of sympathy for the sixteen-year-old

Lucy. It must have hit her hard when her parents divorced. She wondered how long before they split up this photo was taken. The date on Facebook said May 2006, but obviously that must have been the date Lucy posted it. Anton didn't look that much younger. Or younger at all, in fact. But then, he hadn't really changed or aged in the thirteen years that she hadn't seen him.

She scrolled through the various pictures, alighting on the ones of Anton with his family. He looked happy and relaxed. Some were clearly taken on holiday. Not really what she would have expected from a man whose marriage was over and who was planning a new life in London. A prickle of suspicion began to tingle at the back of Emily's neck. She thought maybe she should stop looking. That she was going to find something she didn't like. But she couldn't stop. She had a horrible, ghoulish compulsion to carry on.

Further down, amongst the slightly older pictures, there was one of Anton on his own, looking into the camera, pulling a comedy "sad" face, his bottom lip sticking out as he pretended to cry. Underneath was the caption: *Boo! My daddy has a new job in London so I'm only going to see him at weekends.*

Several people had left comments underneath the picture, including one from Sarah Massey. Anton's ex-wife had written, *At least we won't have him moaning about us clogging up the shower with our hair during the week…! xx*

Emily's throat felt as if it might close over and her heart began to pound. That couldn't be right. But even as she clicked on Sarah Massey's profile, she already knew what she was going to find. Her profile photo was her on her own, on a cliff overlooking a beach somewhere in the UK. But her background photo was her with Anton, standing on a beautiful golden beach with a turquoise sea in the background. Anton was standing behind her, with his arms wrapped around her, beaming proudly. According to the dates on Facebook, she had only recently changed it. Emily clicked on Sarah's "About" page and her eyes scanned the screen, searching for information that she already knew. Sure enough, beside "relationship status" were the words "Married to Anton Massey."

Emily put her hand over her mouth to catch the sob that was just escaping. She gulped for air as the tears began to fall, splashing onto her keyboard like little fat raindrops. Everything had been a lie. The pain was like a knife twisting inside her heart. She had lived her whole adult life waiting for this man, whom she adored, loved, idolized. And he wasn't worth any of it. He was a liar, a cheat and a fantasist. He had used her in the worst possible way, letting her believe that she had a future with him, when in fact he was just using her for sex.

She wrapped her arms around herself, rocking backwards and forwards to try to ease the awful, awful pain. She was hurt, she was deeply ashamed, and most of all, she felt so *stupid*.

★ ★ ★ ★ ★

"Oh, honey, I'm so sorry." Sophie put an arm around Emily's shaking shoulders. "But it wasn't your fault. How could you possibly have known?"

"How could I *not* have known?" Emily shot back. "If you think about it, all the signs were there. I just chose not to look. I chose not to see what was right in front of my face."

"You're not the first one to have done that, Em," Amy said, standing up and taking Emily's glass from her and starting to mix her another gin and tonic. "Look at me. Everyone warned me about Nick, but I chose not to see it. It sounds like such a cliché, but love really is blind. You shouldn't feel stupid, because you're not the only one who's fallen for his lies—don't forget his wife is being duped too."

"I feel so terrible about her," Emily whimpered. "I would never, ever have got involved if I'd known he was still married. I… Well, I'm not that sort of woman."

There was an uncomfortable silence as everyone turned to look at Melissa.

"And neither am I. Any more." Melissa shot them all a defiant look.

"Sorry." Emily shook her head wearily. "That wasn't directed at you, Melissa. I just feel bad for that poor woman that she doesn't know what a bastard she's married to."

"You're not going to tell her, are you?" Amy handed Emily the freshly mixed gin and tonic and sat back down on the floor.

Emily hesitated. "No."

Sophie nodded. "Good. It wouldn't achieve anything except bringing misery to someone else. And imagine the effect on his daughters. They don't deserve that."

"But what about Jack? Anton's his father too…" Melissa countered.

"Yes, but he doesn't know that, does he, Em?" Sophie looked at Emily, who was staring into her lap.

Emily bit her lip and shook her head.

★ ★ ★ ★ ★

Emily arrived at Anton's flat as planned that evening. It was nearly seven thirty as she let herself in, using the key he'd given her all those months ago. As she made her way through the hallway towards the stairs of the Victorian conversion, she stopped to look at the pile of post on the shelf. There were three flats on three different levels, with a number of letters addressed to the owners of the other two. There were none for Anton, although maybe, she told herself, he had collected it that morning.

Why she was still making excuses for him, she didn't know. She had all the proof she needed that he had pulled off a truly spectacular deception, but a small part of her kept hoping that perhaps there was some mistake. Could anyone really lead such a double life? And she genuinely did feel that he loved her. He made her feel like she was the only woman in the world when he was with her and she sensed that they had a connection on a much deeper level than just sex.

She opened his front door and walked up the remaining few stairs. Normally, she would prepare dinner for them and be waiting with a drink by the time he arrived home, usually at around 8 p.m. But tonight she kept her denim jacket on and sat straight-backed on one of the wooden chairs in the small lounge-diner. As she waited, she looked around her. It was as if she was opening her eyes for the very first time. He was an English lecturer with a passion for poetry. *It made his soul burn*, apparently. So where were his books? Where were the photos of his daughters? The pictures? The art? The things he had collected over the years on his travels? Where were the signs of his *life*? There were none. It was just a weekday crash pad. Nothing more. And she was just his weekday whore. Nothing more.

By the time he came through the door, she was shaking with the coldness that had seeped into her bones, despite the heat of the day.

Anton bounded up the stairs and into the sitting room, in his hand a bottle of very good red wine. "Hello, you," he said, bending to kiss her frozen lips. "You have filled my head all day long and I can't wait a moment longer. I suggest that before we eat, I pour us both a very large glass of this wine and we drink it in bed."

Emily didn't reply. Couldn't reply. His presence filled the room with such warmth and radiance. She had loved this beautiful man so very much. Still loved him. And when it was over, she knew without a doubt that she would never, ever love anyone like that again. The thought of her life without him in it was unbearable.

"Emily?" Anton rarely called her Emily. He knew something was up. "What's wrong? You're shaking. Are you ill?"

He knelt down in front of her and enveloped her in his arms. "What's wrong, darling?"

Tears sprang into Emily's eyes. He was so damn convincing.

"I know," she said, her words muffled by his hair.

Anton held her at arm's length and gazed into her eyes, as if he could see right into her soul. She held his gaze, wanting to memorize for ever those lovely glittering blue eyes, that strong, square jaw and those exquisite high cheekbones.

"I know," she said again, more clearly this time.

A flicker of doubt passed over Anton's face. "Know what?"

Emily shook her head. "You don't need to ask that, Anton. I know everything. About you. About your daughters. About your wife."

Anton swallowed hard. "But…that's impossible. H-h-how?" he stuttered.

Emily exhaled. "Through your daughter's Facebook account. It's all there, laid out right in front of my eyes. What a complete and utter bloody idiot I've been."

Even now, she wanted him to prove to her that she was wrong. That she had misunderstood. But she could tell by his expression that she was right.

A succession of different emotions passed over Anton's face—defiance, outrage, guilt—before he crumpled completely. "Oh my God, Em. It's not what you think. There's nothing between us any more. It's just for the sake of the children... You must believe me, Em. I love you!"

"I do believe you," she said, prompting a sigh of relief from Anton. "I believe that you love me."

"I do!" He gripped her arms. "I really do."

"But you love your wife more."

"No! No, Em, it's just for the sake of the children. We lead separate lives... It's a marriage in name only—"

"And the person that you love more than anyone else—" Emily cut across his protestations "—is yourself."

Anton leaned back on his haunches and shook his head in disbelief. "No. You're wrong. You've got it all wrong."

"Well, that's the first truthful thing you've said. I definitely got you all wrong." Emily stood up. "You used me, Anton. And I was so stupid that I actually believed that you wanted to spend the rest of your life with me. Imagine if I'd said yes when you asked me to marry you. What the hell would you have done then? You'd probably have gone through with it! God, I feel like such a fool." As she finished speaking, she began to cry. "No!" she shouted through her tears, wiping her face furiously. "I'm not going to cry over you. You're not worth it."

As she bent to pick up her bag, Anton grabbed her hand. "Don't go like this, Em. Please." He looked up at her with a pleading expression. "I can't live without you. I need you in my life. I'll leave Sarah. I promise. We'll get married and get a house together...you, me and Jack. We'll be a family!"

"Shut up!" Emily yelled, desperately wanting to believe him. Desperately wanting to un-know everything that she now knew about him. "You're such a fraud. You actually don't know where the truth ends and a lie begins."

Anton got to his feet, still holding tight on to her hand. "I'm so, so sorry for hurting you. I know what I did was wrong, but I can make this right. Please, Em, give me a chance to make this right."

Emily could feel herself softening. He was so convincing and she wanted to be convinced. Sensing that she was weakening, Anton pulled her into his arms and clutched her to his chest, as if his life depended on it. The smell of him and the feel of him was as intoxicating as ever. Cupping the back of her head with his hands, he lifted her face towards him and kissed her with the sweetest tenderness she had ever known, his tears falling onto her cheeks and blending with her own. "I only love you," he murmured as his hands moved inside her shirt and began to explore her body. "Only you."

Suddenly, Emily's senses snapped into focus. "No," she said softly, looking up into those beautiful blue eyes, now swimming with genuine tears. For a fleeting moment, she felt a pang of sympathy for him. He did love her, but she knew without the tiniest scintilla of doubt that it wouldn't work out between them, even if he did give up his wife and commit to her. She would never be able to trust him. She would never really know the true person inside him. He had so effortlessly led a double life that she doubted if one woman would ever be enough for him. He would always want more. He would always be on the lookout for the next gullible student who would hang on his every word and maybe even waste thirteen years of her life waiting for him.

"Goodbye, Anton."

CHAPTER THIRTY-THREE

SOPHIE WOKE EARLY THE NEXT MORNING. SHE
wished she could learn to lie in again, but since having Emma
and especially since having Theo, her body clock was timed to
sleep no later than seven. She got up and walked downstairs
to the kitchen. It was a beautiful cottage, painted with soft
pastel colours, which, coupled with the low, beamed ceilings,
gave it a warm and inviting feel. She imagined that Christ-
mas here would be idyllic, with the open fires and the smell
of freshly baked cakes spilling from the Aga. All very twee,
but lovely nonetheless.

She made herself a cup of coffee and opened the French
doors out onto the pretty courtyard garden. Despite the early
hour, the sun was already hotting up and the scents of laven-
der and honeysuckle were unmistakable in the morning air.

She sat down at the wrought-iron table and sighed happily.
Last night had been cathartic for all of them. Emily had really
listened to what they had to say and something seemed to click
inside her mind. "If Amy can come back from being almost
killed, then I can get over a tiny little thing like betrayal," she
told Sophie as they sat in the kitchen later.

"Nobody underestimates the shock you've had, Em. Yes, they're very different circumstances, but both very difficult."

Emily nodded and took a deep, calming breath. "Being with Anton did do one thing for me, though..."

Sophie finished the last of her wine. It tasted a bit sour. She had definitely had more than enough. "What's that?"

"He reminded me that when I was at university, I showed so much promise. Everyone expected me to have a big, successful career. And what did I do? I settled for a boring job at an insurance company in the City. It's literally the last place I think anyone expected me to end up."

"But that's because you had Jack. How could you realistically go off and have a big career when you had a baby to look after? You needed something with manageable hours, rather than doing what I did and working all night, every night." She could feel herself flushing slightly as she spoke, remembering suddenly that she hadn't been necessarily just working when she was out so late.

Emily shook her head. "I think I used it as an excuse, though. Anton once told me he looked forward to reading my first novel and I really think he expected me to be a writer of some kind. He used to say I was a very talented writer..." She tailed off, a wistful expression on her face.

"Well, it's not too late, is it? You're only thirty-four and there's no time limit on writing. That's the beauty of it."

Emily smiled and sat up a bit straighter. "No, it's not too late. I shouldn't waste another minute of my life. I'm going to retrain as a journalist. I should have done that from the start. And I'm going to take a creative writing class. And I'm going to write a novel. I'm going to do it all." Emily's dark eyes shone with excitement and determination as she spoke.

Sophie shook her head in admiration. "You are the strongest person I know, Emily. And I really believe you will."

"Will what?" Melissa and Amy came through into the kitchen from the sitting room, where they had been nestled on the sofa, deep in conversation.

Emily held up her glass in a mock toast. "I'm going to make the most of my talents. There's no way I'm spending the rest of my life working in the City. I'm going for a career change."

Amy and Melissa looked at each other and laughed. "Well, that's funny, because Amy and I have just been discussing her doing exactly the same!"

Sophie motioned for them both to sit down and filled all their glasses from the open bottle of red on the table. She had already drunk far too much and would regret it in the morning, but for now, she just wanted to keep the positive mood going.

"What are you thinking, Amy?"

Amy smiled. "Well, I think I'm a pretty good cook…"

"You are!" they all chorused as one.

Amy laughed. "So, I'd like to make a career of it. I'm going to start up my own catering business."

Sophie eyed her warily. "I know you're not short of money, Amy. But starting up a business isn't cheap. It's going to swallow up a hell of a lot of cash—"

"She knows all that," Melissa cut in, waving her hand dismissively. "But luckily there's a very rich man who I happen to know who will be her first client and introduce her to lots of other potential clients."

Sophie frowned. Nick was due to be released from prison within a matter of weeks. "Not… *Nick?* Surely not?"

Amy pulled a face. "No, of course not! It's Melissa's 'friend'

Mark." She made quotation marks with her fingers as she spoke.

"Mark Bailey?" Sophie's mouth dropped open. "Melissa… is there something you haven't told me?" A mixture of emotions moved like a wave through her mind. On the one hand, she was delighted if Melissa and Mark had become more than just friends. She desperately wanted Melissa to meet someone to settle down with.

On the other hand, Mark was a notorious Lothario. He definitely wasn't the settling-down kind, which instantly made her worry for Melissa. Another, much smaller part of her felt ever so slightly jealous. Although there had never been any sort of physical attraction between them, she adored and admired him, meaning she was more than a little possessive when it came to his relationships.

Melissa shot Amy a warning glance. "No! I don't know what Amy's on about…but I know that Mark would back her. Just wear a short skirt when you meet him, Amy, and with your long legs, he'll be putty in your hands."

Sophie exhaled with relief. "That's a bit unfair," she admonished Melissa. "He has an amazing business brain and he'll only back something if he thinks it will make him lots of money. Mind you," she added, grinning at Amy, "I don't suppose wearing a short skirt would do you any harm!"

Later that night, Melissa lay in bed, thinking. Sophie's reaction to any suggestion of a relationship between her and Mark Bailey was an interesting one. It gave her a tiny scintilla of hope that it might one day be a possibility.

She looked at herself in the mirror each morning and gave herself a stern lecture about the folly of getting involved with him. He had women falling over themselves to sleep with him and he was unashamed about taking them all up on their offers. Since they had begun working together, she hadn't yet succumbed to his charms, but she knew it was only a matter of time and so did he. He looked at her with that twinkle in his dark eyes that reminded her of a cat toying with a mouse. He was just biding his time until the inevitable happened.

She wanted to be the exception, the one who turned him down. But she also knew herself well enough to know that she was powerless to resist him. He was like no one else she had ever met. Yes, he was good-looking and charming, but he was also fiercely clever, hilariously funny and unswervingly loyal. She didn't know anyone, male or female, who wasn't a little bit in love with him.

And she didn't think it was too much of an exaggeration to say that working with Mark had saved her. It had given her a focus and a drive that had always been missing in her career. Before, she had drifted along, enjoying the excesses of the music industry without thinking about the future. Since joining forces with Mark to cover Sophie's maternity leave, she had found something she was good at. Something she didn't mind working hard at because she didn't want to let either Sophie or Mark down. Earning his respect and his praise for her work, rather than her body or her sexual prowess, had given her a bigger buzz than any drug had ever done and helped her to flourish.

Every weekend was spent thinking about him and aching for Monday to come around so that she could see him again. When he was away travelling, she felt restless and bored until he returned. Lately, he had started making noises that she should accompany him on his trips to LA and the prospect made her heart soar. She knew, without him ever having to voice it, that that was when their relationship would reach another level. She couldn't wait.

The next morning, Sophie was sitting alone in the court-yard garden when Amy appeared. She brought with her a pot of fresh coffee and joined Sophie at the table. "Is your head as sore as mine?" She grinned sheepishly, pouring out two mugs of steaming black coffee.

Sophie nodded. "It was worth it, though, wasn't it? You're doing so well, Amy. You should be very proud of yourself."

Amy blushed. "I wouldn't be here if it wasn't for you guys. I will never forget that."

Sophie nodded and sipped her coffee, thinking as she watched her how much Amy was growing and blossoming a little more each day. She reminded Sophie of the wisteria plant at the side of her house—it seemed as if it had withered and died in the winter, only to burst back into life with the most delicate, beautiful flowers as soon as summer came. Amy's porcelain skin glowed, her vivid green eyes shone and her thick, auburn hair tumbled like a wild, glossy river down her long, straight back. She was walking tall again, with her head held high and her balletic posture restored.

"And I will always be eternally grateful to you and Steve for taking us in the way you did…" Amy continued.

Sophie batted the words away with her hand. "We have loved having you with us. It has never, ever been a chore, not for one single minute."

"I know. You've always made that clear and we have felt so welcome. But…"

Sophie blinked in surprise. "But what?"

"But I think it's time for us to get a place of our own. I need to stand on my own two feet and support the children myself. I can't rely on you and Steve for ever."

Sophie could feel the tears pricking the backs of her eyes. She had always known this moment would come. She could feel things building towards it over the past months as Amy became stronger. But she had grown to love Megan and George so much. And Steve had too. He would be bereft at losing them all over again. Plus Amy had been a huge help in looking after the children while he developed his career, which was starting to take off at last. "But what will we do without you?" she asked plaintively.

Amy reached out and took Sophie's hand. "Well, we won't be going too far away, so we'll still see each other all the time."

Sophie nodded through her tears. She very much doubted they would still see much of each other once they left.

"I have seen somewhere that could be perfect..." Amy continued, a wide smile starting to spread across her face.

"Really?" Sophie sniffed back any further tears and gave herself a mental shake. It was ridiculous to expect Amy to stay with them for ever. Of course she had to stand on her own two feet or she would never move on with her life. Staying would be a permanent reminder of what Nick did to her.

"It's the house next door!" Amy sat back with a triumphant look on her face.

Sophie gasped and clapped her hands gleefully. Steve had mentioned something about their neighbours moving abroad, but she hadn't really taken much notice. It was the perfect solution. The children could be in and out of each other's houses all day long if they wanted and they could still spend weekends and holidays together. "Oh, Amy—that's a great idea!"

Amy beamed. "It is, isn't it? I won't feel like I'm sponging off you, but I'll still get to see just as much of you as before."

"But...if you're going to set up your own catering business—and I do think that's a great idea, by the way—what will you do about the kids?"

Again, Amy smiled proudly. "I'm going to hire a nanny. A

nice one," she added, her face darkening momentarily as she thought back to the nightmare she had had with Suki. "And they can look after your two as well, now that Steve's working so much. It would be another way for me to thank you."

"Wow." Sophie looked at Amy in admiration. "You've got it all worked out, haven't you? You have come such a long way, Amy, it's fantastic."

"Thank you. I feel the same way Emily does. I really want to make something of my life. I want my kids to be proud of me, the way yours are of you."

Sophie quailed. "I don't know about that. We all screw up sometimes, Amy, me included."

There was a sudden groan from behind them as Melissa appeared in the courtyard. She was still wearing the shorts and T-shirt she had worn to bed and had clearly not removed her make-up before going to sleep. But somehow she still managed to look gorgeous. "I feel like hell," she said, laughing. "But boy, was it worth it."

She joined Amy and Sophie at the table and poured herself some coffee. "I'm amazed I'm up before Emily. I think that's a world first."

Sophie frowned. "Yes, I hope she's OK. It's been a tough week for her."

Amy and Melissa both nodded. "She's well shot of him, though." Melissa dropped her voice and glanced towards the door, in case she was overheard. "I never liked him. Even at university. You could tell he was a creep even then."

Sophie rolled her eyes. Melissa had never said any such thing. Quite the opposite, in fact. She stood up. "I think I ought to go and check on her."

Leaving the other two enjoying the sunshine, she made her way back into the house and up the stairs. The ceilings were so low that she had to duck in places, so as not to bang her head. Emily's room was at the end of the landing, overlooking the front garden and the road beyond it.

She knocked gently and lifted the wrought-iron latch. "Em?" she called softly into the gloom. There was no reply. Puzzled, she walked into the room and over to the bed. The duvet had been hastily thrown back and the pretty cotton bedspread lay in a tangled heap on the floor. "Em?" she called again, although it was clear she wasn't in the room. "Emily?" Still there was no answer. She opened the door of the wardrobe. All her clothes had gone and there was no sign of her little weekend case.

She made her way back out onto the landing and peered into the bathroom, but the door was wide open and it was empty. Although she could already sense that Emily wasn't in the house, she checked all the other bedrooms, just in case. Maybe something had freaked her out in her room and she had moved to one of the two spare rooms during the night. But she was nowhere to be seen.

Back downstairs, she checked every room and cupboard, before heading back out into the sunshine of the courtyard. Melissa and Amy looked up at her curiously. "What's up?" Melissa said. "You look worried."

"I am worried." Sophie put her hands on her hips as she tried to think what to do next. "Emily's gone."

★ ★ ★ ★ ★

Emily drove as fast as she could through the country lanes, willing them to end so that she could join the motorway as soon as possible. Every narrowing of the road or sharp bend that forced her to slow the car to a crawl felt like agony. "Get out of the bloody way!" she hissed as the road was blocked by a tractor pulling into a field, as if the farmer had all the time in the world.

Finally, finally, she was on the dual carriageway and she could put her foot down as much as she dared. As much as her little Ford Fiesta would allow.

She had woken at dawn with a strange premonition that something was wrong. She reached for her phone, plugged into a charger on the floor, as her battery had been completely flat from around eight the previous night. She switched it on and almost immediately it began to buzz with voicemail notifications. With a shaking hand and a pounding heart, she clicked on the first message.

"Emily? It's Mum." Her mum's voice, normally so calm and assured, sounded strained and panicky. "Jack's had an accident. He's been knocked over by a car. He's OK, but you need to get here as soon as possible. We're at Lewisham Hospital. Your dad and I are with him. Drive safely."

Emily scrolled through her contacts, searching for her mum's mobile number, panic blurring her vision. Finally, she found it and clicked on the contact number. Her mum picked up immediately. "Mum, I'm so sorry, I only just got the message."

"Don't worry, he's going to be fine," her mum said, her voice a lot more measured than in her message.

"Is he home?"

There was a pause. "No. They've kept him in for observation. Why don't you drive to the hospital and I'll be waiting for you."

Emily's senses tingled. There was more to this than her mum was telling her. "Are you sure he's OK?" she persisted.

Another pause. "Yes. I'll see you at the hospital. Drive safely." The line went dead.

By the time Emily arrived at the entrance to the hospital, her mum was waiting for her. "Your dad's with him," she told Emily as she hugged her and led her into the hospital. Emily followed her in a daze. She felt certain that something was wrong.

As they walked into the children's ward, she spotted Jack immediately. He was sitting up in the bed furthest from the door, under a large window. Beside him, her dad sat in the regulation armchair, dealing out cards for the game they were playing. Emily's legs went weak with relief. He looked absolutely fine.

"Jack!" she wailed as she reached him, enveloping him in a hug and bursting into tears.

"Hey, Mum." Jack looked up at her sheepishly as they pulled apart. He had an egg-shaped bump on his forehead and a nasty scrape down one side of his face. There were numerous bruises on his arms.

"Well, I was expecting you to be in a much worse state," she said, still breathless with relief.

"My leg's not great," Jack said, lifting the cover to show Emily that most of his right leg was heavily bandaged. The rest was covered in large bruises. "But other than that, I'm fine."

Out of the corner of her eye, Emily noticed a look pass between her mum and dad. Again, her senses told her that something wasn't quite right here.

"Mum, shall we go and get Jack some sweets?" She motioned pointedly towards the door. Her mum nodded and stood up, a heavy expression on her face.

"I'm not four!" Jack protested as they made their way out

of the ward. Emily looked back at him and smiled, but he and her dad had already resumed their card game.

"Something's going on, isn't it?" Emily turned towards her mum and blocked her way as soon as the double doors closed behind them. "Do you want to tell me what it is?"

Her mum's eyes slid away nervously. "Let's sit down here," she said, guiding Emily into a chair.

"Mum, you're frightening me." Emily tried to adopt a teasing tone, but she couldn't quite pull it off.

Her mum swallowed hard and looked as if she was steeling herself to speak. "The consultant says they've picked up something from Jack's blood tests." She cleared her throat. "They want to do some more tests."

"What sort of tests?"

"I'm not sure. He'll be back later, so you can ask him yourself." Her mum's face crumpled. "But I've got a horrible feeling it's something serious."

In that moment, Emily truly understood what it meant for someone's blood to run cold.

CHAPTER THIRTY-FOUR

"IS SHE STILL NOT ANSWERING HER PHONE?"
Melissa's tone was slightly accusatory towards Sophie, as if she didn't quite trust that she was telling the truth.

"No!" Sophie shot back, her frustration bubbling to the surface. "Just that text saying she had to leave for an emergency and that she'd explain later."

They were walking alongside the river that flowed from Dedham to Flatford. The meadows either side were thronged with tourists making the most of the sunshine and the picturesque countryside. On the river, rowing boats full of inept rowers kept passing by, with teenagers squealing as one of them invariably rocked it, threatening to tip all the occupants into the cold water.

"I wish she'd at least answer her phone to let us know what's happening," Melissa huffed, reaching out to break off a cowslip flower.

"I hope she's OK," Amy added.

Sophie sighed. Emily wasn't a drama queen, so she knew it must have been something important to make her dash off like that. She would call her when they got home to try to get some answers.

As they walked along, all deep in their own thoughts, Amy fell into step beside her. "Can I ask you something, Sophie?"

Sophie looked up at her in surprise. "Sure."

"Why have you and Steve never got married?"

Sophie raised her eyebrows. "Wow, where did that come from?"

"Just curious." Amy shrugged.

Sophie pondered the question. "I don't know. I've always thought we would get married one day. But somehow we've never got round to it. Never even discussed it, actually."

"Well, I think you should," Amy said emphatically. "And let's face it, we could all do with a really big party. I could organize it for you..." she began, her eyes sparkling with excitement. "My way of thanking you both."

Melissa caught up with them and linked her arm through Sophie's. "What's that about a party?"

"I was just telling Sophie that she and Steve should get married and that I should organize the party."

Melissa nudged Sophie. "She's right! We could all do with a big knees-up..."

Sophie shook her head and laughed. "It's not the best reason in the world to get married, just so that we can all have a big party."

"Well, obviously that's not the *only* reason," Melissa conceded.

"No, of course it's not," Amy agreed. "It's just that you two are so perfect together. It would be nice to celebrate your relationship and make it official."

"Don't get too carried away, Amy. There's one small thing you're forgetting..."

"What's that?"

Sophie shrugged. "He's never actually asked me."

Later that evening, Sophie opened the front door to let herself and Amy into the house. Steve was in the garden with the children, enjoying the last of the sunshine as they played a game of chase that seemed to have no rules and involve everyone madly chasing everyone else.

They dumped their bags and stood watching them through the open bi-fold doors that stretched across the back of the house, giggling at Theo, who squealed with excitement every time he managed to catch one of the others, apparently unaware that they were stopping to let him catch them, rather than the other way around.

"Steve's great with them, isn't he?" Amy nodded towards the garden, where Steve was now lying on the grass as all four children clambered over him. Suddenly, he let out an almighty roar and sat up, causing them all to let out blood-curdling screams and run in every direction. "You are a lucky, lucky lady, Sophie." Her tone was wistful, but she was smiling. "Especially when you compare him to Nick or Anton. They're not fit to lick his boots."

"He's going to miss Megan and George, Amy. And you."

Amy shook her head. "He'll be fine. We'll only be next door, hopefully."

"Are you definitely going to put an offer in, then?"

Amy threw Sophie a sheepish look.

"Oh," Sophie said, understanding immediately. "You already did..."

"It hasn't been accepted yet, but the estate agent thinks it will all go through."

"Why didn't you speak to us first? We would have helped you."

Amy nodded. "I know, that's why I didn't tell you about

it. I wanted to stand on my own two feet for the first time in my life."

"I can understand that," Sophie conceded.

"Plus," Amy added, "I thought you might try to change my mind. I couldn't risk it."

Just then, Steve noticed them and waved. Sophie waved back, feeling a surge of love for him. He never complained about her going away with the girls, meaning he was left to look after the children by himself. Then again, she suspected he loved it.

He walked towards them, handsome in his jeans and T-shirt. His face and arms were deeply tanned, his hair lightened by the sun.

"Welcome back, ladies," he said, bending to kiss Sophie. She loved that he was so much taller than her. It made her feel petite when she was anything but.

"You look like you're having fun." Sophie nodded towards the children, who showed no signs of tiring as they continued to race around the garden after each other. Not one of them seemed to have noticed that their mums had returned home.

Steve pulled a sarcastic face. "Always! Anyway, I could do with a cup of tea—I'm sure you could too."

"I'll do it!" Amy dashed off before anyone could protest.

Sophie took Steve's hand and they walked inside the house together. "Amy's got something to tell you..." she began. "I think it's best to tell him sooner, rather than later," she added when Amy gave her a panicky grimace.

Amy nodded reluctantly and looked up from the island in the centre of the room, where she was making the tea. "Hear me out before you react, Steve."

Steve gave her a puzzled look. "OK."

"I've decided that the time has come for me and the children to get a place of our own. To let you and Sophie reclaim this house for yourselves."

Immediately, Steve started to shake his head, but Amy put her hand up to stop him.

"I need to stand on my own two feet again, Steve. It's been incredible being here, but I always knew the day would come when we had to move on…"

Sophie watched Steve's face. The emotion was written in every line and crease of his skin. His mouth was slightly open and she could see his lip quivering. She tried to catch his eye to give him a reassuring smile, but he was staring at Amy in shock.

"So, I've found a house," Amy continued, her cheeks reddening as she spoke, all the while concentrating on making the cups of tea. "And I've put an offer in." She glanced up briefly.

Sophie felt Steve's shoulders sag as his whole body seemed to deflate. "Hear her out," Sophie urged, giving his hand a squeeze.

Amy smiled to herself. "We won't be going far… In fact, I'd say we'll probably see just as much of you as we do now."

Steve frowned and shook his head. "I doubt that." He sounded utterly despondent.

"That's what I said. But she's right…" Sophie motioned to Amy to continue.

"Because the house I've put in an offer for…is the house next door!" Amy finished with a flourish.

There was a short pause before Steve burst out laughing. "Ah, well, maybe that's not such a bad idea after all."

Amy beamed proudly. "And I'm going to set up my own catering business and Melissa thinks Mark Bailey will be my first celebrity client…and I'm going to hire a nanny who can look after my kids and yours so that you can carry on working…"

Amy stopped. "I'm gabbling. Sorry. I'm just excited." She gave
Sophie and Steve an apologetic look.

"Don't be sorry. It's great. Really great." Steve walked over
and gave Amy a hug. "I'm proud of you."

As they finally got into bed that night, Steve asked, "So
how was the weekend?"

Sophie wrapped her arms around his bare chest and kissed
him. "It was good, but I missed you."

"Liar!" He laughed, kissing her back.

"Actually, Emily had to dash off early this morning. Apparently, Jack had some kind of accident and was in hospital."

"Really? Is he hurt?"

Sophie shook her head. "Not badly, thank God. He got
knocked off his bike. Few bumps and bruises, I think."

"Phew." Steve visibly relaxed.

"I love that you're so concerned about him, Steve. You're
such a good man. Better than his real dad, that's for sure."

Steve looked at her quizzically. "What do you mean?"

"Anton. Emily discovered that he was still married. It's hit
her very hard. Actually, I suspected it all along but didn't want
to say anything in case I was wrong."

Steve nodded. "I vaguely remember him from university.
He seemed a bit of a creep back then. God knows why she
got involved with him."

"Anyway, forget about him," Sophie began, snuggling into
him. "Amy said something while we were away that's made
me think a lot about you and me."

"Really?" Steve looked instantly nervous. "What did she
say?"

Sophie looked up at him, wondering why they hadn't had
this conversation years ago. "She said we should get married."

"Oh, did she now?" Steve matched her jokey tone. "And what did you say to that?"

"I said that you'd never asked me…"

Steve smiled his long, slow, sexy smile. "I'm sure I must have asked you…"

"Nope." Sophie shook her head. She was smiling, but she could feel the tears welling up behind her eyes. She had never admitted it before, but she did feel a deeply buried sense of disappointment that he hadn't ever asked her. To begin with, she was just grateful that they were together, when they could so easily have broken up. But as the years went by, the yearning to formalize their commitment grew, especially once the children were born.

"Well, you've never asked me either…" Steve gave her a searching look.

Sophie shrugged. "I know, but maybe I'm a bit old-fashioned like that. Maybe I think it should be the man who proposes."

"Oh, really? You're not exactly a typical little housewife, Soph. I'm the one at home with the kids while you go out to work and earn all the money. Why shouldn't you be the one to ask me?"

There was a long pause as Sophie thought about it. "What would you say? If I did ask you?"

Steve smiled again, making her heart swell. "Why don't you ask me and find out?"

Sophie let out a low squeal of excitement. "Do you want me to get down on one knee?"

He laughed. "Of course…"

Sophie rolled her eyes but climbed out of bed and walked around to his side. She dropped to one knee and took his hand in hers, trying not to giggle. "Will you, Steve Montgomery, marry me?"

Steve beamed at her in delight. "How could I possibly turn down a naked proposal from the woman I love?"

Sophie glanced down. She had completely forgotten she was naked. "Is that a yes?"

Steve lifted the duvet and climbed out of bed. He pushed her gently down onto the rug she was kneeling on and kissed her. "As Mark Bailey might say on his talent show, 'It's a great big yes from me.'"

JUNE 2007

"Police in Portugal say they are continuing to follow up leads in the search for four-year-old British girl Madeleine McCann, who went missing from the family's apartment in Praia de Luz last month."

BEVERLY HILLS, LOS ANGELES

CHAPTER THIRTY-FIVE

EMILY GAZED UNSEEINGLY OUT OF THE CAR WIN-
dow, her mind whirring. She was in the back seat with Amy,
while Sophie and Melissa were in the front. Melissa was driving, as she had done all weekend. It was impressive how well
she knew her way around LA—she looked and acted like a
native, which wasn't surprising, considering how much time
she spent here. Emily felt pretty certain Melissa would end up
living here permanently one day fairly soon.

They were on the Pacific Coast Highway, heading for
Malibu. The view was breathtaking, with the road hugging
the miles and miles of wide, golden, sandy beaches border-
ing the deep blue ocean with its rolling waves crashing re-
lentlessly onto the shore.

It had been an almost perfect day. They had enjoyed breakfast by the pool, before lazing in the sunshine reading for a couple of hours. Then Melissa had driven them to Santa Monica,
where she had booked lunch for them at a breathtakingly pretty
Plantation-style hotel right on the beach. Now they were heading for Malibu, where Melissa had decided that they should try

their hand at surfing. Emily hadn't had the heart to remind her that she couldn't swim.

She had tried to throw herself into the weekend, but it was so, so hard. Every time she started to relax and enjoy herself, a heavy swell of dread would rise up inside her, reminding her that everything was essentially meaningless until Jack got well again.

★ ★ ★ ★ ★

"Leukaemia?" Sophie repeated, unable to compute what Emily had just said. "How can a healthy thirteen-year-old boy have leukaemia? That just doesn't seem possible."

Emily blew her nose. "I know. I keep hoping there's been some kind of terrible mistake, but there hasn't."

They were sitting opposite each other in a busy coffee bar near Emily's flat in south-east London. She had called Sophie a week after they got back from their weekend away and said she needed to talk. Sophie knew instantly it was something serious, but she had had no idea just how bad.

"But there's been such progress, hasn't there? In the treatment available now? The prognosis must be good?" Sophie tried to sound upbeat, despite her shock. She was already mentally rolling through the back catalogue of films she had made about children with cancer, to try to recall some of the positive stories.

Emily shrugged. She looked worn out and seemed to have aged several years in just one short week. There were purple shadows under her dark eyes and her normally olive skin had a grey tinge. "It's amazing how quickly you become an expert when you're faced with it. They do seem pretty positive and obviously he's in the best place," she said, her voice beginning to wobble, before she covered her face with her hands and began to sob again.

Sophie watched her, feeling utterly helpless. "Will he have chemo?"

Emily gathered herself and wiped her face with her tissue, which had long since disintegrated. She fished in her bag for another before replying. "Yes. Hopefully that will be enough."

Sophie took Emily's hand in hers. It felt cold and clammy. "What can I do to help? What can any of us do? Just say the word."

Emily took a deep, shuddery breath. "You can visit him. I think he's already getting bored of just me, Mum and Dad." She gave Sophie a watery smile. "And I don't know if you think it's right for the kids to come, but I think he'd really like that."

Sophie nodded vigorously. "Of course. And what about when he gets out of hospital? Do you want to come and stay with us?"

Emily shook her head. "Thanks, Soph, but there's no need. We'll be fine at our flat."

Sophie pictured Emily bringing Jack home to their cramped conversion flat, which required two steep flights of stairs to reach their front door. It seemed like a very bleak prospect. "Listen, now that Amy and the kids are moving out, we'll have loads of room. You know how much Emma adores Jack. It might do them both good." She gave Emily an encouraging smile. She desperately wanted to help in some way.

"But it wouldn't be fair on Steve..." Emily began to protest.

"I know Steve and I know that he'd be happy to help. We all would," she added. "Please, Em, give it some thought?"

Emily took another deep breath. "OK. I'll think about it."

"And how are you bearing up?" Sophie searched Emily's

face, thinking how desperately tired she looked. It wasn't surprising. After all, she had had two massive shocks in the space of a week.

Emily smiled wanly. "I'm OK. And I suppose there is one good thing to come out of all this…"

Sophie shook her head in admiration. How anyone could find an upside to such an awful situation was beyond her. "What's that?"

"It's made me get over the Anton situation quicker than I would ever have imagined… It certainly puts everything into perspective."

"Have you heard from him?"

"Oh, yes." Emily tutted and rolled her eyes. "He's left various voicemails begging my forgiveness. Claims he's confessed all to his wife and is moving out. Can't live without me, apparently."

Sophie smiled, relieved that Emily was able to laugh about it. It was just over a week since she had cried that she would never, ever get over him. "Have you returned any of the calls?"

"Nope." Emily looked up, her expression defiant. "I honestly don't care if I never see Anton Massey again."

Sophie thought, but didn't say, that she might have no choice in the matter. If Jack needed a bone marrow transplant, his father could be a match. She mentally batted away the thought. Hopefully, it wouldn't ever come to that.

★ ★ ★ ★ ★

He had seemed to be making such good progress initially. The doctors smiled when they spoke to her and told her that the signs were positive. And Jack really had seemed to be improving. He had struggled with losing his hair, but it was already growing back, curlier and darker than before, but growing nonetheless.

They had taken Sophie up on her offer to move in temporarily with her and Steve in Richmond. In truth, it was less of an offer and more of an order. Emily had been reluctant, but Sophie had insisted. And Jack had given her such a pleading look when she told him, that she just couldn't refuse. He had been through too much already. She didn't want to deny him anything that could help his recovery.

But even before the doctors confirmed it, she knew that he had had a relapse. She could sense it, even without the physical clues. She could tell just from looking into his eyes and from the slightly strange feel of his skin. Chemotherapy alone wasn't enough to cure him, they said. He needed a bone marrow transplant.

She hadn't yet told the others. She didn't want to spoil Sophie's hen weekend. But the knowledge was weighing heavily on her and she felt as though she was permanently on the brink of buckling under the strain.

"A sibling," said Jack's ridiculously young-looking consultant when Emily and her mum met with him, "would provide the best match."

Emily's mum's eyes had widened in despair. "But he hasn't got any siblings!" she cried, her face crumpling as she dissolved into tears, before looking at Emily with a confused expression. "Has he, Emily?"

Emily stayed dry-eyed, although her stomach lurched and her heart began to race as the implications of what the consultant was saying began to sink in. "Is that..." she began, clearing her throat nervously. "Is that the only option?"

The consultant shook his head. "No. It's not the only option. But it is the best option. If he doesn't have any siblings..."

he continued, eyeing Emily, as if he sensed that maybe that might not be the case, "we will test all other family members for a match. If we don't find one in the family, he will go on the national register and we may well find a match from a stranger. There are still plenty of options left open to us." He finished with a reassuring smile.

Emily nodded. She liked this consultant and trusted him. She turned to her mum, who had recovered her composure and was desperately trying to put on a brave face. "Mum, would you mind if I had a chat with Mr Carmichael alone?"

A brief flicker of doubt passed across her mum's face before she nodded furiously. "Of course, of course!"

Emily waited until her mum had gathered up her handbag and left the room before she addressed the consultant again. "If..." She paused, trying to work out how to phrase what she wanted to say. "If someone was a match because they were a relative—a sibling for example..."

The consultant nodded briefly and Emily could tell from his expression that he had seen and heard all of this before. It was probably an all-too-common occurrence.

"Would they be able to donate without having to be told they were a relative? Or without anyone else in the family having to be told?"

"They wouldn't *have* to be told," the consultant replied without missing a beat. He had definitely done this before. "But we would strongly recommend that they be told. Ultimately, the decision is that of the parents." He paused for a moment. "I understand that you are not in a relationship with Jack's biological father—is that right?"

Emily nodded. "Yes."

"And am I to take it from your earlier question that he doesn't know that he is the biological father?"

Emily hesitated before answering. "It's complicated."

"Right." The consultant pursed his lips. "Do you have any contact with him at all? Any way of getting in touch with him?"

Emily took a deep breath. "Yes," she said. "If it's absolutely necessary, I know where he is. I could get in contact with him."

The consultant nodded slowly. "Does he have any other children that you know of? Obviously, I'm thinking that they might provide a sibling match for Jack."

Emily looked down at her lap. "Yes," she said. "Two."

"In that case, I would strongly recommend telling him. Those two children represent the best chance for your son's recovery."

★ ★ ★ ★ ★

Emily watched the others from the beach, envying them their carefree laughter. She sometimes wondered if she would ever laugh again. She could feel her mood getting darker by the hour and even the breathtaking beauty of her surroundings couldn't lift it. Not being able to swim had been a handy excuse to duck out of surfing, but the truth was that even if she could, she wouldn't have been able to bring herself to join in the fun.

Sophie was a surprisingly good surfer. While Amy and Melissa tipped off their boards and slipped under the frothy, rolling waves time and time again, Sophie was able to ride the surf all the way to the shore. Emily felt a sudden spike of jealousy shoot through her as she watched Sophie wading back out to join the others, who were floundering about in the deeper water, trying to get back on their boards.

Life always seemed to go right for Sophie. She was rich, she had a highly successful career, she was about to marry the man she loved, and most of all, she had two perfect, healthy, happy children. It just didn't seem fair. For a split second, she felt only pure hatred for her. How had she managed to get it so wrong and Sophie get it so right?

As if she sensed her watching, Sophie surfed into the shore and scooped her board under her arm, before walking up the beach to join Emily. She dropped down onto the sand beside her and ran her hand through her long, wet hair. They didn't speak for a while as they watched Amy and Melissa tumbling into the water time after time.

"They're hopeless, aren't they?" Emily continued to stare straight ahead. "Not like you. You're a pro."

Sophie laughed. "Not quite. But growing up in Northern Ireland beside those amazing beaches meant you didn't have much of an excuse not to learn. It's a lot bloody colder there, though—at least here the sea's warm and the sun's shining."

"Yeah," Emily agreed, looking around her, trying to draw some enjoyment from the beauty of it all. But it was as if she was inside some kind of invisible bubble. She could see it all, but she couldn't *feel* it.

"I know this weekend has been hard for you," Sophie said, throwing Emily a sideways look. "But I'm so glad you came. It wouldn't have been the same without you."

Emily immediately felt bad about her earlier unkind thoughts towards Sophie. She was a good person and it wasn't her fault that she had led such a charmed life, while Emily staggered from one crisis to another. "I'm sorry I'm not more fun."

"Completely understandable." Sophie paused for a moment before continuing. "Look, I've been thinking, Em. Would you like us to postpone the wedding? Just until Jack's fully recovered and you're feeling a bit brighter?"

"God, no. Of course not." Despite herself, Emily was touched. Sophie was so giving, so unselfish, that she would even consider delaying her wedding to make Emily feel better. "You two have waited long enough already. I don't want you to put it off any more."

Sophie smiled. "Yes, but as we've waited this long, a bit longer wouldn't make much difference!"

Emily shook her head emphatically. "No, really. I'll be fine. *We'll* be fine," she said, trying to sound more positive than she felt. She still hadn't told the others that Jack needed a bone marrow transplant. She had met with the consultant only the previous Thursday and she couldn't find a way to tell them without completely ruining their trip.

"Is there something you're not telling us?" Sophie said now, as if reading her thoughts.

Emily desperately wanted to unload. To tell her everything. But she couldn't. It just wouldn't be fair. "No." She shrugged. "Just feeling a bit…low, I suppose. A bit overwhelmed."

"You'll feel better when we get home again. It was probably expecting too much of you to come with us on this weekend. But like I said, I'm so glad you're here. I wouldn't be able to enjoy it at all if you weren't." She reached out and put a hand on Emily's narrow back. "We're like the four Musketeers— one for all and all for one."

"Yup," agreed Melissa, who had come out of the sea and was now deftly tying her long braids into a knot on top of her head. "Sophie's right. It only really works if we're all together. Look what happened when you all decided to kick me out of the group back in Camber Sands that time! You were utterly miserable without me."

Emily couldn't help but smile and she threw Melissa a grateful look. She was such a tonic. She always knew how to deflect the conversation when it strayed into tricky territory or got too heavy.

Amy, who had also emerged from the sea, threw her towel onto the sand and stretched out her long, toned limbs. "I think you'll find you thoroughly deserved it, young lady. And I certainly wasn't miserable without you."

"Liar!" Melissa cried, picking up her towel and swiping it at Amy, who yelped in mock protest.

"Now that I think about it," Amy said, sitting back up and dusting off the specks of sand Melissa had flicked over her, "I should have been begging you to take him off my hands. It would have saved me a lot of grief in the long run—"

"OK, let's not go there…" Melissa cut her off quickly, her cheeks flushing slightly. "I don't need to be reminded what a fuck-up I was."

"What do you mean 'was'?" Sophie said, before they all burst out laughing.

Emily joined in. Sophie was right. Their group worked best when they were all together. Apart from Jack, these three women were the most important people in her life, and no matter how bad she felt, being with them always helped to make her feel better. She would force herself to enjoy what was left of this wonderful weekend in this incredible place and try to shut out of her mind what she needed to do when she got back to England. For a couple of days at least, everything else could wait.

CHAPTER THIRTY-SIX

〜〜〜〜〜〜〜〜〜〜〜〜〜〜〜〜〜〜

MELISSA HELPED HERSELF TO HER THIRD CROISSANT, before breaking off a large piece, smothering it with home-made strawberry jam and popping it into her mouth. Sophie watched her in fascination. "How on earth you manage to stay so slim when you eat so much is an absolute mystery. If I ate anything like the amount you do, I'd be enormous."

Melissa shrugged, unconcerned. "I have a fast metabolism."

"You are *so* LA, Melissa!" Amy laughed, shaking her head.

"Well, it's the truth!" Melissa protested, polishing off the rest of the croissant in two huge bites.

Amy gave her a sceptical look. "I'd say it's more likely to be all the sex you're having…"

Sophie frowned. "Really? Who are you having lots of sex with?"

"I'm not!" Melissa shot back, blushing furiously and shoot-ing a scowl in Amy's direction. She didn't want any mention of her relationship with Mark to spoil Sophie's hen weekend, which Melissa had been planning for months. And it wasn't as if she was in a relationship with him anyway… Well, not a *real* one.

★ ★ ★ ★ ★

"I think we should go to LA together from now on." They were in Mark's sumptuous offices in central London, the hub of his by-now global TV empire. He was sitting behind the huge, heavy wooden desk, which she often teased him was modelled on the American president's desk in the Oval Office, not that she'd ever seen it, apart from on *The West Wing*.

"Don't we already go together anyway?" Melissa was watching a DVD of the latest episode of their American singing talent show, which had just been delivered. Mark was supposed to be watching it too, but he kept being distracted by calls and texts on his mobile. She was pointedly trying not to take too much notice of who was calling.

"I meant, we should travel together, rather than just meeting each other there." He flashed her a flirtatious, perfect white smile. Melissa looked at him and pondered how much he had changed physically since the days when she'd known him as a lowly record executive. Although he had lost weight, had developed a six-pack thanks to his daily workouts with a personal trainer and now had suspiciously fewer wrinkles, she often thought she preferred the old Mark.

Back then, he smoked too much, drank too much and, like her, probably did too many drugs, but she had always thought he was gorgeous and great fun. He had sleepy-looking dark brown eyes, framed with long black lashes, and a throaty, slightly filthy laugh to complement his wickedly sharp sense of humour.

Melissa pulled her eyes away from him and pretended to concentrate on the show she was watching, but a tiny thrill of excitement passed through her. This was the first time Mark had really acknowledged that there was something going on between them. Usually, they arrived separately in LA and met up at the hotel. She would go to his room, supposedly to catch up on work matters, then invariably she would end up spending the night with him.

But unlike any relationship she had ever had before, it was about so much more than sex with Mark. She would never, ever admit it to anyone, but over the past year she had been steadily falling in love with him. She knew it was futile. Mark had a string of beautiful women at his beck and call and he had never led her to believe that their relationship was in any way exclusive. But she couldn't help it. He was like a drug to her and it wasn't a drug that she wanted to give up.

"So…what do you think?" he prompted, jolting her out of her thoughts.

"I thought you were always paranoid about being photographed with any women…"

Mark shrugged. "You're a work colleague. Nothing more." There was a mischievous glint in his eye.

"So is Sophie." Melissa met his gaze with a mischievous look of her own.

Mark smiled. "Yes, that's true, darling, but as Sophie runs the UK side of the business, there's no need for her to travel to LA every couple of weeks the way we do."

Melissa loved it when he talked about "we." "Well, I'm not sure what difference it would make for us to travel together…" she began, although in truth she loved the idea and was never in a million years going to turn him down.

"The difference is that we'd be together for the whole trip. I like that thought." He flashed her another smile and held her gaze with his beautiful, liquid brown eyes.

Melissa groaned inwardly. She wished he didn't have such a hold over her. She knew she ought to put a stop to it. Tell him she wasn't going to be used any more. But the truth was she kept hoping he might one day feel the same way about her as she did about him.

She had never let Sophie know how she was feeling because she felt sure she knew exactly what Sophie would say. *"Don't waste your time."* Or *"You'll only get hurt."* And she would be right. But Melissa didn't want to hear it. She turned towards Mark and gave him her most seductive smile. "I'd love to."

After those first few heady trips together, Melissa also found herself spending more and more time at Mark's house in London. He had just bought a magnificent town house in Holland Park, which wasn't far from her two-bedroom flat in Kensington.

He had developed a habit of calling her late at night and telling her he couldn't sleep, before begging her to come over. A little voice inside her head told her it was nothing more than a booty call and she should have more respect for herself than to go running every time he clicked his fingers. But she just didn't have the willpower to resist him.

It was as she was sneaking out of the house early one morning after one of his calls, that she came face-to-face with Amy, who was unpacking a vast array of food in the kitchen. True to his word, Mark had put a lot of work Amy's way and booked her to cater for numerous dinner parties, which had in turn thrown her into the path of other potential clients. As a result, her fledgling business was already booming.

"Oh!" Amy gasped, putting her hand to her chest as Melissa tiptoed past the kitchen, wearing just her underwear. "Melissa! God, you gave me a fright!" she added, relaxing as she recognized who it was, as if it was the most natural sight in the world to see her friend semi-naked in someone else's hallway.

Melissa froze in horror, holding her breath, hoping it would somehow make her less conspicuous.

As she watched her, Amy smiled to herself and continued unpacking, before realization dawned and her head suddenly snapped up again. "Melissa?" she repeated. "What the hell are you doing here?" As she spoke, her eyes slid down to the scrunched-up pile of clothes Melissa was clutching.

Melissa closed her eyes and groaned. "Shit," she hissed, dropping the pile of clothes onto the wooden hall floor and fishing out her T-shirt, which she quickly slipped over her head. "I could just as easily ask you the same thing," she mumbled, knowing she was trying to buy time to think up a plausible excuse.

"Um…how about I'm here to do this?" Her voice heavy with sarcasm, Amy swept her hand over the granite worktop covered with food.

Melissa pulled on her jeans and padded into the kitchen, still doing up her zip. "Look, Amy, don't mention to Sophie that you've seen me here, will you?"

Amy adopted a disapproving expression. "I don't like keeping things from Sophie. It makes me feel disloyal."

Melissa rolled her eyes. "It's not being disloyal. It's protecting her feelings."

Amy looked doubtful. "Why would Sophie care whether you're sleeping with Mark or not? She's very happy with Steve."

"I know that." Melissa tried to keep her tone as patient as possible. "It's just that sometimes she gets a bit possessive… In a work sense," she added, seeing that Amy was about to object. "I just think there's no need to mention it to her."

Amy sighed. "I don't know… It feels wrong, somehow."

"Look," Melissa began, changing tack. "Why do you think Mark gave you so much work when he didn't even know anything about you?"

Amy didn't reply, although she squinted slightly, as if trying to work out what Melissa was up to.

"It was because I asked him to. It was a favour to me." Melissa hoped Amy wouldn't argue that Mark would have done exactly the same for Sophie.

"I know…and I'm very grateful to you." Amy resumed her unpacking, looking flustered.

"So if you want to repay that favour…maybe you could promise not to say anything to Sophie? Or Emily. Or anyone, actually."

Amy smiled to herself suddenly and Melissa exhaled with relief. She knew she'd won her over.

"Oh, OK. But I really do think you're making more out of it than you need to. You're a grown-up. What you get up to in your own spare time is up to you."

"I agree." Melissa swung her leather jacket over her shoulders and pushed her feet into her strappy sandals. "But probably best to say nothing all the same."

"I've agreed, haven't I?" Amy retorted. "So…how long has it been going on, then? Are you and Mark an item?"

Melissa had turned to leave, but she stopped and walked over to the counter where Amy was standing. "No," she said, leaning her elbows on the worktop.

Amy looked at her carefully. "But you'd like to be?"

"No," Melissa replied automatically. "He's not the type to settle down. We're just having fun."

Amy nodded. "Well, as long as you're both having fun. The problems start when one is keener than the other." She glanced up at Melissa. "And he's a bit of a player, Melissa…"

Melissa could feel herself reddening. "I know that!" Suddenly, a horrible thought occurred to her. "He hasn't…made a move on you, has he?" Melissa wouldn't blame him. Amy was looking radiant at the moment, and if she had been ten years younger, she could easily have had a career as a top model.

Amy laughed. "No! Of course not. I'm far too tall for him…" She winked at Melissa, who could feel the relief flooding through her. "But," she continued, "he does seem to have quite a few girlfriends… Doesn't that bother you?"

"No," Melissa lied, unable to meet Amy's eye. "We're both free agents and can see whoever we want." She didn't mention that she didn't see anyone apart from Mark. "We're just friends with benefits," she added breezily.

Amy raised her eyebrows. "Well, good luck to you, sweetie. As long as you promise not to fall in love with him, I'm very happy for you."

Melissa held up three fingers. "I promise. Brownie's honour."

★ ★ ★ ★ ★

"So, how do you want to spend your last day in LA, then, Sophie?"

"Well," Sophie began, looking around the breakfast table, preparing for the reaction to what she was about to say, "I would like to go shopping for my wedding dress."

"What!" They exploded in unison.

"Surely you haven't left it this late to buy the most important dress of your life?" Melissa gasped. "You're the most organized person I know—and a total control freak, at that…"

"Gee, thanks!" Sophie muttered.

"So, why would you leave getting your dress until the last minute? It doesn't make sense." Melissa sat back and frowned suspiciously at Sophie.

"It makes perfect sense to me," Sophie said, enjoying the moment. Melissa was right—she rarely did anything spontaneous and was always super-organized. "I wanted you all to be with me when I bought it and that hasn't really been a possibility, what with Amy always busy at weekends, catering for rock stars and tycoons, and of course, Emily having to spend so much time in hospital with Jack..." She glanced at Emily, who nodded her acknowledgement.

"So," she continued, "I thought we could get it here in LA, while we're all together."

"That's such a lovely idea, Soph." Amy gave Sophie a wide smile. "I'm so chuffed that you wanted us with you."

"Of course it's a great idea," Melissa agreed, eyeing a fourth croissant contemplatively. "It's just a bit of a surprise, that's all. Right, well, I will just finish this last pastry..." She picked up the croissant and took a huge bite, causing buttery flakes to drop all over her chin. "And then we can go shopping. Literally, my idea of heaven."

"So, shall we try Rodeo Drive first?" Sophie glanced at Melissa, marvelling at her driving skills, as she sped expertly through the wide boulevards of Beverly Hills. She had been to LA many times for work, but she didn't particularly like the place and would certainly never consider living here, unlike Melissa, who seemed as though she already did.

"Nope," Melissa retorted, flashing Sophie a mischievous grin.

"But...where, then?"

"Leave it to me. I know exactly where to go." Melissa took her hand off the wheel and tapped the side of her nose conspiratorially.

They drove in silence for a few more minutes, before Melissa pulled into a car park underneath what looked to her like an ordinary office block. "Where are we?" Sophie hissed. "I'm not hoping to buy stationery supplies!"

"Shh!" Melissa opened the car window and leaned out to speak into an intercom. "Hi there, Geneva. It's Melissa!"

"Melissa Williams?" replied a woman's voice, the line cracking slightly with static. "How lovely to hear from you! Wait— are you in the parking garage?"

"Yes. Look, I know we don't have a reservation…" Melissa began as Sophie started to giggle at her sudden transatlantic drawl. "But a very, very dear friend of mine is getting married and I would really love her to be able to look at your dresses. We're going home to the UK this evening, so it's kinda now or never!"

There was a snort of laughter from Amy in the back seat. "She can't be serious!" she whispered to Emily, who was also sniggering quietly.

There was a tiny pause on the other end of the line, before the tinny voice replied, "*Sure* she can! Why don't you park and come right on up?"

"Melissa…" Sophie gripped her arm in panic. "I'm not sure this is such a good idea. I don't want to feel pressurized into buying something. Can't we just go to Barney's or somewhere instead?"

Melissa drove through the barrier. "You are not getting your wedding dress from bloody Barney's! Don't worry," she soothed, patting Sophie's leg reassuringly. "Trust me."

As soon as the lift doors opened, Sophie relaxed. In front of her was a vast, sumptuous room decorated with exquisite taste and filled with the scent of lilies and luxuriously scented candles. Along every wall hung rows and rows of bridal gowns in various shades of white, pink and cream. She stepped onto the deep, plush carpet, hardly daring to breathe, in case she broke the spell.

She needn't have worried. "Geneva!" Melissa squealed,

throwing herself at a stunningly attractive, tall, slim black woman, who looked like she had just stepped off a catwalk, wearing a white designer trouser suit and eye-wateringly high black stilettos.

"Melissa, honey, you are a bad, bad girl! Why didn't you call me up if you were in town?" Geneva wagged her finger at Melissa mockingly.

"Sorry, honey, I couldn't." Melissa motioned towards the three others, standing shyly behind her. "This is my friend Sophie's hen weekend and it was my job to organize it."

Geneva fixed her huge dark eyes on Sophie and gasped prettily. "Her *hen* weekend?"

Melissa nodded. "Yup."

"So…you mean she's getting married pretty soon?"

"Yup." Melissa shrugged and threw her hands up in exasperation. "One month's time…"

"OK." Geneva was instantly businesslike as she fixed Sophie with a long, appraising stare that made her instantly regret dressing in jeans and a T-shirt. "In that case, let's get started!"

While Geneva ushered Sophie into a changing room and ordered her to strip, Melissa instantly became like a child in a toy shop, as she danced excitedly from dress to dress, picking them up and holding them against her tiny, perfect frame.

"Look at this one!" she cried, sashaying into the changing room with a fussy, lace concoction that would have looked a million dollars on Melissa but would have made Sophie look like a giant toilet-roll cover.

"Um, I don't think so," Sophie said tactfully as she stood in her underwear, waiting for Geneva to reappear.

"Melissa!" Amy shouted from outside in the salon, where she was lounging on a chaise longue, sipping a glass of champagne. "We're here to get Sophie a wedding dress, not you!"

Melissa stuck her bottom lip out. "Doesn't mean I can't try them too, though, does it?" She looked up at Sophie for approval.

Sophie grimaced. "I'd rather you didn't—there isn't a dress in here that wouldn't look better on you than it does on me."

"Oh, now, honey, that's just where you're wrong," drawled Geneva, returning to the changing room with an armful of dresses, which she hung neatly from every available hook.

Sophie scanned the dresses she'd chosen for her. All of them were strapless. "I'm not sure strapless is the right look for me." Sophie gave Geneva a doubtful look. "I don't have the arms for it…"

But Geneva either hadn't heard her or was choosing to ignore her, because before Sophie could object, she was manhandling her into one of the gowns. It was the first time she had ever been dressed by someone taller than her, who didn't make her feel like a lumpy giant, and Sophie began to feel a frisson of excitement as Geneva expertly buttoned the gown and smoothed it down over her hips with a flourish. "There, that's the one," she said as she stood back to admire her handiwork.

"But it's only the first one I've tried!"

Geneva nodded. "I know. But you'll choose this one. Here, step into these shoes," she ordered, slipping Sophie's feet into some exquisitely dainty, crystal-encrusted sandals.

"Can I see?" Sophie tried to open the curtain to get to the mirror, but Geneva blocked her way.

"Just a minute." She reached out and grabbed Sophie's long, thick hair and twisted it deftly into a knot on top of her head, securing it with a beautiful, diamond-encrusted clip. "There. Now you can look."

Sophie stepped once more onto the thick, pale carpet and walked out into the room where Melissa, Emily and Amy were all reclining on separate chaises. One by one, they sat up and their mouths dropped open.

"Oh, Sophie." Amy put her hand over her mouth as she let out a gasp. "You look absolutely beautiful."

"You do…" Emily agreed, smiling at Sophie like a proud mother. "Really stunning."

"What do you think, Liss?" Sophie turned to Melissa, who was uncharacteristically quiet.

"I think," Melissa said, standing up and raising her champagne flute towards Sophie, "that there isn't one single dress in here that would look as good on me as that one does on you."

Sophie could feel her eyes filling with tears. She had never felt like a great beauty. She had always compared herself unfavourably with the others, feeling bigger, lumpier, uglier. But as she twirled in front of the giant, gilt mirror, for the first time in her life, she was prepared to admit that she looked almost beautiful.

JULY 2007

"The wait is over for millions of Harry Potter fans around the world, as the seventh, and final, book in the series, *Harry Potter and the Deathly Hallows*, is released tonight."

PORTSTEWART, NORTHERN IRELAND

CHAPTER THIRTY-SEVEN

SOPHIE'S EYES FLICKERED OPEN AS THE MISTY morning light began to make its way over the top of the curtains and into the room. It took her a couple of minutes to get her bearings as she tried to remember where she was. She smiled to herself as realization dawned. She was in her old bedroom in her parents' house in Portstewart, on the north coast of Northern Ireland.

She threw back her single duvet, thinking how thin and cheap it felt compared to the expensive duck down version she had at home, yet it was so comfortingly familiar all the same. It had been a long time since she had slept in this bed, but it was almost as if her body had memorized every contour and spring in the mattress and it was the first unbroken night's sleep she had had in years.

She walked to the window and drew back the pale pink linen curtains that she could still remember choosing when she was fourteen and had persuaded her parents to redecorate. Immediately, her heart lifted as she looked out at the view of Portstewart Strand, stretching for miles towards the emerald-green hills beyond, like a wide, sandy version of the Yellow

Brick Road beside the wild, rolling Atlantic Ocean. The sky was pale blue, smeared with lilac and orange, suggesting that it was going to be a warm, clear day. She had planned for it not to be, after the relentless rain of the past three months. But she felt thrilled that the sun would be shining on such a special day. It felt like a good omen.

On the door of the heavy pine wardrobe hung her wedding dress, zipped carefully into a protective cover. Melissa had persuaded Geneva to let Sophie take the same one she had tried on, by promising to get Geneva an audition for the American version of the singing show she was working on. "Is she good?" Sophie had asked, picturing Mark's reaction if she was terrible.

Melissa had waved her hand dismissively. "Good enough. Mark will be fine, if that's what you're worrying about."

Sophie had nodded. "If he's not fine about her singing, he'll certainly be fine about her appearance. She's absolutely gorgeous—he'll probably start dating her!"

"No, he won't!" Melissa had retorted, her dark eyes suddenly fierce.

Sophie had looked at her curiously. "Why do you care?"

"I don't… It's just…" Melissa had hesitated.

"Geneva's way too tall for Mark!" Amy had leaned forward from the back seat. "They'd look ridiculous together."

"Yes," Melissa had agreed, giving Amy a grateful look in the rear-view mirror. "That's what I meant."

Sophie unzipped the protective cover and ran her hand over the gown inside. It was a strapless white silk sheath, which was very plain, but Sophie thought it was the most beautiful dress she had ever seen. There was something about the way it was cut that made it look as if it had been created especially for her body. There were no bulges, no creases and definitely no straining buttons—just a perfect silhouette.

The children's voices floated upstairs from the kitchen, where they were already cooking breakfast with her mum. Sophie smiled to herself. They didn't see that much of her parents, so when they did, it made it feel like more of a treat. Her mum especially spoilt them rotten, but Sophie never objected. It was exactly how grannies were supposed to be.

She zipped up the bag as lovingly as if she was dressing a newborn baby and made her way out of the room and down the stairs. She had offered to buy her parents a new house when she first started to make serious money, but they had politely declined, saying no amount of money could buy a view as good as theirs.

They had a point. From every large window, there were spectacular views of the beach, the sea and the craggy little islands dotted in the distance. The colours changed constantly with the colour of the sky and it was impossible to either re-create it or become bored by it.

"Well, good morning, bride-to-be!" Her mum turned to give Sophie an excited grin as she walked into the large, airy kitchen.

"Mummy, me and Granny are making special wedding pancakes!" Emma was perched up on the granite worktop beside the hob, patiently holding a plate out for Sophie's mum to serve the pancakes she was cooking.

"How lovely! You are such a good girl, Emma." Sophie planted a kiss on top of Emma's silky blond head.

"She is," her mum agreed, giving Emma a proud smile. "She's been soooo helpful." Only Sophie picked up the faint trace of sarcasm in her mum's voice. She could well imagine just how "helpful" Emma had been.

"I'm helping too!" Sophie looked over at Theo, who was sitting at the big oak table in another part of the kitchen, shovelling the last bit of a pancake into his mouth. He had a suspiciously Nutella-like moustache on his top lip.

Sophie laughed and walked over to scoop him up, covering his face in kisses, tasting the sugar that was stuck to his skin as she did so. "I don't think scoffing them counts as helping, little love," she told him, putting him back down on the chair and sitting on the one beside him.

"So…" Her mum put a plate of fresh pancakes in the middle of the table and sat down opposite Sophie, smiling at her with eyes that were the same as hers, with just a few more lines around the edges. "How are you feeling?"

"I feel like I wonder why I didn't do this years ago." Sophie helped herself to a pancake and sprinkled some sugar on it. "I can't wait to marry him."

"Yes, well, better late than never, I suppose." Sophie's mum looked at Emma and Theo, who were busily tucking into their pancakes either side of Sophie. "It's a bit different to our day… Back then, having your own children at your wedding would have been unthinkable. Now it's the norm." She gave a rueful shrug.

"Amy did it the 'right' way and look how that worked out."

Her mum nodded. "Aye, that was a bad old business, for sure. But that's not typical. Georgina got married first and it worked out all right for her."

Sophie thought, but didn't say, that her older sister Georgina's marriage to Shaun was a success because they were both as boring as each other, along with their two boring sons, who had followed their parents into dull jobs in the civil service, to nobody's surprise. There was absolutely nothing about Georgina's life that she envied or wanted to emulate.

Sophie looked at both children fondly. "I'm glad the kids will be there. And at least we've got our ready-made bridesmaids and pageboys!"

Emma and Megan were to be the bridesmaids, while Theo and George were the pageboys. Sophie had asked Jack too, but he had laughed and said, "Thanks, but no, thanks."

As it turned out, he was too ill to travel anyway. Sophie had told Emily she understood if she couldn't make it either, but Emily was adamant that she would be there. "Mum and Dad are glad to be able to look after him. They like to be needed."

"Will Daddy be here soon?" Emma looked up at Sophie. She was such a daddy's girl. The deep bond that she and Steve had developed when she was a baby was stronger than ever, even though she was now eight years old. There was a time when Sophie had resented it. Had felt pushed out of their little bubble. But it was hard to remember now. Now she felt only pride that they had such a close relationship.

And Theo had definitely helped to balance the books. Just as Steve and Emma shared a special bond, so did she and Theo. He had come along just when she needed him most and she sometimes thought he had saved her sanity. Unlike her difficult first few months with Emma, she had connected with Theo instantly and could see so much of herself in him. They were like two sides of the same coin.

"No, we're meeting Daddy at the church," she said, smoothing the hair back on Emma's face. "By tradition, the groom isn't really supposed to see the bride before the ceremony."

"Not that there's much tradition going on today," Sophie's mum muttered.

Sophie ignored her. "That's why he stayed at the hotel with the others."

"Poor Daddy." Emma shook her head sadly.

"Why 'poor Daddy'?" Sophie gave Emma a quizzical look. Steve, Emily, Amy and Melissa were all staying in a very swanky hotel resort a few miles outside the town. He certainly wasn't slumming it.

"Because he doesn't get to eat Granny's pancakes, silly!" Emma said as both Sophie and her mum burst out laughing.

CHAPTER THIRTY-EIGHT

~~~~~~~~~~

AMY PROPPED HERSELF ON HER ELBOW AND looked across at Emily, who was staring fixedly up at the ceiling from her bed, her eyes almost crazed with tiredness. "Are you OK, Em?"

She wondered if Emily had slept at all. Every time Amy had woken in the night, Emily had been lying in the same, strange, fixed position, with her arms crossed over her chest. It was disturbing yet fascinating.

"I'm fine." Emily's voice was as robotic as her stare.

The two of them were sharing a room. Megan and George were flying in with their male nanny, Dean, that morning, as Megan had had a school concert and had insisted she couldn't miss the previous night.

Dean had started working for Amy just after she moved into her new house and she now couldn't imagine life without him. He was a thirty-year-old Kiwi, who had planned to travel the world but had fallen in love with London and had trained as a nanny to support himself.

Amy had booked a triple room for herself, Emily and Melissa, but Melissa had declared that she would prefer to have a room of her own, so that she could "get a good night's sleep before the wedding."

Only Amy knew the truth. Which was that she would barely be getting any sleep, as she would be spending the night with Mark. He had also flown in for the wedding the previous night. Amy was becoming increasingly worried about Melissa. Despite Melissa's many protestations and promises that she wouldn't, Amy could see that she had fallen for Mark completely.

Amy understood why. Mark was utterly beguiling and charming—in some ways very similar to how Nick had been when she first met him, but without the psychotic tendencies. He was generous, kind and unswervingly loyal to his friends. But he was also a ruthless businessman and a confirmed commitment-phobe. She was fairly certain he wouldn't be asking Melissa to marry him any time soon, no matter how much she willed it to happen.

"The trouble is," she had told Melissa, "he regularly sees other people, while you only see him. Maybe you should find another man. Be a bit less available. See if it makes him jealous and spurs him into action."

Melissa had sighed. "But it's not that easy, Amy. I don't really meet that many men who aren't gay or already married. And if I'm honest, I'm not interested in sleeping with anyone else…"

"Well, you've certainly changed your tune," Amy had replied, giving Melissa a sly look. "And don't forget you promised me not to fall in love with him."

"I'm not in love with him!" Melissa had spat back unconvincingly. "I'm just…enjoying him, that's all."

But Amy knew it was a lot more than that. She loved Melissa like a sister. She wanted her to find lasting happiness and she wanted her to have kids before it was too late. But she didn't think she'd be doing either of those things with Mark.

"Shall we go down to breakfast?" she asked Emily, climbing out of bed and walking over to the window. Outside, in one direction, manicured lawns gave way to a magnificent, lush golf course, where several golfers were already out enjoying the uncharacteristically sunny Irish weather. In the other direction, sheer white cliffs plunged into a wild, deep, blue sea.

"I'm not hungry."

Amy turned to look at Emily with a frown and padded barefoot over to her bed. She sank down onto the mattress beside her and took her rigid hand in hers. "Tell me what's wrong, Emily."

Emily's eyes briefly found Amy's before sliding away again. "I can't."

"You can." Amy was emphatic. "You have always been there for me, Em. When I was lower than I could ever imagine being. Let me be there for you now. Let me help."

Tears pooled in Emily's dark eyes. "I can't," she repeated, her voice heavy with misery. "I can't tell anyone. It's too... awful."

Amy shook her head. "There is nothing you could possibly say that would shock me, Em. We have been through so much together and we're still here. Still best friends." She gave Emily's hand a squeeze. "Nothing will ever change that."

Emily looked at her again as a tear spilled over her lashes and ran down the side of her face, where it dissolved into the snow-white pillowcase. "I wish that we could turn back time. Undo the things we've done." Her voice quavered as she spoke.

"We all wish that." Amy gave a bitter laugh. "My God, the number of times I've wished I could go back to the day I first met Nick and walk in the other direction so that our paths never crossed." She paused for a second before continuing. "I know you probably feel the same way about Anton…"

Emily didn't reply.

"But what happens to us shapes who we are, Em. In a weird way I'm sort of glad about what I went through with Nick. I think I'm a better, stronger person because of it."

Emily blinked back the tears that were about to fall and sat up, pulling her knees to her chest and looking up at Amy. "I don't think you're a better person, Amy. You've always been the best person I know…"

Amy smiled, glad that she seemed to have got through to her at last. "Thank you. Although that's rubbish, obviously."

"But," Emily continued, "you're right. You are much stronger. I feel like I've gone the opposite way. The worse things get, the weaker I become. I used to be so tough… Do you remember what I was like?"

Amy nodded. "I do. You were unbelievably tough. Scary, sometimes, if the truth be known."

"I don't know what's happened to me." Emily bent forward again, as if a heavy weight was pressing on her shoulders.

"I know what's happened to you." Amy rubbed Emily's back gently. "You have a son who's been very, very ill. That's what's happened to you. It must be the hardest thing imaginable to have to watch him suffer…" Amy broke off, contemplating the horror of what Emily had been through. "Everyone would struggle with it. Regardless of how tough you are. But the good news is that he's had the treatment and he will get better. You have to hold on to the positives, Emily. He's going to be OK."

"No," Emily said, without looking up. "He's not."

Amy's insides lurched. There was something about Emily's

tone that frightened her. "But...I thought... I thought he was in remission."

Emily shook her head. "I thought so too. But the chemo hasn't worked. It's not enough. He needs a bone marrow transplant."

Amy sat back in shock, unable to speak for several seconds, as a million thoughts ran through her head. "But he'll get one, right? Everyone can be tested... You, your mum and dad... Someone's bound to be a match."

Slowly, wearily, as if the effort was almost too much for her, Emily lifted her head. "He needs a sibling."

"Oh." Amy nodded slowly as understanding dawned. She could see why Emily was reluctant. It would involve getting back in touch with Anton and persuading him to get his two daughters tested. "Well," she said finally, trying to sound upbeat, "at least he's got two siblings. It would be so much worse if he didn't."

Emily closed her eyes and rested her head against the head-board. She looked defeated.

"Look," Amy began, feeling a tiny prickle of frustration. "If you need to get in touch with Anton, that's what you'll have to do, Em. If it's what Jack needs, then you'll have to bury your own feelings about him. He could be the key to saving Jack's life."

"It's not that simple, Amy."

"No. I can see that, but it might be the only option." Amy tried to think furiously if there was any other way around it. But there didn't seem to be one. Anton's daughters would have to be tested. "Does Anton have to tell them what it's for? Maybe he could just say it's for an old friend's son and he wants to help."

Emily shook her head despondently. Then she opened her

eyes and fixed Amy with a look of utter despair. "You don't understand."

Amy frowned, feeling wounded. "I do understand, Em. I understand that you don't want anything to do with Anton after what happened, but he's Jack's father. I'm sure he'd want to do whatever he could to help."

Emily closed her eyes again. "You don't understand, Amy." There was a long pause as Emily took a deep breath before continuing. "Anton isn't Jack's father."

CHAPTER THIRTY-NINE

MELISSA STEPPED OUT OF THE SHOWER AND reached for the fluffy white towel hanging over the heated towel rail. She wrapped it around herself and peered into the giant mirror above the sink, examining her skin. She was starting to get crow's feet and a few lines. Maybe she needed to start looking after her skin a bit better.

"Well, aren't you a sight for sore eyes." Mark emerged naked from the bedroom and wrapped his arms around her, smiling at their joint reflection.

Melissa held his sleepy-eyed gaze, wishing she could turn off the feelings she had for him. Amy was right. She had fallen for him hook, line and sinker. And worse—he knew it. She so desperately wanted to play hard to get. To make him work harder for her. But she just didn't know how.

She had never been one of those women who could play it cool. All her life she had lurched from one bed to another, searching for love and affection, always hoping that sex would fill the void. But it never had. Until now. Mark was different. Yes, theirs was a very highly sexual relationship, but she did feel loved by him too.

She tried to ignore that he was so much older than her and that maybe he was some kind of substitute father figure. That was just too weird. No, she loved him in anything but a fatherly way. "Good morning. You're up early. For you."

Mark's velvety chocolate-brown eyes crinkled in amusement. "We could go back to bed if you want…"

"No!" Melissa turned in his arms so that she was facing him. "We need to make sure we're there on time today. It'll give Sophie a nice surprise that you're not two hours late like you normally are."

Mark bent and kissed her on the top of her nose. "I always think being late is very thoughtful. It means your loved ones never have to worry about you if you're not there on time."

"Oh, really? And am I one of your 'loved ones'?" Melissa rolled her tongue on the word "loved," hoping to disguise the seriousness of her question.

Mark's brow furrowed as he pretended to think about it. "Um, yes. One of them, anyway."

Melissa tutted and dodged out of his embrace, striding into the bedroom. She knew he was joking. She just wished he didn't have the power to hurt her so much.

"Hey, sweetheart, what's wrong?" Mark followed her into the bedroom and watched her as she sat at the dressing table, smoothing moisturizer onto her cheeks and blinking back tears.

"Nothing."

Mark came and sat on the bed. "Come on. This isn't like you. You might as well tell me what's wrong."

Melissa looked at him in the reflection of the dressing-table mirror. "What are we doing, Mark?"

Mark blinked slowly. "We're having fun. Aren't we?" He

raised his eyebrows and tilted his head slightly as he asked the question.

Melissa put down the moisturizer. "Yes. It's just..." She could feel her heart racing as she tried to pluck up the courage to say what she wanted to say. "It's just that I think I might want a bit more than that."

"Ah." Mark leaned back slightly and nodded. "I see."

There was an awkward silence. Melissa considered filling it by telling him that she was joking. That she had just wanted to see how he'd react, but she somehow felt that this was the right moment to find out where she stood. Whether she had any kind of a future with him. "What about you, Mark? Do you ever feel that?"

Mark's eyes slid away from hers. She could almost feel him squirming inside. "Um, sometimes. Maybe. I'm not sure."

Melissa watched him, drinking him in. She really loved him. He made her laugh. He made her feel special. He was everything she had ever wanted in a man. She couldn't imagine putting an end to whatever it was they had together. But she couldn't carry on like this either. It would destroy her.

"I think that answers my question." Her voice dropped to a whisper and she couldn't hold back the tears as they rolled unstoppably down her face.

Mark came and knelt beside her, wrapping his arms around her, rocking her gently as she cried. "Don't cry, darling. Listen, I love being with you. I think you're wonderful."

Melissa nodded and sniffed. He had never told her he loved her. Even now when it was all she needed to hear. "I think you're wonderful too."

"Well, then, why the tears?" He stroked her hair tenderly.

"Because I'm in love with you, Mark. And you're not in love with me."

Mark shook his head, looking perplexed. "I told you, I love being with you, I really do."

Melissa gave a half laugh. "I know. But that's not the same as loving me."

Mark opened his mouth to speak again, but Melissa put a finger to his lips. "Don't just say something you don't mean, Mark. I know you so well. I understand you. I know that you're not the type to settle down with one woman. Which is why I have to put a stop to this. I don't want to. But it's eating away at me and I have to protect myself."

"There's no need to put a stop to it, darling." Mark cupped her face in his hands and gave her a searching look. "We're happy, aren't we? We have a good time together. Can't that be enough?"

Melissa smiled. As she did so, she felt him relax. "You see?" he continued, giving his head a tiny shake. "Don't think so deeply about everything. Let's just go with the flow and see what happens."

Melissa leaned forward and kissed his full lips. Then she pulled away and stood up. "That's just not enough for me, Mark. I want marriage. I want babies." She almost laughed as she watched his tanned face instantly pale at her words. "I want what Sophie has, with a man who loves me as much as I love him. Don't worry, I know I'm not going to get that from you. But I need to find a man who *will* give me that and I'm not going to find him while I'm sleeping with you every night."

Mark stood up and came towards her. She had never seen

him look so sad. "I don't want to lose you. We're so good together, Melissa."

Melissa's heart leapt momentarily. Was this the moment she had waited for? Was he finally going to realize that she was the only woman for him and get down on one knee?

"But I'd be a terrible husband," he said, causing Melissa's sprits to drop again instantly. "And an even worse father," he continued. "I'm too selfish. I like my life too much."

"I know." Despite the pain she felt at his words, Melissa admired his honesty. She was glad he didn't just say all the things he knew she wanted to hear, in order to keep her coming back to his bed night after night. "But, Mark, you have to give me the chance to find happiness with someone else. Before it's too late. I don't want to get to forty and find myself on the scrapheap. It's different for you. There's no time limit the way there is for me."

Mark pulled her into his arms and held her tightly to his chest. "Can't we still see each other?" he said into her hair, his voice plaintive. "Can't you hunt for Mr Right while still enjoying the company of Mr Wrong?"

Melissa laughed. She could feel her resolve weakening. Maybe she could still spend the odd night with Mark while she was looking for someone new. "I don't know..." she whispered.

"You do know..." Mark kissed her, sending pulses of lust racing through her whole body. He was so persuasive. "You can't resist me, darling. Any more than I can resist you."

Melissa allowed him to undo the towel she was wrapped in and lay her gently back on the bed. He began to kiss her all over, effortlessly finding her erogenous zones, as if he had memorized the map of her body. "How could you even think about giving this up?" he murmured as she let out a moan of pleasure.

Melissa gasped and pushed him away. "No!" she said, getting off the bed and shaking her head. "I can't. I can't do this any more, Mark. It's over."

CHAPTER FORTY

THE RELIEF OF FINALLY SAYING IT OUT LOUD WAS so overwhelming that Emily began to struggle for breath. She leaned forward, clutching her stomach as she tried to get some air.

Amy, who had been frozen in shock, suddenly sprang into action. She snatched a paper bag from the bin. "Here, Em, blow," she ordered, holding the neck of the bag over Emily's mouth. "That's it," she soothed as Emily began to breathe more steadily. "Just keep breathing in and out."

After several more minutes, Emily took the bag away with a shaking hand. She looked up at Amy, whose face was still rigid. "Say something, Amy." Amy stood up from the bed and walked to the window, where she looked out for a few minutes before speaking. "What I don't understand…" she began, "is why you told us it was Anton." She looked back at Emily with a bewildered expression. "Why you lied to us."

"I didn't." Emily climbed out of bed, her legs wobbling slightly as they took her weight. Her bones felt weary. It had felt like the longest night of her life. She joined Amy at the window. Outside, the sun was up and the sky was the deep shade of blue that meant it was going to be a beautiful, hot day. But Emily couldn't enjoy the spectacular view of the white cliffs and sparkling azure sea stretching out towards Scotland. Her vision was blurred. "I never lied to you, Amy. To any of you. You all assumed Anton was the father, but I never, ever told you that he was."

Amy frowned, as if she was trying to remember. "Well, then, you certainly lied by omission," she said after a while. She looked hurt.

Emily sighed. "Yes, I probably did. I'm sorry. I had no choice."

"Why? Why did you have no choice? I don't understand." Amy threw her hands up in a half-hearted gesture of exasperation.

Emily looked away, her mind racing. "Because I couldn't tell anyone the truth."

Amy nodded slowly. "Right. And are you going to tell the truth now?"

Emily sat down heavily on the sofa and curled her legs underneath her. "I want to." She paused before continuing. "No, that's not true. I don't want to tell anyone. I've managed to keep it to myself all these years. But with Jack's situation being so desperate…I'm going to have to."

Amy exhaled. She looked as if she might throw up. "I'm going to make us some tea. I think we both need it," she said, walking over to the kettle and flicking the switch. "Then we can talk."

Emily watched her as she busily put teabags into mugs and prepared their drinks. She was grateful for the delay. It gave her time to gather her courage.

"Right, here you go." Amy brought over the two steaming mugs and placed them carefully on the glass coffee table.

She sat down facing Emily, mirroring her position on the sofa. "Do you want to begin at the beginning?"

★ ★ ★ ★ ★

The signs were there, long before the bold blue line appeared in the window of the little white stick. She was sick most mornings—she put it down to drinking so much that fateful night. She was tired all the time—she put it down to working flat out for her finals, which were fast approaching. She was emotional over the slightest little thing—she put it down to guilt over what had happened.

As the days and weeks passed, Emily stayed in denial, ignoring the jeans that were slightly too tight around the waist, the bras that were bursting at the seams, the endless, relentless nausea that followed her day and night.

The results were published. She'd got a first. Her mum and dad stood up and applauded wildly as she graduated. "We are so, so proud of you, darling," said her mum for the tenth time as they headed into the college grounds, where all the students were gathering for a celebratory drink.

Emily sensed him before she saw him. "Hello, Emily," said an unmistakable, slightly gravelly voice.

She turned, her hand automatically moving to her stomach, grateful for the loose, flowing gown she was wearing. "Hello, Anton. How lovely to see you."

He smiled, his sparkling blue eyes shining. "You got your first, then." He sounded like a proud father. "I always knew you would."

Her heart hammered in her chest as she gazed up at him. Immediately, all the feelings she had buried came rushing back in a torrent. "It was down to you. You inspired me."

Anton raised his eyebrows. "Wow. That might just be the loveliest thing anyone has ever said to me. Although, of course, the only person who should take any credit is you."

Emily smiled. "OK. If you insist."

"I do." Anton reached out to touch her arm.

Emily jumped as if she had had an electric shock and they locked eyes again. "Anton, I've missed you so much," she said truthfully.

"I've missed you too." The words seemed to take him by surprise as they fell from his lips. "Sorry. I really shouldn't have said that."

Emily looked around the thronging marquee, before turning back to meet his gaze again. "Well, I won't tell if you don't." There was an unmistakably flirtatious tone to her voice that was so unlike her. She had never made the first move with a man before. But she didn't care. He was no longer her tutor, so there were no rules to say it was wrong. She deliberately pushed any thoughts of his wife and children out of her mind. "How long are you staying in London?"

Anton's expression became serious. She could see him fighting with himself. "One night."

Emily nodded. "In a hotel?"

"Yes." Anton cleared his throat before adding, "All alone."

There was a long pause as Emily balanced on the precipice, deciding.

"Would you like some company?" she said finally, her body beginning to tingle with anticipation.

Anton swallowed hard, still holding her gaze. "Yes," he said in a thick voice. "I would like that very much."

Afterwards, she lay on his chest, listening to the thud of his heart and drinking in the taste and smell of him as he dosed quietly.

Anton's eyes flickered open suddenly and he smiled as he saw her watching him. "What?"

Emily bit her lip. "Nothing."

Anton gave her a searching look. "Tell me what you're thinking."

"I'm thinking I wish we could stay here for ever. Like this."

"So do I." She could see in Anton's eyes that he was telling the truth.

"Does this have to be the end, Anton?" A thought was starting to form in Emily's mind. The thought that maybe they could be together. With the baby. Was it such a wild idea? She wasn't too far gone. It might be possible to make everyone think it was his. Including him.

Anton stroked her hair. "I think it does, yes," he said, immediately silencing the thoughts that were racing through her mind. "I...I do have feelings for you, Emily." He paused. "And things with my wife...well, they're not great. But I have two children. They come first."

"You could have more children..." she said, her voice wistful. "With me."

Anton shook his head ruefully. "That would be something of a miracle, I'm afraid. My days of fathering children are well and truly over."

So that was that. Emily's dreams of a life with Anton evaporated in front of her eyes. Like a giant bubble silently bursting.

"But it's not the end for you, Emily," Anton was saying. "It's just the beginning. You will go on to do such great things in your life. I know you will."

Emily ran her hand over her stomach, which was just starting to bulge with the little life growing inside her. He was right about one thing: this was just the beginning.

★ ★ ★ ★ ★

"So it could never have been Anton's baby?" Amy took a sip of her tea and fixed Emily with a hard stare.

"No." Emily allowed a gulf of silence to build up between them. She knew the next question that was going to come out of Amy's mouth. But she didn't want to hear it.

Amy seemed to be holding her breath too, as if she didn't want to ask it.

"So…" she said at last, her tone almost resigned, "if Anton isn't Jack's father…then who is?"

Emily's mind spooled back to the moment the midwife first handed Jack to her after a long, painful labour. Beside her, her mother's face was already suffused with love, instead of the disappointed expression she had worn ever since Emily first broke the news of her pregnancy to her dumbstruck parents.

If she could travel back in time, would she really delete that moment, so that Jack had never existed? She knew, despite the desperate fear of what her revelation was going to do to the people she loved most in the world, that she wouldn't change a thing. She took a deep, shuddery breath and reached out to take Amy's hand in hers, willing her not to hate her for what she was about to say.

"Steve is Jack's father."

★ ★ ★ ★ ★

She managed to avoid him without arousing suspicion. Everyone was working hard for their final exams and there was very little socializing. Emily hid out at her halls of residence, speaking only to Sophie, Amy and Melissa on the phone.

In the exam hall, she kept her head down and avoided eye

contact with everyone, scuttling back to her room as soon as she possibly could the moment it was over. No one questioned it. Emily had always been driven. Had always been the most academic of the group. Destined for a first, as Anton had told her many times.

She was good at blanking things out. At pretending it wasn't happening. So she ignored the symptoms and buried herself in her books.

By the time her finals were over, she had convinced herself that she had imagined the whole thing. So when she finally came face-to-face with him at a party to celebrate the end of their studies, she was ready.

"Hi, Emily." His eyes shifted nervously as he leaned forward to give her a chaste kiss on the cheek.

"Hello, Steve," she replied, smiling confidently. "So, how were the exams for you?" She helped herself to a drink from the groaning table and looked up at him, hoping to convey an impression of calm insouciance.

A flicker of confusion crossed his face. "Uh, OK. They were OK. Yeah. You?"

Emily nodded. "Good, I think. I hope." She crossed her fingers and held them up.

He gave a small smile. "You'll do well, I'm sure... You've always worked really hard."

"Yes, I have." Emily's face was beginning to ache with the effort of maintaining her rictus smile.

"Look, Em, about that night..." He glanced over his shoulder, checking whether he might be in any danger of being overheard. "I'm so sorry. Obviously, it should never have happened."

Emily's eyes scanned the room cautiously before she replied. "What night? I don't know what you're talking about."

A visible wave of relief passed over his features and he

reached out to hug her. She allowed herself to be pulled into his arms for a few seconds, his smell instantly transporting her back to her single bed, his naked body covering hers. But with an almighty effort, she willed the images away. It hadn't happened. He was never there.

"There you are!" said a voice as Sophie danced up to them and gave Emily a playful nudge. "I thought you were dead!"

"No." Emily shook her head. "I was just in hiding, that's all."

★ ★ ★ ★ ★

There was a long, shocked silence before Amy shook her head emphatically. "No. He's not. Steve is not Jack's father."

Emily opened her mouth to speak, but Amy put her hand up to silence her, her face set like stone. "Don't ever, ever say that again." She swallowed, then nodded, her face softening very slightly. "I know you've been under an enormous strain recently, but to say something like that…it's unforgivable."

Emily was almost relieved by Amy's reaction. She hesitated. Should she pretend she had made it all up and blame the stress she was under? It would be so much easier. But ultimately the truth would have to come out, in order to give Jack any hope of finding a sibling match. She had opened the Pandora's box and there was no closing it again. "Amy…I'm going to say it again. Because it's the truth. I wish it wasn't, but it is. Steve is Jack's biological father."

A wave of fury passed over Amy's features. "Jesus! How could you?" She stood up and marched to the window, turning her back on Emily and folding her arms across herself.

Emily swallowed, her mouth suddenly dry. "It was a

drunken one-night stand, Amy. Nothing more. We were both horrified by what we'd done. We agreed to forget it ever happened."

Amy didn't reply for several seconds. "I can't believe that Steve ignored his own son for all these years—"

"He didn't," Emily interrupted quickly. She stood up on her shaking legs and joined Amy at the window. She tried to meet her eye, but Amy steadfastly refused to look at her. "He's never known."

Amy threw Emily a contemptuous look. "You lied to him too?"

Emily's stomach swirled with shame. "Yes."

"Oh my God." Amy shook her head repeatedly. "What a bloody mess."

"I'm sorry." Emily's legs would no longer support her and she sank back down onto one of the chairs, her whole body shaking.

"It's not me you need to apologize to!" Amy snapped.

"I know."

There was a long, heavy silence, before Amy spoke again. "So when were you thinking of telling them? Not today, I hope."

"No, of course not! I... Well, I thought maybe when they get back from their honeymoon."

Amy closed her eyes. "Poor Sophie. After all she's done for you."

"Don't. Please, Amy, however much you hate me right now, I can promise you it's not a fraction of how much I hate myself. I would have happily taken this to my grave, but my son will die if I don't find a match and Steve's kids represent his best chance. What choice do I have?"

Amy finally turned to look at Emily, her eyes brimming with tears. "Just make sure you don't ruin today for them. You owe them that, at least."

CHAPTER FORTY-ONE

~~~~~~~~~~~~~~~~~~~~~~~~~

"ARE YOU READY, DARLING?" HER DAD CROOKED his arm for her to take it. "It's not too late to change your mind!"

Sophie laughed and looked behind her at Emma, who was dressed in a white organza dress and ballet pumps, and Theo, who held her hand, looking proud in a miniature version of his dad's grey suit. "I think it's definitely too late to change my mind, Dad!"

She linked her arm through his and together they walked through the arch-shaped doorway into the church. As the organ began to play the bridal march, she felt a swell of joy deep inside her. Without her realizing it, this was the moment her life had been building towards. Her perfect moment.

As they walked down the aisle, she smiled at distant relatives from either side of their families, various friends and numerous work colleagues. As she drew level with Mark Bailey, she leaned towards him. "I can't believe you made it on time," she hissed. Mark flashed her a dazzling white smile and winked.

Further down the aisle, she passed Amy, Emily and Melissa, all crying openly as they looked towards her, causing a lump to catch in Sophie's throat. Finally, she reached Steve, who had watched her with a wide, proud smile from the moment she had walked through the door.

She drew to a halt beside him and automatically reached for his hand—his smooth, reassuring hand, which had supported her through the good and the bad times of their life together. "You look beautiful," he told her, before turning to give Emma and Theo a tiny thumbs-up.

The service was simple and short, but what took Sophie by surprise was just how emotional it was. There had never been any doubt about their commitment to one another, but actually saying the words in front of all their loved ones was a powerful and moving experience.

As they walked down the aisle together, she was still fighting back the tears. She looked up at Steve as they emerged into the sunshine and could see that he was the same. "Why didn't we do this ten years ago?" She reached up to kiss him and they held each other for a few seconds before the rest of the congregation burst out of the church behind them, led by an overexcited Emma and Theo. "Mummy and Daddy are married!" cried Emma, waving her posy of flowers in the air and dancing from foot to foot.

As they greeted everyone with delighted smiles and kisses, Sophie felt a hand on her back. "Congratulations, lovely Sophie." She turned to face Amy, who looked extraordinarily stunning in a simple, pale green silk dress that perfectly complemented her tumbling auburn mane and her vivid green eyes. Sophie always thought it ironic that Amy looked so much more Irish than her.

"Thank you. I hope that wasn't too difficult for you..." Sophie motioned towards the church. The last wedding they had all attended together had been Amy and Nick's. She knew the memories would be looming large for Amy today.

Amy shook her head, giving Sophie a tight hug. "Still worrying about everyone else, even on your wedding day." She pulled away and gave Sophie a stern look. "Today is about you, Soph. You and Steve." She glanced at Steve. "Whatever lies ahead, you need to focus on today and remember how happy you are."

Sophie frowned, wondering distractedly what Amy meant. "I will. Where's Emily? And Melissa?"

Amy held Sophie's gaze for a second before replying. "They're both here."

"Is everything OK, Amy?" Sophie searched Amy's face, instinctively sensing that something was wrong.

Amy nodded emphatically. "Everything's fine. You just make sure you enjoy every minute of today."

"I will." Sophie turned away as Emma tugged at her dress. "Come on, Mummy! We need to have the boring old photos done so that we can go and eat cake!"

As they posed for the photographs, Sophie watched the guests milling about in the grounds of the church. Mark Bailey had one hand in his trouser pocket, no doubt feeling for his mobile phone, while with the other he shook hands and posed for numerous snaps. She sometimes forgot just how famous he was these days. It seemed only five minutes since he had asked her to help him set up his fledgling company. What a lucky break that had been for her.

And a lucky break for Melissa too, who had turned her life around when she joined them. She watched her now, standing with Emily, yet never taking her eyes off Mark. Melissa thought Sophie didn't know about their relationship, but of course she did. She had known for a long time, thanks to the rumour mill at work. Nothing stayed secret for very long.

But she was waiting to see if Melissa would tell her herself, and the longer it went on, the more she wondered why she had never discussed it with her. She hoped Melissa didn't think she'd be angry. The opposite was true. But she did worry about Melissa. Worry that she would get hurt. Mark was a wonderful man, but he wasn't the type to settle down. He wasn't even the type to settle for one woman. He didn't mean to be cruel, but he couldn't help himself.

Beside Melissa, Emily looked tense and exhausted, much as she had for the past ten months. Sophie felt her heart clench in sympathy for her old friend. She had been under such a huge strain for so long and she didn't have anything like the level of support Sophie did. She just hoped that Jack would make a full recovery so that Emily could try to move on with her life. It was as if she was stuck in limbo until he was better.

At that moment, Amy's nanny, Dean, brought Megan and George over to stand with Amy. Sophie smiled to herself as she caught the look in Amy's eye when she saw him approaching. She watched the way her face lit up and how she flirtatiously twirled a strand of hair around her finger as they spoke to each other.

"Stop it." Steve leaned down to kiss her, his eyes crinkling with amusement.

Sophie beamed up at him, adopting her most innocent expression. "I have no idea what you're talking about."

"You, Mrs Montgomery, are matchmaking. Don't try to deny it."

"I'm not really." Sophie looked back over at Amy and Dean, who were both bending down to talk to the children. "But you have to admit, they make a good couple."

Steve followed her gaze and gave a reluctant nod. "OK. Maybe you're right. He's actually a great guy. She could do a lot worse."

"I'm so pleased for her. She deserves to find someone nice. They all do…" Her eyes moved to Emily and Melissa, who both looked thoroughly miserable. "I just want everyone to be as happy as we are." She reached up and kissed Steve tenderly. "After all that we've been through, it feels like we're invincible. There is nothing that could come between us now."

CHAPTER FORTY-TWO

EMILY'S LEGS WERE SHAKING AS SHE WALKED into the kitchen, where Sophie and Steve were waiting. She had asked to see them together, a few days after they had returned from their short honeymoon in Paris. She knew what she had to do. She also knew that she should have done it fifteen years ago when she first found out she was pregnant. But she had made her decision then and there was no going back on it.

★ ★ ★ ★ ★

Emily left Anton's hotel just after dawn and began to walk along the river in the misty, early light, heading for Greenwich, where her parents lived. They had left her graduation party, telling Emily to *have fun with your friends and enjoy yourself*, unaware that she was planning to go to a hotel with her tutor and spend the night with him.

Anton had kissed her goodbye with such tenderness that morning that she knew it was about more than just sex. It always had been. They had a deeper, more spiritual connection.

But it was over nonetheless. He would be catching a train back to Durham, returning to his wife and children, and she doubted whether she would ever see him again. There was no reason why their paths would ever need to cross now that she had left university and the sadness she felt at this knowledge was like a dead weight inside her.

As she walked, watching London begin to wake up for the day ahead, she knew she had to look towards the future now and make a decision. It wasn't too late. All her options were still open.

She put a hand to her stomach, which was becoming slightly rounder already. There was a new tautness to her skin and her breasts had noticeably begun to swell. Then there was the endless, relentless nausea and the bone-crushing tiredness. She could put a stop to it all. Her life wouldn't need to change and she could fulfil the hopes and dreams she had always held. No one need ever know and she could live her life as if that awful, fateful night had never happened.

Except…*she* would know. She would have to look at herself in the mirror every morning. And, more than that, she really wanted this baby. Yes, it would be the convenient, most sensible option to have an abortion. But she knew herself well enough to know that there was no way she could ever go through with it. She already loved this baby, however much she tried not to. And it would be easy to let everyone assume that Anton was the father. He wasn't going to be around to deny it. By the time she arrived home, with both her heart and her feet aching, she had reached her decision.

It was several weeks before she told Steve. She wondered if she deliberately left it so long because she wanted it to be too late. She called him to ask if he would meet her at a busy coffee shop near Covent Garden.

He arrived looking ashen, his normally tanned skin carrying a faint green tinge. He could barely meet her eye and kept glancing around nervously. After a few moments of awkward small talk, she took a deep breath. "Steve, I thought you should know that I'm pregnant."

Steve's face froze in horror. He opened his mouth to say something but quickly closed it again, apparently unable to speak.

Emily swallowed and prepared for the greatest acting scene of her life. "It's not yours, Steve." Her eyes searched his as she willed herself not to show any sign of doubt or uncertainty. "I know who the father is…and it's not you."

Steve stared at her for a few seconds, before his face seemed to melt with relief. "Not mine?" he repeated, his voice croaky and breathless.

Emily shook her head firmly. "No. I don't want to say who the father is because…well, it's complicated. But I am one hundred per cent certain that it's not you."

Steve blinked back a tear and exhaled with relief, the colour already returning to his complexion. "How can you be so sure?" He looked at her with a pleading expression, wanting her to provide him with a convincing answer.

She paused for a moment, thinking. "I took the morning-after pill, just in case."

Steve gave her a small, grateful smile and nodded. "OK."

"I haven't told Sophie and the others yet because I wanted to speak to you first. I knew what you would think…" She tailed off, suddenly feeling exhausted and emotional.

Steve nodded again. "Thank you."

There was a short silence as both of them drank their coffee, deep in thought.

"Tell me to mind my own business if you want to," Steve began nervously. "But are you and the father in a relationship?"

Emily placed her cup in its saucer and shook her head. "Not any more. As I said, it's complicated."

"Does he know?"

Emily thought for a second before answering. "No. I think it's for the best. I don't want him to know," she added in a stern voice.

Steve gave her a concerned look. "Who'll look after you? Who'll support you and the...the baby?"

Emily was touched by his concern. "My mum and dad. They weren't thrilled, but they'll come round."

"That's good." Steve nodded. "And I'll be there for you too. You know that, don't you? We all will—me, Sophie, Melissa and Amy—if there's anything you need."

"I know. Thank you. And thanks for meeting me today too." Emily finished her coffee and reached for her bag.

"I'll see you soon, OK?" Steve reached out and touched her arm as she left him.

Emily nodded and walked out of the coffee shop, her stomach churning, but she felt certain that she had done the right thing.

★ ★ ★ ★ ★

Fifteen years on, and it was only now that she was realizing what a truly disastrous decision that had been. Yes, it would have been hell at the time and most likely have ended her friendship with Sophie. But Steve would have been a good father to Jack. He would have wanted to be there for him and be involved in his life. She had denied him that chance because she was a coward and didn't want her treachery to be discovered. She had thought at the time that she was protecting him, when in fact she was only really protecting herself. She felt deeply ashamed as she took her seat at the table.

Steve and Sophie looked across at her expectantly.

"How's Jack?" Sophie's forehead creased with concern.

Emily shook her head. "He's not great. That's why I've asked to see you, actually." She paused, trying to gather herself before continuing. "The chemo hasn't worked…"

There was a collective gasp from them both. "Oh no!" Sophie whispered, looking aghast.

Emily looked at their sympathetic faces, intensifying her guilt a thousandfold. "So he's going to need a bone marrow transplant."

There was a short pause before Sophie spoke. "Then we'll all be tested." She glanced at Steve, who nodded quickly. "Of course we will."

Emily swallowed. This was so, so hard. "It needs to be a sibling, to give him the best chance." Her throat dried as she finished speaking.

There was a flicker of confusion on their faces as they digested her words. "So, you mean Anton's kids will have to be tested?" Sophie said finally.

Emily opened her mouth to speak, but she was momentarily dumbstruck.

"Look, Emily, I know you don't want anything to do with him, but—"

"It's not that simple…" Emily interrupted, raising her hand slightly.

Sophie stopped speaking and looked at her in surprise.

Emily could feel herself reddening and she started to shake. "Anton isn't Jack's father." Her voice quavered as she spoke.

"What?" Sophie cried, her eyes widening with shock. "But you said he was!"

Emily shook her head slowly. "The thing is, I didn't. You all assumed it and I admit I was happy for you to assume it. I've never told anyone who Jack's dad is. I would still prefer not to tell anyone, but..." The tears that had been threatening, now began to roll down her cheeks. "But with Jack so ill, I've got no choice. I'm sorry." She put her hands over her face and began to cry in earnest.

"What on earth are you apologizing for, Em?" Sophie leapt out of her chair and came to crouch beside Emily, putting her arms around her shoulders and holding her as she cried. "You have nothing to apologize for."

"I do," Emily sobbed. "I have so much to apologize for."

"I don't understand." Sophie looked up at Steve, perplexed. "So you didn't tell us who Jack's father was... It's not a big deal."

Emily had managed to compose herself enough to stop crying and she watched as Sophie returned to her chair, her face set in a serious expression.

Beside her, there was a sudden noise that was somewhere between a wail and a sob. Steve pushed back his chair so roughly that it tipped back and clattered onto the tiled floor, causing them all to jump. Steve looked at Emily with a pleading expression. "Please!" he whimpered, covering his mouth and shaking his head in disbelief. "Please don't say what I think you're going to say..."

Emily swallowed hard and met Steve's anguished gaze. "I'm

sorry, Steve. I know I should have told you all those years ago...but I thought it was for the best."

"Should have told him *what*?" Sophie was gaping at Steve in confusion.

Emily closed her eyes, wanting the ground to swallow her up for ever. "Steve is Jack's real father."

CHAPTER FORTY-THREE

THERE WAS A LONG, LONG SILENCE. STEVE WAS
standing by the French doors, staring out into the garden. Sophie's mind reeled. Fifteen years ago, they were in their last
term at university. How had she missed that Emily and Steve
were having an affair? Were the signs all there, right in front
of her, and yet she had simply not noticed?

She thought back to the time when Steve had left her.
When he came back, he wouldn't say where he'd been. Had
he been with her then? Was that when he had broken it off
with Emily and chosen Sophie?

"H-h-how long?" she stuttered, not sure she wanted to hear
the answer. "How long were you having an affair?" Her voice
cracked slightly as she spoke and she couldn't bring herself to
look at Emily. "Or is it *still* going on?"

"No!" both Steve and Emily cried in unison. Steve came
back to the table, his eyes blazing. "We didn't have an affair!
Sophie, you *have* to believe me. It was just a terrible, drunken
mistake."

"He's telling the truth, Sophie." Emily had visibly reeled
at Steve's harsh words, but her voice was clear and resolute.

"We were both horribly drunk and Steve crashed on my floor after a gig at the university. Neither of us knew what we were doing. But I promise you, Sophie, we were horrified by what we'd done. We agreed never to mention it again and to forget it ever happened."

Sophie finally looked at Emily. Suddenly, a horrible thought occurred to her. "Amy knew, didn't she? Has she always known?"

Emily's cheeks flamed. "Only since Ireland. I told her on the morning of the wedding."

There was a long, heavy pause as they all sat in silence.

Finally, Sophie spoke again. "The cruellest thing, it seems to me, is not telling Steve that Jack was his son. How could you have done that, Emily?" Sophie's voice broke as she spoke.

Emily put her head in her hands. "I thought I was doing the right thing. I thought I was protecting him. And you, Sophie."

"You were protecting yourself!" Steve spat venomously, causing them both to look at him in surprise. Steve never lost his temper.

"Steve…" Sophie reached out to put her hand on his arm but pulled back. She wanted to comfort him, but part of her was so angry with him. "Why didn't you both just fess up at the time?" She looked from Steve to Emily, uncomprehending. "Yes, it would have been awful. But we'd have got through it."

"Would we?" Steve shook his head. "Would we really have come back from me sleeping with your best friend, Soph? I'm not so sure we would." His eyes brimmed and he took a long, shuddery breath. "I couldn't risk it. I couldn't risk losing you."

Sophie bit her lip. She understood what he was saying and she wondered if he was right. At twenty-one years old, before they had had the chance to live their lives together, before they had experienced real pain, real regret and real joy together, would she have forgiven him? Would she have forgiven Emily? No, she thought now. She probably wouldn't. "How were you able to look me in the eye again, Emily? As if nothing had happened?"

Emily, who was still covering her face with her hands, looked up at her wearily. "It was easy." She sighed. "Because I wiped it from my memory. I just convinced myself that it had never happened. Everyone seemed to assume that Anton was the father, so I did the same. I would have gone to my grave without telling anyone the truth…" She stopped speaking for a moment, swallowing quickly before continuing. "But Jack's illness…" Her voice dropped to a hoarse whisper. "It changed everything. Jack's illness is the reason why I need to tell the truth now. So, although I know this is really painful for you both…" She looked from Steve to Sophie. "The fact is that Emma and Theo are Jack's only siblings. They're his best chance of a cure."

There was a rushing sound behind Sophie's ears and she wondered if she might faint. She took several deep breaths and tried to focus, but her vision only became more blurred.

"Sophie?" Steve was at her side, kneeling on the floor and gripping her arm as he looked up at her. "Sophie! Are you OK? Sweetheart? I'm so sorry…" He pulled her towards him and she allowed herself to fall into his embrace, resting her face against his chest, noticing distractedly how fast his heart was beating. "I'm sorry," he said, stroking Sophie's hair. "I'm so sorry."

Sophie shook her head, but she couldn't find the words to say what she wanted to say. Steve had just discovered that he had a son he didn't know about. How could she possibly tell him now that she didn't even know for sure if the daughter he loved so deeply was actually his? How could she begin to explain that Emma might not be a match for Jack because she might not be his biological sister? The answer, she decided as her thoughts swirled and thrashed around her head, was that she couldn't. No matter how hard it was. No matter how heavy the burden. She had to carry it alone.

"I'm so sorry," Emily said now, breaking through her thoughts.

Sophie looked at her, her blood suddenly boiling with anger at the turmoil she had unleashed in their lives. "Sorry? You're *sorry*? Well, that's OK, then! Emily's 'sorry,' so we should all just shake hands and move on as if nothing has happened! Is that what you mean?"

Emily shook her head. "Look, Sophie, if I could turn back time and change what happened—"

"No!" Sophie cut her off by putting her shaking hand up in front of Emily's face. "Don't you dare. You knew exactly what you were doing and you didn't give a shit about the effect it would have on me or anyone else, so don't pretend now that you did."

Sophie stood up and ran her hand through her hair as tears began to threaten. Eventually, she turned back towards Emily. "Do you hate me that much?" Her voice cracked as she spoke and she slumped back down onto her chair, the tears now falling freely.

Emily moved towards her and knelt down beside her. "Of course I don't hate you. I love you, Sophie. I know what I did was unforgivable, but I thought it was for the best. I thought I was doing the right thing. Please, Sophie, you must believe me when I say that I never meant to hurt you."

Sophie shook her head. Eventually, she took a deep, shuddery breath and looked up at Emily through watery eyes. "But that's the problem, Emily. I don't believe you. I'll never believe a word you say again."

Emily shrank back. "Look, Sophie, I know you hate me right at this moment, but I promise you, it's nowhere near as much as I hate myself. I am so desperately sorry, Sophie. One day, I hope you'll find it in your heart to forgive me."

Sophie pursed her lips, weighing up what to say, while Emily looked at her with terrified eyes. When she spoke, her voice was clear and unwavering. "No, Emily, that's not going to happen. I will never, ever forgive you for what you've done."

CHAPTER FORTY-FOUR

SUMMER DISAPPEARED ALMOST OVERNIGHT. THE evenings darkened and an autumn chill descended. The temperature in the house seemed to drop in sympathy. Sophie and Steve circled each other warily, a veneer of politeness covering every conversation. Neither of them could meet the other's eye.

The tests were done, and just as Sophie had feared, Emma wasn't a match. But Theo was. "I'll understand," said Emily, on the other end of the line, "if you don't want him to be a donor."

"I'll talk to Steve and let you know," Sophie had told her coldly, before hanging up.

She went in search of Steve and found him in his writing office at the end of the garden. The light was on and she could see that he was turned away from his computer screen, facing the wall with his head in his hands. His shoulders rose and fell rhythmically. Sophie hesitated, unsure whether to intrude on his private grief. But they needed to talk. This really was a matter of life and death.

She knocked gently and opened the French door. Steve started in surprise and looked up at her, his face wet with tears of anguish. Sophie felt her own eyes fill. Instinctively, she crossed the room and knelt on the floor in front of him, wrapping her arms around his heaving body and pulling him towards her, rocking him gently.

After a while, his sobs subsided and he took a deep, shuddery breath, before sitting back and looking at her properly for the first time in weeks. "I'm just so bloody sad, Sophie. All those lost years and now, when I finally find out that he's mine, there's a real possibility that he might die. I don't know how the hell I'm going to handle it." His face creased in pain and fresh tears began to pour down his cheeks.

Sophie swallowed hard and sniffed back her own tears. She picked up his hands in hers and looked at him fiercely. "He's not going to die, Steve. Theo's a match."

Steve frowned. "Theo?"

"Yes. Emily just rang. Theo's a match for Jack."

A wave of different emotions crossed Steve's face. Elation followed by anger, followed by fear. "What does that mean?"

Sophie took a deep breath. "It means that we have to decide if we're happy for Theo to donate his bone marrow."

Steve nodded and eyed her warily. "What do you think?"

Sophie closed her eyes for a second, gathering her thoughts. "I think it's the easiest decision I've ever had to make. One of your sons will save your other son's life. It's as simple as that."

Steve's face immediately crumpled again and he leaned forward to hug her. "Thank you," he whispered into her hair.

★ ★ ★ ★ ★

"So, Theo's a match, then? That's great news." Melissa gave Sophie an encouraging smile.

"Yes, it's good news." Sophie didn't say that she had mixed

feelings. It was too complicated to put into words how she felt. She wasn't sure she really knew herself.

"Not Emma, though?" Melissa tilted her head slightly and dropped her gaze.

"No." Only Melissa had ever known that there might be any doubt in Sophie's mind over Emma's paternity.

Melissa's brow furrowed with concern. "How did Steve react to that? It must have made him question things."

Sophie shook her head. "No, incredibly. I started to suggest a DNA test—in some ways it would be a huge relief to know for sure, one way or the other—but before I could get the words out, he stopped me. Said he didn't ever want to know. That Emma is his daughter. Nothing will ever change that."

Melissa's eyes widened in admiration. "Wow. That is very big of him."

Sophie nodded. "It is. Though I think maybe he sees it as some kind of penance for what happened…"

They were in a small Italian restaurant not far from Sophie's house. Melissa had called, asking to see her, wanting to make sure she was OK, after Emily had rung to tell her about the situation. "So, how are you doing?" she asked now.

Sophie blinked slowly. "I'm OK." It was all she could offer at the moment. She veered between a raging, all-consuming fury and a calm, slightly out-of-body acceptance. Steve was the same, although he looked at her now in a different way. She could see the fear behind his eyes, as if he expected her to explode at any given moment.

He had apologized so many times that she had to tell him to stop. "I know you're sorry. You don't have to keep saying it." But she knew all too well why he kept saying it. She had wanted to keep saying it too when he first found out about her affair with Matt. She was scared that if she stopped saying it, he would stop forgiving her.

But he didn't stop forgiving her. He had managed to put her betrayal behind him and forge ahead with their life together, supporting her when she crumbled, just as much as he supported her when she triumphed. Maybe the only reason he had been able to do that was because he wanted to atone for his own mistake. She understood that only too well. She would forgive him and move on with their life together because she too wanted to atone for what she had done.

"It must have been such a shock." Melissa broke into Sophie's thoughts. "For you both. How is Steve coping?"

Sophie considered for a minute. "He has good days and bad days. On the whole, he's coping well, but he's just so bloody sad. He says the thought of all 'the lost years' is what's really killing him."

Melissa nodded. "I can imagine. But they're not really lost years, are they? Steve's been more of a father to Jack than anyone else. He just did it without knowing that Jack was biologically his. Who knows, maybe there was something deep inside, some kind of sixth sense, that made him feel like a dad to him."

Sophie looked at Melissa admiringly. "You're always so perceptive, Liss, and I don't know why, but it always takes me by surprise. I'm going to tell Steve that. I think it could really help."

Melissa smiled, before her face became grave again. "And what about telling Jack? And Emma? It's going to be very hard for them to take in."

"It is," Sophie agreed. "But we've decided not to tell Jack yet, not until he's had the transplant and is on the mend. We think it could be too much for him to cope with, and to be honest, he's had all these years of not knowing—a few more months won't make much difference."

"And what about your two?"

"We'll tell them after we've told Jack. They're still a bit young to properly understand. I'm hoping it won't make a huge difference, as Emma's always treated him like a big brother anyway. I think there's a good chance she might be thrilled."

Melissa smiled, then her face hardened in a way that it rarely did. "And what about Emily? I'm so angry with her, Soph… I can't imagine how you feel about her."

"Oh God, I just don't know." Sophie took a long sip of her red wine. "Yes, I'm still incredibly angry with her, but I also feel a bit sorry for her, I suppose. I understand why she did what she did. But it's so hard to get past it. I think maybe in time I can forgive her, but I really don't know about Steve."

"You're a lot kinder towards her than I would be in your shoes." Melissa pursed her lips in a straight line.

Sophie shook her head. "Everyone's got things they regret doing, Liss." She gave Melissa a knowing look. "You and me included." She let her words register for a second before continuing. "But Emily has paid a hell of a price for her mistakes."

Melissa's expression softened. "I know. But I'm not sure if things will ever be the same again, after the way she deceived us. All of us."

"Things won't ever be the same again." Sophie gave a tired smile. "But they'll certainly be more truthful. There have been too many secrets between us. At least now we can be open and honest. And Emily will need us more than ever if…" She shook her head irritably. "No, I'm not even going to contemplate that. But she will definitely need us."

Melissa sighed. "I know you're right, but… OK. I'll try my best."

Sophie lifted her glass and took a sip of wine, before placing it back on the table. "Let's change the subject. How are things going with Mark?"

Melissa frowned. "What do you mean?"

"Oh, come on, Melissa! What have I just said? No more secrets."

Melissa eyed Sophie warily. "But I thought you might be angry."

Sophie rolled her eyes. "I'm not angry. I've known for ages. It's just that I worry about you getting hurt. I love Mark, but I know what he's like…"

"Well, there's nothing going on anyway. Not any more." Melissa's bottom lip quivered dangerously.

"Oh, sweetie. I'm so sorry." Sophie reached across and squeezed Melissa's hand. She wanted to reassure her, to tell her that Mark would see sense and come running back to her. But she didn't, because she knew it wasn't true. "When did he break it off with you?"

"He didn't," Melissa murmured, causing Sophie to frown in confusion.

"So, you're still seeing him?"

Melissa shook her head. "No. I told *him* it was over in Ireland. On the morning of the wedding."

Sophie sat back, remembering. Normally, Melissa and Mark were together all the time, but now that she thought about it, they had pointedly ignored each other all day, although she had noticed Melissa staring at him several times. "How did he take it?"

Melissa shrugged. "You know what Mark's like. He was upset for about ten minutes."

"You did the right thing, Liss. I know how hard it must have been…" She could see that Melissa was struggling not to cry. "But there was no chance of a long-term future with him. He's too much of a free spirit."

Melissa nodded. "Yup."

Sophie leaned forward again. "Listen, you are so beautiful, Melissa. And you are such a great person. You deserve to find someone to settle down with. Someone to have kids with…"

Melissa's eyes filled. "It's not going to happen, Soph. Not now. I'm too old, anyway."

"No!" Sophie protested. "You're only thirty-five… There's still plenty of time."

"Not really." Melissa's voice was despondent and her tiny shoulders were hunched forward in resignation. "There aren't many single men my age, and by the time I find one who is, who wants to settle down and have kids with me, it'll definitely be too late."

Sophie wished she could deny it. Reassure her that there were plenty of men who would want someone as gorgeous, vibrant and lovely as her to settle down with, but she couldn't. It would be a lie.

"You are so lucky that you found Steve when you did." Melissa looked up at Sophie. "I used to think it was so boring, for you to have stayed with the same man all those years…" She gave Sophie a sheepish smile. "But I'd give anything to swap with you now."

A lump formed in Sophie's throat as Melissa finished speaking. She was right. Whatever had happened between her and Steve, whatever the rights and wrongs of each situation, they had stuck together through it all. In some ways, the hard times had made them even stronger. She knew without even the tiniest hint of doubt in her mind, that whatever happened in the future, whatever challenges they faced, they would face them together.

FIVE YEARS LATER, AUGUST 2012

"The London 2012 Olympics have ended with a spectacular musical closing ceremony and the official handover to the next host city, Rio de Janeiro."

CAPRI, ITALY

CHAPTER FORTY-FIVE

~~~~~~~~~~~~

"THAT'S WHERE NICK PROPOSED TO ME. RIGHT there…" Amy pointed to a viewing platform on a cliff edge that plunged sharply down towards the whitewashed houses of Capri, nestling above the sparkling blue Mediterranean Sea.

Sophie followed her gaze. "I remember you telling us now. I'd forgotten that it was here. It must be difficult, being back…"

Amy shook out her long auburn hair, still remarkably untouched by grey and gleaming under the rays of the hot Italian sun. "No. It's cathartic, actually. Makes me realize that my marriage wasn't all bad. There were times when we were happy."

Sophie gave a neutral nod. Even after all these years, she couldn't bring herself to think of Nick in anything like a positive way. Yet Amy could. Amy, who had almost been killed by him. "You're amazing," she said.

Amy closed her eyes and turned her face up towards the sun. "Yup, that's me. Amazing Amy."

Sophie watched her admiringly. At forty years old, she looked at least ten years younger and was completely comfortable in her own skin, which was also still flawless. Her business was thriving and she now employed eight people, meaning she had had to learn how to be a boss. To everyone's surprise, she had discovered that she had a talent for managing people, and as a result, her confidence had soared.

She was a wonderful mother to Megan and George, neither of whom showed any sign of the trauma that had tainted their early lives. Megan would soon be starting secondary school and had blossomed from a timid, anxious child into a confident, happy girl. Both children still spent a lot of time with Sophie and Steve, sometimes popping in to pick up something they'd forgotten and not leaving for days on end.

Sophie didn't mind. It gave Amy and Dean the chance to have some time alone together. "Do you think you'll get married again?" she asked now.

Amy smiled and shook her head. "No! I love Dean. And he loves me. But we're happy just the way we are."

"Not even…" Sophie nodded towards Amy's rounded stomach.

Amy cradled her small bump affectionately. "No. I want things to be completely different this time. Although the baby will definitely have Dean's surname. That's enough for him."

Sophie couldn't help smiling. Amy's happiness was infectious. She had waited a long time for this baby and had almost given up hope. But just as they were starting to investigate IVF, she had conceived naturally. Both she and Sophie had burst into tears of joy when she told her the news. After all that she had been through, it felt like the happy ending she deserved.

Sophie stretched, enjoying the feel of the hot sun on her skin. It had been such a busy year so far, so she was making the most of this weekend. It was the first weekend away with the girls in five long years. None of them had felt ready before now. Too much had happened. But now seemed like the right time and the wedding had given them the perfect excuse.

She and Amy had snuck away after breakfast, wanting to get some peace and quiet. Some respite before the real madness began.

They had taken an open-top taxi from Capri town centre, up to Anacapri, a smaller town further up the mountain. Once there, Amy had led them to a rickety-looking chairlift that carried them in single chairs right to the very top of the mountain. It was still relatively early, so there weren't many other people around yet and the views were breathtaking. From Sophie's seat, she could see right across the Bay of Naples, towards Vesuvius in all its smouldering glory. "This is perfect, Amy. Can't we just stay here all day?"

Amy laughed. "I wish! No, we'd better think about getting back." She looked at her watch. "There's only a couple of hours to go before the main event."

"Spoilsport!" Sophie teased, but she was already getting up. "I suppose you're right. That is the reason we're here after all."

★ ★ ★ ★ ★

Melissa smoothed down her dress for the tenth time. "I look so fat!" she wailed, looking disdainfully at her reflection in the huge, ornate mirror in her suite.

"I wish I looked that fat!" Sophie said, standing behind Melissa and motioning towards the mirror. "You're at least half my size."

Melissa gave a sheepish grin. "Sorry. Do you think I look OK? Really?" She spun around so that she was facing Sophie, looking up at her with a pleading expression.

Sophie shook her head. "No, Melissa, you do not look OK.

You look…" she continued quickly as Melissa's face crumpled in dismay, "you look absolutely, stunningly, ravishingly beautiful."

Melissa's delicate features and tiny frame had blossomed over the past couple of years. Her pregnancy had left her with more curves, even though her flat stomach had snapped back into shape after giving birth just six months previously. Her smooth, dark skin was glowing and her hair now hung in thick, shiny ringlets to her shoulders. "He is a very lucky man."

Melissa's twinkling brown eyes dulled slightly and she looked away, the pain of what had happened never very far from the surface.

★ ★ ★ ★ ★

Melissa glanced down as her mobile began to vibrate silently in her open handbag. She could see from the screen that it was Sophie. She reached down discreetly to switch it off, hoping that no one had noticed. She was in a pitch meeting with the network. It was the biggest one she had had since joining this production company, pitching for a new multimillion-pound Saturday-night entertainment show, and she didn't want to screw it up.

She had felt that she had no choice but to leave Merlin, even though both Sophie and Mark begged her not to. Working with him was just too painful and too dangerous. She knew in her heart that she wouldn't be able to resist him if they continued to work so closely together.

So she had handed in her notice and very quickly landed a job with another production company, Tightrope Productions, as head of entertainment. It was a great company and it was a great job. But it wasn't the same. Melissa missed working with Sophie. And most of all, she missed Mark.

At first, she compensated for his loss by following his every move on Twitter and on MailOnline, even though it made her feel physically sick every time she saw him being photographed with yet another glamorous woman on his arm. He was a global megastar, whose every move was well documented, so it was easy to keep tabs on him.

But as she settled into her new job, she began to search for his name less and less frequently, until she was looking him up only a couple of times a month. And then she met Pete, which was when she stopped looking altogether.

Pete was a comedy producer at Tightrope and was the exact opposite of Mark. He was exceptionally tall—well over six foot—with a shock of messy black hair and a chiselled, craggy face. Everyone, Melissa included, assumed he was gay, as he had never been known to have a girlfriend, and he was almost pathologically private.

But one night, when they were working late together on a new show, he suddenly asked her if she would ever consider going out to dinner with him.

Melissa had looked up at him in surprise. "Sure. Do you mean just the two of us?"

Pete had looked around him theatrically at the empty office. "Um, yes. That's usually the case on a date, isn't it?"

"A date?" Melissa had blurted out the words before she could stop herself. "Like, a *romantic* date?"

Pete smiled and Melissa felt her stomach give a tiny flip, noticing for the first time just how sexy his full mouth was. "Yes, Melissa, a *romantic* date." He rolled the "r" as he spoke, making her laugh out loud.

"I don't..." Melissa hesitated for a second. Pete was such a lovely guy and she suspected it had taken a lot of courage for him to ask. She didn't want to hurt his feelings. "I don't get involved with people at work. It can make things too difficult if it goes wrong." She didn't tell him about Mark because she assumed, like most people, that he already knew. She had thought they were always discreet, but apparently their relationship was an open secret in the industry.

Pete nodded. "I agree. So let's only 'get involved,'" he made speech marks in the air with his fingers, "when we're not at work."

Melissa laughed again. There was something so refreshing about him. And, more important, he couldn't be more different to Mark. Maybe he was just what she needed right now. "OK."

"Great." Pete fixed her with his dark eyes, which were shining with mischief. "In that case, how about we skip dinner and just move straight to the sex bit?"

Melissa giggled. Something told her this one wasn't going to be a one-night stand.

As soon as the meeting finished, she rang Sophie back. "Did you get my voicemail?" Sophie was already speaking before Melissa could even say "hello." Her voice sounded panicky, which was unlike her.

"No. I was in a meeting. Why?" She motioned to the others to go on ahead without her. "I'll meet you back at the office," she mouthed.

"Have you heard about Mark?"

The tone of Sophie's voice instantly made Melissa's stomach drop. "No. What about him?"

"He's been in a helicopter crash." She gave a loud sob. "Melissa, he's not expected to survive…"

Melissa froze. It couldn't be true. His show was running

on TV at the moment. She and Pete had watched it in bed only the previous night. She remembered thinking how well he looked. "No..." she whispered. "Not Mark... It can't be right."

"I'm going to the hospital now. He's at St Thomas's. Will you come with me?" Sophie was breathless, as if she was walking quickly. "Please, Melissa."

Melissa hesitated. "I'm not sure."

"He'd want you there. I know he would." Sophie was emphatic. She wasn't going to accept "no" for an answer.

"OK. I'll see you there."

To begin with, it was a struggle to get anywhere near him. While the press gathered outside the hospital, ghoulishly hoping for confirmation of his death, inside, various hangers-on jostled for position at his bedside.

"Mark would laugh his head off at this, if he was awake to see it," Sophie told Melissa as they watched yet another of Mark's old conquests leaving with her hair and make-up done to perfection, ready for her close-up.

"Well, she certainly doesn't seem too distressed." Melissa's lip curled in disgust.

"You watch how quickly they get bored, if this drags on for any length of time."

Melissa looked at her in horror. "Christ, Sophie, you make it sound as if you're wishing him dead."

Sophie shook her head wearily. "You know that's not the case, Liss. I love Mark just as much as you do. I can't imagine my life without him in it." She paused, as if composing herself. "But we need to be realistic about this..." She tailed off and her words hung in the air for a moment. "And think about it, there's no way Mark would want to just survive. You know he wouldn't. He'd want to be his old self—" her voice dropped to a whisper "—or nothing at all."

"No." Melissa's mouth set in a straight, determined line and she shook her head emphatically. "I'm not going to be realistic about anything." She glanced up at Mark, lying motionless as the machines keeping him alive beeped and whirred rhythmically. "Mark is not going to die, because I'm not going to let him."

For the next couple of weeks, Sophie and Melissa barely left his bedside, but eventually Sophie had to get back to work. "Someone needs to keep the company going," she told Melissa with a wry expression. "He'll kill me when he gets back if I've let it slide."

Melissa nodded and gave a tired smile. She was pleased that Sophie was now talking as if he was going to get better. As if he'd be going back to work soon. But Melissa was starting to lose hope. At the beginning, she'd been so sure that she could will him better if she was focused enough. But with every passing hour that he didn't wake up, her certainty wavered a tiny bit.

"I'm not so sure he's going to make it, Pete," she cried one evening after a long day at the hospital. Pete wrapped his arms around her and hugged her tightly. She loved that not only did he never moan about how much time she was spending at Mark's bedside, he also never trotted out platitudes to make her feel better. Everyone knew Mark was unlikely to survive, so he just listened and nodded and supported her.

He had never once queried why she needed to be with Mark as much as she did. "I know how much you love him," he told her when she apologized for never being at home these days.

Melissa had reached up to kiss him. "I hope you also know how much I love you too."

And it was true. She and Pete just worked. He was kind, he was thoughtful and he could always make her laugh, even when she thought her heart might be about to break. She had thought she would never love anyone after Mark, but with each passing day, she fell more and more in love with Pete. There was a permanence to their relationship that she had never known before and she could see them being together for ever.

More weeks passed and soon everyone but Melissa and Sophie had become bored sitting by Mark's bed, watching the hours tick by, as the machines around him continued with their robotic hisses and beeps. "He doesn't look like him any more, does he?" Melissa said as she met Sophie's eye across his bed one evening.

Sophie shook her head sadly. "No. I just hope that when he wakes up, he's still the same Mark we know and love." Melissa and Sophie tended to take it in turns to be optimistic, as it was too exhausting for one person to maintain it.

"*If* he wakes up." Melissa turned to look at Mark, willing him to open his eyes. She had long since stopped kidding herself that it was all going to be fine, but she hadn't seen him in person for such a long time. She felt as if she needed to see those velvety dark eyes smiling at her one more time, winking mischievously whenever he was up to no good.

She leaned forward so that her mouth was close to his ear. "Come on, Mark, wake up, you bastard! We can't stay here for ever, you selfish git."

Sophie grinned. "He'd like that. He really missed you, you know, when you left Merlin."

Melissa raised her eyebrows. "He had a funny way of showing it. He seemed to be out with a different woman every night of the week. Not that many of them have stuck around..." She gestured to the empty room around them.

"No, really." Sophie looked fondly at Mark. "I think he's been pining for you. Especially since I told him you were all loved up with Pete."

Melissa's heart gave a little skip. "Really? What did he say?"

"It wasn't what he said, so much as the look on his face. He looked sad."

"But what did he say?" Melissa persisted. She wanted to know.

Sophie sighed. "He said he was pleased for you. That you deserved to be happy. He said Pete was a very lucky man."

Melissa's heart sank. "That's hardly proof of his undying love." She looked at Mark again. "He was probably glad to get rid of me."

"No."

Sophie leapt out of her seat. "Was that you?"

"No."

Melissa shook her head, scarcely daring to breathe in case she was wrong. "No, it wasn't me. It was him."

They both leaned towards Mark's face. "Mark, sweetheart." Melissa stroked his cheek gently. "Did you try to say something?"

Mark's eyes fluttered open and he looked straight at her. Melissa tried to speak, but she couldn't. The lump in her throat grew.

"Mark!" Sophie said, wiping her eyes with the back of her hand. "What were you trying to say?"

Melissa leaned further over so that he could see her face more clearly. Mark opened his mouth, then closed it again, as if the effort was too much. Melissa picked up the glass of water by his bed and put the straw to his dry lips. Mark managed to take the smallest of sips, before his breath seemed to fail him. With an almighty effort, he opened his mouth again. "I love you," he mouthed, before his eyes fell shut once more.

★ ★ ★ ★ ★

"Oh, isn't this perfect for your mummy and daddy!" Sophie planted a quick kiss on the top of Clementine's baby-soft curls as she stopped for a moment so that she could take in every detail of the tastefully decorated garden. A lush green lawn sloped down towards a cliff edge dotted with exotic trees and flowers, through which the Mediterranean sparkled azure blue in the sunshine. Rows of silver chairs had been laid out in front of a simple rose-strewn dais, where they would make their vows and the scent of honeysuckle and clematis hung tantalizingly in the warm air. The whole effect was mesmerizing.

Sophie held on tightly to the baby in her arms as she walked as carefully as she could in her high heels towards her seat in the front row. She had protested that Melissa's mum, dad and half-sisters should be sitting there, but Melissa had been adamant. "You have been more of a family to me than they have. I want you in the front row. All of you."

Emily and Amy were already there as she arrived at her seat. Emily looked up and flashed her a nervous smile, reaching out to give Clementine's chubby cheek a gentle stroke with her thumb as she did so. "You look beautiful, Soph."

Sophie hesitated before taking Emily's hand, still outstretched towards the baby, and squeezing it tightly. "So do you, Emily."

It was true. Although the pain Emily had been through was still evident in her appearance, her beauty remained. Yes, there were deep lines around her big dark eyes and her once shiny black hair was now almost entirely grey. But it suited her. Age suited her.

"I'm so sorry, Sophie," she mouthed, shaking her head. "For everything."

"I know." Sophie kissed the top of Clementine's head as she sat down beside Emily, spreading out the baby's beautiful white silk dress. "Look, let's not dwell on the past, especially not today, Em. Let's think of it as a new beginning. If the past few years have taught us anything, it's that life is short and precious." She glanced down at the baby. "Let's not waste any more time with anger and recriminations."

Emily nodded. "A new beginning," she repeated with a wistful smile.

"So...we're finally going to meet Michael, are we?" Sophie said, deliberately changing the subject.

Emily's smile widened. "Be gentle with him, won't you?" She turned her head and motioned towards the back of the garden. "He's over there."

Sophie followed her gaze towards a tall, slim man, dressed in a pale linen suit, with an expensive-looking white shirt that showed off his tanned chest underneath. With his floppy blond hair and bright blue eyes, he looked a lot like Anton. A younger, prettier version. "He's gorgeous!"

Emily's eyes shone proudly. "I know. I'm very lucky."

"He's lucky too." It was going to take a long time to get their friendship completely back on track, but after everything that had happened, Sophie had decided that life was just too short to hold on to the horrible, corrosive anger that was eating away at her from the inside.

She loved Emily and she missed her friendship too much to lose it. It would take time, but they would mend their relationship. The scars were still there, but they were fading with every day that passed. Right at this moment, she was just happy that they were together.

And she was happy that Emily was gradually turning her own life around too. She had struggled, unsurprisingly, with severe depression after Jack's illness. At one point, Jack had even had to come and live with them temporarily. But she had come through it and had used her experiences to write her first novel, which proved to be enough of a success to support her financially. Now she was busy writing a second novel and adapting the first into a screenplay for TV. Michael was the producer, which was how they had met.

"I think this might be her!" Amy stood as the string quartet struck up with the wedding march.

Sophie craned her neck to see past the rows of family and friends.

"Isn't it traditional for him to arrive first?" Emily said.

Sophie laughed. "Melissa's not really one for tradition. She said she wanted to beat him to the altar…" She rolled her eyes affectionately.

Sure enough, Melissa appeared and Sophie's eyes instantly filled with tears. Her dress was the one she had picked out all those years ago at Geneva's place in LA when Sophie was getting married. It was strapless with a tiered lace skirt and would have looked awful on anybody but Melissa.

She was flanked on either side by Steve and Jack, both looking handsome and proud in their morning suits. Jack was so like Steve that it sometimes made Sophie catch her breath. She couldn't understand how none of them had ever seen it before—it was so very obvious. He had had a tough couple of years, but he had made a full recovery, and looking at him now, no one would ever know that he had been ill. He and Steve had developed an incredibly close relationship and spent as much time as they could together, as if trying to make up for what Steve used to call "the lost years."

Behind them, Emma and Megan held hands with Theo and George, all of them taking their roles very seriously, as they concentrated on walking in time to the music. Emma looked up and caught Sophie watching her, flashing her a wide, happy smile, the sun glinting on her braces. She was growing up into a lovely young woman, and although she always refused to accept it whenever anyone made a comment, she was the image of Sophie.

As they reached the end of the aisle, Melissa reached out to take the baby from Sophie's arms. "I'm sorry." Sophie motioned to the black smudge of mascara that had dripped onto Clementine's tiny, snow-white dress.

Melissa kissed the top of Clementine's head and laughed. "You're such a softie."

Sophie returned to her seat, the tears still rolling down her cheeks. Amy leaned over and handed her a tissue, which she took gratefully and dabbed ineffectually at her eyes. "I think we might all need one of those..." Emily whispered as the music struck up again and everyone turned as one.

Mark made his way down the aisle, moving slowly and carefully, never once taking his eyes off Melissa, who was watching him with an expression of pure, unadulterated joy. As he reached her, she bent to kiss him and lowered Clementine onto his lap, where she happily snuggled into his chest. Mark reached out and took Melissa's hand. "You look perfect," he told her, to the accompaniment of dozens of sniffs from the congregation.

Later that evening, with the dancing in full swing and Mark holding court just as he always did, Sophie pulled Melissa to one side. "That was a perfect day, Melissa. I'm so happy for you."

Melissa smiled and gave a contented sigh. "I'm so happy for myself!" Her skin was glowing and her eyes were shining. Sophie thought she had never seen a more beautiful bride.

"I got a message from Pete this morning…" Melissa glanced towards Mark.

Sophie nodded. "I'm glad. What did he say?"

Melissa smiled fondly. "He said he had no doubt that I would look fat and ugly in my wedding dress and that he'd had a lucky escape."

Sophie laughed. "He didn't!"

Melissa nodded, grinning affectionately. "He did. It was perfect. A little bit of me will always love him, you know."

"I know." Sophie looked over at Mark, who noticed her watching him and gave her a wink, before continuing to regale the crowd around him with some outlandish story or other. "But old Prince Charming over there just edged it, didn't he?"

"Yes. He did." Melissa gazed at Mark. There was no mistaking the love she had for him. His accident had made him radically reassess his life and he had been begging Melissa to marry him ever since he first woke up. She had always refused, until she had Clementine, when she decided that maybe they should formalize their relationship after all. "I'm just wondering why I didn't do this sooner."

"I was the same on my wedding day." Sophie smiled as she remembered how happy she had been on that day. They had just celebrated their fifth wedding anniversary, which seemed slightly ridiculous, as they had now been together for twenty-one years. "But I suppose it doesn't really matter, as long as you're happy and you're together. Amy certainly has no plans to do it again."

"Where is Amy?" Melissa glanced around the marquee. "And Emily?"

"We're here!" they said in unison, emerging from the dance floor, looking flushed and breathless.

Melissa motioned to a passing waiter, who was instantly by her side with a tray of champagne. "I think we should have a toast," she said, handing each of them a glass. "What shall we drink to?"

Sophie looked at each of them in turn, seeing the story of their lives written in the lines and creases of their faces. But they were still here. Still strong. Still together. "I think we should drink to us," she said, lifting her glass. "To best friends for ever."

★ ★ ★ ★ ★

ACKNOWLEDGEMENTS

WRITING THIS BOOK HAS BEEN MADE CONSIDER-ably easier with the encouragement and vision of my wonderful agent, Sheila Crowley. Thank you, Sheila, for your calm, reassuring influence and for always being there when I need you. Thanks also to Abbie Greaves and all at Curtis Brown for your support.

I am so grateful to the incomparable Lisa Milton at HQ. I couldn't be happier that we are finally working together and I have absolutely loved every minute of our first collaboration. Equally joyous to work with is Anna Baggaley, who added so much to *The Story of Our Lives* through her edits and suggestions. Thank you, Anna, for steering me in the right direction with such good humour and tact.

Thank you to my dearest friends and fabulous colleagues at ITV, Jane Beacon and Clare Ely, who read early drafts of the novel and provided both insight and inspiration, as they have done for the past twenty years on a daily basis. Thanks too to another early reader, my good friend Nikki Shepherd, who gave me some very helpful pointers along the way.

The Story of Our Lives is about a group of friends who have a "girls' weekend away" every year and the inspiration for the novel (though not the characters, I hasten to add) came from my own group of girlfriends, with whom I have spent many happy weekends over the past fifteen years. Rachel Bloomfield, Fiona Foster, Yasmin Pasha, Sofi Pasha, Clare Rewcastle, Stephanie Smith and Elke Tullett, thank you for the memories and here's to many more.

Thank you to my mum, Ann, for cheering me on so loudly and for all the help she has given me over the years, along with my lovely brother and sister, Ian and Louise, and their equally lovely partners, Helen and Baz. Thank you to my fabulous mother-in-law, Daphne, and to the rest of the Warner family for providing the laughs.

Finally, thank you to my three favourite people in the world: Rob, Alice and Paddy. You make everything worthwhile and I love you.